WHO'S BURIED IN THE BACKYARD?

Julia Reagan's dying wish sends her daughter to Maryland's Eastern Shore to save a decaying mansion and deal with angry relatives who never left the little town on the Chesapeake Bay. But before she can buy the first can of paint, Grace stumbles into a grave, a murder, and tantalizing clues to the one question she's never been able to answer: What happened to her father?

Grace leaves Washington and her hard earned law practice to take on a new life in Mallard Bay. She'll renovate Delaney House, sell it, and start over somewhere - *anywhere* - that isn't the Eastern Shore. She'd rather avoid those angry relatives, but no such luck. A handsome contractor complicates things, too, but it's the murder investigation that will change her life. The body buried in the backyard isn't the only mystery in Grace's new house, and what she doesn't know could kill her.

If you like a good murder with family drama and historical events that won't stay in the past, you'll love *Squatter's Rights*.

Old lies. Old loves. Old Murder.
Welcome to the Eastern Shore!

SQUATTER'S RIGHTS

AN EASTERN SHORE MYSTERY

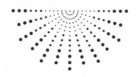

CHERIL THOMAS

For Charlene Janice McMahan

PROLOGUE

AUGUST 1960

F ord Delaney leaned heavily on the shovel and tried to slow his breathing. It would be ironic if he keeled over into the grave he'd just dug. He looked up through the leaf canopy of the small patch of woods, and the normalcy of the stars in the moonless sky calmed him a little.

"It's a dog," he whispered, as if saying the words made it so. "Only a damned dog."

The body in the pit didn't look like a dog, though, and Ford knew it.

What was he going to tell Emma? The thought of his wife made his heart race. Her image stayed with him as he began to shovel dirt back into the hole, moving faster and faster as the grave filled.

Get moving! Get the job done! Ford's personal motto, spouted in boardrooms, Rotary meetings and into the faces of under-performing subordinates, raced around his head. *Stick with the plan and get the job done!* Ford tormented himself with a running monolog of his own trite slogans as he shoveled, his self-loathing driving him into a frenzy.

The shovel hit hard ground. Startled from his mental self-flagellation, Ford stared at the slight mound of loose soil that covered his secret. A bit of tidying up and it wasn't a grave anymore, only a disturbed area in the woods behind his house.

Maybe it would be all right.

A sharp pain lanced through his left shoulder. *Not now*, he whispered as he grabbed a sturdy pine tree and struggled to stay upright. Another pain shot down his arm.

No! Not here. Let me finish.

Please.

CHAPTER ONE

The bathtub in the parlor was a bad sign. The old claw-foot model lay upside down under a ragged hole in the ceiling as if belly-up in defeat. Strips of broken lathing, plaster chunks and a liberal icing of grayish mud covered the room.

"I don't know how this happened," Cyrus Mosley said.

His immediate denial told Grace all she needed to know about the wizened lawyer. An attorney herself, Grace didn't hold many illusions about the legal profession. She'd pegged Mosley for a fool from the get-go.

Reality broke through her irritation and her stomach went queasy with nerves. This was her house. Her tub. Her broken water pipe that was still dripping.

"Well, you *should* know," she snapped. "You're the estate's agent."

"Pardon?" Mosley cupped a hand behind his right ear as if he couldn't possibly have heard her correctly.

Mosley wasn't just old in years; he was ancient in manner and appearance. He wore 80s-era golfing attire and what was left of his hair was sculpted into a tall, white half-pompadour. A pair of bushy white brows and thin, bloodless lips rounded out his cartoonish appearance. Grace wanted to tear into him, but he looked like any moment could be his last.

Not that she was in great shape herself. The last six months had been rough. And while she'd expected the 200-year-old house she'd bought, sight unseen, would need renovating, she hadn't expected a tub in the living room under a collapsed ceiling. Or the Crypt Keeper as the seller's agent.

"This situation, Mr. Mosley. This damage is not acceptable. Your firm is responsible for the house." She paused to see if the short sentences sunk in. A faint scratching noise caused them both to jump and move back from the pile of rubble. "I see you heard *that* fine," she added.

Mosley nodded and took another step back. At least he had on shoes, Grace thought as she moved to a relatively clear corner of the room. Mosley's Bally loafers trumped her sandals for rodent kicking.

Apparently satisfied they weren't in imminent danger, Mosley said, "I was expecting you next week. The cleaners I've hired start this afternoon."

"Cleaners? You'll need more than a week and more than cleaning to put this place into the shape I was expecting. What happened here?"

Mosley's eyes narrowed. "As you know, Grace, there are many issues at play here. Many, shall we say, complications to be handled. Anything can happen in tense family situations."

As you know, Grace. Complications. Family.

She sighed. "How long have you known?"

Mosley smiled and looked pleased with himself. "You were clever. Your grandmother was so surprised with the substantial earnest money deposit she didn't ask for many details. Cash is always an excellent distraction." He gave her a rueful smile and shook his head. "By the time I checked the background of O'Hara

Properties, the contract was finalized and the sale had to go forward."

"Had to? You mean it wouldn't have if you had known I was the buyer?"

"Your grandmother was emphatic about moving Delaney House out of her family's hands."

Grace gave herself a mental back pat. O'Hara Properties had been created for the sole purpose of protecting her identity while she purchased her mother's childhood home. "Does anyone else know I own the property?"

"Your uncle, his wife, your cousins. My staff. Confidentiality was not an issue from our end and not required by your, pardon, by O'Hara Properties' contract."

The scratching noise came again, louder. Mosley moved uncomfortably close to her. She smelled mothballs, an improvement over the rot and decay that permeated the house, but still unpleasant.

This wasn't a courtroom and she didn't have to do the macho, toe-to-toe lawyer thing. She moved away from him, closer to the doorway. "Anyone else?" she asked.

"If you mean did your grandmother know you ended up with the house, no. She went downhill rapidly after the contract was signed and was in a coma for the last week of her life. She never knew you were finally coming home to Mallard Bay."

"This isn't my home, Mr. Mosley."

"Cyrus, please."

"I haven't come home, Mr. Mosley. I bought this property as an investment. I'll renovate and sell it." His shocked look was satisfying, so she added, "It was one of my mother's last wishes and, with any luck, I'll turn a profit."

Screeeek...

This time they both moved for the doorway.

"Help me!" The scream seemed to come from everywhere at once. *"I'm blind! Help me!"*

Grace yelled at Mosley to call 911, ran back into the center of the room and dropped to her knees in the muck that covered the floor around the inverted tub.

"I can hear you!" she shouted. The scratches turned into banging. "Stop, stop! Be still. Help is coming." She heard Mosley giving directions and instructions to the emergency dispatcher.

"No!" he shouted. "*Under!* A person trapped *under* a tub!"

CHAPTER TWO

"You own this house?" The police officer used the same tone he might in inquiring if she ran a cock-fighting operation.

"Barely," Grace answered. "This is the first time I've been here."

"So you're an absentee landlord?" If possible, he sounded even more disgusted. The stocky man with light blond hair streaked gray with plaster mud wore a double chevron on his uniform sleeve. Grace hoped he wasn't the officer in charge.

Cyrus Mosley had disappeared leaving Grace to answer all the emergency responders' questions with variations of "I don't know."

Her anger flared anew at the memory of the lawyer's parting words. When the firemen lifted the tub off the still screeching victim, Mosley had taken one look at the injured man and said, "I have to make a call." Then he was gone, moving faster than she'd have thought possible for someone so old.

She realized the officer was staring at her, waiting for an answer.

"No, I'm not a landlord, absentee or otherwise. I'm a property owner whose house has been vandalized."

He dismissed her with a quick sideways look and took a form from his metal notebook, clipped it to the front and started writing.

"Town records list Emma Delaney as the owner of the house. You Emma Delaney?" he asked.

"No," Grace drew it out. She felt sure from his tone he knew she wasn't. "I'm Grace Reagan. Emma Delaney is deceased. I recently bought the house. And you are?"

"Corporal Banks," he said. "Care to explain how this happened?"

"I just got here with the estate attorney about an hour ago. He was giving me a tour of the house when the screaming started."

On cue, the injured man started wailing again.

"Who is he? Will he be alright?"

Banks finished what he was writing before answering her. "It would take more than a falling tub to take him out. Who is the attorney?"

"Cyrus Mosley."

Banks winced and Grace immediately felt better. Maybe she'd get some pity if nothing else in the way of cooperation from the corporal.

"Take me home! Take me hoooome!"

Banks and Grace turned to see the tub victim trying to sit up. A paramedic eased him back down, only to be rewarded with an ineffective swat from his patient.

"Cut it out, Winnie," the paramedic said as he deftly secured restraining straps over the injured man's arms and torso.

"Do you know who he is?" Grace asked.

Banks turned back to her. "You really don't know him?"

"I don't know anybody except Cyrus Mosley."

Once again the mention of Mosley's name brought a scowl. "You don't know your own tenant?"

"Tenant! He isn't a tenant. This house is supposed to be empty! And intact."

A squeal and a string of curses sent Banks to help the paramedics with their combative patient. Only the threat of handcuffs and the jail's infirmary restored order. While Banks escorted the paramedics and the plaster-covered man to the ambulance, Grace took the opportunity to escape to the front steps and fresh air.

The show had attracted onlookers. Grace was wondering exactly what kind of rabbit hole she'd fallen into when a tall, broad-shouldered man broke away from the knot of people who'd congregated on the lawn. As he jogged toward her, he called out, "Ms. Reagan? I'm Bryce Cutter. Cyrus Mosley sent me."

His smile lit up wide brown eyes and showcased an amazing set of dimples. Grace had to hand it to Mosley. He might have bugged out on her, but he'd sent a handsome replacement.

"He said you'd need some help," Cutter said. "He hired my firm to do some work here. My partner and the crew are on their way, but I'm thinking maybe I should call and turn them around?"

"Good idea. At least until tomorrow." As Grace filled Cutter in, she saw Banks leave the ambulance and walk their way. His scowl deepened at the sight of Bryce Cutter.

"Hiya, Aidan," Cutter said, giving Banks a nod. "Mosley said the place needed work, looks like he wasn't kidding. What happened here?"

"Criminal neglect," Banks said. "Ceiling collapsed nearly killing the tenant."

Grace said, "I told you he isn't a tenant! No one had authority to be in the house except Cyrus Mosley."

Cutter stepped between Grace and the officer. "Look, Aidan. You know Winnie, what he's like. Cyrus sent me in case you, or Ms. Reagan," he added with a nod to Grace, "needed help. He's rounding up Winnie's parents and getting them to the hospital. I'll check on the boy and be right back." Cutter started to move past Banks toward the ambulance but Banks grabbed his arm. Grace could almost smell the flare of testosterone as the two men glared at each other. They were both big, but Cutter was taller and the undercurrent said he had the upper hand.

Banks said, "You need to leave and I mean now."

"Hands off, Aidan." Bryce Cutter's voice was low but effective. Banks released his arm.

Impatient with both men, Grace said, "I want to know what's happening. Is that man going to be okay?"

"He'll live." Banks gave Cutter a last glare before turning to face Grace. "Since you have no standing here, this is the end of our conversation until you produce documentation showing you're the legitimate owner of this property. At which time," he raised his voice to cut off her protest, "we will discuss whether or not charges will be brought against you for endangering the public by the fostering of an attractive nuisance, namely, an unsecured condemned building."

"It was locked and it isn't condemned!"

"It will be when I file this," Banks ripped the top sheet off the form and held the paper up.

Grace couldn't read the print from where she stood, but she didn't think it was good news.

Banks handed her the clipboard and a pen. "I'm declaring the house to be unsafe and a crime scene."

"Crime scene! What crime?"

"The tub didn't just flip upside down and neatly cover the victim," Banks said.

"Oh, come on, Aidan," Cutter broke in. "It's Winnie! Anything could have happened. This isn't a crime. Ask him what happened when he's sober."

Banks ignored him. "No one is allowed in here until my investigation is complete. Which won't happen anytime soon, I assure you." He pointed to the form in Grace's hand. "Sign the bottom line where it says you claim ownership and understand you are barred from the property until it's released by both the Mallard Bay Police Department and the town's Codes Enforcement Officer."

"This is outrageous," Grace said as she scanned the document.

"What's outrageous is the condition of your property. You put a tenant…"

"He isn't a tenant!"

"Lots of folks have seen him here, including me. You put a tenant and first responders at risk and now you'll have to deal with the consequences of your actions."

Banks started in on another form, checking box after box. He signed it with a flourish and handed it to her. "This one you'll need to take to the town office for your construction permits."

"Wait! If you won't let me on the property, how can I make repairs?"

Banks smiled for the first time.

Grace didn't have a lot of patience on a good day and she hadn't had a good day in a long time. Pulling a notebook and pen out of her tote bag, she said, "Your name is Aidan Banks, right?"

"It is."

"Is your supervisor here?"

"My commanding officer is not, no."

"Your supervisor's name is?"

The anger rolling off Banks was almost palpable. "Sorry if I offended you, *ma'am*. But I don't like walking into deathtraps because a property owner was too cheap or lazy to prevent a dangerous situation from developing."

He had a point and Grace told him so, politely. "You'll need to call Cyrus Mosley. You seem to know him. He's responsible for this property, so you'll need to question him about the condition. He was the seller's agent, but I retained him to manage the property and I haven't released him from his contract yet. Here's his contact information." She fished Mosley's card out of her shoulder bag and gave it to the momentarily silent Banks.

Turning her attention to Cutter, she said. "Who is the injured man?"

"Oh, please," Banks muttered as he began punching numbers into his phone.

"I'm sorry, Ms. Reagan, Grace." Cutter took her arm and guided her down the steps and away from Banks. "His name is Winston Delaney."

"Delaney? So he was related to…" Grace let the question trail off as the information sunk in.

"Emma Delaney was his grandmother," Bryce said. "Winnie's your cousin."

May 22, 1952

Dearest Mother,

You'll note this letter isn't addressed to Papa. It's going to be full of girl talk and you know how he hates it, so read him the parts you think he can take and tell him the rest concerns 'womanly troubles'. When you go out to the mountain to see Nanny, let her read this while Papa is out checking the farm. I don't want to write everything twice.

Mother, I know our call last night was full of amazing stories and you surely thought after talking to us that Ford and I are the happiest couple in the world, and at times we are happy, but I'm beginning to see things that bother me and I need your perspective and Nanny's too.

First, forget everything Ford told you about our honeymoon trip. It was a disaster. We drove for four days, and the trip was grueling. The Eastern Shore of Maryland may as well be at the end of the earth. Asheville certainly feels that far away from me now. As soon as the mountains fell behind us, I began to have a bad feeling and by the time we drove into the congestion of Washington, I wanted to run home so badly; it was hard not to cry.

I kept reminding myself I was a married woman and home was ahead of me. I thought we were staying in Washington a few days. I wanted to see the nation's capital, for goodness sakes! Ford allowed me a whole 12 hours. I had exactly one dinner and a cup of coffee before he had the car packed and us back on the road again.

Before you ask, let me say up front that having Clancy with us didn't cause Ford's bad temper. My sweet boy was the best behaved dog you've ever seen, and since his Mama knows the power of a well-placed tip, we had no problems traveling with him. Thank goodness he's only six months old. A full-grown Great Dane could have been hard to handle, especially with Ford being so difficult.

So, it wasn't Clancy, and it wasn't the drive. Not entirely, anyway. Ford was irritable almost from the moment we left Asheville. He was rude to hotel managers and valets throughout the trip. I couldn't believe someone with his breeding would treat staff in such a manner.

Now, you know he's high strung, but that's not what I'm talking about. Ever since his father wired the money for our wedding present and didn't call or even write when he got the news his only child had gotten married, Ford has been moody and became more so as we got closer to Mallard Bay.

Of course, it was cold not to acknowledge our wedding, but Mr. Delaney has certainly been generous in more ways than one. Twenty-thousand dollars and a new job as first vice-president of Mallard Bay Bank and Trust are substantial wedding gifts. But Ford says he earned this job at his father's bank by graduating cum laude from Duke and getting his first job at Sunset Bank in Asheville without any help from Mr. Delaney. He also insists the money his father sent wasn't a wedding present but the last of a trust his grandparents left for him in his father's safe-keeping. He says he's next in line to inherit Delaney House, so even the keys to this magnificent place didn't pacify him. Ford says we don't have the deed to the property, so the house doesn't count as a wedding present, either.

That's all my husband seems to do. Count. Mostly flaws in other people, and it's growing tiresome. I'm hoping this mood is temporary and will pass as our lives settle down. He may still be upset by his father's recent marriage to a (much) younger woman and their globetrotting year-long honeymoon.

Had to take a break yesterday and get dinner ready. I'm writing fast to get this in the mail before Ford comes home today. If he ever got hold of this letter and saw what I wrote, we'd have the first divorce in the Anders family. (Not really, Mother. Don't faint.)

Anyway, Ford's temper. The drive from Washington to the ferry dock outside of Annapolis should have been enjoyable, but Ford just got more and more nervous. The snappishness I attributed to post wedding jitters at the beginning of the trip got much worse. The charming and eloquent man I married turned short-tempered and critical. You can stop smiling! I know you think me guilty of the same attributes.

Really, it was amazing he didn't end up in the Chesapeake Bay. The ferry crew would have had numerous witnesses to testify that my husband needed drowning. He was insufferable and didn't seem to care who witnessed his lack of self-control.

Ford's bad temper and my (admittedly limited) forbearance reached their respective breaking points at the end of our journey when we arrived and found workmen crawling all over the roof of Delaney House. (Yes, they really do call it that. And yes, it is enormous. Not Biltmore House enormous, but very grand.) Anyway, Ford had been building up our arrival as if footmen and servants would line up to greet us. When all we got was a lot of laborers still working on the house, Ford yelled a word he had no reason to believe I'd ever heard. The work on the house was supposed to be finished a week before we arrived. You'd have assumed the world was ending the way Ford carried on. He startled Clancy so badly, the poor dog set to barking. For an instant, I entertained the idea of siccing him on Ford but dismissed the thought for the useless notion it was. A bite of Ford right then might have poisoned my puppy.

Now do you see why I need to talk and Ford can't overhear? How do I live with a man in turmoil? What do I say to him when he behaves badly? Taking a hard line with him isn't working well. Mother, if you're laughing at me, stop it. This isn't funny. Yes, I know I can be a little irritable myself at times, but this is different. Dealing with Ford's temper is exhausting! We're newlyweds! We're supposed to be happy and we are a lot of the time. I just never know when he's going to erupt.

I'll write again soon. Call me and tell me what you think I should do. Make sure you call while Ford's at work so we can talk.

Start working on Papa to bring both of you to see my grand new house! This place is a palace. You have to come soon. Pictures won't do it justice. Here's a tease... guess what hangs over the mantel in the front parlor? Here's a hint: Museums and famous water lilies.

   Love,
   Emma

CHAPTER THREE

M osley gave Grace a wide smile of unnaturally white dentures. "Excellent! Bryce has filled you in and you've made all the connections. That makes things easier."

Grace didn't know if he was delusional or just thought she was.

As if on cue, the old lawyer had returned to the property minutes after Corporal Banks and the emergency workers left. Seeing Grace's face when Mosley's gold Lexus pulled up in front of the house, Bryce Cutter left quickly, but not before promising to call Grace about the job. "We can take care of everything," he'd assured her.

Grace doubted that, but agreed to meet Bryce and his partner the next day. Now she regarded the hopeful expression on Mosley's face and shook her head. It wasn't her - everyone in this place was crazy.

She said, "Cutter made excuses for you and told me the guy under the tub was Winston Delaney. He also told me Delaney is my cousin. That's all I know." Mosley's smile faded a bit. "I want some answers," she went on. "I bought a house you represented to be in decent condition. I bought a *vacant* house, paid you to oversee the property and arrived to find myself in a police investigation." Mosley's smile disappeared completely when she added, "I hope you have insurance to cover the damage."

"Hard to say what's 'damage'," he made exaggerated air quotes with arthritic fingers. "You bought the property in As-Is condition."

"I think it's very easy to say what the damage consists of. I have photos of the house, remember? No tub in the parlor. Intact ceiling." She took a breath before adding, "No tenant."

Mosley closed his rheumy eyes for a moment before saying, "I'll pay for the cleanup from the, ah, accident."

"Yes, you will. And all the repairs to the parlor and the rooms above it."

He threw his hands up. "Done! Now, if we could get past this morning, would you like to see the rest of the place?"

Grace kept her poker face, but her stomach relaxed a bit. "I would, but that obnoxious police officer -"

"Aidan Banks was here?"

"So you know him. He seemed fond of you, too."

Mosley made a 'no matter' wave of his hands. "No, no. We don't have a problem. It just isn't a stretch to guess who you talked to. We only have one officer and a chief. Don't mind Aidan. Come on. We'll stay out of the front parlor and it'll be fine."

Grace didn't trust Mosley's assessment of anything, but curiosity got the better of her and she followed him up the front steps.

"We'll start over. Isn't this wonderful?" Mosley clapped his hands as they crossed the threshold and walked into the large entry hall.

Grace had seen the cantilevered staircase and stained-glass turret windows earlier, but now she studied them with growing excitement. She was captivated by the staircase which wound upward along the walls, seemingly without support. The center of the hall was open all the way to a domed ceiling at least thirty feet above. When she finally turned her attention to Mosley, she saw he was studying her as intently as she had absorbed the room's details. The back of her neck prickled. She needed to watch herself.

She said, "As Mrs. Delaney's personal representative, this property became your responsibility upon her incapacitation, correct?"

This clearly wasn't the reaction Mosley had expected, but he recovered quickly. "Correct."

"And, I believe I'm right in saying you had power of attorney to act for her in the sale of the house, which included the negotiation of the contract. My offer to purchase the house specified the property would be in your care until I took possession, a task for which I paid a premium."

"Pardon?" The pink polo shirt and lime green golf pants screamed 'retired', but Cyrus Mosley was a warrior and today, decrepitude was his weapon. "Haven't we been over this?" he asked, this time tilting his left ear in her direction.

Grace wanted to remind him he'd already pulled this trick once, but she only rolled her eyes and raised her voice. "How long did you let Winston Delaney stay here?"

"Oh. I thought we could talk about that later."

So he *had* allowed Delaney to stay in her house. Grace felt her blood pressure rise. "How long?" she demanded.

Mosley rubbed both ears before answering. "It's a complicated story. Winston was living here last spring. He didn't take the eviction notice especially well." Mosley gestured toward the back of the house. "In the kitchen, you'll find some artwork that expresses his displeasure. I'm afraid your purchase of the house shocked most of the family, but Winston's reaction was the worst. Impossible to predict or prevent that kind of behavior, you know."

"Why would he care?" Grace asked. She'd assumed if any of the family had wanted the house, they'd had an opportunity to buy it.

Mosley took a handkerchief out of his pocket and dabbed his forehead. It occurred to her he could fall out in the hot, smelly house. Just as she started to suggest they go outside, he straightened up and adjusted the waistband of his slacks under his slight paunch while rocking back on the heels of his loafers. She decided this was his go-to move when there was no tie to straighten or suit coat to button up: a symbolic girding of the loins.

"I can assure you, my dear, everything was handled properly," he said in a prim tone.

Odd answer. Grace folded her arms and waited.

"Let's see the rest of the house."

"It can wait," she said. "The damage in there," she gestured to the parlor behind them. "Are you telling me Winston Delaney was so angry he broke in, vandalized the place and flooded the upstairs until the floor was weak enough to collapse?"

"Let's just say he was extremely careless where a leak in the master bathroom was concerned. Winston has certain proprietary feelings about the house and when he learned it had been sold, he became even more difficult."

"More difficult than what? And what do you mean by proprietary feelings?"

Mosley, it seemed, had run out of delaying tactics. He mopped his face again before tucking the handkerchief away and looking her in the eyes. "Your cousin Winston insists his grandmother, *your* grandmother, gave the house to him."

CHAPTER FOUR

B uy the Delaney family home, restore it to its former glory and sell it in a record-breaking deal for Reagan Realty and Renovations, Inc. It had seemed possible when her mother was alive. Even as Julia Reagan lay tethered to life by an oxygen line and feeding tubes, she'd talked about restoring Delaney House. Restoring and selling it. "This time when I give it up, it will be on my terms," she'd said.

Grace had made sure her mother was able to hold the deed in her hands before she died, and now she was paying the price for that indulgence. "Does Winston have any proof his grandmother gave him the house?" she asked Mosley.

"Not a bit and I can assure you it never happened. Emma wanted the house sold and out of the family's hands. 'Off their backs" was the way she put it. The proceeds from the sale were to be divided between her children, your mother and her brother. Of course, your poor mother..." Mosley's voice wavered. "Julia's death coming so terribly soon after Emma's meant Julia's portion went to you."

"I didn't know anything about Emma Delaney's will or her promises when I made the purchase offer," Grace said and regretted the words immediately. She didn't owe Cyrus Mosley, or anyone else, an explanation of her actions.

"O'Hara Properties' bid was the only one I received on the house," Mosley said as if that answered some question. "Stark, your uncle? Well, you wouldn't remember him, would you? Anyway, your mother's brother, Stark, said the offer was too low and didn't want to accept it. But Emma insisted on accepting the highest bid, the only bid as it turned out. She was still lucid then and quite capable of ordering all of us around." A brief smile softened his face and his words. "Receiving half of a below-market selling price upset Stark, but finding out you would end up with the house and would get it for a fraction of its worth was a real blow to him. He feels it's unfair, to say the least."

Grace nodded to the destruction in the parlor and said, "'Below market' is debatable, Mr. Mosley."

She had done her homework before making her offer. Mallard Bay was a hard real estate market to quantify. On the Chesapeake Bay side of Maryland's Eastern Shore, it sat to the north of wealthy Talbot County and south of Kent Island and the commuter communities of Annapolis. Tourism and the vacation home market had given the small village a new lease on life, but a derelict property the size of a small hotel was a hard sell in any economy.

"Value, as well as beauty, is always in the eye of the beholder," Mosley said, but he sounded doubtful. Beauty was in short supply at Delaney House.

Grace decided not to press the point. "So," she said, "Stark Delaney is mad because I paid too little for the house and his son is mad because he thinks he's the rightful owner. And you think the son, this Winston, vandalized the house. Did you call the police?"

"I told you, I saw the damage to the front parlor for the first time with you, today. Winston promised he'd repaired the leak. I suppose you could call the paint in the kitchen vandalism, but really, when you take the condition of the house into consideration, graffiti is the least of your worries. I did send you photos."

"The photos on your firm's website showed a run-down house. The ones you emailed to me showed a *dirty* run-down house. In the pictures I saw, the parlor was intact and without a tub."

"As it was when I was here two days ago." The waistband tugging resumed and Mosley looked like he was trying to remember which ear he was playing deaf with. Finally, he said, "You need to understand the sequence of events. I never expected Emma to sell the house, let alone do it so quickly. Now that I think back, it's clear to me she wanted to dispose of the property before she died. But I couldn't see that at the time. She was my... my friend."

Grace remained silent. Anything nice she said would be insincere, so she opted for waiting for Mosley to continue and, hopefully, make sense.

"Emma fell in early January. Broke her hip. She went on to a rehab facility from the hospital and from there to a nursing home. Pneumonia took her in the end."

"I'm sorry for your loss," Grace said, trying to mean it.

Mosley nodded. "I don't know exactly when Winston moved in, but it was early on during her hospital stay. I stopped by one day to check on the place and found the boy here. It was a battle from then on to get him out. Emma was livid that he'd moved in without asking her. In fact, it's the only time I remember her being vocally angry with Winston. Made no difference to him. Even Emma's death... he seemed immune." The lawyer's rheumy eyes teared up.

Grace studied the domed ceiling and let him have a moment while he blew into a handkerchief and made other sounds she tried to block. The numbness which had enveloped her since her mother's death only allowed her to process new irritations; sympathy for Emma Delaney's lawyer was beyond her. When Mosley seemed to have recovered sufficiently, she said, "Okay, I get the picture. How long did you let him stay?"

"*Let* is not the right word. Despite Winston's bad behavior, he's family. I couldn't have him arrested. But the day I discovered he'd ignored a bad leak in the bathroom off Emma's bedroom, I started eviction proceedings."

"No more Mr. Nice Guy, huh?" Grace said.

"You bet," the pompadour jiggled with his vigorous nodding. "But by then, the floorboards and joists were compromised. Winston had the nerve to bring the eviction notice to my office. Threw it on my secretary's desk and said the house was his. Said Emma had given it to him and he had squatter's rights. Can you imagine?"

Squatter's rights? Grace didn't like the sound of that. "Does he have any basis for a claim of adverse possession?" When Mosley didn't answer, she added, "Has he paid the taxes on this place? Lived here with her knowledge long enough or have any other reason to believe he has a claim to ownership?"

Grace could practically see the lawyer's thoughts rolling around under the liver spots on his scalp. She doubted there could be a successful challenge to the sale, but she didn't share her opinion with Mosley. Instead, she left him in the hall and hoped he would move on to worrying about his malpractice premiums while she checked out the rest of the house. She wanted to see what else Winston Delaney had done while he was a squatter.

Mosley had said the kitchen was in the rear of the house. The odor of rotting food got stronger as she walked down the wide hallway. She opened the last door at the end of the hall and found a kitchen. Or a toxic waste dump; it was hard to tell. She slammed the door shut against the view and the smell.

"It's not this bad upstairs," Mosley said.

Grace jumped and made a mental note to keep an eye on him. He moved like a ninja. Or a ghost. He was certainly well past old enough to be dead, she thought irritably. He'd not only regained his composure but was invading her personal space. Again.

"You have to understand, m'dear. This is an old house, and it hasn't been well cared for in the last fifty years. The sale notice did state maintenance had been neglected."

"That's hardly an adequate warning," she said as she opened the door again.

The kitchen was beyond filthy. Trash and dirty dishes covered every surface and at some point in the last decade, the sink had been used as a garbage can. But it was the 'artwork' Mosley had warned about that made Grace gasp. Across the doors of the crooked, white metal cabinets, four large letters in shiny red paint spelled out a message:

MINE

CHAPTER FIVE

G race breathed through her mouth as she took in the scene. The fury captured in those four letters mesmerized her for a moment; then the smell got her moving.

On their way back to the front of the house, Mosley, who had wisely stayed silent through the kitchen viewing, followed close on her heels. As they passed doorways, he reeled off an inventory of rooms: butler's pantry, lavatory, dining room, rear parlor and front parlor. When she didn't slow down, he told her not to worry; she could see them all later. Grace was thinking more along the lines of going out the front door and not coming back.

She finally slowed in the entry hall and then stopped to take deep breaths as she looked around the elegant room and tried to picture it clean. And less stinky. Her eyes fell on what had to be a crude violation of the original architect's design.

The staircase with its mahogany railings and ornate balusters had been built for stately comings and goings. Elegantly dressed women should float down the wide steps on the arms of their top-hatted escorts and be admired by those watching from the hall below. Unfortunately, that visual went awry near the second-floor landing where a doorway had been cut into the wall adjacent to the top three steps. "Where does that go?" she asked, pointing to the aberration.

As they climbed the stairs, Mosley told her the odd doorway was another of Emma's remodeling projects. In its mid-twentieth century configuration, the house only had one toilet on the first floor and one on the second.

"Emma didn't want visitors coming into the second-floor area. She decided to install a door from the main bathroom onto the staircase and allow guests to use the facilities without coming onto the second floor. Your grandmother believed the doorway gave the hall character."

"Are you serious? A person could break their neck. And, besides, it's crooked." Grace tilted her head to the right. "The door frame and the door are crooked."

"Not really. It's just the right side is a little wonky."

"Wonky. Is that a legal term? The top of the door slants up on the right side! It's got to be a half-foot higher than the left side."

"Your grandmother always found someone with rock-bottom prices and usually got what she paid for, but you'll see, the door opens and shuts fine."

Grace opened the bathroom door but stayed where she was on the staircase. She wondered how many people had stumbled trying to step up off the stairs and through a doorway cut into the wall. *Remove stupid door* went to the top of her mental To Do list.

On the second floor, they walked through musty-smelling rooms, each of which was full of assorted junk, old clothes and rotting upholstery. Grace thought the place looked like the aftermath of a dumpster explosion. Layers of dust, grime and something else she couldn't identify and didn't want to, gave testament to the lack of any housekeeping efforts since at least the first Bush administration.

Mosley kept up a running commentary of useless information. When he said Emma had loved floral patterns and was partial to lavender and rose sachets, Grace said she would have done better with a backhoe and a tanker load of bleach.

"It wasn't always like this," Mosley said, leaving Grace to

wonder how well Emma Delaney's attorney knew the bedroom wing of her house.

The largest room was the worst. "I suppose Winston is responsible for this, too?" Grace waved a hand at the mess but didn't leave the relative safety of the doorway. The contents of the dresser and the closet had been emptied and spread around the room.

"Winston's convinced your grandmother hid valuables in the house. He probably went through everything. I'm sure he waited until after she died though."

"Oh, good. That makes it better."

Mosley nodded in agreement, her sarcasm sailing past him. "You know young folks. Can't wait for anything." Grace gave Mosley a sharp look, but he appeared to be serious. "Your cousin is still a kid in many ways."

Her cousin. Her grandmother. Mosley was on *her* last nerve. As he rejoined her in the hallway, he gestured to a tall pier mirror hanging near the top of the stairs. "This piece is a beauty, though, don't you think?"

The mirror was beautiful, but Grace had to stifle a groan at the sight of herself and Mosley. She was a head taller, even allowing for his hair. The layers of her dark, shoulder-length hair had frizzed in the humidity and she'd sweated through her makeup. Her blue eyes, ringed by smeared mascara, were huge and not in a good way. Only her linen slacks and jacket said she'd started the day with any sense of style, but they were wrinkled and muddy. It was quite possible the old lawyer in his retro golf clothes looked better than she did. Grace decided to blame the heat. The sooner the house tour was over and she was on her way, the better.

The third floor was smaller than the first two and only contained four blessedly empty rooms. On their way downstairs, they paused on the second floor in front of the bathroom which had lost its tub. The floor of the small room sloped from the doorway to a large gaping hole rimmed by jagged ends of floorboards and joists. The toilet and sink appeared to be clinging to the walls to avoid being sucked down to the floor below.

Mosley said, "About twenty years ago Emma decided she wanted a bathroom off her bedroom. She had a tub and sink hauled in from a salvage yard, read up on plumbing and tried to do it herself. When that didn't work, and she'd opened half the walls looking for the water pipes, she had to hire a plumber, but I doubt she got a licensed one."

"So there could have been an ongoing leak?"

"Wouldn't surprise me. Winston's carelessness and the standing water from the recent leak probably finished what the original slow leak started."

When they were back in the large hall on the first floor, Mosley led her to the room he'd previously called the rear parlor.

"You didn't get a good look in here earlier and I want you to understand it's been this way for a long time. It's not part of any recent damage, but I didn't disclose it in the listing. The omission wasn't intentional; I just didn't get a shot of this room."

The rear parlor, in its own way, was as bad as the front. It didn't have a tub or a hole in the ceiling, but long strips of wallpaper hung from its ceiling and the bulging plaster walls had water stains.

"She wallpapered the ceiling!"

Mosley grinned as if they were discussing a precocious toddler. "Emma was addicted to those fixer-upper shows. She watched one on wallpaper and decided to redecorate. Of course, she wouldn't pay to have a professional do it. She got a couple of neighborhood kids to come over and gave them each twenty dollars to try their hands at wallpapering."

"On a ceiling."

"Yes. It was a Victorian fashion, and she liked the idea. Of course, that was more than twenty years ago. Have to say it stayed up longer than I thought it would."

The high ceiling looked like it was molting, shedding hideous lavender paisley-patterned skins in protest of its desecration. For the first time in weeks, Grace felt something other than grief or apathy. The careless and casual abuse of the once grand house made her mad.

Mosley seemed oblivious. "Well, we need to get to my office. I have some papers for you to sign." He rocked back on his heels again, tugging his waistband.

She might have to kill him to get away from him, Grace thought.

"I'll sign the papers tomorrow." She knew she sounded petulant and she didn't care.

"Whatever you say." He took a key from his pocket and handed it to her. "It's all yours, anyway."

Despite her anger and need to get away from the annoying man, Grace found herself trailing him to the front door. He wasn't much, but when he left, she would be on her own and the house was creepy.

"You'll want to have all the locks changed as soon as possible," he said as he stepped onto the front porch. "Winston has a key, and he isn't the only one who does." He stared at her for an uncomfortable moment before raising his hand in a brief wave. The solid thunk of the creaking front door gave his exit an extra note of drama.

Grace stood in the hall and looked around. She'd lost count of the rooms she'd seen and Mosley had said there were more in the basement, an area she didn't even want to contemplate. It was too much. As soon as she was sure Mosley was gone, she locked the front door behind her and tried not to run to her car.

CHAPTER SIX

G race needed a hot shower, clean clothes and a strong drink - not necessarily in that order. She could taste the smell of garbage at the back of her throat.

When she'd planned this trip, spending a week at the historic Egret Hotel had seemed like a luxury she could ill afford. But the Egret was Mallard Bay's only hotel, and Grace had felt she deserved a bit of luxury while she made the arrangements to renovate Delaney House. She would stay a week and then return to Washington and work, rack up billable hours during the week and commute to Mallard Bay on the weekend to see what changes her money had bought. Now that she'd seen Delaney House, the plan seemed naive and impractical.

The historic district of the village was laid out in a simple grid pattern. At its center sat The Egret, a stately Victorian-era building with a wide front porch lined with rocking chairs. Her single room turned out to have everything she needed: a bed, easy chair and a minibar with tiny bottles of decent Chablis. She sipped a glass of wine while using the entire selection of L'Occitane bath products.

Her clothes went into a sealed laundry bag for the hotel's cleaners and she emptied and repacked her leather tote, repulsed by the worry that something from Delaney House might have fallen - or crawled - into the bag that contained her life's necessities. By the time she had eaten the chicken and mushroom pie that was the evening special in the hotel's pub, she was calmer. A second glass of Chablis back in her room coupled with a boring movie let her drift off into a dreamless sleep.

TOWARD MORNING, THE PEACEFUL OBLIVION EBBED, PUSHED AWAY BY increasingly chaotic dreams of unfinished tasks and unmet obligations.

Grace had given up on the idea of sleeping to a civilized hour when her mother's cancer took its last downward turn. She'd found fighting for sleep more stressful than sleeplessness itself; the only remedy was to get up. Her mother's advice for every adversity was: *Move. Do something, even if it's wrong, but keep moving.* Now, Grace did all of her paperwork and bill paying before the sun came up. First financial chores, then news and emails from a shrinking circle of friends.

When the room service coffee fully kicked in, she turned to work email and voice messages. There weren't many. Julia's illness had claimed more personal time than usually allowed to non-equity staff at Farquar, Mitchum and Stoltzfus, Attorneys at Law. Only the protection of the firm's managing partner had saved her job as she worked less and less in her mother's final months.

It remained to be seen if she would stay employed when she returned to work, but not to her old schedule. Most weekends would belong to Delaney House. And even if she could return to the all-consuming schedule, she wouldn't. Twelve years of seventy-hour workweeks had taken their toll: she was 37, exhausted and alone. She knew she should be careful. She needed her job, but she was discovering she didn't care what happened when she returned to the office. Besides, David Farquar owed her.

The year before, Grace came up with a last minute Hail Mary

play and saved their biggest client from a crippling damage suit. Her on again - off again romance with her boss ended for good about the time the case wrapped up, but even in their close daily work environment, they'd kept a good relationship. At least she hoped it was still good.

After answering a half-dozen emails and leaving voicemail instructions to the secretary she suspected was frantically lobbying Human Resources for a real boss, she closed her own laptop and opened her mother's MacBook.

Grace had avoided the laptop after Julia's death. She couldn't shake the idea that opening it and using Julia's passwords would disperse the last of her mother's essence into the universe. Eventually, she had no choice. She needed information from the Mac's files to manage Julia's estate and to close down the business her mother had built over the past thirty years. Grace was a silent partner in the small real estate and home renovation business, but without Julia, there was no one to run the company. Even when she was finally free of Farquar, Mitchum and Stoltzfus, Grace knew she wouldn't be able to fill Julia's shoes. She didn't want to.

Once she wrapped up the renovation and sale of the Delaney property, she'd add the profit to the money from Julia's life insurance and move on with the rest of her life, free from obligations to anyone other than herself. That was the plan which made it possible to put one foot in front of the other, close down her mother's firm and get herself over the Bay Bridge to a musty mausoleum and its decrepit caretaker.

At the thought of Cyrus Mosley, the smell of Emma Delaney's house came back and with it all of the new problems she faced as its owner.

THE MALLARD BAY POLICE DEPARTMENT WAS RELEGATED TO THE rear of the building it shared with the municipal office and a small library. A bronze historical marker said the building was a former school. The mid-nineteenth century facade blended with the streetscape, but the interior had been gutted and reconfigured to maximize space.

When Grace found the Chief of Police manning the reception desk, she felt like she'd stepped back in time. Chief Lee McNamara even looked the part of a village constable. His genial smile and polite greeting softened the appraising once-over he gave her as she entered the station. She wasn't surprised to learn he knew who she was.

The Chief delivered the good news that Winston Delaney had sobered up during the night and admitted to being in an upstairs bedroom at Delaney House and drinking until he passed out. The collapse of the floor in the bathroom woke him out of a stupor but did nothing to make him less drunk. He eventually made it downstairs to marvel at the sight of a 400-pound cast iron tub lying on its side. Before he could come up with an explanation that would leave him blameless, he heard cars pulling into the driveway and panicked. Desperate to hide, he crawled under the tub and pulled it down over himself, breaking a finger and knocking himself unconscious in the process. Chief McNamara tried, and failed, to relay this story to Grace without laughing.

Still smarting from her encounter with Corporal Banks, Grace tried not to laugh with him, but couldn't keep a straight face.

McNamara apologized for his officer's behavior. "We all wear a lot of hats around here, Ms. Reagan," he said. "Corporal Banks volunteers with the Mallard Bay Fire Department. We all do, but Aidan headed a team that handled a fire in a rental house a while back. There were casualties. Made him a bit overzealous. I'll have a word with him."

Grace nodded and resolved to let go of her irritation. "Which of these papers can I get rid of?" she asked, handing McNamara the forms Banks had given her the night before.

The Chief's expression tightened as he looked at the documents. She didn't exactly feel sorry for Banks, but she thought Lee McNamara might do more than just have a word with the corporal.

"I'll take care of these," he said. "If you're using a local contractor, they'll know how to file for the permits you'll need. If you need any help at all, give me a call, or call our Town Clerk, Jake Briard." He handed her a business card. "Mallard Bay is a small place and we run a tight, but friendly operation for the town. I'm sorry your introduction to us was less than pleasant, but I promise you it will get better."

Grace decided to take the Chief at his word. It was a beautiful day, the kind that promised a fresh start. As she stepped out of the police station and into the warm September sunshine, she saw the main street ran down to a waterfront park. She was tempted to walk down the slight hill and take up residence on one of the benches lining the harbor bulkhead, but before she could act on impulse, her cell rang. Bryce Cutter. His crew would be at Delaney House in an hour. The sunny day quickly took a back seat to a dilapidated mansion. She had work to do.

October 2, 1952

Dear Mother,

Do I have stories for you! Get a cup of tea and settle in. There's no way to tell you all this on the telephone. Even if I had the privacy, the bill would be horrendous!

First: Did I tell you Ford has ordered a brass plaque for the front gate? When it's installed, one and all will be advised they are about to enter Delaney House, circa 1670. Can he get any more pretentious? I sure hope not. And this hulking great pile of bricks wasn't built until 1720. But Ford says Lord Somebodyoranother had the land grant from 'the king' (my husband talks like we have a king and refers to him all the time as if he was in the next room), anyway - Ford says since the land grant is dated 1670, we can use that date. I tell you, my husband is a tiresome person and irritating to boot. But he's happy because his sign says our house is 280 years old and that's ever so much better than being 230.

Now that I've set the tone for the main act, here it is:

Your daughter was cast in the role of photographer's model. Yes, your glamorous dream for me came true. (Not the one where I marry a prince and move us all to Europe - the other glamorous dream.) My loving husband hired the famous Sidney Lassiter to photograph little ol' me.

Sidney went to prep school with Ford and has been piddling along as a portrait photographer for years. A few weeks ago, he was in the right place at the right time and photographed the new President when Ike and his entourage were hunting on Taylor's Island! Time Magazine *bought the pictures and now everybody around here with two cents wants their photograph taken by* the *Sidney Lassiter, Presidential Photographer. (Sid had new business cards made. He's also taken to wearing ascots and uses extra oil in his hair.) Ford says Sid's only making hay while the sun shines, but the two of them make me cringe when they get together and try to top each other with their name dropping and one-upping conversations.*

Well, nothing would do, but Ford had to have Sid photograph me wearing the most expensive pieces of his late mother's jewelry collection. I wore her mink stole, too (a mite tatty, truth be told) and a new Dior dress. Ford insists on Dior, but I've discovered it's because he thinks even the locals around this backwater place will recognize the name. Don't I sound grand talking down about my neighbors and so-called friends? I'm afraid I'm becoming bitter.

But that isn't all. Oh, no. My husband wasn't satisfied with a photographic record of his wife dressed up in designer silk and jewels. He's sending the photographs to a portrait artist in New York who painted Ford's mother wearing the same mink. Ford wanted me to wear the pearls and the ruby pendant, a large sapphire brooch, teardrop diamond earrings and a diamond cuff. Imagine! Tacky doesn't begin to describe how I looked when I put it all on. Fifty thousand dollars' worth of tacky, but tacky nonetheless. I told him just to lay the jewelry out on the rug and let Sidney shoot away if all he wanted was a display of Delaney wealth.

We had words, as you may imagine, but I did finally win. I told him I'd wear exactly the same jewelry his mother did in her portrait. It was a risk because we don't have the portrait (seems Ford's father took it with him when he left for Europe and 'lost' it somewhere in one of his moves during the years he met, married and discarded his second wife and found his third.) Ford admitted Mother Delaney only wore the pearls, earrings, and gold cuff. And let's not forget my rock of a wedding ring. I know Ford was disappointed, but he'll be happy enough when the portrait is done. He's determined to replace his mother's portrait over the mantel in the front parlor with mine. He says she would be pleased, although he can't know. He never knew her.

Well, now I feel ashamed of myself seeing this all down in my own handwriting. Poor Ford. If all he wants is for me to be photographed wearing a mink and fabulous jewels, I ought not to complain. But - it's not what I want! I know, I know, I know. I'll try to do better.

I did have some fun during the hours I had to pose. Mother, the man kept twisting me this way and that all afternoon! Anyway, at the end of the session, I told Sid that Ford wanted a set of photographs of me with Clancy. Now, the famous 'Mr. Lassiter' is a puffed up toad and he nearly exploded at the idea of being a pet photographer, but nonetheless, I prevailed. I took off my shoes and put the pearls around Clancy's neck, and we cuddled on the rug in front of the fireplace. You should have seen Sid's face! Now, the trick will be to get the pictures from him without Ford finding out I put his mother's pearls on a dog. But I'll worry about that tomorrow, as Scarlett would say!

Plan a trip up here for the spring and you'll see your daughter immortalized in a fabulous oil portrait. Come for any reason you like, but come see me. I am lonely and Ford says I can't travel alone. I'm tired of arguing about it with him.

Give my love to Nanny and Papa.

Emma

P.S. Is Nanny feeling better? Are you and Papa doing well? I should have asked right off. I should rewrite this. I sound awful. Well, you know me and love me, anyway!

E.

CHAPTER SEVEN

G race drove straight to Delaney House with a plan to
photograph the property, inside and out, before the work crew
arrived. She wanted to document the state of the house before
signing any paperwork for Cyrus Mosley.

She had another, less practical reason for photographing the
house. Her mother had loved secret places. Treasure hunts were
regular games when Grace was a child. The Arlington row house
where she'd grown up had many nooks, odd corners and spots that
were perfect 'hidey holes' as Julia called them. Grace had no desire
to go through every dark corner of Delaney House, but she was
hoping the camera's viewfinder and the photographs would help her
spot the areas where a young Julia might have left hidden treasures -
and maybe a few answers. That Winston Delaney, or someone, had
already ransacked the house made her task more difficult but not
necessarily futile. She was looking for valuables of a different kind.

She started with the short brick pillars, which sat on either side of
the front porch. The one on the left had a tarnished bronze plaque
that read: *Delaney House - circa 1670.* The house had Victorian hall-
marks, but now that she studied it, she could see it had been built in
stages, with the overwrought Victorian style taking predominance.

From her tote, Grace took a notebook and pen. She listed the location and subject of the first photos and made a note to find out more about the house's history. She'd need all the marketing material she could get when she put the renovated property on the market.

After shooting the columns, she turned her phone's camera to the house, her stomach clenching with each new view of peeling paint and missing slate roof tiles. The outside of the house made her apprehensive, but it took everything she had to step inside when she unlocked the front door. She'd steeled herself for the smell, but the sheer size of the house was intimidating. All she could think of as she walked through the rooms was the amount of work it would take to make the structure habitable.

She was outside pondering the locked door to the basement when a purple van pulled into the drive and parked behind her BMW. Men and women in purple overalls emerged from the van, followed by the driver, a heavyset man with a mop of curly black hair. He carried a small white dog in the crook of his arm. The dog gave a welcoming yap as they reached her, and the man extended his free hand. "Henry Cutter, at your service."

Other than his coloring and warm brown eyes, Henry didn't resemble his younger cousin. The overalls accentuated his rotund form and his weather-beaten face and rough hands testified to years of hard work. His firm handshake and the sight of workers unloading industrial-size cleaning equipment gave Grace a glimmer of hope. She doubted this group could handle Delaney House, but maybe they could send for reinforcements. After a quick walk through the downstairs, she led Henry out of the rank smelling house to a rickety, but mostly upright picnic table in the backyard.

Cutter clipped a leash onto the dog's collar and set it on the grass. "In answer to the question you've been too kind to ask, no, I don't take Leo with me on every job. I'm dropping him off at the Humane Society as soon as we're finished. No, no," he laughed at her expression. "Sorry, that came out wrong."

"I hope so," Grace said as she reached out to scratch Leo's ears.

The little dog looked like a cross between a Chihuahua and a soccer ball but had a ready smile and a thank-you lick for her hand.

"I've been fostering him to get his diet regulated and teach him some household manners. He's going to his forever home today with a great family who's adopting him. It's all good, right Leo?"

Leo settled next to Grace's foot, conveniently within reach of her hand. She continued to scratch his ears as she and Henry discussed the scope of work to be done in the house. When they'd agreed a thorough clean out was the first order of business, two overall-clad workers were dispatched to empty and sanitize the kitchen. Two others were instructed to take down and haul away the mildewed window coverings. The remaining crew was sent to start shoveling out the debris in the front parlor.

"Masks and gloves, people!" Cutter called after the workers.

"How about oxygen tanks?" one of them yelled, setting off a round of teasing by his coworkers.

To Grace, Henry said, "Don't worry, I've seen worse."

"Really? When?" Grace was genuinely curious. Her mother had flipped more than a dozen houses, but none as far gone as Delaney House.

"Okay, this *is* pretty bad, but we can handle it." He consulted his clipboard. "You'll need to strip this place and do a lot of remedial work before you can even start renovations."

"I want to set up a work schedule and get things into place so I can return to DC next week. I have to go back to work." *If I still have a job,* she added silently.

"Okay. I can handle everything for you here." Henry nodded approvingly as he made notes. "Cyrus told me the basics of the situation and, frankly, the grapevine filled in the holes. Delaney House is famous, you know." He turned to look at the hulking structure and Grace followed his gaze, taking in the damaged roof and cracked attic windows. A broken downspout canted at an angle from the gutter, held on to the house only by a twist of ivy vines.

"Does everyone refer to it as 'Delaney House'?" she asked. "Seems rather grand."

"You probably don't know, but a lot of the Town's history is tied to this house and this land. Parts of the building have been here more than three hundred years."

She shook her head. "I did see the plaque out front, but I know next to nothing. My mother, Julia Reagan, was Emma Delaney's daughter. She was raised here but had no interest in coming back. I haven't been here since I was a baby and I don't have any memory of it."

"You inherited it?"

"No. I bought the place when it came on the market because ..." she faltered, as she did every time she tried to explain why she'd bought her mother's childhood home. And like every other time, she gave the easy explanation. "My mother dreamed of restoring the house." She wanted to move off the topic. The fewer people who knew her personal story, the better. "I understand you and your cousin have a contracting business, too. Are you interested in bidding on the renovation work?"

Henry hesitated before answering. The calendar app on his phone got a workout as he flipped through screens.

"Bryce and I own this cleaning and estate management service, as well as a custom cabinetry and restoration company. Our regular clients take up most of our time, but we've been considering expanding. I'll talk to Bryce about the construction, but I can definitely handle the clean out and basic chores over the next few days. If we feel we can't do the renovations, we'll give you recommendations. That's all I can promise for the moment. Fair enough?"

Grace thanked him but wondered if she should trust a recommendation from Mosley. Henry seemed kind and trustworthy and he hadn't exactly jumped at the work. She decided it would have to be good enough.

Henry said, "I need to run Leo over to his new parents. The crew has plenty to do until I get back. I could call Bryce and we could all have lunch and an informal conversation, if you want. No commitment, just talk. How does that sound? I promise not to wear the overalls."

She still had reservations, but Grace found herself smiling and nodding. It sounded like a plan.

CHAPTER EIGHT

"No need to get bids. We want the job," Bryce Cutter said. "You won't get a better price anywhere and we deliver our work on time."

Henry frowned. "I told Grace we'd just talk about the work today. We have a full calendar."

Now that she saw them together, Grace realized how the two men complemented each other. Handsome, charming Bryce was the salesman, the idea guy. Solid, serious Henry was the guarantee of a quality product. The cousins exchanged a look Grace couldn't interpret.

Bryce said, "See? This is how we work, Grace. Henry is the cautious one, and I run flat out. Good thing is, I follow through with the work. Every time. Right, Henry?"

Henry still looked unhappy but agreed with his cousin. "Every time. He'll be there at three a.m., but the work will get done."

Henry had selected a small restaurant only a few blocks away from Delaney House. Morsels Cafe offered tables in a side garden and Grace was grateful for the breeze that washed away the scent of decay. Tall potted hibiscus plants and a prolific trumpet vine provided splashes of bright color in the garden, which also had a view of the busy harbor. It would be easy to slip into vacation mode, if she could stop worrying about the broken, dirty house.

Bryce and Henry plowed through burger platters while Grace picked at a crab salad. Even the Eastern Shore's famous blue crab backfin and Bryce's flirtatious teasing weren't enough to distract her from the need to get the renovation work started.

"Come on, now," Bryce said when she asked how he would rank the order of basic repairs to the house. "That last joke of mine was funny."

Bryce was trying hard to entertain her, and she wanted to tell him she didn't have time for it. Every minute she sat in the pretty garden eating and laughing was a minute longer she would be on the Eastern Shore. She wanted to find all the information Delaney House and its last occupants had to give and then leave, shutting the door to this part of her life forever.

"Relax, Grace, this is going to be an adventure," Bryce said.

"I think what Ms. Reagan is trying to tell us is she's in a hurry and she wants to talk business," Henry said.

Again the men shared a look indicating more would be said when Grace wasn't around to witness it.

"Okay, I can do that," Bryce said in a mild tone. Over the next half hour, he described first the basic repairs and then assured her Cutter Enterprises could modernize the house without sacrificing its architectural integrity. Both men stared at her when they heard she'd bought the property without seeing it.

"That's a real 'good news' 'bad news' event, huh?" Henry said. "A dream house that's uninhabitable."

"Way to make it better," Grace said and held her empty glass up for the waiter to see. The Bloody Mary she'd had was a rare lunch treat. She decided one more couldn't hurt. "My mother was a real estate broker and she had a house-flipping business. She'd find properties that didn't need a lot of work, offer all cash and a quick sale and do a basic reno. Most of the time, she flipped for a profit. Some were a wash and some lost money, but overall, she was pretty successful. I've been winding the business down since her death."

"Cyrus said you're a lawyer. I guess that means you can't hang around for the duration of the project?" Bryce finished his last fry and ignored Henry's surprised expression. "We can do it, Grace. You aren't thinking of bringing over your contractors from DC are you?"

That was exactly what she'd tried to do, but 75 miles and the Bay Bridge had proved to be insurmountable obstacles. Even the contractors Julia had the best relationships with turned her down flat. Those who knew the Eastern Shore tried to warn her off the idea of rehabbing a property in a rural area so far away from her home base.

"I'll use local workers," Grace assured him. "And I know it won't be easy, but I made a promise to my mother and I'm going to keep it. She wanted to save her childhood home; wanted it to leave Delaney hands in good shape," she tried to explain. "I have no memory of the house or her family - Mom broke ties years ago - but I love the challenge of setting a historic property to rights. Besides, I'd have done anything to make her happy. It didn't seem impossible at the time."

"It isn't," Bryce said. "I promise."

The memory of her mother's face, swollen from the chemotherapy, but smiling with excitement, made her happy. She squared her shoulders and refocused on the contractors. "My plan is to do enough renovation to restore it properly and once it's in good shape, list it and get an agent to sell it for me."

"The listing part won't be hard," Henry said. "People retire, move here and get a real estate license. The place is crawling with them."

Her fresh Bloody Mary arrived and Grace took a sip. Its peppery warmth was soothing, but guilt began to poke at her. She shouldn't be here. She had clients in Washington expecting work from her, and none of them would be pleased to know she was spending a Wednesday workday dealing with another personal crisis and having a two-drink lunch.

"Let me understand," Henry said. "You live less than a hundred miles away, but you never came over to see the property before you bought it?"

Grace sighed. If she hired the Cutters, she'd spend a lot of time with them. Starting out on a less than truthful basis could cause her problems later on. "As soon as she learned it was for sale, Mom wanted to buy the house. She was dying and I was in denial. It wouldn't have mattered what shape this place was in. If all that was left was a hole in the ground, she'd have still wanted it. So I - *we* - bought it. Coming over here to see it first wouldn't have changed anything." She didn't add that Emma Delaney wouldn't have sold it to her.

Bryce picked up his sales pitch. "We can handle it for you. We'll get the place cleaned up and in good enough shape to sell. You can decide how much reno to do as we go along."

Grace nodded. "I'll be here for a week, then it's back to work for me. I'll need a workable plan in place before I leave." The temptation to hand her key to the Cutters and walk away was strong, but she'd seen too many people blow their budgets and lose everything to smooth-talking contractors.

Bryce said, "Why don't you take this a bit at a time. Basics first. We'll check everything, of course, but Delaney House sits on brick and stone foundation and the main floor is over an English basement. Not likely to be any sill damage. Probably no serious structural issues either. The hole in the parlor ceiling, repairs to the bathroom, some water damage, maybe a new roof - that's a good start."

She hesitated. Mosley was paying for a lot of the work Bryce described, but Julia had wanted Delaney House to be restored. Grace needed to get estimates, pick the best contractor and get the lowest price. Rushing into an agreement with the Cutters, no matter how sweet and charming they seemed, felt like bad business. But she was tired. And a little tipsy.

"Okay. To start, give me estimates on roof repairs, basic kitchen and bath updates and paint inside and out. Obviously, I'll need some landscaping, too. You know Mosley's firm is paying for the clean out and damage from the ceiling collapse, so keep that estimate separate. I'll pay you and he'll reimburse me."

Both men looked relieved.

Bryce said, "Sure. I can get a crew in as soon as Henry's guys finish cleaning. Good thing Winnie woke up and told the police what really happened. No telling how much time we would have lost in Aidan's investigation." He scrunched his face in an imitation of the policeman's scowl and was finally rewarded with a laugh from Grace.

"What's the deal with him, anyway?" she asked.

"Aidan's been a jerk from the day he was born," Bryce said without hesitation.

"Bryce and Aidan don't exactly get along," Henry added. "They've been scrapping since grade school."

Bryce shook his head. "Henry always tells that story. Aidan was a few years behind me and it's true we've never liked each other, but last night wasn't personal between us. He gets hot fast and burns out faster. One of those guys with a real short fuse."

"But he's a police officer!" Grace was appalled.

"Well, yes. He's pretty good at what he does and Lee McNamara keeps a tight rein on him. Aidan gets worked up and anything to do with Winnie sets him off. Don't worry about him. The important thing is Winnie's okay, he's set the record straight and you won't have a problem with Aidan."

"So he knew I didn't have a tenant in the house!" The memory of the police officer's accusations rankled anew.

"No, I think that's why he was mad. He assumed you and Winnie had an arrangement."

Grace shook her head. Her momentary relief at having a plan for Delaney House evaporated at the thought of dealing with Winston and his parents. She'd have to meet her mother's family sooner or later, and their first topics of conversation weren't likely to be pleasant.

Cyrus Mosley's name flashed on her phone as an incoming call made them all jump.

"See? Even old Cyrus wants you to hire us," Bryce teased.

But that wasn't what Mosley wanted at all.

CHAPTER NINE

"I had clients in my office, Miss Reagan, when that fool Banks came in here yesterday and made a scene. He said you told him I was responsible for the house." Mosley's voice shook with emotion. "You knew I wasn't at fault. As soon as Winnie was coherent, he took responsibility."

Grace felt a twinge of guilt but ignored it. "How is our squatter today, Mr. Mosley?"

"Fair," Mosley said. "He had a lot of alcohol in his system and the concussion kept him drifting in and out of consciousness. He'll be fine. You need to come over to my office so we can finish our business."

She excused herself to the Cutters and walked out of the garden to the sidewalk in front of the restaurant. Mid-day traffic in Mallard Bay was heavy with pedestrians and slow-moving vehicles clogging the narrow village streets. Grace knew the colonial town had become a popular tourist stop in the last decade, but she was still surprised at the number of people.

"Grace? Ms. Reagan? Are you there?"

She sighed loudly enough for Mosley to hear her with either ear. "Unfortunately, yes. I believe you're asking to be relieved of your responsibilities under the contract of sale." This time Mosley didn't respond, which infuriated her. "You were either dishonest about the condition of the house when you listed it for sale or you allowed it to deteriorate while it was in your custody after I bought it. Either way, I'm not releasing you from anything, just yet."

Mosley was quiet for so long she thought he'd hung up. "Alright," he finally said. "I can understand your position. There are extenuating circumstances of which you are not aware, but still, I see your point. Come to my office and let's talk. If you like, I'll sell the house for you and send you a check. I'll buy it from you myself if you don't want to wait for it to go on the market. I can't get any fairer than that, can I?"

It was Grace's turn for a stunned silence. "Why would you do that?" she finally said.

"Emma Delaney was special to me. I want to do right by my friend and wrap up her affairs properly."

He was old, she reminded herself. And he'd been bullied by Winston Delaney, if not more members of the family. She felt her irritation fade. "Give me directions. I can be there first thing in the morning." Cyrus Mosley could wait, she decided. She needed some time to think.

The brick Victorian-era building at the corner of Washington and Goldsborough in Easton seemed a fitting location for Cyrus Mosley's office. But while the building was ancient and the decor decades away from current fashion, Mosley's secretary was about twenty. Maybe forty. It was hard to tell with her heavy makeup and barhopping clothes. She snapped a wad of gum in time with her swaying walk as she led Grace down a narrow hall to a conference room.

"Mr. Mosley will be with you shortly," snap, snap.

Grace watched the girl totter away on five-inch heels and felt her own feet start to hurt.

After a ten-minute wait during which Grace envisioned Mosley crouched around the corner, timing his entrance to show her where she stood in his busy schedule, the man himself strode in and placed a thin folder of papers on the table.

"My dear," he said, offering his hand.

He wore khakis with a knife-edge crease and a blue oxford cloth dress shirt. A sedate silk tie hinted of a navy blazer hanging nearby. It was such a change from her first impression that she smiled and shook his hand before remembering she didn't like him.

"You look lovely," he added.

Grace knew her tailored slacks and silk twinset were flattering and was glad she'd taken extra care to appear professional. She felt sure of herself, ready to wrap up her business with Emma Delaney's attorney.

The secretary pranced back into the room carrying a remarkably level and steady tray with a pot of coffee and two china mugs.

Mosley said, "Grace, dear, you look so much like your grand-mother, I assumed you'd love coffee, too. Would you prefer tea?"

Grace stared at him.

He seemed pleased with her reaction. "You didn't know that did you? You could be a young Emma's twin and I don't know why I didn't say before. I was so shocked when I first saw you, I couldn't concentrate for marveling at the resemblance and I am sure I seemed like a doddering old fool. Let's start over, shall we?"

Mosley poured the coffee and Grace sat, trying to process what he'd said. He opened the file, took out an eight-by-ten photo and handed it to her with a courtly flourish. "Grace Fiona Reagan, meet your grandmother, Emma Fiona Delaney."

She heard him say something about needing another file. He left the room quietly, shutting the door behind him.

The photo was a professional portrait of a woman who looked so familiar, Grace knew Mosley's comparison had been truthful. Large blue eyes stared out over sixty years and gave the impression Emma Delaney was ready to speak at the first opportunity. High cheekbones balanced a long, thin-bridged nose. Her dark hair was in a French twist with only a wave across her forehead to soften her face. Despite the elegant dress and meticulous grooming, the woman in the photo had sharp angles and no-nonsense expression.

Grace thought she could be looking at a photo of herself in Joan Crawford's clothes.

There were differences, of course. Emma's photo projected an elegant countenance. She was thin and stylish. Elegant, thin and stylish were not always in Grace's playbook, but she pulled off cold and no-nonsense on a daily basis.

She took the photo to a window, turning it this way and that as if different levels of light could tell her more than the two-dimensional picture had to give. *Fiona.* Grace had thought she was named after her mother, Julia Fiona. Now it seemed they were a trio. She, her mother and the grandmother she'd never known.

"Mama," she whispered, "you have some explaining to do."

CHAPTER TEN

M osley produced all the necessary paperwork, Grace produced her passport for official identification, and the gum-snapper turned out to be a notary. A few minutes later, with considerable reluctance, Grace released Mosley from his custodianship of Delaney House. Their agreement that, upon her written notification, he would buy the house back from her at twenty thousand above her purchase price should have eased her mind. Still, as seven thousand square feet of mold, dirt and crumbling plaster became her sole responsibility, she thought she could feel the weight of it. Her heart gave a lurch when he asked if she wanted to sell it right then.

When she didn't answer immediately, he handed her another document. She wasn't surprised to see Mosley, Kastner and Associates had a real estate division; the completed listing agreement only needed her signature. Rearing back in his chair, the lawyer gave his waistband a tug and began to talk about her options, as he saw them.

"So I can list it for sale or, as we agreed, I'll buy it outright if you want to put this all behind you." Another form was produced, this one a contract for sale with the amount of the purchase price left blank. "The land alone is worth quite a bit and the house is on the National Register of Historic Places, but its size and condition will limit buyers and lower the offers. The repairs will be expensive, to say the least."

Grace thought Mosley had never said the least in any conversation, but kept the observation to herself. She asked for more coffee and settled back to read every word of every page of the documents, mainly to irritate him, but also to allow herself some time for her emotions to settle. In her law practice, she specialized in land use regulations and real estate settlements, so even though there was pleasure to be derived from dragging the process out and making Mosley wait, she moved through the wherefores and therefores of the deed, listing agreement and purchase offer quickly. Mosley huffed and fidgeted, as if she were insulting him anew with each passing minute.

When she finished, she put the documents into her briefcase with Emma Delaney's photograph. Mosley said nothing, only pursed his lips when she told him she'd consider his offers and get back to him.

"Before I go, though, I do have some questions." She had decided Mosley was more likely to be truthful than her mother's brother and his family, and Grace wanted answers. "Did you know my father?"

Mosley reddened. "Father?"

I can do this as long as you can, Grace thought as they stared at each other in the wake of his one-word response.

Mosley caved first. "I knew of him, of course. It was tragic, his death, I mean. Young man."

"What do you know about him?"

Mosley took another pause and seemed to be considering his words carefully. Grace wanted to push him but made herself relax her tense posture.

"I know very little," he finally said. "When she came home with you, Julia said he had been killed. A car accident."

Grace nodded. This meshed with the information she'd gotten

from her mother. "Did Mom give you any details about him? Where he was from?" She'd never see Mosley again once she'd left Mallard Bay. There was no reason to be secretive about her questions.

"I'm sorry, no. I recall your mother saying there was no other family on his side."

She'd been afraid of getting that answer, but she still had her mother's brother to ask. And she had another question for Mosley.

"Do you know why my mother left here and broke all ties with the family?"

"Yes, I do. It isn't a pretty story, either. As I mentioned I was, still am to some extent, the family's attorney."

"And the family members in question are dead," Grace said.

"I still have a duty to protect their interests," Mosley wagged a finger at her but relented before she could object. "It's a trite scenario, I'm afraid. Two women, one baby, both wanted to mother it. Julia and Emma argued a lot in the best of times. When you were about two, Julia decided she'd had enough. She had a trust fund from her grandfather, so she took you and left. Emma tried to stop her; she called me nearly hysterical and demanded I file an emergency petition for custody."

"Of what?" Grace said and then gaped at Mosley as she realized what he meant. "Of *me?* Emma Delaney wanted custody of *me?*"

"Yes, I'm afraid so. They'd had a fight, a terrible one. Julia was packing when Emma called me. I tried to talk to both of them, but it was futile. Emma was distraught for a while, but life goes on. When she saw both of you were happy and thriving, it was a huge relief. She had me set up your trust…"

"Trust?"

"Yes. Emma set one up for you. It was modest, but still enough to pay for private schools and other enrichments. It was an irrevocable instrument, which was fortunate for Julia because later Emma ran through almost everything. Everything except Delaney House."

IT WAS TOO MUCH TO ABSORB. GRACE'S MIND SWAM WITH conflicting thoughts as she walked away from Mosley's office. Emma, a maternalistic grandmother, and Julia an angry teenaged single mother. Her mother working so hard to grow Reagan Realty, but not because they needed the money. *Hard work pays off, Grace. Take care of your own problems and follow your own good sense. Don't rely on anyone else.* And yet a trust fund made their lives comfortable.

How could any of this be true? And if it was, what else didn't she know?

She bought a latte from a coffee bar across from the courthouse square and sat in a nearby park. The fresh September air rolled over her while she sipped her drink without tasting it.

A young widow with no family making her way on her own. Grace had never questioned this image of her mother's past. Julia Reagan had never waited for anyone's permission and usually steam-rolled over anything standing in her path. There had been men from time to time, but none were allowed too close to Grace. And none, Julia had assured her daughter, could ever take Jonathon Reagan's place. Julia had been gentle, but firm. *Just the two of us. No father, no family.*

Except, apparently, a grandmother on the Eastern Shore and a trust fund.

Grace waited for this to hurt, but the only emotion she felt was relief. Her mother hadn't been alone. She might not have wanted the family connections, but they were there. Now that she thought about it, Grace realized her mother hadn't lied, she just hadn't told the whole truth. There were lots of missing details, critical details, but these could wait for another time. Grace had the Delaneys and their house to deal with now.

She could hear her mother saying, *keep moving - do something, even if it's wrong.* There was plenty to do. For starters, she could look at the house through new eyes. She wanted to know about her father, but she also wanted to know about her grandparents and the family she'd never known. She wanted to learn the truth if such an elusive thing could be found among the spider webs and trash in Delaney House.

Oct 19, 1952

Dear Mother,

I hope this finds you and Papa well and Nanny, too, God bless her. Please share this with her. I need advice and help in the worst way, but please keep this between you and Nanny. Papa will hit the roof and I can't take any more lectures. You and Papa were right and I was wrong. I shouldn't have married Ford in such a rush and run so far away from home. There! Said and done. Now you have to help me.

I know you said I shouldn't dwell on it, but I can't shake the disappointment I feel with Ford and this museum he calls our house. It isn't any more mine than the jewelry he drapes around my neck. Last night we went to a retirement party for a local judge and Ford 'gave' me his mother's large ruby pendant to wear. 'How wonderful!' I hear you say. Not at all.

He gave it to me right before we left for the dinner. No words of love from my husband, only a lecture to be careful with the heirloom and to be sure and remind him to put it back in the safe when I was finished using it. Using it! I am not a partner in our marriage or even the mistress of this household. I am an ornament to be dressed, presented and then stored away until I am needed again. Ford owns me. Or so he thinks.

His temper is awful. You know I can hold my own in an argument - I do hope you aren't heaving one of those huge sighs! This is serious, Mother! Remember that hateful Grant Sommers who pitched such a fit at the Fourth of July picnic a few years ago? His poor wife standing there all dog-faced and embarrassed while he ranted at her for putting onion in the potato salad? That's Ford. Can you believe it? But I have seen this side of him several times and have no expectation of improvement on his part.

In your last letter, you said I needed to be a patient and good wife. You said I should make friends who could help me adjust. I fear you don't understand the gravity of my situation. It's more than Ford's bad temper.

Now, please take this seriously! I know it sounds childish, but imagine living with it every day - the women in our circle are mean because Ford was THE catch in this little place and I am a nobody in their eyes. Most of them never heard of Asheville, or say so anyway, to be hurtful. There are any number of girls who'd gladly take Ford on the rebound and many a day I'd like to let them have him.

There are parts of my life I love. And I do make the best of things and look for the fun where I can - like with Sidney and those ridiculous photographs. But everything is tinged with fear - yes, real fear, Mother - of what Ford will do if I push him too far.

I may use the wedding money you gave me to come home for a while; I miss you all so much. Please call soon. Ford gets the bills, so I can't make long-distance calls while he's out without a good explanation. Remember - call mid-morning during the workweek. Any other time Ford or the housekeepers will be here and I won't be able to talk. Tell Nanny I love her. Tell Papa I miss him. Yes, I do! I am so miserable I miss Papa's nattering at me about everything. At least he paid attention to me and he loves me. I miss you all terribly.

Emma

Nov 1, 1952

Dearest Nanny,

I am wondering if Mother is keeping my letters from you. I have been pouring my heart out for some time now, thinking she was sharing my worries with you, but your letters don't respond to my problems. I hope she has at least given you an idea of what my life is like here in Maryland.

It's beautiful here. As beautiful as our mountains, only so different. The Eastern Shore is cut off from the rest of the state by the Chesapeake Bay. It takes forever to get here by ferry and even though there's a brand new bridge from Annapolis, I think this place will always feel like a foreign country to me.

This place is too far from the mountains and you. I want to come home. There, I hope I haven't upset you too much. I was a silly girl to let Ford sweep me off my feet. I was so haughty and sharp with Mother when I was leaving; I know it must be hard for her to forgive me. But honestly, she ignores everything I tell her and just keeps saying I have to work harder at being a good wife and helpmeet. I suspect she has bragged so much about the Delaneys and this huge mansion, she can't think how she will explain a divorced daughter landing back in her house.

Despite my sharp words, you know it will break my heart to disappoint her, but I am living a lie here with Ford. I can't give him what he needs - I don't even know what that is. We aren't a good match and I don't know how to fix us without losing myself.

I am coming home. I'll have to drive in order to bring Clancy. Ford hates him - why didn't I see that back in Asheville? I'll spare Mother from the shame as long as possible by living with you, if you'll have us. Clancy will be so happy to run free on the mountain again.

After saying all this, you'll think me odd, but I can't leave until after Christmas. Ford has planned several social events here at the house and I am determined not to hurt him any more than I have to. He doesn't know how I feel, of course. Talking to him about my unhappiness is as useless as talking to Mother. Neither one of them listens.

Don't write me back. Ford reads my mail before he gives it to me. It's a constant fight about that, but so far, I'm not winning.

I'm coming home, Nanny. I'll work hard to be a useful and productive person. No more silliness, I promise.

I'm coming home.

Emma

CHAPTER ELEVEN

T he desk clerk at the Egret Hotel was happy to give her a walking map of the area, but after a quick look, Grace stuck it in her tote. Mallard Bay was so small; it would be hard to get lost.

She wanted to get a feel for the village where her mother had grown up. For an hour she wandered and window-shopped along wide, tree-shaded streets, enjoying the crispness of the morning air and the beauty of the old buildings and waterfront. Canadian geese flew overhead in varying 'V' formations, loudly proclaiming the advent of fall. Grace found herself wondering what daily life would be like if she stayed on in the renovated mansion.

She turned off the main street and walked deeper into a neighborhood of large older homes. Queen Anne, Italianate, Gothic and Shingle Style houses were interspersed with twentieth-century Craftsman. Grace indulged her passion for architecture as she walked in the warm sunshine. She'd just passed a Greek Revival suitable for a plantation when she came to a triple-wide, wooded lot that looked as if it hadn't been touched since the area had seen its first inhabitants. From the sidewalk, she peered through stunted mulberry trees and taller pin oaks and saw there was a fence or wall of some kind twenty yards or so back in the woods. Covered in ivy and vines, it formed a long wave of green and rust rising from the ground to block the view of the remainder of the property.

"Awful, isn't it?"

A woman working in an adjacent yard dropped her rake and hurried toward Grace with a purposeful stride, clearly intent on a conversation. "Don't suppose you'd like to buy it and clean it up? I hear you can get it for a good price." Long wisps of gray hair escaped from under a wide-brimmed straw hat, giving the woman a witchy appearance at odds with her practical rubber gardening shoes and mud-stained jeans. She walked bent slightly at the waist, the only sign of infirmity Grace could see, but the wrinkles in her thin face put her well north of retirement age.

The woman pulled off her gardening gloves and extended her hand. "Avril Oxley," she said. "Some of my neighbors like having this wooded area. Think it gives the block a less urban feel. I say they should go live on a farm if they want to be one with nature."

"Yes, well, I can see your point," Grace said. "Nice meeting you, but…"

"They might not care about the animals who've taken up residence and the kids hanging out in there smoking God-knows-what all, but I do. The owner's passed on, and now that the property's in the hands of an attorney, I am sure it can be had for a good price. You can't see it from here, of course, but the house is huge."

Grace wondered how many neglected properties there were in the historic district. Maybe the area's property values weren't what she'd thought. "Well, your yard is certainly lovely," she said, as she started moving. "I have to run; I have a lot to do."

Avril Oxley followed along at Grace's side. She said, "Thank you. I certainly try; we all do here. I chair the Friends of History Foundation. It takes a lot of time, but I feel it's my civic duty. I hope you'll walk around the block and look at the house. I have the attorney's name if you're interested in buying. He's a personal friend and I can assure you he'll give you a fair price. He needs to unload it to settle the estate."

She talked on, but Grace was looking at the street signs on the corner. They were approaching the intersection of Jefferson and Carroll. She tried to orient herself without pulling out the map. If she turned to the left up ahead and again at the next corner, she would be on...

"Who owns the property?" Grace asked, stopping short.

"Well, the attorney..."

"I mean whose estate is it?" Grace tried not to shout. After all, she knew what she was going to hear. She hadn't only bought a crumbling house, she'd also gotten a vermin infested forest with pot smoking teenagers in residence.

"Emma Delaney," her new friend answered. "Did you know her?"

DESPITE THE LIGHT BREEZE STIRRING THE FALL AIR, GRACE FELT overheated as she sat on the back steps of the house and studied the tangle of trees and vegetation covering the rear half of her property. It had taken some time to rid herself of Avril once the woman learned Grace's identity.

She gathered her hair and flapped it like a fan to generate a breeze on her neck. She would have never guessed how large the property was by the view from the house. No doubt there would be more surprises as the project went along, but this one was a doozy. Clearing out the woods and restoring it to a natural area suitable to an urban neighborhood was out of the question. She'd clean it up, of course, but brush clearing and landscaping would have to wait for the next owner. Her most immediate need was to finalize the renovation plan for the house and get it in motion.

Still, the woods intrigued her. The cleaners working in the house didn't need her and for the moment, she had nothing to do but make a decision she didn't want to face. She decided to walk the perimeter of the woods and get a better look at the overgrown property.

Twenty feet or so past the tree line which marked the edge of the patchy lawn, sunlight was filtered down to cool greenness by a heavy leaf canopy. While it was beautiful, the low light disguised the fact that the ground was a living snare. As she tramped deeper into the gloom, vines and raised roots caught her feet and scraggly bushes with thorn-covered branches grabbed her clothes, making progress slow and occasionally painful.

The wall she'd seen from Jefferson Street turned out to be an odd arrangement of a vine-covered fence running parallel to and about four feet in front of a brick wall. The bits of fencing which were visible appeared to be barbed wire, and Grace decided against a closer inspection. Whatever the original purpose had been could remain a mystery - the mosquitoes were beginning to feast on her unprotected skin. Turning to retrace her steps, she caught her right arm on a needle-covered branch and yelped as a long, deep scratch welled up and blood trickled down her arm.

She might have made it to the lawn without further injury if she hadn't stepped wide to the right to avoid a massive spider web she didn't see until she was nearly in it. She jumped and felt her ankle roll on impact. The green world of Emma Delaney's woods turned sideways as Grace pitched over, face first, through the web and flat out into a patch of bright scarlet plants.

The ground gave way as she fell through into darkness.

"A SINKHOLE?"

"Yes, a sinkhole," Henry repeated, not for the first time. "We really need to get you to the hospital."

"I wasn't out for long and everything works. I'm not going anywhere but to the hotel to clean up." Grace flexed her arms and legs and tried not to think about her embarrassing and painful rescue from the woods. "If you'll hand me my purse, I have some hand wipes."

Henry jumped to do as she asked and grunted as he lifted the tote. "What the devil is in here?"

"Everything," Grace said. She tried not to moan or to snatch the tote from Henry's hand. "I don't understand how a sinkhole can simply open up." She scrabbled through the bag, sure she had antiseptic wipes and a tube of cortisone cream.

Henry sat down beside her. "Grace, you're repeating yourself. Listen to me; you can deal with it all later. You blacked out, so you probably hit your head. Your arm is cut up and the wounds were dragged through poison sumac, so you are going to be in a bad way soon if you don't get medication. Are you sure the spider didn't bite you? When was the last time you had a tetanus shot?"

Stepping between his agitated cousin and Grace, Bryce Cutter took her uninjured arm and helped her up from the back porch step where they'd carefully placed her a few minutes earlier. "Henry's right, you know. You're awfully lucky. If you hadn't been able to crawl out the hole and yell, the guys in the house wouldn't have found you. Who knows how long you would have been out there?"

"And we can't have our newest client die on us," Henry chimed in. "Bad for business, so come on. We'll take you to the ER and stay with you."

Bryce's solid body felt good as she leaned against him, but the pounding in her head increased with each step they took. She also thought Henry had a point about the tetanus shot. And the spider. And she was allergic to the sumac.

She hated hospitals but ended up spending the rest of the day moving at a glacial pace from the waiting room to an exam room, through x-rays, tests and pokes and finally, to the blessed peace of her hotel room. Bryce was as good as his word. Henry begged off to supervise the crew at Delaney House, but Bryce stayed by her side right up until she reluctantly watched him drive away from the Egret Inn. The combination of shock and painkillers had lowered her inhibitions to the point she wanted to throw herself at the contractor and beg him not to leave her.

She called herself stupid and a lot worse as she limped through the lobby and made her way to her room. Exhaustion finished her off as soon she lay across the clean, white bed where she dreamed the house and the woods and a giant spider were conspiring to kill her.

CHAPTER TWELVE

"You're kidding," Grace said and shook her head, wincing at the pain the simple motion caused.

Everything about Chief McNamara said he was serious. His expression, his words, even the way he leaned across to her, elbows on his knees, dipping his head to look her squarely in the eyes. "I was with the State Police for twenty years and I've been the Chief of Police in Mallard Bay for the last ten. I know what a grave looks like."

"It was a sinkhole."

"The bones you fell on would indicate otherwise."

"Jesus, Joseph and Sweet Mary," Grace moaned as she carefully leaned her aching head back against a tapestry-covered wingback chair.

McNamara had managed to commandeer the small library of the Egret Hotel and a coffee tray for two. He poured a cup for Grace as she absorbed the news. The medication the emergency room physician had given her yesterday had worn off, leaving her clear-headed, but shaky. She was trying to avoid taking more of the tempting little pills, at least until after she gave her statement to the Chief. She took her time and sipped the coffee, but it was a poor substitute for narcotics.

McNamara continued in his calm tone. "Before Tuesday, when was the last time you were at the house, Ms. Reagan?"

"I've been told I lived there as an infant. I don't remember, though."

"How well did you know Emma Delaney?"

"Not at all. I mean, she was my grandmother, but my mother and I had no ties to the family."

"And why is that?"

McNamara's voice was deep and gentle. Grace wished she had an answer to please him. "I don't know," she said. "Not for sure. It was a given in our home. A fact of life. Not something we dwelled on or even discussed."

The door to the library opened, letting in a hum of voices from the lobby. It was Friday afternoon and the weekend tourists were checking in. A petite blond woman with a curly updo entered the room, stopped as she caught sight of Grace, then raced over to her.

"Cousin! I'd know you anywhere."

Grace managed to set her coffee down and stand up before she was engulfed in a hug from the stranger.

"I can't believe I'm finally meeting you!"

The words were muffled against Grace's sweater. She tried to wiggle free, but the blond, a bird-like creature, remained glued to her sturdy frame.

"Well, this is a bit awkward, Ms. Reagan," McNamara said. "I don't believe you've met your cousin, Niki Malvern."

"I'm your mother's brother's child," the woman said as she released Grace after giving her shoulders a final squeeze. "My father is Stark Delaney. And, God help me, my brother is Winston. The guy who was napping under the bathtub. Chief Mac knows all of us from way back."

McNamara said, "I asked Niki to join me here. I need to talk to both of you."

Niki looked confused. "Why? Winnie's fine. Or he will be. He keeps getting himself into messes and he always walks away with only a few dings." She sounded irritated that her brother hadn't suffered more. "Even though he managed to break a finger when he pulled the tub over and knocked himself out, he broke his middle finger. Can you believe it? He's walking around with a huge splint that makes him look like he's constantly shooting a bird. Mom is apoplectic."

McNamara laughed. "Your brother is probably enjoying himself immensely."

"You know it. Even Dad laughs every time he sees it. That part's kinda nice. Or it would be if Mom would just chill. I should have told her to come with me today to get her mind off Winnie. She's looking forward to meeting you, Grace."

Grace noticed Niki didn't say how her father felt.

Turning to McNamara, Niki said, "I was surprised when you called, but of course I wanted to come and meet my cousin. Oh! Is this about your accident?" She grabbed Grace's arm again. "Dad heard you fell in the backyard and ended up in the hospital. Are you okay? Hope I didn't hurt you with my hug."

Grace wanted to shout that of course the hug hurt. Niki was hurting her *now*. She wanted to yank off her shirt and show the rainbow of bruises, her stitches and the sumac rash. Instead, she patted Niki's hand and removed it, saying, "I was walking near the rear of the property and fell. I'll live."

McNamara raised an eyebrow but only said, "Why don't you both sit down."

Niki took the second wingback, still smiling at Grace. "I can't believe it! You're really here!"

Grace couldn't believe it, either, but refrained from saying so.

Focusing on Niki Malvern, McNamara said, "I was just talking to Ms. Reagan about her accident. It turns out the situation is a bit more complicated than we originally thought. I asked you to come because your parents indicated they'd rather not deal with the police again so soon."

"So you did call them." Niki's face reddened. "Did Dad hang up on you?"

"He usually does if he doesn't like what I have to say," McNamara sounded unperturbed. "I need to interview your family and you're the low hanging fruit in that contest." This got a wan smile from Niki. "I've told your cousin, we've discovered she fell into a grave."

Grace wanted to leave. She wasn't ready for the Delaney relatives. Cyrus Mosley had left her four messages demanding to know how she was. Adding more people to the problems she had to deal with was too much. Her back hurt and her head was in a steady rhythm of pulsing pain. She dug in the tote for Ibuprophen, washing three pills down with the strong coffee.

"Oh, don't be silly," Niki said. "I'm sure she fell into the swimming pool."

"What swimming pool?" Grace perked up. Mosley had conveniently forgotten to mention a pool.

"Gran's, of course. She never liked it or the tennis courts, so she let the woods take them both over. She threw her trash out there for years. She said it was biodegradable. The neighbors couldn't see what she was up to because the area is so overgrown, but one of them eventually caught on and complained to the town."

"Avril Oxley?" Grace guessed.

"Yes! You've met her?"

Grace winced at the squeal in Niki's voice.

"Miss Oxley is an active supporter of community policing," McNamara said without a hint of sarcasm.

"Oh, Miss Avril's an institution," Niki said. "If you're doing anything in this town, you're dealing with her, whether you want to or not. She used to complain a lot about Gran and the house and property. It was embarrassing. She kinda calmed down over the last few years, but if she's stirred up again, you'll have your hands full, Grace."

"More useful information Mosley didn't share," Grace said. "A death trap pool and a neighborhood vigilante."

"We've seen the pool," McNamara said quietly. He sat on the arm of an overstuffed sofa and looked at them each in turn. "Niki, I know it's been a rough few months for your folks and for you. First your grandmother's death, then Winston's troubles -"

"You mean totaling his car and blowing three times the limit on the Breathalyzer. Don't sugarcoat it. Grace's gonna hear it all sooner or later."

"Okay, straight talk, then." McNamara agreed.

Grace didn't want straight talk. She wanted *no* talk. She wanted them both to go away and her head to stop hurting.

McNamara said, "Grace didn't fall into the pool. It was a grave. We found skeletal remains just below the surface of the pit."

"It's a small pool," Niki said in a defensive tone.

McNamara shook his head. "I am sure this is hard to believe, but you need to listen to me. The grave is a good fifty feet away from the swimming pool."

"Oh," Niki sat up straighter and after a moment nodded her head. "Well, okay. I remember now."

Grace's mouth fell open. Niki suddenly *remembered* a grave?

Even the Chief appeared surprised, but only said, "Please explain."

"It's not a big deal," Niki insisted. "A long time ago Gran had a big dog named Clancy. My dad remembers riding on him. He even has a painting somewhere of Gran and Clancy. Gran told us lots of stories about Clancy, but the one Dad tells the most is about when Clancy died. Gran wouldn't let Grandfather dispose of the body, and did I mention Clancy was a Great Dane? Dad said he weighed close to two hundred pounds. Anyway, Gran insisted Clancy had to be buried in the backyard. Grandfather wouldn't allow it and they had a huge fight. But in the end, Gran won, as usual, and Grandfather ended up burying the dog in the woods. It caused him to have a heart attack. He recovered, but Dad said things were never the same."

"In what way?" McNamara asked.

"I don't know for sure. Dad only said Grandfather was never healthy after his heart attack."

"So, is it possible?" Grace asked. "That's a big dog, maybe -"

"No." McNamara was firm. "The bones that are left are human, not canine. The pit isn't a swimming pool, it's a grave. If either of you knows anything that might help us determine what happened, now's the time to tell me."

He'd spoken to both of them, but Grace saw his eyes were on Niki. The younger woman flushed. A brief shake of her head was her only response.

"How long has it been there?" Grace asked. "The grave and the bones, I mean. When did the death occur?"

McNamara closed his notebook and rose. "Inconclusive at the moment. Given the state of the remains, it's been a long time. If either of you remembers anything or just want to talk, call me. I'm sorry to delay the renovation plans, but Delaney House and the grounds are blocked off until the MSP finish their investigation."

"The State Police?" Niki's head came up. She stood and reached out to touch McNamara's arm. "I want you to handle it. You know us. Why do the State Police have to come in?"

McNamara patted her hand. "It's protocol in a homicide investigation for a small department like ours. It will be a joint operation. We'll help, but the State folks will be lead."

"Homicide." Niki sat back down abruptly.

"Until we know otherwise, that's how we proceed."

Grace followed him to the door of the library. "Sounds as if it will take a while. I'll return to Washington if that's okay?"

"I have your statement. If the MSP have questions after they've seen my report, someone will contact you. If you should remember anything your mother may have told you that could have bearing on the investigation, get in touch immediately."

Grace agreed but knew she wouldn't be making a call. For thirty-six years, her mother had avoided the subject of the Delaneys and Mallard Bay. It was only while she was dying that she talked about her family home. Grace thought she had more questions than the police did and far fewer resources to get answers.

CHAPTER THIRTEEN

M*-I-N-E*
Three weeks later, the red letters still defaced the white metal cabinets and the kitchen still smelled. Henry Cutter's crew had cleared the garbage in the short period they'd been allowed to work, but years of abuse, neglect and decay weren't so easily removed. While the State Police had sliced and diced the grounds and searched the house looking for clues to a murder, Delaney House had been quarantined to all but law enforcement.

Grace wished they'd just bulldozed it.

"Are you excited to finally get started with the renovations?" Niki asked.

"Sure," Grace said without enthusiasm. She'd left her condo in Washington hours ago with the pre-dawn commuters, turning not towards the L Street offices of Farquar, Mitchum and Stoltzfus, but taking New York Avenue to Route 50 and Mallard Bay. As she reached the peak of the Chesapeake Bay Bridge, her BMW broke through the fog to a beautiful sunrise. For a moment, her heart raced with a rare feeling of joy and something that almost felt like freedom. A half-hour later, freedom was not an option. Delaney House was a huge ball and chain.

She'd turned down Cyrus Mosley's offer to buy the house outright. She'd promised her mother she'd follow through with the plan to renovate it and sell it in a respectable condition. That promise was looking more and more like a life-altering mistake.

"You should have told me you were coming," Niki said. "If I hadn't run into Henry yesterday, I might have missed you."

Niki had contacted her daily in the weeks since they met. At first, Grace was flattered to have an actual blood relation who wanted to be connected. She wanted - needed - to know about the Delaneys, but she was an introvert and Niki's constant contact quickly became intrusive. Still, Grace tried to make herself engage. Niki gave exhaustive details about her visits to Delaney House where she watched the MSP technicians perform work she didn't understand and gossiped with the neighbors. As the investigation dragged on without a quick identification of the body in the grave, Niki's emails took a more personal turn.

Everyone is on edge here. I can't wait for you to come back. We need to be together and get to know each other. What's your work like? What did you do today? Come for a visit, come for a visit, come....

A loner by nature, Grace felt smothered. She went longer between responses, which only made Niki resort to phone calls. Grace had hoped to slip into Mallard Bay, meet with Chief McNamara and the Cutters and be back in Washington before Niki heard she'd been there. She wanted to be charitable, but the word *stalker* flashed through her mind as she realized Niki was waiting for an explanation. "I'm not staying today. I'm only here to set up a work schedule with Henry and get some prices from Bryce."

"And to see Chief Mac," Niki added.

"I've already done that." Grace was happy there was something Niki didn't know. "Let's go outside," she hurried on in an artificially cheery tone. "We can wait for Bryce and Henry out there. I'm hoping there'll come a day when I can stay in this house longer than ten minutes without getting nauseous, but it's not today."

Outside the air smelled better, but the grounds looked like a set for a B-Grade disaster movie. The stretch of woods behind Delaney House had been trampled. Many of the trees near the grave had broken limbs. One small mulberry had been uprooted and dragged out onto the lawn. A white tent complete with secured side-flaps covered the grave and neon yellow caution tape tied to stakes cordoned off the back half of the property. Two warning signs declared the area to be a crime scene. Grace wondered if they would still be there when she was ready to market the house.

"Bryce!"

Niki's shout interrupted Grace's sour thoughts. She turned to see her cousin run across the lawn to meet the handsome contractor and his partner. By the time Grace had joined them, Bryce had gotten one of Niki's bear hugs and an enthusiastic kiss.

Henry Cutter gave Grace a gentle pat on the shoulder. "Don't mind them," he said. "All the girls do that. You can go next if you want."

Niki giggled as she dabbed her pink lipstick off Bryce's mouth. "Bryce and Henry gave me my first job out of high school. I didn't like cleaning, so Bryce hired me to paint. Some of the best houses in town have my handiwork."

"You maybe did three kitchens, max, before you decided college was a better option," Bryce said. "But you were our favorite employee while you hung around."

"And not for the reason you might think," Henry said, adding a Groucho wiggle of his bushy eyebrows. "Niki's an enthusiastic baker. Every morning we had muffins, sweet rolls and donuts. I gained a lot of weight that summer before she decided manual labor wasn't for her."

"What do you think running an inn is, if not manual labor?" Niki demanded. "A lot of good a history degree did me. I still clean house, bake and paint. But I do love it."

Niki's emails had been full of details about the bed and breakfast she owned. Grace had politely declined several invitations to visit, but Niki continued to raise the subject.

"Hey! Let's go to the inn to talk. I baked a coffee cake this morning and there's plenty left. We can discuss the house and I'll show you around."

Niki continued to hang onto Bryce as she talked. Grace thought they could be models for a wedding cake topper: Bryce tall and dark, Niki petite and blond, both gorgeous.

"Sorry, kiddo," Bryce peeled Niki off his arm. "We've got business to transact and I've got to be at another job site in an hour."

"And I have to be back in DC for a four-o'clock meeting," Grace added. "I'll need to leave soon."

Undeterred, Niki said, "So, do you know anything new? What'd Chief Mac tell you?"

"The police are finished for the time being and they're going to let me start renovations on the house as long as I stay away from the woods. They have a lot of forensic work to do, but beyond the basics, nothing new."

"I've also heard from Avril Oxley." Grace turned her attention to Bryce and Henry. "She wanted me to know she would be taking an interest in any work we do on the house."

"Avril and I get along fine," Bryce said. "She's the chair of a local unofficial historical preservation group. They're rabid about saving the area's history, and I find working with them not only makes my life easier, it brings in business. We're better off having her on our side from the outset. Avril's a purist, she only cares about history and buildings."

"Because she's so obnoxious humans won't have anything to do with her," Henry said.

"Cut it out," Bryce said. "You know how much business she sends our way and no, we wouldn't get it anyway. She tells everyone we do quality restorations."

"She's a pain in the ass."

"She has influence," Bryce countered.

"I get it. She's an influential pain in the ass," Grace said. "I'd like to move on to the schedule for work. Whatever we do will be scrutinized and we'll just have to deal with it. Well, gentlemen, let's get to it. Ready for a walk through?"

Once again, subtlety was lost on Niki. She stayed close to Bryce, pointing out obvious areas for renovation as they walked through the house. Grace tamped down her irritation and tried to take in the tidbits of useful information Niki dropped. It *was* helpful to learn where the mechanics of the house were located, and that the basement was full of spiders, camel crickets and the odd snake. She considered locking her cousin down there so she could have a conversation about finances with the Cutters. Privacy wasn't possible with Niki around.

Niki's tour concluded in the entry hall. "This is my favorite room in the house. I used to love to play dress up and pretend I was a queen in here."

"Who are you kidding, Nik? You still do that," Henry teased.

"Okay, this has been fun," Grace interrupted. "But I'm running out of time and Bryce and Henry and I need to talk contracts. So, Niki, I'll call you later in the week. How does that sound?" It sounded rude and she knew it, but she'd had all of the giggly gossipy Niki she could take.

To her surprise, Niki took the hint in stride, gave Grace a fierce hug, planted another kiss on Bryce and left, honking and waving as she pulled out of the driveway. Grace felt limp with relief.

"I've only got about ten minutes," Bryce said, "but this won't take long. I worked up an estimate last night and from what I've seen this morning, I think it's sound. We can stay with the basics, or we can do the full restoration or anything in between. It's your call."

Grace looked at Henry, but his face told her nothing. If he still had reservations about renovating Delaney House, it didn't show.

"Where do you propose to start?"

Henry said, "My crew will need about a week to get the place emptied and surface clean."

"I wanted to talk about the clean out," Grace said. "The police took all the documents and photographs they found. Chief McNamara has promised to give me copies of what they have." This was what she hadn't wanted to discuss in front of Niki. "I photographed the interior of the house the last time I was here. I'm looking for any information on my mother. My parents. Anything at all." She felt her face redden, but hurried on. "As you saw, the first floor rooms are empty except for trash. I've studied the photos and didn't see much of interest or value other than the furniture on the second floor. And I want to go through the books and the clothes stored in the main upstairs bathroom, so you can leave it as it is."

Henry nodded and said, "We'll leave that room for you and we'll keep a lookout in the rest of the house for anything that isn't ordinary trash."

"You will be careful, though?" Grace asked.

Henry frowned, "Well, look. I can't guarantee anything. Maybe you should be here while we work, you know, check everything before we take it to the dump."

"There's no need for that," Bryce broke in. "We'll be careful. It shouldn't be hard to tell what's valuable."

She wanted to stay and sort everything herself, but it wasn't possible. She had a long-running case coming to trial and obligations to her client. She needed to leave soon in order to make a scheduling conference.

"I wish I could stay," she said. "I'll check in with you often. Send me a text with a shot of anything you're unsure about. Or better yet, if there's any question about an item, keep it."

"No problem," Bryce said, looking relieved. "Leave everything to us."

Grace hoped it would be as easy as he made it sound.

The Cutters' estimate to clear the house and restore the front parlor ceiling and the bathroom above it was straightforward. Returning Delaney House to the condition it was supposed to have been in when she bought it would cost more than forty thousand dollars. She thought Cyrus Mosley was going to be very unhappy.

Grace nodded to Bryce and said, "When can you start?"

CHAPTER FOURTEEN

"The bones in the grave belong to a young woman."
Grace wondered if the police academy had trained Lee
McNamara to deliver bad news. He sat across from her in Farquar,
Mitchum and Stoltzfus' smallest conference room and studied her as
if calculating her reaction. He'd left his uniform behind in Mallard
Bay. In his conservative navy blue suit and red pinstripe tie, he could
have been a client anxious to settle a complicated transaction. Grace
intended to let the reception staff think exactly that. She needed a
new client, not a police chief questioning her about a murder.

"Do you know how she died?" she asked.

"Trauma to her left temple seems the likely cause. Whether she
died instantly or not, we don't know."

"Any idea who she is?"

"Ideas, yes. Proof, not so much. That's why I need help."

"From me." Grace couldn't imagine how he thought she could
help him.

"You and the Delaneys."

She was grateful he hadn't said 'your family'. She was still
processing the new familial ties and, so far, she didn't like them.

McNamara continued. "I had a talk with Henry Cutter. Went over to Delaney House yesterday to see how the work was coming along. He's saving a lot of things for you."

Once again, Grace was reminded there was nothing confidential in a small town. "Did he tell you what I was looking for?" she asked.

McNamara shook his head. "Not specifically, no."

"Good, because I didn't tell him." She felt slightly mollified. At least Henry wasn't spreading rumors.

"Suppose you tell me." McNamara's voice was gentle but firm. He was on her turf, but he still held the upper hand. She didn't like it, but told herself they could be searching for the same thing. What difference did it make who got to the answer first? She had to trust someone, and Lee McNamara appeared to be her best bet.

"I hope my mother left something in the house that will tell me who my father is."

"You don't know?"

"I know who she said he was. They fell in love while she was in college and married when she got pregnant with me. He was older, in the Army and was deployed right before I was born. He died in a car accident in Germany when I was a few weeks old."

"Sounds reasonable. Sad, but reasonable." McNamara settled back in his chair and crossed his legs. He had the air of a man waiting for the rest of the story.

"It gets sadder," Grace said. "He had no family. They had no friends in common who could tell me about my father as I grew up."

"This bothered you," he said when she stopped.

"That's just it. It didn't. I never questioned it. Mom and I were happy. 'Two girls against the world' she'd say. We had a nice home, a good life. Mom dated some, no one for very long. She had a lot of friends, but most of them were work related or neighbors. Even when I grew up, went to law school, got this job, we were always together. We talked ten times a day by phone or text and had dinner whenever I could get away from work. She was my best friend."

It was only when McNamara leaned forward and said, "I'm so sorry," that she realized tears were leaking from the corner of her eyes.

"Oh, God!" She grabbed a tissue. "I can't believe I went into all of that. It isn't important. What I wanted to say," she stopped as she realized she'd said exactly what she wanted to this kind man, who even now was waiting patiently for her to finish. "When my mother died and I had to go through her papers, bank accounts, and safe deposit box, it was what I didn't find that bothered me."

"Documents?" McNamara asked.

Grace took a deep breath and said, "In the papers in the house, was there a death certificate for my father?"

"No. I'm sorry. You were hoping to find something in Delaney House that might identify him?"

"I know his name, place of birth. I mean, he's real."

"Of course, of course," McNamara said. "Do you have any records at all?"

"No. No marriage license or obituary. Nothing from the Army. Not a single piece of paper with his name on it."

"And you thought you'd find information in Delaney House?"

"I recently learned we lived there after he died. I hoped maybe she left it all behind her when we moved to Washington. Maybe she didn't only cut ties with her family, she cut ties with her entire past."

McNamara opened a canvas briefcase and took out a thick sheaf of papers.

"These are copies of all the documents of any kind that we found in your grandmother's house. There's nothing concerning your father. In fact, most of this is ordinary daily detritus, grocery lists, bills and such. But there are some items we're hoping will spark a memory for you or the other family members. Anything you remember hearing about the time of the murder or afterward would be helpful. Anything at all."

Grace eyed the thick stack of documents. "There are hundreds of pages here."

"Most of it useless, I'm sure." McNamara's tone was agreeable but didn't offer an option for refusal.

"Most?"

"The documents are in chronological order. There is an inventory sheet on top. The earliest items are letters between Emma Delaney and her family back in North Carolina. You'll see in later correspondence her mother returns the letters and, obviously, Mrs. Delaney kept them. I've given a set of these documents to Stark and Niki, too. Winston refused to cooperate, but I'm hoping one of you will read something that will spark a useful memory."

"Is there anything about my mother in here?"

"I'd rather you read everything without bias from me."

Grace looked at the stack. "This will take forever."

"According to the medical examiner, the murder occurred sometime in the late fifties or early sixties. A young woman has waited more than a half-century for justice." McNamara rose and held out his hand. "Whatever you can do to help will be appreciated."

SHE WAS ABLE TO IGNORE THE PAPERS ON HER DINING ROOM TABLE until the weekend. In the intervening days, the long awaited court case settled on the eve of the trial only to be promptly replaced by two more battling clients funneled her way by David Farquar. Her boss seemed pleased. Grace felt like she was drowning. By the time the official workweek was over, she would have mucked out the kitchen of Delaney House if it meant she didn't have to read another legal document or listen to another angry person.

She knew she should spend the weekend getting up to speed on her new cases, but she gave her Saturday morning to Lee McNamara's documents. By the time she'd finished a pot of coffee, she was hooked. It didn't happen immediately. McNamara was right. Most of the papers were trash and rated no more than a cursory glance. But others did what all the hours she'd spent in Mallard Bay had failed to accomplish. Slowly, Grace began to get a sense of who her grandmother had been.

Grocery store receipts showed Emma Delaney usually bought bologna, saltine crackers and box wine. Fuel bills, bank statements and tax returns said she must have closed off most of the house in the winter and could have qualified for food stamps.

As the image of Emma's last years began to take shape in Grace's mind, so did the memories of her own childhood with summer camps and riding lessons. Had the luxuries she'd enjoyed while growing up come from a woman who was cash poor at the end of her life? Why hadn't Emma sold Delaney House sooner?

But it was her grandmother's letters that caused Grace to keep reading through the afternoon.

She watched the sunset from her tiny balcony overlooking Connecticut Avenue and remembered the sunrise on the Chesapeake Bay. Her 900-square-foot condo felt cramped after the expanse of Delaney House. The balcony suffered in comparison to the wide porches back in Mallard Bay.

She needed to talk to someone objective, but friends had fallen by the wayside during the years she had narrowed her life to her work and David. When Julia's cancer reappeared with a vengeance a year ago, the last of Grace's social life disappeared. She'd been torn in half between Julia's needs and the demands of a man who was always busy. Always too busy.

Now she was almost free. Free and rudderless for the first time in her life. She could pick up the phone, find Cyrus Mosley and accept his offer. She imagined the conversation, signing the papers. Disposing of the house, its people and their secrets.

It felt wrong.

SHE DIDN'T EXPECT DAVID TO BE COMPLETELY UNDERSTANDING WHEN she called him on Sunday morning to tell him she needed another leave of absence, but she also didn't expect him to fire her. She'd thought she was ready for a negative reaction and was surprised to find his words hurt.

It's too much, Grace. I've done what I can, but you've pushed me too far.

That was her whole problem, she thought as she sat staring at her cell. The tiny photo of David's face seemed to watch her reproachfully from the contact list. She was tempted to stab the little green phone symbol next to his name and tell him how wrong he was.

She hadn't pushed David, or anyone else, far enough. But that was about to change.

Feb 20, 1953

Dearest Nanny,

I am so sorry. I have so much to tell you, but those words are the most important. I need to say them to everyone, especially to Ford, but I can't bring myself to do it. I'd have to tell him why I'm sorry and I've waited too long to do that. I think you guessed the real reason why I couldn't leave after Christmas as I'd planned. Your lighthearted treatment of my excuse let me know you didn't believe influenza prevented me from traveling. As usual, you were correct. And as usual, I ruined everything - again.

Poor Ford never knew. I kept dithering about telling him. I wanted to leave so badly and if he knew I was in that condition, he'd come after me, so I didn't say anything.

I got 'sick' after the New Year's Eve party. After I realized what kind of 'sick' it was, I couldn't decide what to do. Last week, the decision was taken out of my hands. I wasn't far enough along to need a doctor, thank goodness, so Ford didn't have to be told. Of course, he didn't notice anything was wrong.

He isn't a bad man, Nanny, despite what I've said. He simply isn't the man for me and I certainly am not the woman for him. The awful truth is, I'm relieved not to be tied to Ford with babies. And since I'm not, I'm coming home. I still have the money Mother gave me as a wedding gift, so I won't be penniless even though I won't take any money from Ford. Maybe Mother knew how things would end with us.

Anyway, I'll be with you on Stark Mountain in a week or two. It all depends on timing. Ford is going on a business trip and will meet up with his father in New York. I'll use his visit as a chance to - I almost wrote 'escape'. That sounds so horrible, and yet that's what it feels like.

I'm coming home.

Love,
Emma

Oh, Nanny!

I didn't get yesterday's letter sealed before the phone rang and Ford gave me the news his father isn't coming. His new wife is pregnant and can't travel. Can you believe the irony? Ford is beside himself. I have to get this into the mail. I don't know now when I will come, but I AM coming home. Don't worry and please don't tell Mother and Papa. I will figure it out.

All my love,
Emma

April 2, 1953

Dear Mother,

Ford and I are well and very relieved to hear you are all the same. Please read the newsy parts of this letter to Nanny and Papa and let them know how much I love them. Tell Nanny everything is fine with me and make her believe it. I'm working things out here and I will never forgive myself for worrying her when she was so sick. Promise you'll never keep bad news from me again. The thought I could have killed her whining on about my life when her heart is so bad - enough about that. You take care of her and I'll straighten myself out here. Fair deal?

Here's a blurb for her: Winter has passed and spring here on the Eastern Shore is glorious. Papa needs to figure out how he can get away from the store and bring you all to see me. Now that Nanny is living in town with you, maybe you can take a vacation? You will love this beautiful place. It's so different from Asheville, you'll swear you are in another country.

I'm sure Papa is saying one can travel easier than three and I really would come home to see you, but Ford can't make the trip right now. Too many pressing things at work, and he doesn't want me to travel alone. Besides, he has me involved in so many activities, leaving at this point would upset his schedule.

Anyway, I have a new friend, Audrey Oxley, and I know you will love her when you meet her. Mother, not a word about my best friend being a single woman. She's the niece of a local merchant who is very successful, and he is the head deacon of the First Church in Christ. The family is well placed, so don't worry. It's a relief to have a friend who isn't a social obligation, if you know what I mean.

You will be pleased to know, Mother, Mallard Bay is just a little Asheville in terms of the ins and out of our social hierarchy. I am putting your lessons to good use. Why, only last week, I hosted the

Garden Club and my new rose bed was much admired. When it's in full bloom, it will be featured on the Bay Republic's society page and I'll send you a copy of the article. Now that should make Nanny smile!

I must close and get busy. Dinner for eight tonight - a campaign strategy session for our local congressman. I am sure there will be imaginative plans for arm-twisting donors hatched over the prime rib. The beautiful Waterford goblets you sent at Christmas will toast a band of merry conspirators. Audrey and I will entertain the ladies with something lighter and I'll serve your lemon icebox pie.

I hope you are all pleased with the transformation of your tomboy rebel child.

Tell Nanny not to worry, there's still a bit of the old me here, but I'm trying hard to grow up.

Love,

Emma

CHAPTER FIFTEEN

"Mother, he's a grown man, not a child. He's behaving like a jackass and since I can't stop him, I'm not having anything to do with him at all. I am certainly not apologizing to him or anyone else."

Niki rolled her eyes at Grace and held up an index finger, "Mother, *mother!* Stop. I'm with Grace right now and she can hear you."

It was true. Grace could hear the tinny voice blasting through Niki's phone.

"I'm sorry I raised my voice," Niki said when the squawking paused. "I apologize to you for being rude, okay? Now I have to go. Grace is giving me a ride home and I don't want her to hear this."

"Glad I was useful for something," Grace said as Niki dropped her phone into her jacket pocket.

"Mom's trying to guilt me into coming over for dinner and making nice with Winnie. It's not happening. I'm cutting him out for a while. For my own sanity, you know?"

Grace pulled her car over to the curb in front of a large colonial that looked old enough to have come by the description due to its actual age. A white sign in the yard announced *Victory Manor Inn* in gold letters. She'd arrived in Mallard Bay only a few hours before and called Niki. This time when Niki offered a room at her inn, Grace said yes and they'd sealed the deal with lunch at a harbor-front cafe.

While she'd have preferred to stay at the Egret Inn with its lovely privacy, the severance pay David offered in exchange for a non-compete agreement would only keep her solvent for a few months. Most of the lump-sum payment would go into Delaney House and Grace knew she shouldn't count on getting all of her money out again anytime soon, if ever.

"I won't be staying long. I'll get a place as soon as I can," Grace said as she opened the BMW's trunk and took out a suitcase. Niki hadn't blinked when Grace told her she was in Mallard Bay to stay through the renovation, but the loaded trunk seemed to surprise her.

"Think you brought enough stuff?" Niki asked.

"I was able to rent out my place for six months. I'll find a place here as soon as I can."

"Nonsense," Niki said. "You'll stay with me."

Grace tried to make her smile look more genuine than it felt. The 'family' rate at Niki's B&B was much less than the cost of staying at the Egret Inn, but it would still take a bite out of her funds.

Sub-leasing her condo in Washington had been a last minute decision. Money won over worry when a house-hunting co-worker asked if leaving the firm meant Grace was moving away. Short-term rentals in buildings like Grace's were rare and a tenant she knew personally was too tempting to pass up. Having the condo's mortgage and fees covered meant one less worry while she was in Mallard Bay. An apartment on the Eastern Shore or even the room at Niki's inn would be a fraction of the cost of her DC home.

Grace felt better about the arrangement when she saw the pretty yellow room on the second floor of the Victory Manor Inn but still wasn't sure how long she could take her effervescent cousin. She had just hung up the last of her clothes when Niki called out from the hallway that she had a surprise. Grace opened her door to find Niki holding a large plastic box.

"I've got a date this afternoon," Niki said. "I'd cancel, but it's complicated, so I thought maybe you could entertain yourself with these while I'm gone. I mean, if you want to." She held the box out to Grace. "Family photos from Gran's house. I'm not much for keeping stuff like this, but you might be interested."

It was all Grace could do not to rip the container out of Niki's hands.

"They're yours," Niki said. "You can have them. I wasn't sure why I was keeping them after Gran died, but now I do. I was saving them for you."

For the first time, Grace hugged her cousin with affection.

As the afternoon passed, Grace sat at a round table in Niki's sunny kitchen and sifted through black and white photos of strangers and newspaper clippings spanning more than sixty years. Stark Delaney and a Tony Delaney were named in reports of high school baseball games and field hockey tournaments. Julia Delaney played softball and won swimming competitions. Older articles chronicled the rise of Winston Stratford Delaney III, 'Ford', through civic groups into local politics.

Grace felt an unfamiliar tug of jealousy as she leafed through articles recording Winston's science fair project and Niki's dance recitals. Still, overall, she felt oddly satisfied when she put the last clipping back in the bin and replaced the lid, resealing the past in its plastic tomb.

She'd checked an avenue of information and nothing had changed. She still didn't know what caused the family's rift, and she hadn't learned anything about her father. There were no new facts to change her mother's account of their history.

LATER THAT EVENING AS SHE AND NIKI WERE SHARING A BOTTLE OF wine and a pizza, Grace asked if there were any other contractors she should consider before consigning all the work on Delaney House to the Cutters.

"Well, I've known them my whole life and I've always had a crush on Bryce, so I'm hardly impartial." Niki laughed at Grace's expression. "Oh, come on! The man is a *god.* Don't tell me you don't think so, too."

"Are you two involved?"

"Okay, don't answer me, but you know he's amazing. And, sadly, no. I'm not his type. He isn't mine, either, but I'd be willing to make allowances."

Niki's tinkling laugh was contagious. Grace was coming to realize it was hard not to like the girl - in small doses.

"So who is your type?" Grace asked. "Who was your mystery date this afternoon?"

Niki rolled her eyes. "I'm embarrassed to tell you after the way he behaved when you met him. We've been on and off since junior high. I love him, but I'm never gonna be in love with him if you know what I mean. We get the idea every now and then to try again. We're on the downside right now, and I swear this is the last time. He's got to move on and I need a fresh start."

"I've met him?" Grace asked, thinking back over her short time in Mallard Bay.

"Aidan Banks. You know, the officer who came to the house when you found Winnie under the tub."

"Oh." Grace had no trouble remembering Banks' angry face. "Well, that explains why he was so agitated. I guess he was upset about your brother."

"He stays upset about Winnie. They've hated each other even longer than Aidan and I have been together."

"Chief McNamara said he was rude because he'd worked on the scene of a fire at a rental property. I guess landlord negligence sets him off?"

"Let's say Aidan has issues and I'm trying not to let them become my issues. Now, your turn. Who's the man in your life?"

There was no way to explain David Farquar without opening up her life to Niki, and that wasn't going to happen. "No one at the moment. My life has been mostly work and taking care of my mother."

Niki frowned. "Well, you came to the wrong place if you want to find a husband. The Eastern Shore is long on retirees and short on eligible men you'd look twice at."

"Not a problem," Grace said. "I want to get my life settled. Romance can wait. Besides, you got married, right? Your name's not Delaney, so there must be a Mr. Malvern."

Niki had never mentioned a husband. Grace realized she'd never given her cousin's personal life any thought before now.

"I was somewhat precocious," Niki grinned. "I got married the summer after high school. It only lasted a few years, but that was long enough. Bob decided letting me have this house free and clear was a better settlement than alimony."

Grace had never handled divorce settlements, but Niki's story sounded odd. "You must have had a good attorney," she said.

"Cyrus," Niki answered. "And he didn't have to be good. Bob is 59 and worth a bazillion dollars. If I'd had the stomach for a fight with the old fart, I wouldn't have to run an inn for income." Again, the silvery laugh lightened her words. "The 'victory' in Victory Manor Inn was the divorce settlement."

"You married a man, what? Thirty years older? When you were eighteen? That's, that's…"

"Profitable. Obviously." Niki laughed.

"I was going to say 'unusual'," Grace said.

"You wanted to say 'trashy'."

"No! But maybe precocious is the right word."

"Mom uses it a lot. She also said Bob was a good catch before she knew he didn't intend to give up his other women. We kept that part from Dad. If he'd killed Bob, it would have ended the settlement agreement."

"Well, you did say your father has a bad temper."

Niki's laughter died abruptly. "It wasn't funny at the time. We hide a lot from Dad, just so you know."

It was an opening Grace had been looking for. "I wonder if you would be willing to set up a meeting for me. With your parents, I mean."

The silence in the dining room grew uncomfortable as Grace waited for an answer. Niki pretended to be occupied picking pepperoni off her pizza and stacking the orange disks in a greasy column.

Grace finally said, "Okay, this isn't a good idea. I can call them and we can meet without you. I can understand..."

"No." Niki spoke softly, but firmly. "You don't understand. That's the problem."

"Then tell me. I'm going to meet them sooner or later, you know."

"I'm afraid they'll be rude. My parents, both of them, are difficult. They are bookends, in a way. Dad is abrupt and can be," Niki hesitated. "He can be cruel. Not intentionally. He just doesn't care what anyone thinks. He says what's on his mind and people sometimes get hurt."

Grace thought Niki was probably the one who was most often hurt, but she said nothing.

"I mean, don't get me wrong, he's there when I need him. Most of the time, anyway. He loaned me the money to redo this place as a B&B after my divorce. He'll always come over if I need something done, too."

For the first time, Grace saw that Stark might have some traits in common with his sister. Julia had always been at Grace's side.

"Mom is his marshmallow," Niki went on. "She's gooey and soft around him, but will take the head off anyone who upsets him. She says it's because when he's mad it's hard on her, but I know it's more than that. She's proud to be the wife of a strong man. She used to say that to me when I was little. She'd say, 'Niki, find yourself a strong man like your daddy. You take care of him and he'll keep you safe.' She brags, saying she's the only one who can handle him. Frankly, the two of them together suck all the air out of a room. I try to avoid family gatherings as much as possible and when we have them, I go to their house so I can leave when I want." The speech seemed to drain her.

"Okay. I'll wait until they're used to me being here."

Niki looked relieved.

"But don't get too happy," Grace added. "We're about to have a change of subject neither one of us will like."

The doorbell rang.

"How did you do that?' Niki rose to answer the door.

"Avril Oxley," Grace said, nodding to the window behind Niki's chair. "She's coming up the front walk."

CHAPTER SIXTEEN

Avril was happy to take Niki's chair, a slice of pizza and coffee. Niki seemed happy to give it all to her and disappear, giving Grace a sympathetic smile as she left.

"I've never approved of fast food," Avril said after her first bite of pizza. "This is soggy."

"Sorry about that. But we weren't expecting you."

"Worry about yourself. Dough and cheese will kill you." Half a slice of pizza disappeared before the old woman continued. "I only just heard you were here. We need to talk before you do anything to Delaney House."

Grace remembered all the warnings she'd heard about the nosy neighbor, especially Bryce's insistence that it was better to pander to her meddling than to fight it. "I appreciate your interest, Mrs. Oxley and I assure you I'll follow all the required procedures." She emphasized 'required' and earned a deadeye stare from Avril.

"You may call me Avril. And it's Miss. Miss Oxley," Avril said. "I had a lover but never married her. Illegal in Maryland back then."

Grace had just taken a mouthful of water and snorted it through her nose.

"Oh, get hold of yourself, girl," Avril said as Grace mopped up. "I wasn't always old and bent, you know. Was a looker in my day and so was my Glenda. This," she waved a hand to indicate her tiny, arthritic body, "comes in one way or another to everyone lucky enough to survive into old age."

"Yes, ma'am," Grace said. She was still recovering from choking and couldn't manage more.

Avril nodded in approval and popped a pepperoni round from Niki's abandoned plate into her mouth. "So, I'm here because I know more about Delaney House than anyone alive today and I feel it's my duty to help guide you through the renovation. It's arguably the most important structure in this town. One of the oldest standing structures on the Mid-Shore for that matter. Of course, it's been rebuilt and renovated so many times; most of what's left of the original building isn't visible. But some of the original wing is exposed."

"Really," Grace said, her initial resistance to the irritating woman clashing with her interest in anything to do with the house's history.

"Yes. What's now the kitchen and the room above it date to about 1740, and you would know that if you'd done the proper research before considering renovations. You can't run in there willy-nilly and start changing things. You could wipe out a piece of history. A piece of our history. So, I'll help you."

"Thank you, but…"

Avril smacked the tabletop with her open palm. "No 'buts' about it, missy. You need me."

It was a silly argument and Grace decided to use it to her advantage. "You're right, of course. I apologize. Let me get you more coffee and maybe you could tell me about the house? Did you see it back when my mother, Julia, was young?"

"I was here well before then. Born and bred in the house I own now. Family homes. Nothing like them for history." Avril continued eating and talking through two more slices of pizza and half a pot of coffee. Grace found herself caught up in Avril's stories of sneaking into Delaney House as a child - snooping through other people's homes being a habit Avril cheerfully owned up to.

"Delaney House was better than any castle I'd ever read about. Everything was big and shiny. It all sparkled to my eyes. The housekeeper was a large woman named Miss Rollie. Your grandfather's mother died when he was born, you know. Miss Rollie had been with the Delaney family forever, so she took over raising Ford, too. At least as much as Mr. Winston would let her. She was a kind woman. When I'd show up over there, she fussed over me like I was hers. She would treat Ford and me as if we were brother and sister until Mr. Winston came home, and then she'd send me home."

Grace hadn't given much thought to the occupants of the house before her mother's family. "Was it a big household back then?" she asked.

"Oh, yes. Household help mostly. Houses like ours - although my family home is much smaller - always had a housekeeper and maids and a gardener. Ford, your grandfather, was an only child growing up and my mother died in a boating accident when I was six. We had our semi-orphaned state in common, and we played with each other for years. We even had a path through the woods from my backyard to his. It's grown over now, of course."

Grace couldn't imagine children traipsing through those woods without a bushwhacker leading the way.

"The natural division of boys and girls eventually split us up. He was a few years older, so he tired of me first and I was crushed. But time takes care of those things and we grew up. We never got on in our teenage years. Then my older half-sister came to live with us and Ford was all of a sudden interested again. She was invited everywhere. She was beautiful and outgoing and she dragged me along with her until she established herself in our society."

"Do you remember how the rear parlor looked before it was wallpapered?" Grace reddened at her own rudeness, but she was tired and Avril appeared to be settling in for a long, involved, personal memoir.

Avril blinked at the abrupt change in the conversation but changed gears without hesitation. "It looked like the same room without wallpaper hanging in strips from the ceiling."

"Oh," Grace said in a placating tone. "So you've seen it recently, then. Do you remember the furnishings? It's empty now."

"Of course I remember the furnishings before Emma ruined everything," Avril snapped. "I assume you don't care how it looked in the past couple of decades. No one in their right mind would want it like that."

"The deterioration started about twenty years ago?" Grace asked. No maintenance and haphazard DIY projects would account for the current state of the house.

"We're all deteriorating, every day, all day. Look in the mirror. Is that the same view you had twenty years ago? I'm guessing no."

Grace laughed. She was beginning to enjoy Avril. Which could be dangerous, she told herself. The old woman could strike like a snake.

The snake was smiling a bit, Grace's laughter having apparently restored what passed for Avril's good humor. With another refill of her coffee cup, she took up her story again.

"When Mr. Winston and Ford were alive, they kept the pocket doors open between the parlors to make one large room. The front parlor had a grand piano placed between the windows so it could be seen from the street. Near that was a full-sized harp. It was the most beautiful thing I'd ever seen and I would always try to play it, but of course, it never sounded right with a child pulling the strings. The harp was gone by the time I was attending the parties Ford and Emma gave, but the piano was still there and they would always have a string quartet or a jazz band. We did have fun. I met my first lover there."

Hoping to keep Avril on track, Grace said, "It's hard to imagine all of that in the house I bought. There's no furniture on the first floor now."

"Good thing, with tubs falling through the ceilings. All the paintings gone, too?"

Grace nodded.

"Shame. Emma's oil portrait was over the mantle. Ford was so proud of it. He'd commissioned it from an artist in New York, I think, from a photograph of Emma some famous photographer took when they were first married. Most people were impressed, but my sister said Ford only did it because he needed something splashy to cover up the loss of the Monet."

"They lost a Monet? A real one? How did that happen?"

"Well, 'lost' isn't the right word, really. Mr. Winston remarried and had another child and wanted to settle his affairs between his new family and Ford. He came to visit and when he left, the Monet, a Degas and some of the furniture - antiques, I was told - were packed up and shipped to France where Mr. Winston lived with his new family."

Grace digested this for a moment. "You must have been close to them to know all of this."

"Off and on over the years, yes, we were close. Sort of. But for a while, my sister was Emma's best friend and she told me a lot."

Grace gave in and asked about the sister Avril clearly wanted to discuss.

"Audrey. We resembled a little, but she was older and taller. And a lot more glamorous. Her mother was my father's first wife. It didn't last long. Their marriage, I mean. My father supported Audrey and her mother, of course. And when Audrey wanted to come live with us after she graduated from college, Father agreed." Avril sat back from the table and seemed lost in the memory. After a moment she said, "Audrey's why I called the police when I heard you'd fallen into a hole in the backyard."

Grace wished she had something to take notes on. Avril seemed to like dropping non sequiturs and watching her victims try to catch up. Grace took a moment to gather her thoughts, but it was hopeless. "Okay, I give up. What does your beautiful sister have to do with the hole I fell into?"

"The police didn't tell you? That's interesting." Avril looked at her empty cup and said, "Fresh coffee would be nice."

Grace gave Avril her best hostile witness glare and was rewarded with a smile.

"I didn't mention Audrey just up and vanished, did I?"

You know damn well you didn't. Grace shook her head. "What did you tell the police?"

"I reminded Lee McNamara about Audrey as soon as I heard about your accident. He's hard to read. I can't tell if he's taking my concerns seriously."

So you're spreading those concerns around a bit, Grace thought. She was getting an education in small-town gossip. "The chief didn't mention your sister to me."

Avril gave an exasperated sigh. "I have to get him to pay atten-tion! It's the only thing that makes sense, now that I look back."

"How long ago did she disappear?"

"1960."

"Surely the police investigated back then. You did notify them, right?"

"Did I? No. My father was still alive and in charge of the universe. You better believe he turned over every stone, but discretely, of course. He pulled in every favor he could and when none of the official avenues turned up anything, he hired detectives. The one place he didn't search was the neighbor's backyard."

"Why not?"

"Because we didn't think she was *buried* anywhere, of course. We believed she'd run off. Audrey was a bit of a wild child. She'd be considered a saint by the standards of today's youth, but she was a bit scandalous in our stuffy little town. Her mother had been a dancer in New York, but our father saw to it Audrey was raised in boarding schools and not with her mother's theater friends. Father hoped Audrey's education and the right social setting could make her one of us. And for a while it was working. We hoped she was settling down. She was even engaged. When she ran off, Father said it all must have been too much for her. She didn't want to get married and couldn't see how to get out."

"Didn't her fiancé look for her?"

"He and my father made a project of it for months. They finally gave up when the last detective Father hired found a man who said he sat next to a woman who looked like Audrey on a bus to New York."

"That must have been hard for all of you."

"It was, but Cyrus took it the hardest."

CHAPTER SEVENTEEN

"*Cyrus Mosley?*" The idea of Mosley as anyone's love interest made Grace glad she hadn't eaten much.

Avril nodded. "He was Audrey's fiancé. I can't say he's waited for her all these years, but he never married."

Grace tried to make sense of what Avril had said.

"I suppose it's a lot to take in," Avril said. "But you've got to get up to speed, girl. You can't just wander into a situation like this and blunder around. This is another reason why you need me."

"You don't really believe Emma Delaney would live in a house with her best friend buried in the backyard, do you?" Avril had thrown a lot of information at her, most of which sounded like a soap opera plot.

"When I look back, I'm not sure I ever knew Emma at all," Avril said. "She was kind to me when she first came and when Audrey was alive. Even afterward, if Ford weren't around, she'd invite me over to swim with her and the children. But she changed when Ford died. And later we had a falling out and never mended it. I wanted to go over when she died, but there was no point by then. There was no one I wanted to see and I don't feel safe going over there alone now. Look what happened to you."

"May I ask what you and Emma fought about?"

Avril looked uncomfortable. "I suppose you have a right to know," she finally said. "I'm not proud of it, but we argued over your mother. Actually, you were the catalyst for our last argument."

"Me?"

"I told Emma she was selfish to hold Julia back and I, unfortunately, made a rather adamant point about you being Julia's child to raise, not Emma's. I thought it needed saying, but I should have stayed out of it. Emma never forgave me, and then Julia stayed away. I never saw her - or you - again. Emma's heart was broken and I made it worse for her." Avril's cantankerous air had dissipated and she looked exhausted.

Grace offered to call her as soon as she had decided which renovations she would be doing to Delaney House. Avril was a walking bank of information and, as irritating as she might be, she was right about one thing - Grace needed her.

THUNDERSTORMS SWEPT IN FROM THE WEST, POUNDING WASHINGTON and Baltimore before expending the worst of their fury as they crossed the Chesapeake Bay. A steady rain passed over Mallard Bay in the night, easing Grace's sleep and leaving the morning with a crisp edge. When she arrived at Delaney House, the place looked better after its rain bath. If she didn't look at the mud field that was the backyard, Grace thought she might be able to hold on to her good mood.

The work crews were in full swing. Grace picked her way around sawhorses and the electrical cords that seemed to snake everywhere. She found Henry on the second floor in one of the larger bedrooms standing amid piles of clothes, shoes and odds and ends of furniture.

"My God," Grace said, trying to hold onto her temper. "Sorry, Henry. It's just, I hoped it would be clean by now."

Henry looked embarrassed. "When you called and said you were here, I came over to try and organize this a bit before you got here."

"*Organize* it?" she looked around the room and came back to Henry who was holding an armful of old shoes.

"We may have had a miscommunication. You said save everything that wasn't trash. We tossed anything that had ever been edible and all the stuff Winston left behind. Didn't think you wanted his dirty laundry."

"Not in any sense of the phrase," Grace said.

"Everything that we kept is in this room. If you could go through it and take what you want, I can clear it out and then we move on to the next step."

"Which is?"

"The exterminator."

Grace groaned. "If you clean out everything, isn't that enough? Is an exterminator really necessary?"

Henry gave her a pitying look. "At the very least, you'll need a certification that the house is termite free or that termites have been taken care of, if you do have them. You can't sell the property without it. But you have mice and I'll be surprised if you don't have a regular zoo in the attic." He handed her a business card. "We work a lot with this guy, Benny Pannel. He specializes in humane removal of mice, squirrels and such. He goes in, sets traps, shows us where the entry points are and we seal them up. He removes the trapped animals and replaces the traps until he's gone a month or so without finding anything. Nice guy; you'll like him."

"Is he expensive?"

"He's competitive. You need someone experienced and Benny can handle the job. Problem solved."

"Maybe that one," Grace said.

Her enthusiasm for searching for clues to her mother's past went out the door with Henry. The piles of Emma Delaney's belongings seem to swell around her.

Get moving!

Feeling her mother's hands at her back, Grace reluctantly started her search.

AFTER EIGHT HOURS OF SORTING THROUGH EMMA DELANEY'S WORN clothing, outdated magazines and grocery coupons, Grace wished Henry Cutter hadn't taken her instructions quite so literally. Her definition of 'junk' and his varied considerably.

Other than some clothing and costume jewelry she thought Niki might want, she sent most of the contents of the second floor to the dumpster. From six bedrooms once occupied by a wealthy family, there remained only two beds and a dresser. Grace thought she could feel the house's resentment as she walked through the empty rooms.

She was grateful Niki wasn't home when she returned to the inn. A shower, quick nap and clean clothes put her in a better mood until she wandered into the inn's dining room and found a formal table setting for four.

"Good! There you are. I was about to come find you," Niki entered from the kitchen carrying a low centerpiece of pink roses and white mums.

"Looks like a dinner party," Grace said, taking in Niki's white sheath dress and chunky onyx necklace. Her hopes for a quiet recovery from the long day died away.

"Mom called this afternoon and seems to be over her snit. I think putting my foot down with Winnie's bad behavior was just what she and Dad needed. They're coming to dinner and I have to say, I'm rather proud of myself." She glanced at Grace. "You did ask to meet with them, remember? You're okay with this, right?" A pointed look said if Grace had a problem, it was too bad.

Grace sighed. "How long do I have? I need to change." The leggings and oversized turtleneck sweater, which had been fine five minutes earlier, felt shabby.

Niki insisted she looked wonderful, and anyway it was too late. The front door opened.

CHAPTER EIGHTEEN

F ar from being the imposing figure she'd imagined her mother's
brother to be, Stark Delaney was at least two inches shorter
than Grace and thin to the point of gauntness. Unlike her mother, he
had dark coloring, graying brown hair and hooded brown eyes, but
the family resemblance was there in the shape of his features. His
face said he was present under duress.

Connie was a bit taller than her husband and wore heels, which
allowed her to stand behind him and still have a clear view over his
head. Her expensive knit suit was at odds with Stark's khakis and
golf shirt.

Introductions were awkward, but Niki and Connie shared a gene
for streaming conversation. Stark and Grace silently assessed each
other as mother and daughter segued through one safe topic after
another. When Niki served drinks, Stark grabbed his scotch with a
touch of desperation.

Grace asked about Winston's condition as if he had been injured
in a benign, generic accident - not one involving a falling tub.
Connie responded as if her son was ten and recovering from the flu.
Appreciative of their efforts to maintain polite small talk, Grace
answered Connie's questions about her life in Washington in the

same breezy, superficial way and the evening moved along. Stark's vocabulary was limited to basic short responses and facial cues aimed at his wife and daughter, all of which appeared to be ignored.

Dinner occupied their attention for a while. Niki's lasagna was undercooked and the Caesar salad was heavy on garlic. The meal's deficiencies gave Stark a reason to complain and describe his various digestive ailments while Connie first rushed to her daughter's defense and then give her own critique. The lack of concern or response on Niki's part said this was normal dinner conversation. By the time coffee and biscotti were served, Grace was more than ready to change the subject.

As if reading her mind, Connie said, "Grace, has anyone told you how much you look like your grandmother?"

"It's been a long day." Stark cut his wife off and pushed back from the table.

"Daddy, let's talk a bit longer." Niki slid the plate of biscotti toward her father.

"You and your mother talk enough for all of us. And she," he nodded at Grace, "looks tired. Let's call it an evening."

"If you could stay for another few minutes, I'd be grateful." Grace flushed, embarrassed to sound so needy.

Stark nodded unenthusiastically and stared at his coffee.

"I'm sure Niki has told you what's happening at Delaney House," Grace said.

Stark's head came up. "She's told Connie about the work you're doing to clean Mother's house up, yes. Good thing you're a D. C. lawyer, you're gonna need a lot of money to fix that old pile up."

"I'll only be able to do so much. Of course, I'll keep you informed of the progress. I've hired Bryce Cutter to do the renovations."

Stark and Connie looked at each other but said nothing.

"I do have some questions," Grace hesitated. Now that she had the opportunity she wanted, she found it hard to introduce the topic of her parents. She started with the easy question first. "I'm searching for anything that might have belonged to my mother -"

A cattle prod couldn't have gotten a sharper reaction. Stark and Connie jerked to attention and Niki's hands flew to her mouth. In the next second, Grace realized how she'd sounded and hurried on. "I don't know much about my mother's early life, or my own. I'm hoping to find any of my mother's childhood things. Toys, books. Anything like that. Would you have any idea where Mother's things might have been stored?"

Stark laughed. "Stored? Girl, nothing is stored in that place. *Buried* under crap, now that's another question and I don't have any answers for you."

If any of the Delaneys found irony in his statement, it didn't show. The tension eased, but only a bit.

Grace took a breath and said, "Well, then, I'm hoping maybe you can tell me something about my father." There. It was out.

Connie started to answer but stopped when Stark raised his hand. "Are you saying your mother didn't tell you? I wonder why?"

"She did," Grace said. "But she wasn't long on details about him, and I never thought much about it until she was sick. By then, she didn't want to talk and I didn't want to upset her." It was the truth. Mostly.

Stark said, "Again, I'd have to ask why? And if your mother didn't want you to know, why should I tell you?"

Her uncle was enjoying himself. Grace tamped down her anger and focused on the man sitting across from her. Stark's eyes were glittering and his mouth was drawn in a thin, mean smile. He wanted a fight.

"A valid question," she said and was rewarded with a grunt of surprise.

Connie and Niki were bystanders who couldn't look away from a train wreck.

"It wasn't fair for my mother not to tell me about my family." Grace sent a silent prayer for forgiveness to Julia. "Obviously, she didn't feel she could, but I have no idea why. She never said anything at all about any of you and she didn't say much about my father."

"I never met your father and my sister left a long time ago." Stark's words were sharp. "Why do you want answers now? Seems a little late to get worked up over missing your daddy. You're crowding forty if I'm not mistaken."

Grace clenched her hands under the table and tried not to laugh. If this was all he had, she could handle him. She had planned answers to this very question, but tossed them and went with an end run around the question.

"Please," she said. "Anything you're willing to tell me will be more than I know now. Can you at least tell me why my mother left Mallard Bay?"

Playing helpless to the bully worked.

Stark leaned back, relaxed and in charge. "Seemed to me like Mother and Julia just couldn't get along. You were still a toddler when Julia got it into her head to leave. I guess you know that. I was away at college, but I had to come home to deal with Mother. She nearly lost her mind worrying you'd starve or need something she could give you." Stark took a sip of coffee, but no one stepped into the silence. Finally, he said, "Young people can be thoughtless."

He could have meant Julia or Grace or the universe in general. Grace didn't ask for clarification, but said, "You must have known something about my father."

Stark shook his head.

Connie came to life, saying, "We felt terrible for her, of course." Now that the tension had eased, she seemed eager to join the conversation. "Your parents didn't have much time together. It was tragic."

"You weren't there," Stark barked at his wife.

Connie's face colored. "That doesn't mean I didn't feel bad for your sister when I heard the story."

"Don't repeat gossip. You weren't there."

Niki gave Grace a 'see what I mean?' look and bowed her head.

"Did you see my mother after she moved to DC?" Grace tried to steer the conversation back to the pre-Connie ambiance.

"Of course." Stark glared at Grace as if it had all happened yesterday. "I hauled furniture and Julia's clothes and your toys across the damned bridge a dozen times until Mother finally accepted that Julia wasn't going to come home. Nothing was enough for either one of them. Mother'd call me home to take a load over to whatever rattrap apartment Julia had you in, and Julia'd be mad when I showed up. She'd yell at me to take it back and we both knew I couldn't without sending Mother on a bender."

"Stark!" Connie yelped. "Don't say…"

"She was an alcoholic! Who the hell doesn't know that? She had every reason to be, but damn, woman. You think it's a secret? The girl here," a forefinger jabbed in Grace's direction, "*owns* her house. You think she hasn't figured out there was something wrong with her grandmother?"

"Daddy, please!" Niki broke out of her protective posture and stood up. "I'm sorry, but…"

"Don't you 'Daddy please' me, young lady. What the hell did you think would happen when you set this up? She wants to know about her family. I've got nothing nice to tell and I won't lie." He turned to Grace. "Go talk to Cyrus Mosley. He's got all your answers."

Grace hung onto her temper, but it was a struggle. "It sounds like you had a rough time of it and I'm sorry I've upset you." *And that my mother's death doesn't seem to bother you*, she added silently.

Stark snorted. "The past was bad, but the present's no picnic either. You've got your hands on Delaney House, understand? *Delaney.*" He stood and tossed his napkin over his plate. "You selling it when you're done tearing it up?"

Grace didn't take the bait. "Yes."

"I thought so. Just remember this while you're enjoying that money you get. It's mine."

"Really?" Grace kept her tone mild. She wanted him to keep talking, but Stark only glared at her. She said, "Is that why you left me a message in the kitchen?"

"What the hell do you mean, a message in the kitchen?"

Niki's face paled as she caught on. "Oh no, Grace. Don't."

"Mosley said it was your son who trashed the place, but now, I'm wondering. Someone spray painted a message in the kitchen."

Stark merely looked surprised, but Connie said, "No!" and stood abruptly. "My boy was good to his grandmother! He's always working on something over there. Stark and Winnie have been treated unfairly. Surely you can see that, Grace!"

"I don't know what happened before I got here," Grace said. "But your mother-in-law sold her house, remember? She didn't give it to me, I bought it."

Without taking his eyes from Grace, Stark said, "I'm leaving. If you want a ride, Con, you're leaving, too."

———

WHEN THEY WERE GONE, GRACE INSISTED NIKI TAKE A LARGE brandy and go to bed. As she cleared away the dinner dishes and rehashed the evening in her mind, she found herself humming her mother's favorite song. They'd watched *Casablanca* so many times, she and Julia could quote long lines of dialog. Behind the sounds of running water and clanking dishes, Grace could hear her mother's clear voice singing *As Time Goes By*. One line from the song resonated.

If she only knew which fundamental thing applied to the decisions her mother had made, maybe she would finally understand what had happened to her family.

Jan 3, 1955

Dear Mother,

I am so sorry I had to cut the call short last night. The important thing was to let you and Papa know we had gotten home safely. I could tell you didn't really want to talk and with Ford rushing me to get off the line, it did seem best to hang up, but I felt the lost connection to you and home like a wound.

You are handling everything so well. I don't want to be a burden, but I am so grief-stricken I can hardly move. I'll get better, but I know we have lost the best of us with Nanny's passing and I just can't accept that she's gone. I'm so glad we got a nice long visit in last summer and of course, last Christmas on the mountain was wonderful, even though the trip was short. Who would have guessed I'd spend two Christmases in a row in North Carolina? Or that this year's trip would be so sad.

You are her daughter and no doubt think I am a thoughtless and selfish child to write to you this way about my loss, when yours is even greater, I know. But I want you to know how much I admire you. I don't believe I have ever told you that. You have borne so many sad times, my little brothers - two sweet children gone too soon. And whom did you have to raise? A headstrong hellion who caused you no end of problems. I know Papa isn't always an easy man - for heaven's sake, don't let him read this! But you have handled him with grace and care, and you have made him happy. And I think you have been happy, too? I hope so, although, Mother, dear, it is hard for me to tell. You are always in motion and always busy. Now that it's too late for me to contribute to it, I pray you are also happy. At least a bit, from time to time. I have come to realize we shouldn't ask for more if we are to avoid perpetual disappointment.

And there I go, veering off to the gloomy side again, which is not what I want to do. This letter is meant to tell you I love you, I admire you, and I will do my best to make you proud.

Emma

CHAPTER NINETEEN

A shiny black van was parked in the driveway of Delaney House when Grace arrived a little after eight the next morning. *THE VERMINATOR- No Job Too Big, No Critter Too Small* was painted in large yellow script across the side panels. An army of bees, ants, snakes, and rats swarmed, slithered and crawled their way around and through the words, leaving no doubt which critters the company could handle. Grace studied the van from her car and thought about going for more coffee. In Washington.

"Hey! You gonna sit there all day?"

She hadn't seen Bryce approach and yelped in surprise when he opened her door and offered his hand. His smile - and those dimples - wiped away her alarm. Feeling silly, she let him pull her along like a reluctant child to meet The Verminator.

A tall, gangly young man jumped out of the van, greeted Bryce and introduced himself to Grace as Benny Pannel. Over the next hour, they walked the house and grounds, Bryce pointing out areas of concern and Benny taking copious notes with an eagerness that made Grace nervous. She trailed along after them until they headed to the basement. She felt itchy after hearing Benny talk about the creatures that could be inhabiting Delaney House.

After checking on the crews who were painting the newly repaired front parlor, she ran out of excuses to avoid the chore she'd planned for the day. The original second-floor bathroom, with its crooked second doorway off the main staircase, awaited a clean out and scrub down.

Like other areas of the bedroom wing, the once-elegant bath was stacked wall to wall with items Emma Delaney had considered worth saving. Books lined all the walls and filled the tub. Old toys, appliances and small odds and ends covered the rest of the room. Grace started work near the hall doorway. Her plan was to have 'save', 'donate' and 'trash' piles, but only one heap grew as she worked. The contents of the Victorian-era bathroom were going straight to the dump.

She'd cleared the area around the sink and toilet when she heard Bryce call her from the main hall. She joined them, her heart sinking at the sight of his grim face.

Benny Pannel, on the other hand, was elated. He happily reported there were bats in the attic and signs squirrels shared the space with them. Termites were eating the service porch. Mice ran rampant throughout the house and were nesting in areas on every floor. A roach infestation, camel crickets and three dead birds rounded out his initial assessment.

"I'll probably find more as I get into it," Benny informed her cheerfully. "At least the woods've been cleared some, what with the police working back there and all. You won't be popular with the neighbors for a while. Critters gotta go somewhere."

Grace groaned and said, "Let's focus on the house. How long will it take you to clear it?"

"I can lay traps for the squirrels in the attic and basement today. I'd wait until the basement is cleared to do any kind of treatments. Start with an empty shell, you get the best results on a job like this. Now, I'll have to get permission for the bats. They're protected, you know. The gov'ment loves a brown nose bat, good for the environment. They eat -"

"I don't care what they eat!" Grace was horrified. "I want them gone!"

Benny looked at her quizzically. "The bats won't hurt you. I mean, there's always a possibility of rabies, but the same's true of any mammal. And these bats eat insects. Neat, really. And the government protects them."

"Of course they do," Grace said.

"But we're lucky. This is the best time of year to exclude them from a building. That's the official term, 'exclude'. They don't want you to get any ideas about hurtin' the little guys. I've got pamphlets I can give you."

"No, not necessary," Grace said as she tried to remember the symptoms of rabies.

Bryce put an arm around her shoulders, gave her a hug and said, "Benny here will fix us up. Don't worry." Before Grace could react, he'd released her, stepped back and was saying, "So you and Henry's crew will be done by today, right?"

Grace thought about the state of the bathroom. "Tomorrow, maybe."

Bryce checked his beeping phone. "Busy morning. I've gotta go. Benny's people can start setting traps everywhere but the bat locations on the third floor. My interior construction crew can start on the attic once Benny makes sure it's safe to proceed with the bat removal. Excuse me, *exclusion*. Given what we saw upstairs, that's our first order of business. We'll replace everything rotted up there, which includes sections of the fascia under the eaves. We'll seal the bat entrances and then we'll repair the points of entry around the chimneys and screen them. That'll stop the birds and squirrels, too. We'll patch the sub-roof to keep it all secure and dry until you decide what to do with the repairs to the slate roofing. And we'll need to strip out the insulation. What there is of it, is soaked with bat urine and guano." He paused for Grace's groans and Benny's laugh. "When we've secured the place against the larger pests, Benny can set up a maintenance plan to get rid of the roaches and mice. We'll rip out the areas with termite damage, Benny'll treat it and we'll rebuild the service porch floor. Sorry, Grace. I hate to tell you, but I think that will be the minimum you'll need to do."

Grace's heart dropped. 'Basic reno' had expanded to a complicated operation and wouldn't touch the living area.

"Sounds good," Benny said. "And just so you know, there are live bats in your attic right now, so don't be startled if you see them flying around in the early evening."

"Outside, you mean?"

"Well, sure. But remember, you got 'em inside, too. I'll trap the ones that can't or won't leave, and I'll remove them from the house. No poison, no dead bodies, no mess."

"Except the urine and guano," Grace said.

Benny, who apparently didn't do sarcasm, nodded happily as if she'd finally gotten his sales pitch.

"Where do you take them?"

"Well, outside of course…"

"And far, far away?"

"If you want, sure. But you need those bats, and I can bring you some bat houses. They're like bird hou…."

"Far, far away, Benny. The bats, the mice, anything that isn't human goes far away from this house and from me, got it?"

The estimate Benny gave her explained his irritatingly good mood. As she watched the Verminator van pull away from the house, she wondered if a buyer could be talked into co-existing with government-approved bats. The idea of bats in flight over her head made her shiver and then jump when Bryce patted her arm.

"Whoa, now," he said. "It's not so bad. Happens around here all the time. Some of the best houses have bats. Most people don't even realize they have them nesting in their attics."

She tried to smile. If she had to have bats, at least she had Bryce to handle the problem.

"It will all work out, Grace," he said softly. "You'll see. We'll be done here before you know it. I'm going to give you a beautiful, critter-free house."

She wanted to believe him. He was standing close enough for her to smell the clean scent of new wood and licorice from the box of candy he had in the pocket of his flannel shirt.

"Did you take in the early matinee?"

"What?"

"You usually see Good and Plenty in the candy counter at the movies."

"Oh, these. Want some? Good for what ails you." He tapped a small pile of the tiny pink and white candies into the palm of his hand and waved them under her nose.

"Too early in the day for me," Grace smiled. "But you go right ahead."

Bryce popped the handful into his mouth and grinned. "I buy them in bulk. Love the stuff." He looked like a little boy, happy with a mouthful of sugar.

She said, "I'm not a licorice fan, but I've always loved the way it smells."

Bryce's expression went from playful to interested.

Grace gave him a wide smile. "Well, back to work for both of us."

She was halfway to the second floor when he called after her, "Not fair to take advantage of a guy when his mouth's full of candy." But he stayed where he was in the hall, and she kept climbing the stairs.

CHAPTER TWENTY

G race traded her sneakers for a pair of white rubber boots she'd found under Emma's bed. After carefully inspecting and wiping them off, she stuffed her feet into them, tucking her jeans down inside. The knee-high boots were clunky and a size too small, but looked as if they would withstand attack from anything short of an alligator. She added heavy rubber gloves to round out her safety gear and went back to the second-floor bathroom.

Once she got into a rhythm, she picked up speed, while still looking for anything that might have been her mother's. Nothing struck a chord. Soon all that was left was a chest-high, triple-row of old magazines and books stacked along the back wall of the bathroom. She heard skittering noises and prayed the sounds were coming from inside the walls. She told herself mice couldn't get through her rubber boots and gloves and pushed on.

Emma Delaney had an eclectic taste in reading materials. Issues of Popular Mechanics from the 70s and 80s were stacked on top of Regency romances and outdated library reference volumes covering astronomy and theology. Stained and worn cookbooks were interspersed with children's books. A copy of 'The Diary of Anne Frank' was bracketed by 'The Home Taxidermist' and Carl Sagan's 'Cosmos'. All were lumpy from water damage. Grace didn't want to know what kind of water or how they'd gotten wet. With a sigh, she began to fill one trash bag after another, dragging them to the hall when they became too heavy to lift.

She was on the last row when the wall moved.

Later, she had no memory of leaping across the bathroom and slamming the door behind her, but when she opened her eyes, she was in the hall, amazed that her pants were still dry. The pier mirror hanging on the wall in front of her showed a tall, wild-haired woman with a face whiter than the rubber boots on her feet.

Deep breaths. Get a grip. Think of something else.

"Thanks, Ma. That worked when I was six," she muttered. She told herself her rapid heartbeat was only shock and her pounding head was due to allergies. She wasn't having a heart attack and, although she'd just carried on a two-minute rant aimed at her mother, she wasn't crazy. "The wall did not move," she said out loud.

She considered calling the workmen from the front parlor. But this was her house. Her problem. And she really wanted to see what was in the bathroom for herself.

No rodents or reptiles met her as she eased the bathroom door open. What she'd first thought was a large crack in the plaster was really a crude doorway. She'd been so worried about mice and spiders, she hadn't noticed the back wall was made of drywall, but now it was plain to see. No attempt had been made to match the room's crown moldings. There were gaps where the cheap materials met the original plaster. A print of the Eiffel Tower taped to the wall hid the upper door hinge, and the last stack of books she'd moved had been acting as a doorstop. In the darkness beyond the opening, the skittering noises were louder.

After another long moment of hesitation, she said, "Oh, for God's sake" and yanked the makeshift door wide open. When nothing rushed her, she leaned cautiously into what she was already thinking of as the secret room.

The area behind the false wall was lined with metal racks and shelving, all packed with clothes bags and hat and shoe boxes. The cedar-scented air felt out of place in Delaney House. She'd found - what? Emma's secret stash of haute couture? With ten rooms on the upper floors to choose from, why had Emma created this hidden closet? Then Grace remembered her mother's hidey-holes. The need to have a private spot where you could keep treasures safe. In Emma's case, it looked as if clothes were her main concern.

She replaced a stack of books in front of the drywall door to keep it shut. Emma's fashion stash could stay where it was for the time being. Grace was suddenly seized with the need to see the whole house. She'd poked around the woods and found a grave, dabbed at cleaning the house and found a secret room. What else was sitting right in front of her? Enough poking and dabbing. She wanted to see the entire property she'd bought from her grandmother.

She wanted to know everything. Besides, she told herself as she stomped down the stairs to the first floor, she'd already handled a dark, hidden room in a bat-infested house. She was ready to take on the basement.

THE VINE-COVERED WINDOWS LET IN ENOUGH LIGHT TO ALLOW HER to move around old furniture and gardening implements. When the pull-cord for a single overhead light bulb brushed against her face, she shrieked and jumped a foot, but was happy for the additional weak light it spread around the former servant's quarters.

The room under the kitchen and butler's pantry in the main house appeared to have served as a large kitchen and gathering area for the household staff. A cast iron stove and a large brick fireplace with hooks for cooking pots shared the space with cast-off furniture and yard equipment. In fact, it appeared every gardener who had ever worked at Delaney House had tossed his tools down the basement steps.

Enough light spilled into the center hall to allow her to find her way toward the front of the house. She didn't venture into the various rooms that opened off of the hallway but surveyed each one from the doorway. Nothing she saw encouraged further exploration. Gloom, more gloom and junk filled the spaces, which once housed the people who'd kept Delaney House operational. The door at the end of the hall was shut. Before she could lose her nerve, she stepped forward and opened it.

In the gray, filtered light from the street-side windows, she saw neatly stacked boxes lined up beside a long, wooden worktable. Other than two folding chairs, the rest of the room was empty.

"One room," Grace said as she looked around. "One damned room out of twenty-four is clean and it's in the basement."

AFTER HER INSPECTION OF THE BASEMENT, SHE ROAMED THE ENTIRE property, making herself examine every area not still cordoned off by the police. Since she didn't find anything out of the ordinary, it didn't take long.

In need of a break and lunch, she took a carton of yogurt to the first-floor quarter landing and settled down. The staircase was the only place in Delaney House that wasn't covered in workers or grime or both. Her vantage point six steps up from the main floor gave her a view of the stained glass windows and raised-panel wainscoting in the front hall. So far, this spot on the stairs was her favorite place because it allowed her to believe she could pull off the renovation. And with her back against the wall, nothing could sneak up on her.

She didn't want to share her discovery of the secret room until she'd gone through the clothes and personal items Emma Delaney had hidden away. She also didn't want to rummage through any more dark corners of the dirty house, so she sat on the steps and tried to come up with a plan that was more appealing. She ran out of yogurt with no new ideas, only the need to keep moving.

The room behind the false wall turned out to be a cedar-lined and relatively clutter-free space that smelled lightly of lavender. She remembered Mosley's comments about Emma being fond of sachets and felt ashamed of her cynicism. A wrought-iron floor lamp spread a warm light that eased her apprehension. Nothing moved and she could only hear the sounds of the workmen on the first floor.

Where to start? Garment bags lined the right-hand side of the room. On the left, shelves of hat and shoe boxes were organized by season and color. A light layer of dust lay over everything, but not as much as she had expected. On a whim, she selected a box labeled 'Summer Straw 1958' and found a boater style hat with a yellowed grosgrain ribbon. The Garfinkel's label looked new, even though she knew the Washington landmark had closed years ago.

Other boxes produced cashmere and silks. Christian Dior, Lagerfeld and Chanel. All carefully wrapped in brittle tissue paper. She replaced everything the way she'd found it. Sealed furrier bags contained a mink jacket and two stoles with matching hats.

A rear corner of the room held a few men's things. Several Scottish wool jackets and linen suits were preserved with the same care as Emma's clothes. A black tuxedo and a dove gray morning suit hung beside a cashmere robe. Emma and Ford Delaney had been a fashionable pair. Grace sat on a needlepoint bench in front of a bow-front dressing table and wondered if the last reflection in the wavy glass had been an older version of her own face.

A 1950s-era jewelry box covered in blue tufted leather looked both out of place and deliberate. As if Emma Delaney had wanted this item to be identified as solely hers. The latch was stiff with age, but Grace teased it gently until it finally gave. She opened the first compartment to find a single empty envelope with a few words scrawled across the front.

If you have this, I am gone. Remember how I loved you.

Grace ran a finger lightly over the words. The handwriting wasn't distinctively male or female. Who wrote it? Who was supposed to find it? What had been inside? She felt like a voyeur.

If Emma had ever used the box for its intended purpose, the jewelry was long gone. Only letters filled the compartments. Small bundles, some tied with ribbon, others with corded string, were packed into spaces meant for gems and gold. She examined each bundle without untying it and saw the letters were addressed to different people, some to a woman named Ingrid Anders. She remembered Anders was Emma Delaney's maiden name. A few were addressed to Emma.

A quick check of the postmarks placed the last letter nearly twenty years before Julia's marriage to Jonathon Reagan. There was little likelihood the letters held any useful information for her and it felt wrong to read them, but she couldn't leave them behind. Cradling the bundles in her left arm, she closed the empty box and left the dark, sad room.

The bright sunlight streaming through the dirty turret windows did nothing to warm her as she reclaimed her seat on the first-floor staircase landing. A check of her cell showed she'd missed a call and had voicemail from David Farquar. She leaned back until she could see the domed ceiling, then let her gaze slide downward, taking in the architectural beauty of the open hall. She reminded herself the house was her mother's dream, a legacy. She was doing the right thing.

CHAPTER TWENTY-ONE

"Secret room? What secret room? I haven't poked around upstairs in years, but I think Gran would have said something."

Over dinner that evening, Grace tried to introduce the subject with a humorous tone, but Niki wasn't having it. She was still depressed over the party with her parents, and seemed intent on taking a negative view of every conversational topic Grace posed. The fried chicken dinner Grace had bought went to waste as both women picked at their food.

"This is so greasy," Niki finally complained. "I can't believe you got this chicken at Three Pigs."

The chicken had been crisp and hot at the deli, but instead of putting the foil bag into a low oven as the clerk had instructed, Grace had left it out on the counter while she and Niki shared a bottle of wine and griped about their respective days. The chicken was greasy now, but Grace knew the dinner wasn't what was bothering Niki. Her cousin had canceled a date to stay home with Grace, and Grace wished mightily that she hadn't.

"Look, take one blanket apology for my family, please?" Niki pushed her plate away and folded her arms on the table. "Last night was terrible, but you can see what I mean about my parents, right?

They're toxic. Between them and my brother and Gran's antics, there were times I wanted to find Aunt Julia and run away to her."

"Are you serious?" Grace gave up on her own dinner and poured another glass of wine. Reality's continual assault on her long-held perceptions was unsettling. She and her mother hadn't been cast from the family, her mother had run away. They hadn't been forgotten, Emma had continued to watch out for them. They hadn't been unwanted, Niki had longed for her aunt and cousin.

"Grace! You *saw* them - how they really are, I mean. You got the genuine Stark and Connie show. And now you're telling me Gran had a secret room? How bizarre is that? She lived in a huge house all by herself, for God's sake! Who was she hiding her clothes from? The termites and bats?"

Grace didn't mention the letters. Niki was in no mood for an objective review of whatever information Emma had hidden in her blue jewelry box.

"Maybe the rest of the house used to be neat and organized, too," she offered. "Maybe she wanted one place with pleasant memories where she could go and..."

"And what? Be a reasonable, nice person she apparently couldn't be when she wasn't holed up behind a fake wall in her bathroom? That sounds better, yeah. Let's go with that."

Grace shifted gears. If she couldn't talk Niki out of her bad mood, she may as well take advantage of it. "Tell me about life with Emma. I keep getting these bits and pieces, and all of you seem angry with her. Clearly, it was more than eccentricity."

Niki groaned. "She was just mean, okay? Well, not always. Nobody is mean all the time. And I can remember her rocking me and singing when I was real small. At least, I think I do. Maybe I only want to have the memory. Who knows? Winnie says he was her favorite and he's right. I was the one who wanted to play at her house. He was the one she wanted to see."

"Sounds like normal sibling rivalry."

"Sure. Some of it," Niki admitted. "But her face lit up whenever she saw Winnie. No one else was in the room when he was around. It would even make Dad mad, sometimes. One time, I heard him say, 'you've got two grandkids, you know,' but Gran ignored him."

Two. Grace took the thoughtless comment for what it was - Niki's bad memory, not her own.

"She was just generally cranky and grumpy," Niki went on. "She smelled old and her clothes were usually dirty from some project she was working on. She wore these white watermen's boots and looked awful. It was embarrassing. What? Why are you laughing?"

Grace told her about wearing the boots while she cleaned.

"Oh, Jeez! Don't let Dad see you in those. It'd finish him off. He told Cyrus he wanted Gran buried in them and I thought he'd really done it."

The wine finally had its impact on their empty stomachs. They laughed until Niki started to hiccup. When Grace described how she'd looked in the mirror after the bathroom wall 'moved' and she'd leapt into the hallway, Niki went off into another spasm of giggles.

"Why, Grace?" Niki gasped. "Why put yourself through this? Let Henry and Bryce clean it all out. It's funny now, but you must have gotten a real shock. God knows what's in that place. You've already been injured once, isn't that enough?" The laughter was gone; Niki's face sober again. "I've finally found you. I don't want anything bad to happen to you."

Grace reached across the table and took Niki's hands. "Something bad has already happened to both of us. I want to know everything, don't you? I want to know why my mother left here. What, or who, hurt her and your father. What made Emma do the things she did."

Niki pulled her hands away and stood up. "No! It isn't any of our business! Knowing what happened all those years ago won't make our lives any easier, only sadder. I want to deal with this life, today, the best I can. And I want my only cousin with me. Is that so much to ask?" She left the room without waiting for an answer.

"I want my father," Grace said, but as usual, there was no one to hear.

"COME ON, HELP ME OUT," GRACE SAID THE NEXT MORNING AS SHE and Niki waited for the coffee to brew. Niki showed no ill effects from the wine or their last conversation. Grace thought resiliency might be one of her cousin's best attributes. "You know I'm looking for anything my mother may have left behind at Delaney House, but so far I haven't found anything."

A clap of thunder made Grace jump, but Niki didn't flinch. An early morning storm with lashing rain threw the day out of kilter. With no deadlines to anyone other than herself, Grace found herself at odds. She was anxious to get on with the renovation but reluctant to leave the bright, cozy inn. Nagging at Niki for information was an acceptable delay.

Niki studied her hands for a moment and began to pick at the cuticle on her right pinky. "So what can I tell you? She was gone before I was born."

"Well, do you know which bedroom Mom used?"

Still worrying her cuticle, Niki said, "Dad complained about dragging everything up and down two flights of stairs when Aunt Julia moved in with you and when she left. That would mean you lived on the third floor. Aunt Julia's bedroom was next to Gran's when Julia was growing up. The large room on the other side of the ensuite that collapsed."

Grace made a mental note to check out both spaces. "I walked through the basement," she said. "It's all junky except for the last room under the front of the house."

"I'm surprised you braved it," Niki said. "And I'm astounded you found an empty room."

"Not empty, not completely. Just neat."

"Even more surprising. As I remember it, the basement was full of yard stuff and junk. Dad said when he was a boy, Gran had a workshop down there for gardening projects and other hobbies. He said it was clean and he remembers it smelled good. By the time Winnie and I came along, Gran wasn't much on gardening anymore.

We'd sneak down there, but it was scary. Lots of spiders." She found an index finger that needed attention and began to pick.

Grace busied herself getting coffee mugs and creamer out. She tried to sound casual as she asked, "Do you think Emma would have kept my mother's things?"

"I want to say yes, but the truth is, I don't know. Despite what I said last night, there were sometimes when she was nice, even grandmotherly. But she never talked about Aunt Julia or Tony. You've heard about him, right? Gran's oldest child?"

Grace poured the coffee and handed Niki a mug. "I saw some photos and articles in the box of stuff you gave me. So, there were three children?"

Tears welled up in Niki's eyes. "You're breaking my heart, Grace. How can you not know how many brothers your mother had?"

Because my mother and your father and our grandmother were secretive and selfish.

"Because something bad happened," Grace said. "I don't know what, but I'm going to find out."

Feb 8, 1956

Dear Mother and Papa,

You've only been gone a day and here I am writing a letter. I know I will be too busy to be lonely as soon as I am back on my feet. I wish you could have stayed longer with your beautiful grandson and me. Master Winston Stratford Delaney the Fourth! Now that you're gone, Ford will be the only one calling him that. I'm sticking with 'Tony'.

Call when you get home and I'll have news, I'm sure. If all goes well today with the nurse Ford hired, I'll ask her to move into the nursery wing on the third floor. I hear you, Papa, we should have planned better, but who could have predicted Tony would make his entrance so soon? Anyway, until the nurse situation is settled, Audrey will stay over. And Mother, I hope you see now how nice she is and how concerned she is about the baby and me. Just because she isn't married with children of her own, doesn't mean she isn't helpful with Tony. And she is such great company, as you said yourself, Papa.

Why, right now she is downstairs coordinating the food, which is still coming in from friends and church members. And at some point, she will arrange the nursery furniture Ford's father sent from France. I still say it's so elaborate, it's embarrassing - really, Mother - a hand carved cradle with Austrian lace draperies? The suite Ford and I bought was perfectly fine, but Ford says it can go back to the store. Oh, dear, I think I've already told you this. That nasty drug they gave me for the delivery is still wreaking havoc with my memory.

Anyway, until I can navigate stairs, Audrey will be in residence. She hates living at her father's house and Ford and I love having her around. I know you worry, but it will all work out well.

Your grandson is crying, and our prince will not be denied.

Call me soon!
Love
Mommy/ Emma

June 5, 1958

Dear Mother and Papa,

This will be short. I am trying to rest as much as possible so the bun in the oven will bake completely before she is born. And yes, I know this one a girl. I can feel it. A sister for Master Tony! And I'll name her Fiona, after Nanny. That will please you, won't it?

Once again, Audrey has come to the rescue and is keeping Tony occupied while I stay off my feet. The baby nurse is lined up though, so Audrey will move back home after my little Fiona comes. What would I do without Audrey? She's the sister I never had. Stop rolling your eyes, Mother. You know she's lovely. And she's engaged! That should ease your mind about her 'seemliness'. (Really, Mother? Unseemly? Just because of the dress she wore to the picnic? I'll have to be more careful about the photos I send if you're going to be so picky.)

Anyway, the happy fiancé is Cyrus Mosley. You remember Ford's friend Cy? We all thought he'd be the one to win Audrey, but until now she's said he was too serious for her. "No magic," she said. I sounded like you, Mother, when I gave her the lecture about marrying a man who could take care of her - see? I did listen. And Audrey listened to me. Anyway, Cy is crazy about her. He calls her his princess and you should see the diamond ring she has!

So your grandson has a princess for a nanny until the baby nurse arrives. She's wonderful with Tony and he loves her. Sits in her lap big as you please and pretends to read his books to her. He does resemble Ford when he concentrates with that serious scowl!

Have you decided if you're coming back after little Fiona arrives? It is hot here in summer, and I understand if you want to wait until October. But don't wait so long that the snow keeps you in Asheville for the winter. Fiona could be walking before you see her. I'll hush now and nap. I am awfully tired today. I miss you both!

Emma

June 8

Well, this is the craziest post-script ever! I didn't get this to the mailbox before my water broke - oh, Papa, close your eyes to that part. I know you heard the news from Ford and I will call you when I get home, but I can't wait until next week to talk about my Stark. Papa, you have to bring Mother up here right now and see my new baby!

I reread this letter and I almost tore it up, it's so silly, but you know your girl and I don't want to rewrite old news, I want to tell you about my baby boy. I am sure I thought he was a girl because he is so different from Tony. Instead of being big and blond with curls, Stark is tiny and dark. He will also have curls, I think, but now his hair lays in soft swirls around his perfect sweet face with its rosebud mouth. And his eyes! They are huge and so beautiful.

Tony is all Delaney, as we have known from the day he was born, but I believe I have given the Anders a new member of the clan in Stark. This child is the image of you, Papa. He was early, of course, so he's little, but I'm sure that will change. He's eating well and seems happy.

Now, about the name. I do hope you are happy with my choice. Ford isn't thrilled, but he could hardly complain. After all, I had no say at all in Tony's name, not that I would have changed it. I was so set on naming this baby after Nanny, but that wasn't possible. She never talked enough about Grandpa Joe to give me a good sense of him, and I never knew her parents at all. The only thing I could think to do in her honor was to name the baby after the place she loved best. When he's older, I'll introduce him to his mountain and tell him that's why he is so big and strong.

Please come soon and see your crazy daughter and her two beautiful children!

Emma

CHAPTER TWENTY-TWO

G race knew she couldn't avoid David forever.
Call me as soon as you can. It's important. She hadn't listened to the two voicemails which followed. David's direct line at the office had just started to ring when Chief McNamara walked through the kitchen door.

"Sorry to startle you. You didn't have to hang up." McNamara stopped to wipe his feet on the mat inside the doorway, but he didn't take his eyes off Grace. "Niki told me to come on in. She'll be behind me in a minute."

So much for the privacy she'd thought she had when Niki went out to the grocery store.

"I caught her as she was leaving," McNamara went on. "Looks like I'm getting you at a bad time, too."

"Not at all," Grace said. "Not a call I wanted to make."

McNamara raised an eyebrow and Grace found herself wanting to tell him everything. Niki arrived before the temptation to unload her troubles got the better of her. Her cheeks flushed at the thought of what David would say about her using a police officer for a confidant.

McNamara thanked Niki for the scones and coffee she offered

but asked her to wait until they'd talked. The timber of his voice changed and with it the friendly atmosphere in the room.

"I have some news and I need a favor," McNamara said after they were seated at the kitchen table. His notebook and pen were in his hand and Grace wondered if early in his career he'd practiced the move, sliding into interview mode while his audience's attention was deflected. "The medical examiner's report is finished for now. The remains in the grave are of a woman, which we knew. She was approximately twenty-eight years old. From the skeletal remains and other indicators, we know she was probably blond, Caucasian, around five-foot-four." He waited a moment and continued. "I'm doing the legwork for the State Police since I know all of you. I've come from your parents' home, Niki, where I asked your father for a DNA sample. He refused."

Niki took his words in, rapid blinking and clenched hands her only response. McNamara let the silence stretch. Finally, Niki said, "I'm not surprised. Dad's first reaction to everything is 'no'. He probably feels this is another invasion of his privacy."

McNamara smiled reassuringly at her earnest defense of her father. "It would be easier if he would give us a sample, but we can get the information another way." He removed two stoppered tubes from his coat pocket. "I need to get a sample from both of you. If our victim's DNA has markers that match one of you, then she's related in some way. But if she matches both of you, she's a Delaney."

"How did she die?" Grace asked.

"Head trauma."

"Maybe it was an accident, then," Niki said. "Maybe there was a family graveyard and Gran just didn't tell us. She hid a lot of stuff, you know. Grace even found a secret room the State Police missed."

McNamara turned to Grace. "Is that true?"

"Yes. It was easy to miss." Without giving herself time to think about what she was doing, she lied. "It was just another closet, clothes and shoes. Some furniture, not much. All old. You're welcome to come go through it." The letters sitting at the bottom of her tote bag called her name.

"A secret room," McNamara repeated. "Where?"

She told him about the back wall of the main bathroom.

"And you went through everything?"

"Only enough to get an idea of what's there." *And to find the letters.*

"Please keep the workers off the second floor and don't go back until I tell you," McNamara said. "I'll get some people back in there today if I can. I won't hold you up any longer than I have to."

"Chief Mac!" Niki's voice caught. "You're going to go through Gran's clothes? Whatever happened out there in the woods didn't involve her. She was just crazy. I mean, really crazy. Mental. Not crazy like a killer. You can't let people think she could have murdered someone." Tears trickled down her face. "Please don't do that."

"I'm sorry, Niki," McNamara said gently. "This is a homicide investigation. I can't control much and I can't stop rumors."

Grace fetched a box of tissues. When Niki had pulled herself together, she said, "Will the State Police do anything to Dad for not cooperating?"

"I won't need him to if I can get samples from you two."

"Have you talked to Avril Oxley?" Grace asked.

McNamara finished swabbing the inside of Niki's cheek before answering. "Yes," he said. "Have you?"

"Yes." Grace saw Niki was looking at her quizzically. "I'm sorry, Niki, I should have told you sooner, but with everything that's happened, I forgot. When Avril was here, she told me her sister went missing sometime in the late fifties or sixties. She didn't give me an exact date." Grace gave them the rest of Avril's story.

Niki was outraged anew. "Are you saying Avril thinks her sister, this Audrey, was murdered and buried in the woods? That's insane!"

"Avril didn't say anything about murder," Grace said.

"So, it wasn't murder - our grandparents just buried their friend in the backyard and didn't tell her family? Avril can't believe that. You can't let her say it!"

"Slow down a bit," McNamara said. "Your grandparents may

not have known anything about it. They could have been out of town when the woman was buried and not noticed the disturbance to the woods when they returned." McNamara finished sealing the swab he'd used to take Grace's sample and stood. "We're close and your DNA will help. I'll ask you two not to share Miss Oxley's theory. The fewer people who know, the better. For the moment, anyway."

Niki asked if he'd told her father.

With a glance at Grace, McNamara said to Niki, "He shared your feelings. I asked him to stay away from Miss Oxley. She's old, Niki. She sounds tough and acts tougher, but she's old and she firmly believes this is her sister. We all need to respect her fear and the grief that will come if she's right."

Niki's chin came up and her eyes narrowed. "Dad's right this time, Chief. Avril has no right to go around saying our family was involved with her sister. She has no right-"

"Stop it," McNamara's voice was icy. "Now. Listen to me and hear me. The Delaneys didn't corner the market on suffering. Don't make Avril's misery worse. Rise above it and leave her alone."

Niki covered her face with her hands and her shoulders shook.

"You're testing Avril, too?" Grace asked, breaking the awkward silence.

"Yes," McNamara said. "Only the three of you for now. If the Delaneys and Oxleys are preliminarily ruled out, we'll expand our search. Full DNA testing takes time, so we're already checking databases of missing people from that era, but the information cataloged online is thin and hasn't turned up anything. Dental records from that period are long gone, so it's slow work, I'm afraid."

She'd give him the letters as soon as she read them, Grace decided. A couple of days wouldn't matter to Audrey's sister, but Grace was tired of waiting.

THE LETTERS SHE'D READ BACK IN WASHINGTON GAVE A VIEW OF

her mother's family that changed Grace's life. What would this visit to the past do to her?

Laid side by side in chronological order, the letters from Emma's jewelry box formed a square four wide by three deep and covered the center of Grace's bed. Most were in a graceful, neat handwriting she soon came to associate with Emma Delaney. Emma and her mother, Ingrid, had produced letters that spanned nearly twenty years. Grace picked up the oldest one first.

She read slowly and took notes, identifying each letter and its contents, treating each page as evidence in a legal case. Which, she reasoned, they well could be. Three hours later she called Lee McNamara and made an appointment to meet him the next morning. She would give him everything she'd uncovered but first she wanted to talk to Niki.

CHAPTER TWENTY-THREE

"What do you mean, what happened to him? Grandfather died, of course. You don't see him hanging around, do you?" Niki was still irritable.

The afternoon and early evening had slipped away while Grace had studied the letters. Once she had her questions, she'd been so intent on getting answers she hadn't realized she'd stopped Niki on her way to bed. Now they were squared off in the upstairs hallway and Grace was wishing she'd left the conversation until morning. "I meant, *how* did he die?"

"Why do you want to know? Why is this coming up now?"

Grace didn't want to tell her about Emma's letters and the frustrating details they omitted. "I just realized I didn't know."

Niki narrowed her eyes at the weak explanation.

"Is there some reason you don't want to tell me?" Grace added, hoping to forestall any more questions about her sudden curiosity.

"He committed suicide," Niki said in a flat tone. "Shot himself out in the woods behind the house. We don't talk about it."

It was what she'd suspected after reading the letter in which Emma talked about funeral details, but it was still a shock to hear Niki's words. "Why?" was all she could think to say.

"Who knows? We sure don't. It was ages ago." Letting out an exasperated sigh, Niki said, "I can see where you'll go with this. Chief Mac has put all kinds of ideas in your head, but you can just forget about our family being involved with a murder. I know this is all new to you, but really. You can't think that of us."

"I just wish someone had told me. Do you think Chief McNamara knows?"

Red patches bloomed on Niki's neck and cheeks as she leaned in closer to Grace. "Ford Delaney, *our* grandfather, was the president of Mallard Bay Bank and Trust - the very bank we all still use now. He was on half a dozen boards and heavily involved in state-level politics. He also had a problem with depression and it eventually got the better of him. Daddy and Tony were young and your mother was only a baby. Gran loved Grandfather - anyone can see that by the way she grieved. He had a lot to live for, but I guess not enough because he shot himself. Okay? We don't talk about it; so don't bring it up again. Not to Chief Mac, and especially not to my father. Do. Not."

With a short jab at the air with her index finger, Niki stalked off.

Emma had never used the word 'suicide' in her letters to her mother, even though the inference was easy to make from her wording. Grace hadn't meant to upset Niki but now she had confirmation. Ford Delaney had committed suicide in 1961 - the general time frame the medical examiner set for the death of the woman in the grave. A hell of a coincidence, Grace thought.

———

WHEN SHE TURNED HER PHONE ON, SHE SAW THERE'D BEEN TWO more calls from David. Since she was already in an emotional turmoil, Grace decided she might as well confront him, too. He answered her call on the first ring.

"Are you all right?" His voice was tense with anger.

"You sound like I shouldn't be. What's wrong?"

"I couldn't get you and no one knew where you were."

She pictured him, still in the office, shoes, jacket and tie off, a carton of carryout Thai nearly buried under the paper he'd generated during the day. It was after nine, so the bottle of Jack Daniels would be front and center, having made its appearance when the largest corner office of Farquar, Mitchum and Stoltzfus transitioned from work to what passed for a home life in David's world.

Grace said, "You fired me. It would be in bad taste to keep showing up."

"You could have answered the damn phone!"

Her palms started to itch. After their first big fight, she'd gone through half a tube of cortisone cream before she realized it wouldn't cure the rash that was David.

"I'm not doing this." She kept her voice low so it wouldn't shake. "Tell me what you want or I'm hanging up."

"The very generous severance I gave you means you *do* take my calls. You left some unhappy clients here, Grace, and you owe them, even if you don't think you owe me."

Now the base of her neck felt warm. The rash would be there soon. "What do you want?" She pushed each word out and then bit her tongue.

"We have a problem with the Collins property. The rezoning fell through and the contract buyers are backing out unless we come up with a solution, fast."

She waited. Rezoning was iffy in the best of cases and this one had been a long shot from the outset. But Collins was David's client, not hers.

When she didn't respond, he said, "You left a few things here."

There was silky, wheedling tone she'd expected.

He took her silence for encouragement. "I could drive over, bring you your stuff and we could talk. You could give me some insight on the best way to handle the appeal."

David Farquar needed her advice on a circuit court appeal only slightly more than he needed advice on breathing. What he wanted was Grace, but she knew better than to get her hopes up. David was lonely and lazy in his personal relationships. She knew he missed having his girlfriend only steps away from his office, 24/7. It was unusual for him to offer to drive to her, though.

"And if you wanted to come into DC, it would save time." Bingo. Nothing had changed. David's needs still came first. "Grace? Listen, let's meet at -"

"No."

Her mother had said David would marry Grace if she'd bring the minister to the office after hours and agree to live alone the eight hours a day she wasn't working. When he'd missed Julia's funeral for a new client meeting, Grace wondered how she could have been so stupid for so long.

"David," she forced herself to soften her words. "I don't want to hurt you. And I don't want to argue. What I want is to move on. You were generous with money and I was generous with my sweat equity over the past decade. What you call severance was only a fraction of the value of the partnership I was due."

"We're not getting into that again."

"No, we aren't," she agreed. "I'm going to hang up, but I want you to remember this: I think you're amazing. I learned a lot from you and only some of it pertained to the law. The most important thing I learned is I don't want to be like you. I want a real life and someone to share it with. That's never going to be you, but it doesn't mean I didn't love you. It just means I don't anymore."

There was a sharp intake of breath, and Grace knew he'd finally heard her. She touched the red dot on the screen, ended the call and cut the last tie to her old life.

CHAPTER TWENTY-FOUR

Aidan Banks was on desk duty at the police station the next
morning and he wasn't happy to see her. Grace thought if he'd
been a dog, there'd have been a warning growl, maybe an air-snap.
She had to wait for the Chief and it was tempting to call Banks out,
ask him what his problem was, but the truth was, she didn't care. She
had enough turmoil to handle without digging around for more.

After an uncomfortable few minutes, McNamara appeared and
ushered her into his office. He shut the door behind them, blocking
Banks' glowering presence, much to Grace's relief. The letters and
Ford Delaney's suicide were depressing enough on a rainy fall
morning.

The chief's office was a tiny room tucked between the reception
area and a one-person cell. Grace decided the police station could be
set down in 1960 without changing anything except the electronics.
It felt like the right place to discuss the Delaneys.

"I'd heard about it of course," McNamara said when she'd
explained why she'd come. "Ford Delaney's suicide came to mind as
soon as I read the coroner's report on the remains. I've done some
reading in the *Star Democrat's* morgue. The society page and obitu-

aries as well as the front pages. Fortunately, it was a weekly edition back in the fifties and sixties." He eyed the letters Grace stacked on his desk. "You read all of these?"

"Of course," she said. "I have copies, but I'll want these originals back when you're through."

He nodded. "You take anything else out of that room?"

"No." It was all she could do not to add 'sir'. The expression on McNamara's face said she didn't want to waste his time.

He said, "I'll need an affidavit from you detailing what you saw and did in the room."

Grace hoped she could tell the story without sounding foolish. *There were scratching noises, the wall moved and I don't remember how I got into the hall.*

"Problem?"

"Not at all." *I've got nothing but problems*, she wanted to say.

"Good. So tell me what's in these." McNamara's desk was metal, old and battered, its surface clean except for Emma Delaney's letters. "I'm assuming you've found something besides recipes and family news?"

"Delaney family news might solve your murder, Chief."

"Is that so? Which one of these envelopes holds the answers?"

"You'll want to read all of them to get a sense of the relationship between Emma and Ford Delaney. But it's the last half dozen or so that get to the heart of the matter. They confirm Emma and Ford were friends - good friends - with Avril's half-sister."

"So you believe these letters prove the woman in the grave is Audrey Oxley?"

"No. But I won't be surprised if the DNA tests prove it."

"Any clues to the murderer's identity?"

"Plenty, but they go in several directions. It could have been Emma or Ford, or someone in Audrey's family."

He gave a 'come on' wiggle of his fingers. "Or?"

"Or maybe Cyrus Mosley. They were engaged." She was still grappling with the idea of the manipulative old attorney in a love affair gone wrong.

McNamara nodded. "You've been busy."

"Did Avril tell you about Mosley? Have you talked to him?"

"This is a small town, Ms. Reagan. Less than five hundred people on the census. Did you know that?"

Grace shook her head, frustrated by the change of subject.

"Of course, it can actually hit two thousand occupants when everyone who owns property in Mallard Bay shows up at once. That's true of most of the coastal areas of the Eastern Shore. Come Heres have bought up most of the historic properties and good waterfront in this area, mostly for vacation or retirement homes."

"But not Delaney House," Grace said, trying to follow his ramblings.

"Delaneys were Come Heres a hundred years ago." He laughed at her surprise. "You thought they built that palace? Old Winston the First bought in the late eighteen hundreds. He sold off a good portion of the property to finance the restoration of the house and renamed the place after himself. His son, the second Winston, managed to hang onto it during the Depression and Winston the Third came out of WWII rolling in money from war contracts. Industrial nylon, if I recall correctly."

"They teach Delaney lineage in school around here?"

McNamara leaned back in his swivel chair, tilting it until the front wheels lifted and the back bumped the cinderblock wall behind him. Grace hoped he wasn't settling in for another narrative on the bygone days in Mallard Bay.

"My family's been here since the tadpole stage. We've been fortunate enough to hang onto the family home. My cousin owns it and I have the house my father was born in. We're luckier than most."

"Sounds like you may know people who were here during the time of the murder," she guessed.

"You aren't enjoying my history lesson?" McNamara smiled. "You lawyers. No wandering off topic allowed."

"I'm sitting in a police station and have just given you possible evidence in a murder case. I'm hoping everything you say is relevant to the here and now."

He sat upright again, his chair wheels hitting the ground with popping noise that made her jump. "Well, then, let me be direct, Ms. Reagan. In a case this old, how I get to the truth is as important to me as solving the crime."

"You're going to have to work on your definition of 'direct', Chief."

"No one I've talked to who was alive and here during the period we believe the murder was committed remembers anything useful. A few local people remember Audrey Oxley's disappearance, but mainly because she was Cyrus Mosley's fiancé. Mosley himself added some color to the story, but nothing helpful. For all I know, the girl ran away, found a new life and is a great-grandmother by now."

"Or she's been in a grave behind Delaney house for the last half-century."

McNamara nodded. "My point is, regardless of the dead woman's identity, Miss Avril's family and Mosley's involvement with a missing woman have been brought back to public scrutiny. And, as you point out, the Delaneys aren't looking so good at the moment. I have a professional duty to solve the crime, but I also have a moral duty to hurt as few people as possible while I do it."

Grace tried to see the case from his perspective. "Because the killer, or killers, will be upwards of seventy-five years old."

"At least, probably older." McNamara agreed.

"They may be dead, too."

"If not, they'll likely die in prison. Once I find them, that is."

"You. Not the State Police?"

McNamara's smile returned, but it was a sad one. "I'm afraid so," he said.

When the Chief walked her to her car, he thanked her for the letters and affidavit but didn't give her any more insight into the investigation. Grace left with a sinking realization that he would sacrifice a speedy resolution to lessen the impact on the town and its citizens, past and present. She briefly considered going over his head to the State Police and rejected the idea.

On a basic level, she trusted Lee McNamara, and the last thing she needed was another enemy.

CHAPTER TWENTY-FIVE

There was a terse note from Niki on the kitchen counter. The guests in room four had checked out, there were no reservations until Wednesday, and she was off with Aidan Banks for the rest of the weekend.

Grace didn't waste any time wondering what had changed Niki's mind about ending her relationship with Banks. Relieved of the need to tiptoe around her angry cousin, she had the freedom to spread out and work on her financial records. She was opening her laptop on the kitchen table when Cyrus Mosley's gold Lexus pulled into the inn's parking lot.

An hour of peace, Grace thought as she watched the lawyer stalk up the walk. *Just an hour to figure out what I'm doing.* Mosley jabbed the doorbell unnecessarily as he glared at her through the window in the kitchen door.

"I suppose you were going to tell me sooner or later," he said by way of greeting. "I had to learn from the Chief of Police you were declining my offer to buy the house."

The truth was, she'd never taken the offer seriously and had forgotten about it in the whirlwind of her exit from Washington. She poured two glasses of iced tea, not because she wanted any or he'd asked for it, but to have something to do while Mosley ranted at her. He was wound up enough to levitate out of his canvas Top-Siders.

He planted himself next to the kitchen island, bristling with anger. "And then I find out you've gotten yourself involved in the investigation. I certainly could have done without your interference on that front, too."

"My interference?" She focused on putting the pitcher back in the fridge and rummaging through Niki's kitchen cabinets for cookies. After that, she'd have to look at Mosley again and she knew when she did, she'd embarrass both of them.

He was dressed in what she had to assume was a Saturday golfing outfit. The jaunty popped collar on his baby blue golf shirt screamed 'eighties' while coordinating perfectly with the little whales embroidered all over his twill slacks. Grace thought she saw the whales tremble right along with their owner as Mosley told her how he felt about her intentions to renovate Delaney House.

"Emma didn't want this!" he sputtered. "She wanted that God-forsaken house out of Delaney hands. If she knew you were taking it apart and putting her money into renovations, she'd turn over in her grave."

"Her money?" Grace said. The urge to laugh at Mosley wasn't as strong now, but a desire to slap him was growing.

"Of course! All you have, you owe to her. I'm asking you to honor her wishes. Sell the house to me now, or at least allow me sell it for you. I can also keep the family out of this ridiculous murder investigation. Lee McNamara and I are friends; everything can be taken care of discretely if you'll just go back home and let me get on with the practicality of things here."

At the mention of McNamara, Grace remembered the police chief's words, his 'moral duty' to solve the murder without inflicting more pain on the families - and Mosley - than he had to. Grace thought it unlikely the state police shared McNamara's sentiments, or would bow to Mosley's wishes. Besides, she had a moral duty, too, but it wasn't to anyone in Mallard Bay.

"You're right," she said. "I should have given you the courtesy of a formal rejection of your purchase offer. I also should have told you I was coming back here to stay during the renovation."

Mosley did his heel-rock and waistband adjustment maneuver and gave a grudging nod. Unfortunately, yanking his waistband to and fro caused the fabric of his baggy pants to ripple, which made the whales appear to bob on the ocean that was Mosley's lower half.

"What?" he demanded when she turned away. "Are you alright?"

Grace drank tea and got herself under control. When she could talk without laughing, she made a comment about bad allergies and apologized again for upsetting him. "I'm sure it's hard to understand, but my mother wanted to return the house to the way it had been before her family destroyed it." Mosley flinched, and she hurried on. "I'm unemployed for now, so I have plenty of time to see to her last wishes."

"I heard about your break with your firm," Mosley said. "I hope it wasn't because of this situation with the police investigation?"

Grace was tempted to tell him it was the nagging, unanswered questions about her father. What she said was, "I want to finish this house. It's time for me to try something new." Inspiration hit her. "Once I've finished here and sold the property, I might open my own firm."

You never know what's going to be the magic bullet in an argument, she thought as Mosley visibly calmed and sipped his iced tea. She pushed a package of cookies toward him.

"Will you stay here?" he asked.

"No." If she never saw another legal document, she'd be happy, but she'd distracted Mosley and diffused the situation.

"Alright. I can see your mind's made up and arguing with you won't be any more fruitful than trying to talk sense into your grandmother or your mother. God knows I lost enough rounds with them." He bit into a cookie and sprayed crumbs as he sighed and said, "So, I'll help you."

Grace grabbed a cookie for herself and prayed the sugar rush would give her strength. She now had the 'help' of Avril Oxley and

Mosley, two irascible octogenarians who were also potential murder suspects. "Thank you," she managed.

Mosley's smile had no warmth. "As far as the police investigation goes, remember, I'm your attorney. Refer McNamara and anyone else who contacts you to me. I'll handle everything."

"I don't need an attorney, Cyrus." She hurried on over his protest, "But I do want to say I was sorry to learn your fiancé might be the victim."

Mosley drew himself up and glared at her. "Whoever the unfortunate woman is, she is not Audrey Oxley. And who's to say it's a murder? Anything could have happened and I will not allow the police to jump to unwarranted conclusions."

"Okay," she drew the word out. "But how can you be sure it's not your fiancé?"

"A man knows when a woman leaves him. Audrey left me, plain and simple." The mulish look was back on his face, but his eyes showed pain.

Grace took in the cement pompadour, liver spots and whale pants, the rigid posture and the rheumy eyes, and was surprised to find she felt anger toward this Audrey. The woman had been gone for nearly sixty years, but Mosley still grieved.

"So who do you think was in the grave?" Grace asked.

"I don't know, but it had nothing to do with the Delaneys."

His tone said the discussion was over, so she nodded as if she believed him and got a genuine smile for her lie.

AFTER HER MORNING WITH McNAMARA AND MOSLEY, GRACE wanted to deal with something concrete and verifiable.

She needed to make arrangements to fund the renovations, and she had yet to decide exactly how she was going to pay for the work. Mosley had given her a check for the deposit she'd paid to Bryce and Henry, but there was much more to be done and it would all come out of her own pocket.

She knew from her partnership with her mother that it was best to avoid properties needing work buyers would never see. Buyers were willing to pay a premium for custom cabinets, but updated electrical panels were expected. Getting Delaney House up to the 'expected' category would be a major undertaking.

Bryce had given her prices for basic renovations. Each project he named had to be done and none of it would be visible in the interior of the house. After consulting her notes, she made a pot of coffee, set her laptop up on the kitchen table and worked her way through the proceeds of her mother's estate.

Julia Reagan had been cautious in her investments, taking few risks and preferring a small, but protected return. Over the course of several hours, Grace liquidated it all, channeling the proceeds into a new account earmarked for Delaney House. As she totaled the transactions, her heart sank. It wasn't enough. Julia's assets, even with the insurance policy she'd left Grace, would only cover the roof, electrical rewiring and new sewer lines. If she was lucky.

Without letting herself dwell on the enormity of what she was doing, she moved on to her own accounts and an hour later everything but her 401K was in the construction fund. Her carefully researched and solidly performing investments would give Delaney House a modern furnace, its first air conditioning system and a small contingency fund.

She had enough to cover the basics, but the house wouldn't look any better than it did now. She blinked back tears as she shut the computer down and rested her head in her hands.

SUNDAY MORNING BROUGHT SUNSHINE AND THE CALLS OF MIGRATORY birds on their way south. The decision Grace had reached in the night wasn't any easier in the beauty of the new day. The renovation account was still short and didn't leave her any money to live on. Sleep hadn't worked any miracles, and she only had one option left. She would have to sell her mother's row house in Arlington.

Taking a loan on Delaney House was too risky. If it didn't sell quickly, she'd have to pay the mortgage or sell it at a loss. At least if she paid cash for the renovations, she'd be able to hold on to the property until the right buyer came along.

And who might the right buyer be, she wondered as she stood in the shower and let hot water pound on her still tired body. "A crazy person," she said out loud. "A rich crazy person." Except for her heavily mortgaged condo and an anemic retirement fund, everything she owned - everything her mother had owned - would be tied up in a white elephant.

When three cups of coffee and a long walk didn't change anything, she called her mother's tenant and told him to make his best offer.

CHAPTER TWENTY-SIX

L ee McNamara made good on his promise. Grace was back in
Delaney House on Monday morning. As far as she could tell,
the police had found nothing of interest in Emma's secret room. All
of the boxes and bags were opened, but none were empty.

"I can't believe I missed this." Bryce surveyed the area, giving
the flimsy wall a few taps and shaking his head. "It's so obvious with
the stacks of books gone."

"I can't believe Winnie didn't ransack it," Henry said. "But I
guess that would have required him to be sober enough to realize it
was here."

Bryce frowned. "Hey! Come on, now. Winnie's an okay guy.
He's just got a problem."

"Yes, he does."

Grace wasn't in the mood for family squabbling. Any family. "I
want to use the small bedroom next to the sleeping porch for the
clothes and other items I'm keeping," she said. "I'll keep it locked so
no one accidentally leaves it open. I don't want dust and dirt from the
reno getting all over everything."

Henry and Bryce agreed, and Grace was relieved neither seemed
to take offense. She wanted to keep Emma's stash to herself,

although she'd share it with Niki if her cousin ever started talking to her again.

"When we get this wall down, it will be a huge bathroom," Bryce said as he took measurements. "It must have been a bedroom or an upstairs library at some point."

"I do like Emma's reasoning," Grace said. "Let's put in a large linen closet for storage and a walk-in shower in this area."

Her excitement grew as she told them the changes she'd been considering. She'd reached a verbal agreement with Julia's tenant and was trying to keep her thoughts centered on the repairs and improvements she could make to Delaney House. Thinking about the source of the money for her renovation plan was too upsetting.

As they walked through the second floor, she described the two new Jack and Jill style baths she wanted between the smaller bedrooms. The oak floors were battered but salvageable. Rich buttercream paint for the walls with a warm white on the painted woodwork.

Bryce nodded in approval and said, "The great thing about a house built over so many years is you have a lot of latitude in your reno style while still staying true to at least one period of the house's history. Those back bedrooms and the sleeping porch are part of an addition which connected the kitchen to the house."

"Makes sense. Avril told me the kitchen and the room above it are from the 1700s."

"That's what my research indicates," Henry said. "I told you, I love this place. I've read everything I could find on the house."

"I need to do that," Grace said. "Avril gave me quite a lecture about jumping into renovations without knowing the house's history, and she's right. Thank goodness I have you for guidance."

She was rewarded with an 'aw shucks' smile from Henry.

"Well, if you really want to be in the period, those rooms should be dark wood and heavy floral wallpaper."

"No thanks. I need to sell this place. We're going with a light, uniform palatte throughout. It will appeal to more people and be easy for the new owners to change."

They ended up in the kitchen, where she described custom cabinets that would mirror those in the butler's pantry. Her enthusiastic monolog faltered when she saw the looks Bryce and Henry exchanged.

"Alright, what?" she demanded.

"It sounds great. You've got a good plan for the finished product, but there's a lot of work to do before the fun stuff like paint and finishes," Bryce said.

Grace sighed. "I know, but I have to keep the end in sight or it's overwhelming."

"That's what we're here for," Bryce said. "Roof first so everything stays dry. Electrical, plumbing and air systems next. That work will cause some damage to the walls and ceilings, but repairs can be done in the cosmetic phase. As we go, we'll exterminate major infestations and finally, the glamor stuff - kitchen, bathrooms, floors and paint."

"If I have any money left, you mean."

"We'll see when we get there," Bryce said. "Roof repair and replacement - mostly replacement, with the repairs to the fascia and some of the rafters, and new insulation. New electrical throughout with zone panels. New plumbing throughout, including replacement of the original terracotta sewer pipes. Extermination." He consulted his clipboard. "I'd say about one-twenty. Maybe more if the entire roof is replaced. You could save a good bit if you replaced the slate with something cheaper."

"No," Grace shook her head.

"Okay. Air systems, another thirty. Those numbers are assuming we don't hit any structural issues or foundation problems. I haven't seen any signs, I'm just saying once you open an old place up, stuff happens."

"It certainly does," she said glumly. "You're at one-fifty and I still don't have a kitchen."

"Well, we could…"

"A period restoration but with all modern conveniences," she broke in. "May as well see what I can't have."

"Seventy-five, basic. No frills." Bryce paused, then continued. "The new bathrooms on the second and third floors and the rehabs of the two original ones will be around sixty altogether."

"Including the removal of the doorway off the staircase?"

"I think we can squeeze it in."

After a moment, she said, "The exterior trim needs work and paint, gutters and downspouts replaced, new landscaping, new drive-way, new front walk. The pool and the grave filled in. My God," she moaned. "I can't believe I just added 'grave filling' to a reno checklist!"

"First for me, too," Bryce said. "And don't forget, the chimneys will need to be cleaned and new screens and caps added and my guess is when they get up there, the brickwork will need repair and the linings resurfaced. The mortar on the front steps needs replacing. If the Historic District Commission can be persuaded, you should consider some kind of storm windows."

"Grace, this is a far cry from basic restoration," Henry said quietly. "You're moving awfully fast."

"He's right," Bryce said. "Leave the list with us. We'll get the roof done and we can discuss the rest after we see how bad that is."

For a few moments, Grace had returned to her professional persona — the Grace who knew what she was talking about. The Grace who was in charge. She felt a flash of anger at the Cutters, who apparently thought she couldn't handle her own problems. Shame followed quickly on the heels of her anger. She knew exactly how they'd gotten that idea. They had to be thrilled with such a lucrative project, but she could see neither one of them believed she would commit to the scope of work she'd just described.

She wondered if they were right.

"We'll start the roof tomorrow," Bryce said. "I've got a full crew ready to go. Before we get into details, though, I need to tell you something. I've hired a new employee. Winnie's going to give me a hand."

Henry looked as surprised as Grace felt. "You aren't serious?"

"Yes, I'm serious," Bryce snapped at his cousin. "You know he's done a great job when I've used him before."

"I know you said he did, but…" Henry stopped and shrugged. "If you say you need him, you need him."

"I need him. Same as before, to run errands for me between jobs and to do some of the unskilled work." Turning to Grace, he added, "Try to put your personal relationship aside. Winnie has the most recent knowledge about this place. He did what little work was done around here for the past few years and he can save us some time." He glanced over his shoulder as they heard tires crunching on the gravel driveway. "And besides, he's here."

"We don't have a personal relationship," Grace said. "He just trashed my house and almost got himself killed here."

"Trust me and give him a chance, Grace. I've tried to look out for Winnie and help him. He's not a bad guy when you get to know him. And if it doesn't work out, he's gone. No arguing, I promise."

Grace followed the cousins outside to see Niki standing with a tall young man. The stranger was neatly dressed and clean-shaven with short sandy hair. His worn boots and muscular build said he was either used to hard work or spent serious time at a gym. She looked around for a more likely Winnie.

"I didn't expect to find him here, but I guess it's only right that I introduce you. This is my infamous brother," Niki said as Grace approached them. "Winnie, meet our cousin, Grace Reagan."

"Call me Winston, Grace. No one else does and it will make a nice change."

She'd been told Winston Stratford Delaney the Fifth was lazy, devious, destructive, lying, rude and probably dangerous; an alcoholic and drug addict. No one had mentioned he was also charming, well-mannered and gorgeous.

She shook his outstretched hand and felt herself returning his smile. "Well, Winston, I understand you're here to help Bryce."

"Help Bryce?" His large blue eyes widened as he released her hand. "Why, cousin, I'm here to help *you*. This old place has a lot of quirks and surprises; you know? And since I'm the only one who has any experience in maintaining it, I can save you some trouble."

Bryce broke into the conversation, saying he needed Winston's help finding an electrical panel.

"You made a smart decision," Niki said as the men walked away.

Grace was relieved that Niki seemed to have moved past their argument. "I didn't make any decision, Bryce did. He just now told Henry and me."

"He hired Winnie without telling Henry?"

Grace nodded. "It didn't sit well with Henry, either."

"I guess not. He's never understood why Bryce looks out for Winnie."

"Why does he?"

"Who knows? But even Bryce can't take much of him. So don't worry, either Winnie'll wander off somewhere and not come back until the work is done, or he'll make Bryce mad, which is what usually happens. But there's one thing you need to remember. What Winnie wants, he gets. Nothing bad ever sticks to him, if you know what I mean. If he wants to be here and work on the house, you're better off making use of him. Take it from me, it doesn't pay to cross my brother."

CHAPTER TWENTY-SEVEN

"I came to apologize," Niki said as they walked back up the driveway. "It was unreasonable of me to think you wouldn't have questions about everything, even the stuff we don't talk about, like Grandfather. It's just hard because some topics have always been taboo."

"Like your grandfather."

"Like *our* grandfather and Gran's drinking." Niki looked miserable.

"My mother?" Grace asked.

"Yes."

"And I'm bringing it all to the surface."

Niki studied the roofline of Delaney House and hugged her fleece vest to her body as if she were freezing in the unseasonably warm November sunshine. "Had to happen sooner or later," she finally said. "I've managed to forget how much dirty laundry we have and it's a shock to have it all dragged out and opened up for speculation by people who weren't a part of it."

There were areas of Grace's own life she wouldn't want to hold up for public scrutiny. She said, "I'm sorry. I'll try to be more sensitive to your feelings, but I have to find out why my mother left and what happened with my father. It's awful your family has to go through a police investigation at the same time."

Niki rubbed her eyes and gave Grace a wan smile. "*Our* family. I'll keep correcting your pronouns until you give up and accept us. You are us and God help you, we are you. All the same DNA, Grace. Family."

It was a shaky truce, but Grace didn't want to argue anymore so she asked if Niki would like to see Emma's secret room and the clothes hidden away there.

Two hours sped by while they held an impromptu fashion show, preening and laughing at themselves as they struck poses in front of the tall mirror in the upstairs hall. Emma's clothes were all long on Niki and tight on Grace, but each of them found a few items that worked. They were debating the merits of a lemon yellow cocktail dress when they heard heavy steps on the staircase.

"Hey, Cousin Grace," Winston called out. "Bryce sent me to find you and see if you want to do a walk about the property. He wants to point out a few trouble spots we found."

"That's what I need, more trouble spots. Want to come?" she asked Niki, who was wearing a cashmere sweater with sleeves that came down over her fingertips.

"Uh, sure. I'll take this if it's okay. Those scarves, too?"

"All this stuff came out of the hidey hole Gran kept from us?" Winston asked.

Grace felt like she'd been punched. *Hidey hole?* She'd had never heard anyone else use the term but her mother.

Winton walked into the secret room and looked around. "I can't believe I missed this," he said as he picked up a silk scarf from a pile of clothes Niki had just gone through.

Alarm bells went off in Grace's mind. Winston had already upended the house searching for valuables and now he was holding one of the few things Emma had managed to save.

Niki, apparently, had the same idea. "We're playing dress up with some old clothes of Gran's," she said, wrapping a feather boa around her neck. "Most of it's moth-eaten, but there are a couple of decent dresses and some fun stuff like this. Can you see Gran in feathers?" she waggled the end of the boa at him.

"Only old clothes?" Winston sounded skeptical and before Grace or Niki could answer him, he picked up one of the clothing bags. "Oh, ho! What have we here?" He grabbed the sleeve of the mink coat.

"Be careful!" Niki said as a seam ripped. "You idiot! Old fur rots."

Winston dropped the coat in disgust. "What isn't rotted? Is any of this junk worth anything?"

Still glaring at her brother, Niki said, "Have a look if you want. There are a couple of evening gowns from the fifties," she held one of the dresses up. "Gran had them all stashed in here, probably to keep us from doing exactly what we're doing now." She pushed Winston back and picked up the mink. "I've been through everything. Some neat hats, but no jewelry."

Winston glared at her and turned back to the door. "Well, when you girls are through playing we can get started on some real work."

"Oh, this is real work," Grace said. "Unless Niki wants that dress, this lot is going to the dump. Maybe you can load it up for me."

"Sorry, I'm on Bryce's crew, not Henry's," Winston said. "I'll tell the guys you're on your way."

"Asking him to work was a stroke of genius," Niki said, once he was out of earshot. "He won't leave you alone if he thinks you got something he wanted."

Tell me about it, Grace thought. The kitchen cabinets with their spray-painted message were never far from her mind. She still wasn't sure if father or son had been the author, but the meaning was clear.

Niki stroked the yellow dress. "You aren't really going to throw all this out, are you?"

"He'll see some clothes go on the dump pile," Grace said.

Niki laughed and clapped her hands. "I *do* love having you as a co-conspirator!"

THE WALKABOUT WAS DERAILED BY WINSTON, WHO TOOK THE ROLE of tour guide. He insisted they start in the kitchen and led the Cutters, Grace and Niki through the house, describing the structure and its former occupants. They were in the dining room, ostensibly to look at a leak around one of the window frames when he began to describe parties his grandparents had given decades earlier.

"When Grandfather was alive, he and Gran were very social and were always entertaining. He was into politics big time in the fifties and sixties, you know."

Grace looked over at Niki, but she was watching her brother as if she couldn't wait for his next word.

"I wish we had pictures of the rooms from those days," Grace said as she pulled the corner of a peeling strip of wallpaper and was rewarded with enough dust to make her sneeze.

"Oh, just remove all the crap, clean it up and you'll see what it looked like in the glory days," Winston moved out of the dining room and into the rear parlor. "For instance, here's a hint: this room didn't have wallpaper hanging from the ceiling and none of the rooms were painted purple."

Grace was finding it hard to be quiet while one of the people responsible for the damage to the house was telling them to how clean it up, but she chewed the inside of her cheek and waited while Henry asked what the rear parlor had been used for in recent years.

"Gran closed the room off. Didn't want to look at the peeling paper, I guess. Who knows? We used to ride our tricycles in loops through the two parlors and the hall. Good fun when you're three."

"We did not!" Niki's outburst startled everyone. "Gran would have never let us do that!"

"Maybe not you," Winston snapped. "But she let me do anything I wanted. I played in here all the time, although, now that I think about it, it was only when I stayed here alone with Gran. You missed out, I guess."

Niki's face flushed with anger, her hands clenched at her side. "You never spent any time with her unless you wanted something!"

"And you did?"

Niki didn't answer, but Bryce said, "Come on, guys. Play nice."

"What era is this section of the house?" Grace asked. When Winston gave her a blank look, she said, "When was this part built?"

"Oh. Who knows?" His tone said, *who cares?* "I didn't say I was an architectural expert, but I know more about the family history than anyone else."

Niki turned and left the room. They heard the screen door on the back porch slam. A minute later a car started.

"She's always been hyper, and she hates it when I remind her Gran and I had a special relationship." Dismissing his sister with a wave, Winston moved on to the entry hall. "Follow me. I've got more stories you'll want to hear. For instance, this kinda rounded ceiling is only used in grand houses."

"Boy's always been a fool," Henry said as the front door closed behind Winston. "Thank God he didn't get this house."

As much as she'd wanted Winston gone, Grace was irritated at his departure. She didn't understand Bryce. First, he had to have Winston here and then, just as suddenly, made him leave. She'd started to question Winston about the basement when Bryce had interrupted - rudely, she thought - saying he'd totally forgotten about supplies that needed to be picked up.

"I wanted him to take me through the basement," she said again, not willing to let the subject go. "He might know what Emma stored down there."

Bryce winced and said, "Oh, Grace, I'm sorry. I could see you were getting tired of his silly stories and I sure was."

Grace tried to hang onto her temper. "But *I* was the one who was talking."

Bryce's face reddened. "He was showing off and it embarrassed me. But since you brought it up, please stay out of the basement. All we're finding is junk - broken tools and old lawn chemicals. A couple of bottles of some chemical mixture exploded and sprayed a wide area. It's probably weed killer, but I'm not letting the guys finish in there until I have professionals in to deal with it."

She didn't like Bryce telling her where she could go in her own house. She opened her mouth to say so, but he hurried on. "I'm sorry. It's your call, but you should know the guys have already found a couple of snake skins in the rear rooms."

Grace didn't try to hide her revulsion. He'd said the magic 'S' word. If there were anything important in the basement, she'd wait for the workers to bring it out.

After the Cutters left, she walked through the first floor one more time before locking up. Winston's stories of parties and politics and children running through the rooms had given her a new perspective on the once grand house. How many generations had crossed its threshold, calling it home and presuming it was theirs? They'd all left their marks - some to fade away, others leaving an indelible stain.

Grace was coming to realize that although she would pay the bills and oversee the restoration, this was Delaney House and she was only passing through.

CHAPTER TWENTY-EIGHT

Over the next two weeks, Niki stayed busy with the inn, not avoiding Grace, but not seeking her out her as she once had. Grace let herself enjoy the breathing room. She had plenty to keep her occupied.

For once Delaney House seemed to cooperate with her plans. As the house filled up with workers and their tools, the atmosphere in the old space changed. A new energy seeped through the rooms as if released by the physical activity.

And there was Bryce. He treated her with deference, never far from her side when he made his daily rounds. His face would light into a smile when he succeeded in catching her eye, and Grace found herself smiling back. A tiny swell of happiness took root near her heart. It was a strange feeling. She didn't let herself analyze the oddities of the relationship; she wanted to enjoy it. Without getting carried away, of course.

It came as a shock one morning when Grace realized she was happy. Even Winston's presence didn't mar the exhilaration she felt as she watched Delaney House begin to return to life or the tingle of anticipation each time she caught sight of Bryce.

She was surprised to see how well Winston and Bryce worked

together. Bryce always spent time with Winston after consulting the crew foreman on the progress of the day's project. Winston managed the supplies and ran errands. Bryce would leave a list of instructions with Winston each day and Winston would disappear on his appointed rounds, which usually kept him away from the house for several hours. The tasks he was given at Delaney House were simple, requiring no particular skills, only a strong back.

"I'm not billing you for him unless he's here at the site," Bryce told her. "Winston's my employee and I have him doing errands for other projects as well as this one. He's a big help, but I'm keeping him away from here as much as I can." One of his shoulder hugs ended the conversation. The hugs weren't as casual as before; an electricity passed between them at every touch. Being near Bryce felt dangerous and Grace liked it. Still, she held back, telling herself there was no point to a new romance. Wherever she went after Delaney House was finished, it wouldn't include Bryce Cutter.

For the most part, Winston stayed out of her way. Other than an occasional smirk and calling her 'cousin' in a drawn-out singsong voice, he left her alone. Days went by in which the house seemed to be deconstructing as rot and decay were cut away and buried original details emerged.

The interior demolition phase was nearly complete when Winston's accidents stared.

At first, there were the anyone-could-have-done-it type of mishaps: the wrong cabinet removed from a bathroom, an original glass window shattered, an unsecured brace on the ladder he was using. It was a short ladder and a short fall, but he was out for a day with a bruised knee. Bryce lectured the moaning Winston even as he helped him out to the truck for the ride to the Urgent Care center. Grace thought Bryce was being unnecessarily harsh and was further surprised to see the other workers were unsympathetic as well.

Henry's early assessment, 'boy's a fool', seemed to be the general consensus among the older workers. Their attitude didn't change when Winston came back to work. Grace tried asking Niki for advice, but only got a shrug and a 'hate your luck' look for her trouble.

She was on the third floor washing years of grime off the hallway baseboards so they could be painted when she heard Winston's angry voice yelling *'It wasn't me!'* The last time she'd seen him, he'd been assigned to scraping wallpaper off the dining room walls.

"Who the hell else was working down here?" the foreman, a usually quiet man named Marty, countered in a tone Grace had never heard him use before. She sat back on her heels and listened to the conversation echoing up from two floors below. "Don't you have enough sense not to put a work rag down a toilet? There're two inches of water and mess in there."

"I told you, it wasn't me! I only have two rags and they're both right -"

"Yeah, both right there, huh? I see one right there and I just fished the other one out of the toilet. After I slogged through a flooded bathroom. Get your ass in there and clean the mess up. And one more screw up and I'll -"

"You'll what? Let's talk to Bryce and see what you'll do."

Grace rose and headed for the stairs.

"Clean. It. Up." Marty's voice traveled through the house.

She paused on the top step. The two carpenters who'd been working in the rebuilt ensuite bathroom came out into the hall to stand behind her. One of them said, "I'd leave 'em to it, Miz Reagan. Let Marty sort the little punk - uh, your cousin - out."

Grace took his advice. Marty had ten years, four inches and fifty pounds on Winston. Grace and the carpenters waited at the top of the stairs until they heard the slurping sounds of a wet vac start up. They didn't need to see Winston working to know who'd won the stalemate. The carpenters hi-fived each other and Grace laughed out loud.

The satisfaction of seeing the arrogant Winston put in his place vanished the next morning when Grace learned Marty was gone, replaced by a younger man who spent the next three days asking everyone for help as he got up to speed on the project. After that, most of the Cutter crew avoided Winston. Only the three youngest, boys just out of high school, still treated him as a co-worker. The older workers and tradesmen watched him with unsmiling faces.

After a week of tension, Grace asked Bryce to move Winston to another project, or at least out of the house. "He upsets everyone but his posse," she explained.

Bryce gave her a sharp look. "What posse?"

"You know the three guys who hang around him, Devon, Rick and I don't think I ever heard the other kid's name."

"Joey Pecolini," Bryce supplied. "I can move Winston if you insist, but it will slow things down. I don't have another gopher to put on this job, and the guys constantly need things picked up from the suppliers. And he's good at stripping wallpaper. God knows we need someone on that."

"So put him on the landscape crew when he isn't running errands. Let him irritate those guys for a while and I'll strip wallpaper."

Grace regretted the offer immediately. Later, as she sponged soapy water on purple paisley wallpaper, she blamed Winston, who'd given her a huge grin as he headed out to join the crew working to remove the last of the rubble from the swimming pool and the cracked surface of the tennis court. Winston was outside on a perfect autumn day and she was inside, breathing through a triple-filter mask and wondering if she had enough antihistamine with her to ward off the inevitable allergy-induced migraine. Somehow, she groused to herself, he'd won again.

THE ACCIDENTS DIDN'T STOP WHEN WINSTON LEFT THE HOUSE, THEY only followed him outside.

Work slowed when tools were misplaced. A bucket load of concrete chunks released three feet short of the dump truck bed required a half-day to clean up. A healthy oak tree uprooted instead of its dead neighbor left a gaping hole in the only undamaged area of the backyard. After his bruised knee, Winston never suffered as much as a splinter from his carelessness, a fact which seemed to irritate everyone more than the damage he caused. Winston was Teflon, and it was damned annoying.

"He has to go." Grace put her foot down the afternoon of the oak tree incident.

"Okay," Bryce said, amicably. "Can you tell Niki and Stark? I promised both of them I'd give the boy a chance. They're so afraid he'll go back to using if he doesn't have a steady job with mandatory drug testing. I hate to disappoint them."

His smile, those dimples and a reluctance to get into another family fight won out over her good sense. Winston started back on the dining room wallpaper the next day. Grace told herself she was happy not to have to spend her days in paisley hell, but she knew it was not going to end well.

The 'accidents' continued, but they were minor. The boys, as Grace thought of Winston and the three younger workers, had to be kept separated. At breaks, or when no one was watching, they would erupt into horseplay until either bellows of laughter or anger caught a supervisor's attention.

A trip to Ocean City for a solitary Thanksgiving restored some of her equanimity and gave her time to think. The following Monday, when she walked in to find them taking an unscheduled smoke and beer break in the kitchen, she was ready to handle the Winnie problem once and for all.

"He has to go," she told Bryce. "Him and his friends. All four of them."

Bryce claimed bad reception on his cell and she had to keep raising her voice. She didn't care who heard her as she stalked around the side garden and shouted into her phone. If gossip could get to Stark and Connie before she did, so much the better.

"They were smoking around dirty work rags soaked with God knows what. They know there's to be no smoking in the house at all! And alcohol! Isn't Winston supposed to be doing AA? Aren't they violating some license or law?"

"I'll handle it, Grace. Reception is breaking up, but I'm on my way."

His placating tone hit her last nerve. "I am paying an hourly rate for *work* and I have four boys playing in my house. I want them gone. Now."

Static answered her. She ended the call not caring if he was still on the other end of the line. She stopped pacing at the edge of the rear lawn and stared into the decimated woods behind the house. Shaking off her surface emotion, she tried to look at the situation from a detached view. Something was going on that she wasn't seeing. Her attraction to Bryce and her obsession with Delaney House and her mother's past were clouding her assessment of the conflict churning through the work crew.

The trees that remained on the Delaney property had seen decades of life in all its vagaries. They'd sheltered human banality and secrets of love and murder. They had hidden a grave. Grace studied them for a long time but learned nothing at all.

CHAPTER TWENTY-NINE

"Did you really fire Winnie?"

Grace was halfway up the staircase at the Victory Manor Inn, on her way to a hot bath and a glass of wine, when the kitchen door flew open to the hall below, startling her. Grabbing the banister to regain her balance, she turned to face Niki, who now stood at the foot of the stairs, hands on her hips.

"Can we not do this?" Grace asked. "I'm exhausted and I need to clean up. I'll tell you all about it later, okay?"

"Sure." Niki's voice was steady. "You go ahead and take your bath and I'll tell my mother it's all a mistake and Winnie can go back to work tomorrow to the only job he's been able to land in the past year. How does that sound?"

Grace groaned and sat down on the steps. "Try to see it from my point of view. I don't have a choice here. Winston has caused all kinds of problems. He's careless, won't listen, causes accidents, and the rest of the crew are either resentful or joining him in goofing off. I found three of them in the kitchen with him drinking beer and smoking."

"You fired him for taking a break?"

"Taking a break? They were drinking alcohol when they were

supposed to be working! All of them are off the job. Do you realize how much I was paying them to party in the kitchen? Two of them are roofers, for God's sake. I'd prefer them sober when they're thirty feet in the air."

"So fire the damned roofers. Winnie can drink a beer and still scrape wallpaper."

"Fire the others but not the ringleader?"

"Yes." Niki's mulish expression would have been comical if she hadn't been so angry. "Winnie's your family. The others aren't. Fire them if you want to, but you are taking Winnie back. Mom and Dad are in a rage and I won't have a minute's peace until Winnie's working again. You owe me."

Grace felt her grip on her own anger slipping with each passing minute. If the words crowding her throat came out, there would be no going back. And if she cut ties with Niki, she'd be working in a vacuum as far as the Delaneys were concerned.

Niki wasn't finished. "You came to us; we didn't kidnap you. You turned everything upside down and I still welcomed you. Whether you like us or not, the four of us are the only family you have. It's bad enough you keep poking around in the past and all the old stuff that drives Dad crazy, but you don't even try to act like a part of the family. I didn't say anything when you skipped out on Thanksgiving, but firing Winnie is too much. I've stuck by you, now it's your turn."

Not trusting herself to speak, Grace climbed the rest of the steps to the second floor. As she reached the door of her room, she heard Niki say, "I'll call Dad and let him know Winnie should be at work tomorrow."

Grace closed the door behind her and turned the lock.

———

THE NEXT MORNING, GRACE TOLD BRYCE TO MAKE THE THIRD FLOOR into a self-contained apartment and to make the project a priority. She also told him to keep Winston out of the house.

"He could work on the basement," Bryce said. "We need to have a couple of the rooms cleaned out and scrubbed down before we install the new-"

"Out. Of. The. House." Grace struggled not to add, *I wouldn't be in this mess if you hadn't hired him.*

Winston seemed happy with his new routine. But despite the fact he was often off on errands for Bryce, on the first day he still found time to drop a paint can from a second-floor scaffolding, missing a worker on the ground below by scant inches and ruining half a day's work. The next day he was assigned to the help strip old paint off shutters and actually made progress until he flicked a cigarette stub near a pile of rags soaked in solvent. The resulting fire was small and quickly contained, but an ugly area of scorched grass and two ruined 19th century shutters were hard to ignore. Bryce promised to have replicas made and moved Winston to the front yard to hand-dig ancient bricks out of the sunken and pitted walkways.

"Do you think he can do that without destroying them?" Grace asked as she and Bryce watched Winston through the curved windows of the front hall. "I want those bricks re-laid in the new walkways, you know."

Bryce's answer was to slip an arm around her and kiss her gently on the cheek. "It will be fine. I promise."

For those few minutes, even with alarm bells ringing and the certain knowledge she was making a mistake, she was happy in his arms.

"Let me take you to dinner tonight," he said as he released her. "We can celebrate Winnie's new brick-digging job. And we can celebrate your move to Delaney House where you'll have some privacy."

She wanted to say yes, meant to say yes. 'I can't' came out instead. "I've got a lot to do tonight and I'm not sure this," she waved a hand between them, "is a good idea."

His smile widened, which caused his eyes to twinkle and his dimples to deepen. "You are so wrong," he said and reached for her again.

From somewhere outside came the sound of breaking glass, but neither of them heard a thing.

———

GRACE DECIDED TO TELL NIKI STRAIGHT OUT THAT SHE WAS MOVING to Delaney House, but when she entered the kitchen of the Victory Manor Inn, she could see the timing was wrong. Every surface held dirty bowls, plates and utensils, and Niki's face looked like a thundercloud.

"This is a bad time. I'll come back later."

But escape wasn't an option.

Niki said, "Oh, for heaven's sake, come in. I'm just screwing up one recipe after another in my pathetic attempt to be a chef and make a living. Screw it." She threw the spoon she held into the sink.

Tears sprang up in Niki's eyes, and it was all Grace could do not to turn and run. She was tired and preoccupied, but mostly she didn't want to let go of the glow from her afternoon with Bryce. Certainly not for another of Niki's tantrums.

"Dad sold Gran's pearls."

Clearly, Grace was supposed to know what this meant. She said nothing, hoping Niki would elaborate, but the dam behind Niki's big blue eyes burst and tears poured down her face.

Grace hesitated, unsure what was expected of her. After a moment she moved to Niki's side, only to be rewarded with a shove that knocked her off balance. Catching the back of a chair, she regained her footing and yelled, "What is *wrong* with you?"

"*Me?* What's wrong with you? You had everything and it wasn't enough! You had to take the house and now there isn't enough money. Dad sold Gran's pearls. He said it would only be the ring, but he sold the pearls, too." Niki grabbed a tea towel and scrubbed it across her face.

Grace tried to work out what Niki was saying. Stark needed money? He'd gotten a significant chunk with the payout of his inheritance, but she didn't think reminding Niki of that would help.

"I bought the house from your grandmother, Niki," she said in a low tone. "Your father wouldn't have gotten a bigger share if someone else had bought it."

Niki threw the dishtowel after the spoon and knocked a coffee cup into the sink, shattering it. "*Your* grandmother! She's yours, too! And don't you dare act as if you don't know what I'm talking about. Cyrus cut the price of the house so you could buy it."

"Where are you getting this nonsense?" Grace felt her cheeks redden. "Cyrus didn't know I was the buyer. Neither he nor Emma knew. She insisted it not go to a family member, and you know all of this. The only reason I got the house is because she didn't know, *they* didn't know I was the buyer."

"Oh, please." Niki's tone was heavy with sarcasm. "Cyrus always does exactly what he wants and Gran always let him. After sending money to you all those years, she still divided what little she had left between Dad and Julia, instead of giving Dad his fair share. He told me all about it."

"When?"

"This morning." Niki leaned forward aggressively. The tears were gone, but the fight was still there.

Grace felt sick.

"He came to tell me he needed money," Niki went on. "I was supposed to get Gran's diamond engagement ring and her pearls. She told me they were mine. She didn't put them in the will, but she gave them to Dad to keep for me. He sold the diamond right after she died. He said he had bills to pay and he had to do it. Today, he told me he sold the pearls. I didn't know why he and Gran were always fighting about money, but now I do. It was because she was sending everything to you. And when you wanted the house, you got that, too. Cyrus saw to that. Cyrus makes sure you get everything you want!"

Shock kept the thoughts that were racing through Grace's mind from connecting. "Why?" was all she could manage. "Why would he do that?"

"Dad says I should ask you that very question, but you know what? I don't care. I want my life back. I want you to leave."

Grace stripped and cleaned her room, packed the BMW and drove to the Egret Inn. She spent a miserable night alternately crying and going over everything she wished she said to Niki. To all the Delaneys. How dare they make her the villain in their dysfunctional family?

The next morning, she checked out and drove into Easton. At Target she picked up a sleeping bag, blankets, towels and pillows. At Lowe's she bought a dorm-sized refrigerator, microwave, and a small teacart to hold it all. By late afternoon, she was settled in on the third floor and rolling creamy white primer on her new bathroom walls. She'd been away for more than three decades, but Grace was once again living in Delaney House.

CHAPTER THIRTY

To Grace's amazement, she slept well in the old nursery at Delaney House.

The third-floor suite smelled fresh and was clean in a bare wood and new drywall kind of way. Total exhaustion helped. Her shopping spree, hauling everything up two flights of stairs and a late evening of painting paid off in a dreamless sleep. When she woke, she could hear the workers arriving and light streamed through the windows. She'd made it through her first night.

Using the best pieces of furniture from the second floor, she furnished the largest room as a sitting area and kitchenette. The adjoining room was her bedroom, and the small room under the eaves served as storage. Each day she added something new to her little home. The third floor began to feel like an oasis on top of a beehive of construction activity.

From the first morning, life seemed to speed up. She had no time to worry or second-guess herself. Work on Delaney House consumed her during the day and Bryce filled most of the evenings, taking her to dinner and once to an auction where she bought a period chandelier for the dining room. These dates ended earlier than she would have liked, but Grace knew she had only herself to blame. She'd expressed concerns about a relationship and Bryce was respecting her wishes, a novel concept for her after David's high maintenance behavior. Each time Bryce gave her a gentle kiss and left, shutting the door on her growing interest, she found herself more attracted to him.

In the first week of her residence at Delaney House, her emotions went from fairly miserable to nearly happy. When Niki showed up on Saturday morning with a basket of food and an apology, Grace was wary, but eventually had to admit she wasn't mad at her cousin anymore.

"I shouldn't be surprised, but wow!" Niki said as she turned slowly taking in the sitting room's soft yellow walls, refinished pine floors and the leather cushioned Stickley love seat and matching chairs. "I don't remember a fireplace being up here," she said as she ran a hand along the narrow marble mantle.

"It's a coal stove, so it's only ornamental now, but I like the way it looks. The whole house was beautiful at one time," Grace tried to sound casual.

"I sure don't remember it that way," Niki said as she moved around the room looking at the furnishings. "All this stuff was on the second floor under the junk?"

Grace wondered if a scouting mission was the purpose of Niki's sudden need to reconcile. She said, "The bigger pieces, yes. I had to buy a new mattress, appliances and some odds and ends."

Niki turned away and stood in front of the sitting room window with its view of surrounding rooftops and the steeple of Christ Church. After a moment, she said, "All my life, since I can remember, anyway, Gran was difficult and this place was creepy. Winnie can make up all kinds of crap and maybe Gran did tell him things she didn't tell me, or maybe he listened to Dad's rants about her, back when Dad would talk to us about any of it. But I blocked out everything I could because it's scary when you're a kid and everyone is always mad."

"Then not much has changed, has it?" Grace said.

Niki's laugh was bitter. "No. But it needs to. That's why I'm here." She turned back to face Grace. Behind her, the sunlight caught Niki's blond curls and outlined her slender body. It took a moment for Grace to see she was crying.

"I never wanted to hurt anyone," Grace said, unsure what to do. "I just want to finish this house for my mother and find out what happened to my father. When I know that, I can deal with whatever the truth is and move on. I want a new life, Niki, but I have to finish the one I have first."

Niki ran her fingertips under her eyes but stayed where she was in front of the window. "Yeah, I get it. You came in late to the game and I can't blame you for what you've done. It's not like it was personal, right?"

Grace wasn't sure what Niki meant, but she said, "If I hurt you, it wasn't intentional, I swear." Guilt immediately reared its head. The truth was, she hadn't deliberately hurt Niki, but she hadn't taken any care not to hurt her either.

Niki nodded once and said, "Well, I'm not ready to give up the only sane relative I have, so what do you say, can we call a truce on all of it? You bought this place, it's yours. You hire whom you want and you do what you please. My crazy parents and deadbeat brother aren't your fault or your responsibility. Just be my friend, *my* family, and let's start over, okay? For goodness sakes, it's almost Christmas!"

Grace chose her words carefully. This time she would be completely honest. "You understand I won't stop asking questions? I need to find out why my mother took me and left Mallard Bay and the family. If I know that, I might learn more about my father. Not knowing him didn't matter to me for a long time, but now that Mom's gone, it does. Can you understand?"

Niki shook her head. "I don't have to. It's important to you, and that's enough for me. I'll think about it, and if I remember anything, I'll tell you. Now, let's eat the scones I brought. It's a new recipe and I need to know what's missing. They've got too much or not enough of something."

Grace said, "One question first?"

Niki unloaded the basket on the small gateleg table that served as a kitchen counter and said, "I brought two kinds, blueberry and cinnamon. One question and you have to test both."

"Deal. When you talk about my mother, you call her 'Aunt Julia', even though you never met her. But the other night, when you talked about Tony, you called him 'Tony'. Why?"

Niki handed her a napkin with two small scones. She looked thoughtful for a minute before answering. "I've never called him anything else. It's not as if we talked a lot about him. Mom tried to help me understand why Gran was so difficult to get along with, so she told me about Grandfather and Tony. How they died, I mean. It just creeped me out more, you know? Mom knew Tony, so she was able to make him sound real. She's older than Dad by a couple of years and she was in some classes with Tony in high school. She said he was really handsome and all the girls had a crush on him. They closed the school for his funeral."

Grace tried to imagine how her mother and Stark had managed. Julia would have been twelve and Stark fourteen.

"I've always called her Aunt Julia because I want her to be real."

"What?" Grace refocused on Niki.

"For a long time, I believed she would come home and bring you, and I would have an aunt and a cousin. Mom's an only child and you were all I had in the way of family who might not be, you know," Niki made air circles at her temple and rolled her eyes.

Grace laughed and then she saw Niki was serious.

"After a while, I was mad at her, and at you, for not coming back. I wanted to go find you, but Gran said you were somewhere far away and we didn't know where. I'm not a kid anymore, but sometimes I'm still mad. Can you understand?"

It was Grace's turn. "No," she said, repeating her cousin's words. "And I don't have to. It's important to you and that's enough." It would have to be, she decided as Niki crossed the room for a hug. Grace was short on relatives herself, and her heart wasn't ready for another fight. Besides, it was almost Christmas.

SOMEONE WAS SHAKING HER AWAKE. SOMEONE WITH A HAND ON HER foot.

The scream was out of Grace's mouth before her eyes were open, but even as she scrambled to find the pepper spray she kept by the bed, she realized the room was empty. Whoever had been there was gone, but something was wrong. She found her slippers and a sweatshirt to pull over the t-shirt and leggings she'd worn to bed. When she opened the door to the hallway, she smelled it. Smoke.

Flipping every light switch she passed, she ran down the staircase to the second-floor landing and on down to the front hall. Even as she saw the smoke billowing down the long hallway from the back of the house, she heard the alarms of approaching fire engines. A sudden pounding on the front door brought her to her senses. She threw back the deadbolts, screamed 'Get back' and opened the door only wide enough to slip through, slamming it behind her. Avril Oxley waited on the front lawn.

"Thank God," Avril said as she grabbed Grace in a bony, but surprisingly strong hug. "It's your back porch, but the rest of the house hasn't caught yet."

"No!" Grace gasped and pulled Avril further away from the house. "There's smoke in the house. Someone must have opened the back door."

Avril stared at her as the fire trucks arrived and the fight to save Delaney House began.

Dec 25, 1959

Dear Mother and Papa,

Merry Christmas! I didn't get to talk long enough today to say that. Your grandson loves the telephone and I hated to make him cry on Christmas by wrestling it away from him. I hope you enjoyed hearing a three-year-old's version of Santa's visit! Poor little Stark is still frightened of all the excitement and ruckus his boisterous big brother kicks up around the Christmas tree and all of the celebrations. The little thing has spent most of the last month in my lap, clinging for dear life while Tony races around shouting and squealing with excitement. You were probably right to stay home. The noise level alone would have brought on a migraine for you, Mother.

Thank you so much for the wonderful presents, you were too generous as usual, but it was heartwarming to see the gifts for the boys from their only real grandparents. Ford's father is yet to be heard from. I may have told you - in fact, I am sure I did, I was so mad! Mr. Delaney took his wife (we refuse to call a thirty-year-old 'Stepmother') and their daughter to Switzerland for the holidays, and didn't even send us a card. They still live in Paris, you know, and I was hoping for an invitation, but we don't even rate acknowledgment. I guess the deed to this house was supposed to cover Christmas morning for his grandchildren.

I know you will tell me to count my blessings, and believe me, I do. Mr. Delaney and his second family could have come here instead of skiing, and then I'd have had a time on my hands. We are still recovering from his last visit. I've managed to rearrange the furniture to cover the bare spots from the antiques he took.

I've done this letter all wrong. I'm so scattered these days, I can never seem to get to the point. But here it is: the real Christmas part of my letter. I will be sending photographs of the boys seeing the

Christmas tree, but I wish someone was photographing you now so I could see your faces as you read this. You're going to be grandparents again! Can you believe it? Another June baby is on the way! Ford is thrilled and I am still in shock. I thought I was only exhausted from running after the boys, but the doctor says I'd better trade in my high heels for high top sneakers. He doesn't know how right he is. My ankles are already looking puffy.

So maybe this time, we'll see Fiona. Whoever arrives will be a handful, I am sure. Ford has reluctantly agreed to a live-in baby nurse, so most of the mess and noise can be confined to the third floor.

I should have ended this with the big announcement and said something Christmassy, like 'God Bless Us Every One'. Come to think of it, that's perfect! I need all the blessings and help I can get!

Merry Christmas and love from your daughter,

Emma - Mommy X 3!

March 14, 1960

Dear Mother and Papa,

This baby has to be a girl. She is so easy on her mama and I am grateful. Her brothers are about to run me into the ground, but she just gives me a little thump from time to time to let me know she is awake. No heartburn, either. She's an angel. The boys are fine. Stark is talking a lot now and just shouts right over Tony, who is never quiet, as you know. Anyway, both boys would love a visit from their grandparents, hint, hint.

Ford has been even busier than usual. He is a member of so many groups and his bank board is a very social bunch of fellows. He's out more nights than he is home and gone nearly every Saturday to the club to play golf. He says it's all part of his job. 'Schmoozing' the clients, he calls it. I would have thought keeping their money safe and running a profitable bank would have been the part of his job which took the most time, but apparently not. As odd as it sounds, the arrangement works for us. The boys and I are happy and Ford seems to thrive in his non-stop life.

I have my girlfriends and Audrey comes by almost every day to visit, but she doesn't stay. Our paths have become so different, just as you predicted, Mother. Her engagement to Cyrus has gone on so long with no firm date, I am beginning to believe we will never see a wedding. They are very active, though, and party every weekend. Ford is a bit irked with me at the moment because he has to attend some of the important social events alone. I can't stay on my feet all day with the boys while carrying this baby and then go out in the evening and be on my toes, socially. Ford says all of his deals are done on the golf course and at parties and dinners, so he has to go. I tell him all of my deals are done over Cornflakes and applesauce. He doesn't see the humor in that.

Audrey and Cyrus take pity on him, and they are often a three-

some. Furthermore, according to Audrey, Ford never lacks for dance partners. My husband is a very handsome man while I grow bigger every day. Nature, most assuredly, is not a woman!

Poor old Clancy isn't well. I know the lifespan of a Great Dane isn't long, but I'd hoped for a few more years. Ford wants to put him down and 'be done with it', but you know I can't. He has been my best friend and I can't think what I will do without him. I don't let the boys ride him anymore, but they'll still lie down on him while he naps and Clancy is content to be a bed for tired little children. It breaks my heart to think this new baby may not know him.

I don't want to end on a sad note, but I have to go. Ford will be home soon and for once he is eating with us, so dinner has to be special.

Mother, I do want to know how the redecorating is going, and Papa, I haven't forgotten the new spring lines are coming in. I want to hear about the latest furniture styles. I wish you were closer. Maybe I could get Ford to trade in some of these heavy old Victorian pieces and lighten this place up with a few pieces of Danish modern. I know you two nearly swoon every time you see the chandelier and the dining room, but you have to admit the horsehair settees are horribly uncomfortable.

There I go again! Can't seem to keep to one train of thought or one task without wandering off. Hope it's only the baby making me ditzy!

Love,

Emma

CHAPTER THIRTY-ONE

"Rags soaked in solvent are combustible, you know," Aidan Banks said in an accusatory tone. "And you don't have an occupancy permit."

Grace shook her head. "There weren't any rags on the back porch. I was out there before I locked up. And someone opened the back door." She stopped herself from adding 'and woke me up'. She'd forgotten about the occupancy permit and if she didn't come up with some quick answers, she'd be homeless.

"It was open, alright. Maybe you were careless." Banks started to type on his tablet.

Even though her inner lawyer was shouting 'shut up!' and Avril was pulling her away, Grace exploded. "I'm telling you the back door was locked and there were no rags on the porch. You report anything to the contrary and I'll sue you." Damn. She hated people who did that. Aidan Banks brought out the worst in her.

He didn't acknowledge her threat, just kept tapping.

"You can go back home, Avril," Grace said, peeling the old woman's hand off her arm. "I'll let you know in the morning what the damage is."

"I may as well be here with you," Avril shot a pointed look at

Banks as she said, "You'll only wake me up when you come in. I'm just thankful you were staying with me. You could have been killed."

Grace raised an eyebrow but otherwise kept her face neutral. Banks stopped tapping and glared at Avril. "She's staying with you?"

"Is that any of your business?" Avril snapped.

"So you weren't sleeping here tonight?" Banks swiveled back to Grace.

"If your house was on fire wouldn't you check it out?" She neatly evaded the question, but her emotions were on a seesaw as adrenalin started to ebb and she struggled against a sudden onset of giggles. She was being rescued by Avril Oxley.

Hours passed before the firefighters were satisfied that the last ember had been doused. The rear porches were rubble, and yellow warning tape sealed the back of the house.

As the fire crews packed up, Grace was briefed by a sympathetic McNamara who looked steady and unruffled, even at four a.m. on a bitter and damp December morning. "You're lucky it's a brick house and we got the call in time. But, I have to tell you this may be arson."

Grace felt both vindicated and horrified. "I told Corporal Banks that the back doorway from the hallway onto the porch was open. Smoke was pouring in from that direction. I had locked the door earlier in the evening and there weren't any rags or cans of solvent on the porch. He didn't believe me, and so I didn't tell him I'm also sure someone was in the house."

"Why? Did you see someone?"

He shook my foot. She decided not to press her luck with tales of an unseen hero. "No, I heard them."

"Well, no one's in there now except firemen, but there's something you should see."

The kitchen door on the side of the house was undamaged. Other than the heavy smell of smoke and half a dozen broken windows, it was clear the fire hadn't made it to the house's interior, but there was damage all the same. The old metal kitchen cabinets had gone out in the first wave of demolition, but where they'd hung someone had painted four letters.

MINE

Grace knew who had set the fire.

MCNAMARA FOUND AVRIL AND GRACE HAVING COFFEE IN THE sunroom of Avril's house on Sunday afternoon. After they'd rehashed the events of the night before, McNamara changed the subject. He had the results of their DNA reports.

"You're sure?" Avril asked in a trembling voice that made her sound as old as she looked.

McNamara patted her hand. "I'm positive the woman in the grave is not a Delaney, Miss Avril. She's a genetic relative of yours."

Avril accepted the news with a jerky nod. After a moment, she said, "Do I, I mean I will if I have to, but do I have to look at the remains?"

"No, ma'am. No need."

Avril straightened a bit. "No need, or no point?" She was gathering her wits and coming back to center.

McNamara said, "No point. The remains are skeletal. But I do have something to show you." He pulled a small plastic envelope from his pocket and handed it to her.

Avril studied the thin gold watch. "It could be Audrey's. She wore one as I recall, but is this it? I couldn't say." She gave the envelope back to McNamara.

"I understand," he said. "Was there anything your sister wore regularly, something that went missing after she disappeared?"

"I've thought about that a lot." Avril pushed herself to her feet and walked over to a glass sliding door to gaze out at the woods, which had held Audrey, or someone, for more than a half a century. "I packed up her things when it became clear she wasn't coming back, and I tried to figure out what she was wearing when she left. All her clothes were here as far as I could tell. She didn't wear much jewelry, her watch and of course her engagement ring. She left the ring here and I gave it back to Cyrus." She was silent for a moment.

"I made a note in the family Bible so I wouldn't forget, or in case I wasn't around when this day came. Turns out I'm not only here, I've never been able to let go of those terrible weeks after Audrey disappeared. Anyway, I can tell you for sure that when she left this house the last time, she was wearing a new dress and she looked beautiful. The dress was special. She'd ordered it from Woodies - Woodward and Lothrop in DC. It's gone now, but do you remember it?"

McNamara and Grace both nodded.

"She'd splurged, spent her entire month's allowance from Father on a black linen sheath. It arrived the day before she left."

McNamara's hand dipped back into his coat pocket. "There was also this with the remains." His voice was gentle as he held out a plastic baggie which contained a scrap of dark fabric, a frayed label still attached at one corner. The stylized gold initials were still visible. *W&L*.

"Audrey," Avril whispered.

CHAPTER THIRTY-TWO

A vril wanted to be alone after McNamara left. Grace seized the opportunity to get back to Delaney House and assess the damage from the fire. She heard the angry voices as soon as she opened the front door.

"I didn't do it, I swear!"

Winston.

Grace pushed the kitchen door open to find a pasty-faced Winston and an angry Bryce. For a moment, no one spoke.

"Let me guess what you didn't do," Grace finally said, pointing to the orange letters sprayed across the cabinets.

"I don't have to explain anything to you," Winston spat back.

"You're right," Bryce said. "You have to explain things to me and I have to explain to her. I work for her, you moron, and until today, you worked for me."

Winston's eyes narrowed and he stepped closer to Bryce. "I am tired of this shit and I'm not playing games anymore. Let's take care of everything right now."

"You won't like it," Bryce said quietly. "The repercussions, you know?"

For a long moment, Grace wasn't sure which way it would go.

Then Winston charged out of the house, slamming the kitchen door so hard it popped back open. Gravel hit the side steps as he gunned his truck and raced down the driveway.

"What are you doing here?" Bryce asked.

"My house, remember?" Grace looked around the room. "Between the soot and mud and Winston's artwork, there's a lot of work to do."

"I'll get a crew on it." His tone was still cool and he was looking at her with an expectant expression.

Her already thin patience snapped. "What? Am I supposed to thank you for sorting him out? I told you I didn't want him here and now I'll have to go through all kinds of aggravation with Stark and Niki because he's unemployed again. If you hadn't hired him in the first place-"

"Okay, okay." Bryce put his hands up in mock defense. His boyish grin was back. "You are feisty when you get worked up."

"You know it was arson, don't you? And Winston did it."

"Now wait a minute. No way! Arson? Winnie? He's a jerk sometimes, and he's got problems with alcohol and other things, but arson? No."

"How about vandalism? You know he's the one leaving that stupid message."

"Which is why he's off this job."

"So he broke in here last night and spray painted the cabinets, but he didn't cause the fire?"

Bryce had moved closer as they talked, and now Grace took a step back. She wasn't ready to be placated.

He stopped where he was. "Look, if Winston did cause the fire, it was an accident. It was a bucket of rags, Gracie. Rags saturated with solvent can combust if they're stored packed together. I've seen it happen and I really ride the guys about it. Anyone who does this kind of work knows you don't keep work rags that way. When I took Winnie off the shutter project, the only thing left for him to do was digging out bricks and cleaning up. So far he hasn't managed to break any bricks, but maybe he got sloppy with the cleanup."

"Someone was in the house, Bryce."

"Well, Winnie obviously did get in here at some point, but he didn't set the fire. I'm sure of it. I think you just didn't see the walls in here when you locked up."

"Someone woke me up. In my bedroom. Before I could get myself together, they were gone and when I got downstairs, the door here at the rear hall was open and smoke was pouring in. Thank God Avril saw the flames and called 911."

Bryce closed the gap between them and pulled her into his arms.

"Avril saved the house with her 911 call and the intruder saved me," Grace mumbled into his shoulder. Bryce stepped back but kept a gentle hold on her arms. "Yeah, Gracie - about Avril. She's been good to me and ordinarily, I wouldn't say anything, but you may want to keep your distance there."

"Why?"

"You know she had a feud with your grandmother, right?"

Grace nodded. "But she's been supportive, in an overbearing sort of way, since she learned I owned the house."

"And why is that?" he tucked a wayward strand of hair behind her ear. "Maybe Avril wanted the house out of the Delaneys' hands. She's always had a chip on her shoulder towards the whole family, and now you're her favorite person? It doesn't track. In fact, if I had to pick someone as an arsonist, I'd consider Avril."

Grace stared at him before saying, "That's ridiculous! She owns the property next to the back woods. Why wouldn't she want me to renovate the house and clean the land up?"

"She's old and she's carried a grudge for a long time. She hated Emma Delaney for years and didn't you say you look like your grandmother?"

"So I've been told," Grace answered. "Avril said she and Emma had a falling out when my mother took me and left. But 'hate' is a very strong word."

"Well, someone doesn't want you here." Bryce gestured toward the cabinets. "I hope it's only Winnie. I guess you won't be going back to Niki's?"

"No." She told him about McNamara's visit and the identity of the woman in the grave. "Avril wants me to stay, and I'll feel better if I can keep an eye on her for a day or so. It's ridiculous, but I feel responsible for her loss."

"As long as she doesn't agree with you, I guess you'll be safe there." He pulled her back in for a kiss.

Grace tried to relax into his embrace but her thoughts wouldn't be silenced. Something was wrong. Something besides murder, arson, and anonymous messages. She let Bryce hold her because she had no idea what else to do.

BY MONDAY, GRACE HAD RESIGNED HERSELF TO REBUILDING BOTH back porches, replacing the windows across the back of the house and repainting the downstairs rooms.

The day was fractured with the crews assessing the damage and conferring with Bryce on a new work schedule. Grace shuttled between construction conferences and errands for Bryce. Now that Winston was gone, the importance of the gopher job became clear. By late afternoon, she was exhausted and depressed at the increased scope of work. Her list of chores had expanded to include an insurance claim for the damage from the fire. She quickly learned that arson-involved claims move slowly.

Bryce and the workers had been gone for an hour when she heard loud voices outside. Finding Winston and Aidan Banks in a fight in her driveway was the last straw in the irritating day.

"Stop it!" she screamed, causing Banks to shift his focus to her for the second Winston needed to land a blow squarely in the middle of his face.

Grace, who hadn't hit anyone since second grade recess, launched herself at Winston and put the day's frustration into a shove that sent him staggering backward, tripping over his own toolbox and landing flat on his back in the gravel. Ignoring the groaning Winston, she bent down next to Banks, who had bounced off the tailgate of Winston's truck and sat on the ground holding his bleeding face.

"Hang on," she said, fishing in her jeans' pocket for her cell. "You'll be fine."

This brought a series of loud squawks from Banks, who sounded like he was strangling.

"Try and stay calm, I'm dialing 911 -"

Banks snatched the phone away from her and threw it toward the house. "Naaa!" he managed as he struggled to his feet. After giving Grace a look that made her back up, he walked, more or less in a straight line, to his car.

She watched him leave before moving to pick up her phone and check on Winston.

"I ought to sue you," he said as he sat up and rubbed the back of his head.

"I ought to shoot you for trespassing."

"I'm not trespassing. I came to work on the porch. See?" He pointed to the toolbox he'd tripped over.

Was he on drugs? He certainly appeared addled. Brain damage? "Were you going to work in the dark tonight? You were fired, Winston. Besides, there are no porches. You burned them up, remember?"

They both looked at the back of the house. The remains of the back porch and the sleeping porch above it had been removed and the house looked naked without them. Naked and scorched. The doors to both porches now opened onto empty space and were covered by plywood.

"It wasn't me. I told you." Winston whined.

"It wasn't you who set the fire, or it wasn't you who painted 'MINE' on the kitchen wall?" She didn't wait for his answer. "Get out of here before I call the police. The *other* police - McNamara. If you come back again, he'll arrest you."

"I left some tools, I'll just -"

"Take one more step toward the house and I'll call 911. I don't think the drug test they'll give you in booking will come back negative, do you?"

"Bitch," he spat at her.

She could feel her heart pounding with the need to run, but she stood on the scraggly patch of grass that passed for the side lawn of Delaney House and watched as Winston drove away.

It will never be over, she thought.

CHAPTER THIRTY-THREE

S he might have known Banks would lodge a complaint. Lee McNamara was coming up Avril's walk when Grace left the following morning. He had an official tone to his voice when he asked for details of the altercation.

Grace sighed. This was what her life had come to: one fight after another and the police in the middle of everything. She said, "I walked outside last evening to find your Corporal Banks in a shoving match with Winston Delaney. Banks took a blow to the face that looked like it did a lot of damage. When I tried to call 911 for help, he grabbed my phone out of my hand, threw it, and left." She pulled the iPhone with its cracked screen out of her pocket and held it up. "I don't suppose the department will reimburse me for this?"

McNamara frowned. "Have it fixed or replaced and give me the bill."

"You have a slush fund to cover that hothead's damage?" she asked and instantly wished she hadn't. He was being nice and she sounded anything but.

McNamara sighed. "We've run through that pot of money, but I'll figure something out. Do you know what he and Winston were fighting over?"

She'd thought of little else, but had no answers. "No, do you?"

"What did your cousin say?"

"Mostly he whined about how I'd hurt his back when I pushed him away from Banks."

McNamara's smile lit up his face. "Oh, really? You broke up the fight?"

"I'm guessing Banks didn't mention that part?"

"He probably forgot."

"Of course he did. Is his nose broken?"

"Not too bad. It'll only improve his looks, if not his disposition." McNamara glanced at his watch. "I'm on my way to check in with Miss Oxley. I don't have any news, but I wanted to see how she's coping."

"That's kind of you."

"It will be a kindness when I have some answers for her. But, for now, on behalf of the department, I apologize for Corporal Banks' behavior. He was off duty, happened to be driving past and saw Delaney pull into your driveway. He stopped to ask a few questions and things deteriorated rapidly. Banks says he was defending himself, Ms. Reagan. He didn't initiate the brawl, but I'm sorry you had to witness it and, uh, intervene." He grinned again.

"Polite of you not to laugh until you leave."

McNamara's smile widened, warm and genuine. "You have no idea what a struggle it is."

"Avril said you were nearly killed!"

Grace punched the volume down on her phone, taking care not to slide her finger over the cracked screen. She'd already cut herself twice. She wanted to ask Mosley if Avril had called to tell him about the fire or that his long lost fiancé had been found, but he was still ranting about her poor choices and their consequences.

"I need to see you," Mosley said when he wrapped up his rehash of all the reasons why she should cut her losses and sell the half-finished house to him.

She was sitting on the sixth step of the cantilevered staircase, her favorite spot. Late afternoon sunshine streamed through the turret windows, washing over her, warming the old wood and lighting the ruby glass in the small window above the front door. Oddly, Mosley's voice didn't detract from her surroundings, he seemed to be a part of it, natural even when irritating. He was the thorn on her rose bush, she thought. She was very tired.

Mosley's tone changed and she refocused. "Well, if you won't be sensible and discuss selling, I'll go on to the other reason I called. As the attorney for your grandmother's estate, I've been asked to facilitate a meeting between you and your Uncle Stark. He and Connie would like to talk with you."

"I can only imagine," Grace said dryly. She sat up straight and stretched her legs out, stretching muscles that were surprisingly sore. Was she getting old on top of everything else? "I'm not hiring Winston back. In fact, he's not allowed on the property." She wondered if Mosley was hitching up his pants in the brief silence that followed. "But you can also tell Stark I'm not pressing charges." She let Mosley work out for himself what the possible crime might be.

He finally said, "I have to say, I don't know why he wants to talk to you, which is why I would prefer to be present. If you could be here at two tomorrow, I'll schedule Stark and Connie to join us at three. There are a couple of other issues on a different topic that you and I need to discuss."

"I'm serious," Grace said. She could smell bad news wafting through the phone. "Winston is off the property, and I'm not changing my mind this time."

"Duly noted. I'll back you up on that."

"I don't need you to back me up, or to chaperone my meeting with Stark. I'm perfectly capable – "

"For heaven's sake!" Mosley's cracked baritone blasted through the phone. "I know each of you are perfectly capable of tearing each other limb from limb, but I'd prefer you didn't do it on my watch. Now, will you please come here tomorrow at two? I need to talk to you and it has nothing whatsoever to do with Winston."

On his watch?

Another piece of the puzzle that was Mosley clicked into place, and Grace smiled as she hung up. The old lawyer saw himself as the captain of the ship that was the Delaney family. She looked around the hall and remembered her first impression of Emma's representative — the Crypt Keeper. Her smile faded. Mosley never stopped trying to steer what was left of the family toward what he claimed were Emma's wishes. He knew the family's secrets. He also knew more about Audrey Oxley's disappearance than anyone alive. Had he killed her?

Grace hugged her knees to her chest and wished herself far away.

THE FIRE RECOVERY COMPANY FINISHED ITS WORK AND BY Wednesday morning, Grace was ready to move back to the attic apartment. The guest room Avril had given her had been lovely in the Sixties when it was last decorated, but the mattress was hard and the room felt stale. Grace didn't think anyone had slept in there for a long time.

She might not have been accustomed to guests, but Avril wasn't willing to let Grace leave without a fight. She'd been slow to process the news of her sister's death and had allowed Grace to look after her while she took to an upholstered rocker in her dusty den. The rocker faced a wide window with a view the backyard and the wall that ran along the back of the Delaney property. The wall that had hidden her sister's grave for so many years.

Grace left her with the newspaper and a tray of tea and toast each morning. In the evenings she made a hot meal and updated Avril on the renovation progress. By Wednesday Avril began to perk up and talk about something other than the funeral she was planning for her sister. Grace thought she could safely leave.

Avril thought otherwise. "You can't go back there," she said. "You don't know who started the fire."

"I've got a good idea, and I don't think he'll try it again." She intended to make sure of that when she met with Stark and Connie.

Avril was shaking her head. "You don't know, not for sure. I've told you, kids hang out in those woods. Anyone could have done it."

Grace told her about the new spray-painted message on the kitchen walls.

"The police are keeping an eye on Winston, and Bryce has fired him. I've had the locks changed again, and that's another reason I have to move back. Only Bryce and I have keys and he can't be there every time someone needs to get in."

"You don't have an occupancy permit," Avril said.

Grace was relieved to hear the old woman's voice back to her regular lecturing tone, even if it meant they were going to continue to argue. "I need to get back," she said.

"Even if you're willing to break the law, you need me and I'm not quite ready to get back to work." The pugnacious tilt of Avril's head warned Grace to weigh her response carefully.

"I'll make sure to keep you in the loop. I'll come by each day and update you until you feel well enough to get out."

"Oh, stop it!" Avril pushed herself up and out of the rocker. "I'm not sick, just feeling puny. Go on back to your house and if that jackass Aidan Banks comes snooping around, tell him you're still living with me."

Grace decided it would be a good answer for anyone who asked.

"And," Avril's voice took on a sly tone, "you may as well let Bryce stay with you. He'll protect you and you two aren't fooling anyone."

CHAPTER THIRTY-FOUR

The Gum Snapper took her into Mosley's office as soon as she arrived. The lawyer was waiting for her and once the coffee tray was in place on the small conference table, he got down to business without any of his usual chatter.

"I'm sorry to be so mysterious, but we have a difficult subject to discuss and there is no easy way to broach it. As you know, your grandmother and grandfather were my clients. On several occasions, your mother was as well." Mosley paused. When Grace sat back in her chair without comment, he patted the peak of his white pompadour. The hair didn't give.

"But not Stark?" she finally asked.

"Your uncle has always preferred his own counsel."

"Sounds about right," she said. "So let's get to whatever it is you have to tell me."

Mosley nodded, but fidgeted a moment more before saying, "Emma sent me to see Julia about a month before they both passed away."

"What! Why?" Grace frantically ran through the timetable of that awful period. She'd still been working, but not full time, and every spare moment was spent with her mother. She would have known, surely, if Mosley had appeared.

"I knew your mother her whole life," Mosley began, then fell silent again. He was dressed to work today: a crisp white shirt and navy Brooks Brothers suit. This attire seemed to require more than his usual waistband adjustment. As the silence stretched, he tugged at his cuffs and picked invisible specks off his sleeves. Grace noticed there were new hearing aids behind both ears and wondered how he was dealing with the loss of one of his delaying tactics.

When she couldn't stand his dithering any longer, she said, "You may want to cancel Stark and Connie. We're not doing anything until you answer my questions. Why did Emma send you to my mother? Did you go? If so, what transpired when you saw her?"

"Good. Good, tight questions. I was curious, of course, when I learned you were an attorney. I checked you out in the official channels, *Martindale Hubbard* and all that. I also called some associates who are in your neck of the woods. For a young attorney, you have an excellent reputation. I know your mother was proud of you. Your grandmother was, too. Shame she never got to tell you."

Grace felt the impact of his words, and decided that while Mosley might not be at the top of his game, he was still crafty enough to tangle her up if she wasn't careful. She wondered if Chief McNamara had the same trouble questioning him. She put Mosley in a mental witness box and tried again. "Did you see, or talk, or in any way communicate with my mother in the weeks before her death?"

He rose and walked to the windows overlooking Washington Street before saying, "In late January, Emma asked me to call Julia. She knew Julia and I kept in touch, distantly, of course, but still." He glanced over his shoulder at Grace. "If you didn't know, it's not because I wanted it to be a secret. Your mother insisted. You won't like the rest of this, but it isn't privileged, if you want to hear."

"All of it."

"All of it," he repeated. "I don't think so. How about if I tell you what your mother wanted you to know?"

Stunned, she watched as Mosley crossed back to his desk, opened the bottom left drawer and withdrew an envelope. Grace hated that her hands shook as she opened it. "What is this?" She glanced at the two sheets of paper and then rechecked the empty envelope.

"Your mother wanted you to have your original birth certificate and the court order changing your last name to Reagan."

Grace felt frozen in place, afraid to read the words to see if what he was saying were true.

"My dear, your birth name was Delaney. Your parents weren't married. Julia didn't feel you needed to know. Then she couldn't find the right time to tell you, and then when she got sick … well."

"Well, what?" The inertia snapped and now she wanted to strangle him. Strangle somebody. The somebody who had kept the secrets. Why would her mother have thought Grace would care that she was born out of wedlock? The answer came at once: she wouldn't. She had to have been hiding something else.

"Julia believed she'd have more time," Cyrus was saying. "When she realized she didn't, she didn't want to spend the few days she had left shattering your relationship. She said she knew you would find out sooner or later and she wanted me to handle the situation."

"She trusted you." *But not me* — the unspoken words hung in the air.

If Mosley took offense, he didn't show it. "Many people do, my dear."

"You kept this from me! That's unconscionable! It's, it's… malpractice!" She was on her feet and waving the papers in his face. "You've had this information for seven months with instructions from my mother, your client, to give it to me and you waited all this time. What else, Mosley? What else haven't you told me? Keep anything else from me and you'll be sorry. I'll tie you up in court until your last day on earth and beyond." She stopped abruptly when she realized he was grinning broadly.

"My God, it's like a visit from Emma herself," he laughed.

Grace stood still and tried not to explode. It took all the self-control she had to speak to him in a civil tone. "Let's try this again.

And make no mistake, I *will* sue you for malpractice if you don't have a damn good reason for what you've done."

"Oh, my dear," he wiped his eyes. "The only mistakes I have ever made all involved Delaneys." He sat heavily, sinking back into the swivel chair, rocking it. After a moment, he said, "As I told you, on Emma's instructions, I located your mother and called her. She agreed to meet me and gave me the address of her new apartment."

Grace felt her heart drop. Her mother had stubbornly refused to admit she was dying, referring to her last residence as her 'new apartment'. Friends didn't know until they arrived at the small complex of cottages near Sibley Memorial Hospital that Julia's new home was a hospice. Mosley had just given her proof that he had, indeed, talked with her mother less than a month before her death.

"I saw Julia straight away and, of course, learned what was happening. Julia said she was having a good day, but..." Mosley's voice trailed off.

"Go on!" Grace demanded, unwilling to give him any sympathy. "What did you talk about?"

"Emma wanted me to tell Julia everything - especially that the house had been sold and Julia should bring you and come home one last time. Of course, Emma and I didn't know you were the buyer."

As Mosley's words sank in, Grace tried to take in enough air. She slowed her breathing and willed herself to calm down. Mosley looked exhausted, and she reminded herself of his age.

"Did Mom tell you we owned Delaney House?"

"No. She might have, but I preempted that conversation when I told her about Emma's health."

"So you told Mom her mother was dying, and then you had to tell Emma her daughter was dying?"

"Yes."

Anger still churned through her, but Mosley was looking less and less like the villain. She might have felt sorry for him, but the feeling was too awkward, the gulf too wide. She managed a choked, "She didn't tell me."

"I assumed as much. I'm afraid I've never understood any of you

Delaneys, so I can't explain why you all don't just talk to each other. Emma and I kept a check on you and Julia over the years, of course. We knew where you lived, but in later years, unfortunately, not what was happening in your lives. It was more peaceful that way."

"But why?" Grace still couldn't grasp the enormity of what the two women had hidden from her.

"Emma and Julia were never good together as adults. One was always wanting to help, the other refusing to accept. All too often I was in the middle. But you know about that, don't you? It's a lawyer's lot in life, being in the middle."

And the middle was usually where the truth lay, Grace thought.

"I did my best by each of them, gave them the last gift I could," Mosley said. "And I promised Julia when the time was right, I'd tell you about your father."

Grace unfolded the papers again and looked at her birth certificate. At the empty space next to 'Father'.

"I'm listening," she said.

CHAPTER THIRTY-FIVE

"There is no Jonathon Reagan, my dear. Your mother took her grandmother's maiden name when she left Mallard Bay. She reasoned if she invented a bland version of a father and put him and his non-existent family out of your reach, you would be less likely to go searching for the truth. She also wanted a clean break from the Delaneys."

"She wanted a clean break, except from the trust funds." Grace tried and failed to keep the bitterness out of her voice.

"You Delaneys have a streak of pride a mile wide, but you all — every one of you — goes after what you believe is yours."

"What we *believe* is ours?"

Mosley waved her question away. "Your mother was very young, emotionally, when she went to college. I imagine she was a bit intoxicated with the sudden freedom from Emma's hovering. She did well academically and she made a lot of friends, had a good time."

"And got pregnant."

"Yes. It wasn't a serious relationship, and she and the young man had a falling out. He turned out not to be the sort she wanted in her life or yours, so she cut him out."

"She did a lot of that, it seems," Grace couldn't sit still any longer. She rose and paced the length of Mosley's office. The information he'd thrown at her sat in a lump near her heart, unfathomable yet perfectly clear. So many questions answered. When she could trust her voice again, she stopped and faced him. "Tell me the rest. What else do you know?"

"I don't know his name; I give you my word." Mosley took his handkerchief out again and wiped his eyes, making no attempt to disguise his emotions. When he leaned back in his chair and tugged at his waistband, Grace felt relieved. The lawyer was back.

"But you know why she didn't tell me."

"The boy questioned Julia's assertion that he was the father. Your mother never wanted him to have the opportunity to say those words to you. She told me not to give you that," he gestured to the envelope, "unless it was absolutely necessary."

"Absolutely necessary in your opinion? Well, you seem to think it's necessary now. Why?"

"Your Uncle Stark is very angry. I hoped it would fade in time, but now I'm not sure. He and Connie are disappointed, to say the least, in how little they received when Emma's will was settled. I'm afraid the price you paid for the house was the last straw. I've tried to explain that given the market and the condition of the house it was the best we could do, but they've never been sensible about money. It was bad enough when they believed Emma had taken a stranger's best offer. When they found out you were the buyer, they felt they'd been cheated."

Grace remembered Stark's angry face and the bitter words he'd flung at her across Niki's dinner table. "So you're beating him to it by telling me there is no Jonathon Reagan? Stark said I should ask you about my mother. He said you had all the answers. Is this what he meant?"

Mosley looked nonplussed for a moment. "No. Both Emma and Julia told him the same story they gave the rest of the world."

"The rest of the world and me."

"Yes. They thought it best. Stark has always been suspicious, and in the absence of the truth, a wounded person will fill in the blanks with the worst-case scenario. I'm afraid Stark believes Julia and I encouraged Emma to accept your offer when she could have gotten a higher price."

"Did you?"

Until today, she'd thought her purchase of Delaney House had been a surprise to her mother, now she wouldn't put anything past Julia and Mosley. *Keep moving, Grace. Don't rely on anyone else. Take charge.* Her mother's voice was as clear as if she stood in Mosley's office.

"No," Mosley sighed. "But it's easy to see why Stark would think so. Julia was always my favorite. Stark was resentful of my friendship with the family. Thought I was usurping his father's place."

Grace tried to see Stark's point of view. "And by accepting my offer…"

"Your below market offer," Mosley added.

Grace rolled her eyes, but let the comment pass. "You gave me the house and returned half the purchase price to me through my mother's will."

Mosley nodded. "He won't listen to reason. Stark told me you were asking about your father. If you keep on, he may eventually tell you his version of things and it won't be kind to your mother."

"Why? What does he know that you aren't telling me?"

"Who can say what Stark thinks he knows? What he doesn't know is what I've told you. Your uncle doesn't know the truth."

She had to get out of Mosley's office and into the fresh air. The elegant room with its expensive furnishings was closing in on her. She started for the door just as it opened and the gum-snapping secretary announced Stark and Connie's arrival.

Grace cut off Mosley's response. "Could we have a minute, please?" she asked. When the door shut again, she turned back to Mosley. "You said you gave both Emma and my mother the last gift you could. What did you mean?"

Mosley seemed surprised by the question. "My dear, I'd have thought that was obvious. I promised both of them I would take care of you."

CHAPTER THIRTY-SIX

Mosley kept up a running stream of innocuous chatter with Connie while fresh coffee was brought in. Grace used the time to pull herself together.

"Are you well, Grace?" Connie asked in a solicitous tone. "You're a little pale. I hope you aren't working too hard."

"I'm feeling a little off, now that you mention it. I might be coming down with something. Hope I'm not contagious."

Connie's smile faltered a bit.

"Well, then let's get on with this so you can go home and rest," Mosley said in a too hearty, we're-all-family-here tone. "Stark, you and Connie have something to discuss with Grace?"

Stark crossed his arms but it was Connie who spoke. "Niki was telling us how nice the house is looking. She said you found a lot of furniture, good furniture on the second floor."

Grace felt her tenuous hold on civility slipping. She'd been expecting to hear a plea for Winston's reinstatement, not a conversation about the few antiques left in the house.

"I found some nice serviceable pieces, yes." *And I'll be damned if you're getting your hands on any of it.*

"Have you gone through all of the drawers?" Stark demanded.

He looked angry, but Grace was beginning to think he was always angry.

"I have cleaned it all thoroughly, yes."

"If you found any jewelry, it's ours." Right to the punch line.

"Now, Stark," Mosley began. "You and your mother came to terms before she died. Everything remaining in the house was Julia's, which means it went to Grace."

"I was cheated and you know it. She," he shot a venomous look at Grace, "wasn't supposed to get anything. I want whatever it is she found in the house!"

It was Mosley who lost his temper first, slapping the table in front of him, sending a wave of coffee over the rim of his cup. "We've been through this a dozen times. You got a second legal opinion and your Baltimore lawyer told you the same thing I did. The house was sold before your mother's death. The proceeds were split evenly between you and your sister. The contents of the house were also split between you. Your mother even allowed you to select the items you wanted for your share. Julia died and left her half to Grace."

Stark would not be mollified. "Then I'll sue the estate. There's jewelry missing. I keep telling you! Jewelry my mother promised to Niki outside of the will and I want it back!"

Mosley looked disgusted, but not surprised. Connie wrung her hands but stayed quiet.

"Why are you so worked up about it if the jewelry belongs to Niki?" Grace asked, distracting all of them. "Is it that you've run out of valuables to sell?"

"What does she mean?" Cyrus' voice was flat, and he glared at Stark.

"Emma's diamond," Grace said. "And the pearls." She turned to face Stark. "Let me make this clear. There was no jewelry worth having in the house. And if by chance I ever find anything of value that should go to Niki, I'll make sure she gets to keep it and you don't get your hands on it."

Stark half rose from his chair. Spittle flew from his mouth when he said, "I'll sue if every piece isn't returned to us."

Grace was ready. "How were the contents of the house divided, Stark? You take the first floor and leave me the second? Where, exactly, is the furniture that used to be downstairs?"

"Where?" Stark spat the word at her. "Tell her where, Cyrus."

Grace's stomach lurched as she remembered the receipts in the paperwork from Emma's house. Bologna and saltine crackers. Double-digit bank statements.

"Tell her or I will." Stark was grinning, but it wasn't a nice smile.

"Emma was proud," Cyrus started. "She wouldn't take help-"

"She sold off the most valuable pieces for money to live on," Stark said. "Even the ones I wanted — especially the ones I wanted. She sold my grandfather's portrait. She said the offer was too good to pass up."

Grace kept her voice detached and cool. Stark was trying for emotional wounds, but she wouldn't let him get her at that level. Turning to Cyrus, she said, "I'll need an inventory of what he took from the house. I'll provide you with a documented list of what was left." The photos she'd taken on the first day would come in handy after all.

Cyrus sighed and said, "For God's sake! Would the two of you stop? I have a detailed list of everything of value in the house. Kindly remember that I'm the executor of the estate and I'm not senile, yet. I believe you will both be disappointed when you see what the other ended up with."

This earned him a sharp look from Stark, but Grace was relieved. She had no desire to go after anything Stark had taken, but neither would she let him take what was hers. Besides, there was another issue she wanted to discuss.

She said, "While we're all together with legal counsel, I want to make something clear to both you and Connie. Cyrus, pay attention, you'll want to make sure Winston gets this message and I'm only going to say it once." She paused to make eye contact with each of them before continuing.

"On the night of the fire, someone came into my room and woke me up. I didn't see them, but whoever shook me tried to save my life. That's the only reason I haven't sworn a complaint against Winston for the arson."

Connie was on her feet. "How dare you! You have no proof —"

"Shut. Up." Stark didn't spare his wife a glance as he silenced her. To Grace, he said, "What makes you think the boy did it?"

"Someone spray painted 'mine' on the kitchen walls again, right before the fire. It was Winston, or it was you. Painting stupid messages and setting fire to the house doesn't seem like your style. Plus, I'm not so sure you'd wake me."

No one contradicted her.

"So here's the deal," she continued. "The part where you need to pay attention. If you or your son — either one or both of you — vandalize the house again, I'll have you arrested. Breaking and entering, criminal trespass and let's not forget arson. You'll be in jail for a while on that last one alone." She rose and stared down at her uncle. "Leave me alone and I'll leave you alone. Mess with me again and you'll find out how much damage I can do."

She made a grand exit from Mosley's office; one she thought of with satisfaction in the weeks to come when it seemed nothing would ever go right again.

———

GRACE WASN'T SURPRISED TO HEAR FROM MOSLEY THE NEXT DAY.

"I looked at the photos you emailed me last night," he said. "I suppose you could enlarge them, but I doubt they'd hold up in court if Stark sues you."

Grace had him on speaker as she drove. She was midway across the Chesapeake Bay Bridge, returning to Mallard Bay from the settlement on Julia's Arlington house. The construction account for Delaney House had just gotten a healthy infusion of cash. She glanced down at the glints of sunlight on the water far below her. Since handing her mother's keys to the new owner, she'd been indulging in a mix of relief and grief, an addictive cocktail she knew she needed to give up.

"Grace? Are you still there?"

"Just a sec." She concentrated on slowing to make room for a large SUV intent on changing lanes in front of her. She was sure she'd eventually get used to driving over the two-lane span of the eastbound Bay Bridge, but today was not the day to test her multi-tasking skills.

The SUV darted back into the left-hand lane and sped around a school bus as they reached land on Kent Island. A state trooper peeled off the median and carved the reckless driver out of the pack of traffic. Grace yelled, "YES!"

Mosley gave a yelp, and she remembered the hearing aids.

"No, my dear," he said as if she hadn't just plunged ice picks in his ears. "I don't think your pictures prove anything, but I also don't think he'll sue. He's short on cash and no reputable firm is going to take his case on a contingency basis."

"So where do we stand?" she asked.

"Stark huffed and puffed a while after you left. They were truly shocked at the idea of Winnie starting the fire. Oddly, hearing that he woke you seemed to settle them down."

Grace considered that. "So baby boy is only an arsonist, not really a bad guy?" she asked.

Mosley sighed. "I'm having a hard time believing any of it, to tell you the truth. Arson requires some thought, and usually a purpose. Winnie's no pyromaniac. He doesn't do fire for thrills, we'd have seen evidence of it by now. And he's close to the laziest human I've ever known. Planning just isn't in character."

"The spray paint?"

"Pure Winnie," Mosley agreed. "If someone left a can of paint within reach."

"Then who started the fire?"

"I took the liberty of calling Bryce Cutter and he feels strongly that the workmen, Winnie, actually, left a bucket of turpentine-soaked rags on the back porch. The foreman overlooked it. He'll be dealing with the crew this morning, but I'm afraid it will be your insurance that will cover the costs of repairs — pending the police report, of course. Bryce assures me he'll do the work at cost."

Grace opened her mouth, then closed it. She wanted to tell Mosley it wasn't his place to call her contractor, but it occurred to her she hadn't heard from Bryce since the morning after the fire. Was he avoiding her? If so, Mosley's call had probably made things worse.

"Look, Cyrus, there was no bucket of rags on the back porch when I locked up. I know it's hard to prove, but I'm telling you, I would have noticed a hazard like that. And if it was an accident, then who woke me up? Someone set the fire. If not Winnie, my money's on Stark."

"I've known the boy his whole life." Mosley's voice sounded his age. "Stark couldn't do that, Grace. He probably would if he could, but it's his family home. He just couldn't, I promise you."

Grace kept the obvious response to herself. 'The boy' was in his sixties and as mean as they came. He not only could, Grace knew he *would* burn down Delaney House if it meant she wouldn't have it.

CHAPTER THIRTY-SEVEN

G race tried hard to ignore Christmas, but she hadn't counted on
Avril's tenacity. When Grace went to collect her things, she
found the old woman trying to drag a silver aluminum tree down her
attic stairs. By the time they'd put the relic together with the help of
duct tape and a bottle of Merlot, she felt like she'd fallen into the
Twilight Zone. Blue twinkling lights transformed the tree into something that looked like it would blast off at any moment.

"It's been years since I had it up, but I decided you could use a
little Christmas cheer," Avril said without a trace of guile.

"How kind of you," Grace replied in her best Eliza Doolittle.

Avril nodded as if a broad Cockney accent was exactly what she
expected. "I picked up a cheddar and Brie mac and cheese at Three
Pigs when I was getting the turkey," Avril said. "It's supposed to
snow tonight and you'll need a hearty meal if you're going back to
your apartment. It'll be cold up there under the rafters."

Avril won. It was the day after Christmas before Grace went back
to Delaney House. Work on the house stopped over the weekend and
Avril was right, it was not only cold on the third floor, it was lonely
in a way only Christmas can be.

Last year, Grace had tried to make a perfect day for her mother, who would have much preferred to sleep through the holiday. This year, she cooked Christmas dinner while Avril, wearing an apron that said *Bah, Humbug,* gave instructions in a running commentary which, included her opinions on everything from frozen turkeys to politicians, a combination Grace found apt as well as entertaining.

She and Avril toasted each other over the turkey and oyster stuffing. *You're really missing something, Mom,* she thought. Not that Julia would be at this table if she was still alive. Grace shoved the thought aside. She was moving on.

BEING BACK IN DELANEY HOUSE AFTER THE FIRE AND THE INTRUDER unnerved her, but she couldn't avoid it forever. Especially if it meant staying on with Avril or moving to a hotel.

Although Niki called daily for a short chat, there had been no mention of Grace returning to the Victory Manor Inn. There had also been no mention of the showdown in Cyrus' office. When Grace tried to bring it up, Niki abruptly changed the subject. Ignoring the gorilla in the corner was helpful for maintaining Christmas cheer, but Grace knew she'd have to deal with Stark and Connie sooner or later.

Niki invited her to a Christmas Eve lunch at Morsels. They exchanged gifts, laughing when each presented the other with a scarf, and talked about the renovation. Their careful conversation avoided any topic that might lead to conflict. By Monday morning, when Grace was once again in the third-floor apartment, her introvert nature was begging for a break from entertaining Avril and dancing around her family's minefields.

The renovation was more than halfway complete. In another six or eight weeks she could list the house with a Realtor. She hoped by then she'd have an idea of where the rest of her life was headed. Whatever she did, she'd need a job. It might take months for Delaney House to sell.

The day after Christmas was a holiday for the Cutter work crew. While hunting and football seemed to occupy the rest of Mallard

Bay, Grace took advantage of the opportunity to search the empty house in daylight. She'd all but given up the idea that her mother had left behind any clues to her father, but she'd take one more look. And there was always the possibility Stark and Winnie were right about Emma squirreling jewelry away. She was in the third-floor storage room checking the pockets of one of Emma's mink coats when she heard vehicles pull into the driveway.

From the window, she could see Bryce and Joey Pecolini get out of a pickup. Her annoyance over Bryce rehiring one of Winston's posse faded when they started to unload wood from the truck. At least they were working today. After a moment, she went back to checking pockets and tried to decide how to handle Bryce.

Despite the rush of activity after the fire, he'd been absent for more than a week. The text message he'd sent on Christmas Day sounded like something for a maiden aunt he'd forgotten to call. She'd ignored *Hop ur xmas is gud,* but it hadn't been replaced with anything better. She reminded herself that she was the one who'd asked to keep the brakes on their relationship; maybe Bryce was just paying attention. She toyed with this novel idea until she heard the truck start and roll out of the drive. A moment later, Bryce called out her name. If she'd stopped to think about it, she'd been embarrassed at how fast she made her way to the third-floor landing and the staircase.

"You look like a movie star floating down those stairs," he said as he watched her descend.

"I was beginning to think you'd moved onto another project," she said as she reached the main hall.

"I told you I had to do a family thing down in Virginia, right? No? Oh, Grace, I'm sorry."

Against her better judgment, she let him hug her. And nuzzle a brief kiss on her neck. "Really sorry," he whispered. "But, I have a present for you. It's in the kitchen."

He pulled her along with him down the long hallway to the back of the house and the kitchen door. Flinging it open, he said, "Ta da!

They don't look like much now, but these will be beautiful when they're refinished."

Grace walked slowly into the kitchen. The large square room with its brick floor and tall windows no longer served as a garbage dump. Henry's cleaning crew had erased the grime, and Bryce's gift was the promise of the transformation to come.

"A guy I know is demolishing an old house out in Sussex County. I took a chance you'd want these. If you don't -"

"They're perfect," Grace said, pulling her hand out of his so she could inspect the tall oak cabinets that were lined up against the walls.

"They're in rough shape, but my carpenters can refinish them. My friend's not one for cabinetry restoration, so he calls me before he demos."

For the next hour, they planned the layout of the new kitchen. The placement of the cabinets, a farmhouse sink and a custom island to run through the middle of the room. Bryce sat on the service staircase and sketched layouts to capture Grace's decisions. When she tired of pacing off furniture placements, she joined him and watched the outline of her designs take shape.

At one point she realized it was Bryce she was studying, not his sketches. Worrying a piece of licorice, his face stern in concentration, she saw a different man. Not the charmer or the salesman, but the man at work.

"There!" He held the pad of paper up for her inspection. Now it was a boyish Bryce who held his sketch up for her approval.

Grace was thrilled and told him so.

"I took more out of the Sussex house if you're interested." He pulled out his phone and flicked through screens until he found what he wanted. Putting an arm around her turned the picture in her direction.

"Fantastic," Grace said, delighted with the Welsh-style cupboard. "I'll take it, it's perfect!"

"There's more." Bryce leaned closer, saying the angle was bad, but couldn't she see the potential in the corner chest with a missing door?

What Grace saw was Bryce. His licorice breath was warm on her ear as he described the potential of the dilapidated pieces.

"Right," she said, hating the way her voice caught.

She started to rise, but he put a hand on her shoulder to stop her. "Wait there's more."

He scrolled through pictures so quickly, all Grace saw was a blur of flashing images. And his long, lean body stretched out next to her. She tried to concentrate on his work boots.

"Grace," he said, his words tickling the air near her ear. He was holding the phone so she could see an ornate newel post and banister. "I saved this from one of his sites."

"Beautiful," she managed.

"Yes."

Neither of them was looking at the phone that Bryce slipped back into his pocket.

CHAPTER THIRTY-EIGHT

S he knew it was a mistake the minute it was over. Well, maybe not the *first* minute - but it didn't take long.

Grace didn't have time to nurture a romance, and she doubted a relationship with Bryce would last. He was too gregarious for her, and they had little in common other than a love for restoring old properties and her weakness for dimples. Why hadn't she seen that back in the days when she'd wanted to heat up their relationship? Part of her wanted to go back to the time of sweet anticipation and surface attraction, but most of her had moved on. The truth was, she rarely thought of him when he wasn't around and when he was, her reaction was purely visceral. Not the basis for a love story.

While she was appalled at her callous treatment of a nice guy, she wasn't going to take the time to search for emotional substance in Bryce. It was possible she might rediscover the magic that had resulted in a stair tread-shaped bruise on her back, but probably not. Magic required two people - the magician and the person willing to believe. She was neither. To her, Bryce was like the licorice candy he loved - a strong flavor without much else. She'd had enough of that with David.

She didn't answer his calls over the next two days but kept their communications to texts. She ignored his innuendo and emoji-laced messages, responding with a lead on a chandelier and updates on the start of the kitchen reno. His replies all ended in 'Miss you!' and were punctuated with pop-eyed happy faces. Hers ended in 'talk soon'.

She told herself she wasn't trying to avoid him; she simply couldn't think of what to say. She was an emotionally cautious woman, slow to build relationships and to trust. In the past two months, she had opened up to more people than she was comfortable allowing into her life. Grace planned her spontaneity, and her fun never included trysts on a staircase. The reason for her about-face was short and simple. She'd wanted to do it, so she'd done it and she'd liked it.

Now she had to get out of the mess she'd made.

EVENTUALLY SHE HAD TO SEE HIM, BUT SHE MADE SURE HENRY WAS there to provide a buffer. If either man found it odd that Henry was brought in for the final kitchen design meeting, nothing was said, but his presence didn't stop Bryce from beaming at Grace every time he caught her eye. Still, he kept his hands to himself and the conversation to work matters. She'd started to relax when he asked her to go to the basement with him.

Henry had begun checking his watch and making leaving noises, when Bryce said, "We can take it from here, right, Grace? Henry's got places to go and dogs to see."

Henry looked at Grace and back at Bryce. "I do have something planned, but it's not a rescue. I'll cancel and we'll finish."

"No need," Bryce's words were to Henry, but his eyes were on Grace. "Never keep a good dog waiting, isn't that your motto?"

"Actually, no."

Henry was clearly uncomfortable now, but Bryce made shooing

motions at his cousin and said, "I won't be here much longer. I just need to take Grace downstairs and get a decision on the placement of the new mechanical room."

"Oh, no need," Grace said, happy to be able to end the matter. "I was down there yesterday. The room Marty's recommending will be fine. The second one on the left." Having Marty back as foreman and Winston out of her house were the only good things to come from the fire.

"You were in the basement with Marty?" Bryce sounded surprised. "I asked you to stay out of there."

Grace hesitated. She wanted to say it was her house and she'd go where she wanted, but she also wanted the conversation to end on a good note. She said, "Marty told me you were still concerned about the last room at the front of the house and we didn't go in there. Are there still problems with the chemicals that were sprayed in there?"

"Not sprayed, Grace," he took on an irritable tone she hadn't heard before. "Exploded. I'm not sure how they did it, but some of the guys were fooling around and mixed together a bunch of old lawn chemicals and other stuff. I sealed that room off until everything else is cleared out and then I'll hire certified hazardous materials cleaners to come in and deal with it. So until then, you need to stay out." His face was flushed and his eyes narrowed, but as agitated as he was, Bryce apparently realized he crossed the line. He added, 'please' through clenched teeth.

Grace looked at Henry, whose confused expression was no help. He didn't seem to know what was going on, either.

"I'm sorry," she said, not sorry at all. "I'll stay out of there." She'd go down to the forbidden front room as soon as he was gone.

Henry insisted on canceling his meeting and taking them to the tavern at the Egret Inn for an early working dinner. Bryce jumped on the idea so fast, Grace could see he was as anxious to change the tension between them as she was. She was pretty sure they had different reasons, though. She needed a general contractor to finish the renovation. She didn't know why Bryce was back to his eager, flirty self before they'd finished their salads, but if he thought they were returning to their old relationship, he was very wrong.

THE BIG ROOM AT THE FAR END OF THE BASEMENT SMELLED BAD, BUT was empty except for the old table and bare shelves. As Grace replaced the strips of tape resealing the door, she felt stupid and not a little concerned about her lungs. Whatever she'd inhaled in her five-second scan of the dank room couldn't have been good for her. Over-bearing or not, she should have taken Bryce's instructions at face value and stayed out.

The next morning, Bryce told her he'd called the cleaners. "I didn't realize they'd be booked this far ahead," he said. "It will be a month before they can get here. Does that work for you?"

She knew he meant 'Can you stay out of there that long'. He didn't mention the re-taped door, but she hadn't made an effort to hide what she'd done.

"Sure," she said. "If you think they're worth waiting for. We need somebody good. You were right, it's dangerous."

He gave her a smile, but no dimples.

She smiled back and changed the subject to the color of stain for the new-old kitchen cabinets. They could talk forever and never run out of renovation topics. Grace was grateful for the small blessing.

For once Delaney House seemed to cooperate with her plans. The house hummed with workers and their tools and the atmosphere in the old space changed. A new energy seeped through the rooms as if released by the physical activity.

Bryce treated her with deference, never far away from her side when he made his daily rounds. His face would light into a smile when he succeeded in catching her eye and Grace found herself smiling back. They were moving in reverse, as if they were building up to the scene on the kitchen staircase, not dealing with its after-math. There would be no more romance, but they could still work together. The emerging beauty of Delaney House made her happy.

It lasted a week.

He showed up after the crew left on Friday afternoon. She'd just poured a glass of wine and was on her way to a hot bath when the piercing scream of the new security alarm went off.

"It's me! It's me!"

She found Bryce at the security panel behind the front door, struggling to hold on to a bottle of champagne and an armful of roses while he frantically pushed buttons.

"What's wrong?" he yelled at her. "The code doesn't work."

Grace's cell went off before she could answer him. When she'd entered the all-clear code and given the password to the security company, the silence in the house was louder than the alarm had been.

"You changed the code?" he asked.

"Obviously." She couldn't deny it and didn't owe him an explanation.

"Any particular reason?"

"A security code isn't any good if half the world knows it. I change it often."

"I get it. A city girl thing."

She wanted to be straight with him, but there he stood, cleaned up and bearing gifts. And smiling, in full dimples, so she said, "It's a big house and I set the alarm whenever I'm alone. You should ring the bell or call before you come."

"Okay, but it's hard to surprise you that way." He held out the roses.

She took them, but said, "That's the point, Bryce. I don't want any surprises. Not from anyone."

Her words were there, she heard them, and yet he only nodded and smiled some more and said, "But we could have some fun. We haven't had any time alone lately. Let's have this champagne and then we'll go out. I made reservations in St. Michaels. A beautiful place on the water. What do you say?"

What she said was 'no'. She was tired and irritated but she tried to be kind as she begged off.

He insisted on leaving the champagne for another time, and Grace knew she'd only postponed a problem. She reset the alarm after he left, put the roses in a plastic water pitcher and finally got into her hot bath, but her peaceful evening was ruined.

CHAPTER THIRTY-NINE

The other projects which had kept Bryce so busy and away from Delaney House all seemed to disappear. The harder Grace tried to put emotional distance between them, the tighter Bryce attached himself to the daily work on her house.

At first, he said the crews needed him. When it was clear the foremen had their various projects in hand, he insisted on going with Grace to distributors in Baltimore and Wilmington to look at tankless hot water systems and high-efficiency furnaces. She knew she needed her general contractor with her and she wasn't about to let him spend her money without her, but the trips were awkward. Two weeks into the new year, she changed her mind.

Maybe it was because she'd just signed a contract for an HVAC system that cost enough to give her the trip around the world she was never going to have. Or because every time Bryce caught her eye - and he was always trying to catch her eye - his dimples flashed with his smile. When she let her guard down, she reacted to his smile, to those dimples, and she was tired of her insides driving her crazy. Grace decided to clear the air, once and for all, after an afternoon of appliance shopping.

"Stop it," she said as she pulled the car off the road and into the parking lot of a McDonald's.

"Stop what?"

Despite his question, Bryce didn't look confused as they squared off in the front seats of the BMW. She looked him straight in his beautiful brown eyes and knew she was making the right call.

"I have a nice car don't I?" she asked.

He frowned, making even that mundane move look sexy.

"Yes?" he asked. "I mean, 'no' would be rude, and a lie, but I don't know what you want me to say."

She wanted him to have to work for the answer. Maybe that way it would make an impression on him. After a minute she said, "It's my mother's. Or it was. She needed a car that would impress her clients when she took them out to view properties. She worked hard, my mom. And when I had to decide what to do with her car, I kept it. Not because it's expensive, or beautiful. I prefer Jeeps."

Bryce was trying so hard to follow her, she almost felt bad, but she went on. "I kept this expensive car instead of my Jeep because I wanted to remember how hard Mom worked. This car was the token of her success. Do you know what I'm saying?"

"Of course," he said.

"You have no idea."

"Look, Grace. I only asked if you wanted to stop and have an early dinner. Like I said, I know a great place -"

"A romantic place, no doubt."

"You prefer McDonald's?"

He really was trying, she thought. Trouble was, he was trying to push the wrong agenda. To the wrong woman. She said, "If you're hungry and want to go through the drive through, I'll get some coffee. If you want to talk about us, I'm not interested. I've given you mixed signals and I'm sorry. You're a nice guy. I like you, Obviously, I do, or I wouldn't have let things go as far as they did. But we are not a couple. I'm not staying in Mallard Bay. I'm selling the house as soon as possible. I'm thinking of putting it on the market in the next week or so."

"You can't do that!"

Grace could practically see the gears shift behind the handsome face. Not, 'Don't leave, I'm crazy about you' but 'You can't list the house'. It had always been about the house.

"We aren't nearly ready," he went on. "I need six weeks. Give me six weeks. Five!" He searched her face. "Give me five weeks and you can list it."

She tried to work out the reason for the five-week timeline. It wasn't long enough to make the house perfect. She'd be showing it while the finishing touches were being added.

"Five weeks," she agreed.

It hadn't been a big Christmas or a big romance, but each stirred up emotions she could have done without. Ordinarily, a problem requiring Benny Pannel wouldn't be a good thing, but an unexpected visit from the always-cheerful Verminator on a gloomy Monday morning seemed like a gift.

"Had a possum extraction over on Jefferson and one of your neighbors is a new client, so I decided to drop by and see if you are still critter-free," Benny said as he accepted her offer of coffee and a tour of the house. "I guess having the van parked outside here all that time was good for business."

"It's certainly hard to miss," Grace agreed and laughed as he thanked her sincerely for the 'compliment'.

She enjoyed showing the house off to someone who'd seen it at its worst. Benny knew most of the workers and high-fived and fist-bumped his way through all three floors, checking former problem spots as he admired the new construction.

"I'll take a look in the basement, too," he said as they wound up the tour in the kitchen.

They found dead mice in the new mechanical room. Benny crouched down and examined the two small bodies without touching them. After a moment he stood and swept the beam of his Maglight around. Nothing scurried or squeaked. Using gloved hands, he sealed the mice in a heavy plastic bag.

"I'll put these little guys in the truck and then check the rest of the rooms," he said.

She reminded him of the chemical explosion and told him about the sealed room at the end of the hall.

"That hasn't been cleaned up yet?" Benny asked.

"Seems hazmat cleaners are in big demand."

"Well, I know some people," Benny said, then appeared to reconsider what he was going to say. "Listen, I'm sure Bryce and Henry have it all under control. These mice definitely got into some kind of poison. See here, you can tell because -"

"I don't need to look," Grace broke in. "I'll take your word for it."

Benny shrugged, "Okay, but it's interesting. I'll put out some traps and see if we can save any others that come wantin' a warm place to spend the winter."

Grace told Benny he had changed her view of certain elements of nature. She was rooting for live mice to be captured in her house.

As they came up the steps into the yard, Benny looked into the woods and said, "I guess it's not a grave anymore since the body's gone, right?"

She winced at the sight of the mound of dirt still visible behind the now-scraggly tree line. She'd finally been permitted to fill in the pit where Audrey Oxley's body had been found. While the removal of the bright orange flags and yellow crime scene tape had been an improvement, the area was still a gravesite.

After seeing the Verminator on his way, she called Lee McNamara. The grave was a constant reminder that the murder was still unsolved. Her call went straight to voicemail. She asked McNamara to call her and ignored the option of speaking to the duty officer. Another encounter with the surly Aidan Banks wasn't likely to be productive. Besides, she'd wasted enough of the morning. If Bryce was on a five-week deadline, so was she.

Grace had unofficially joined the Cutters' painting crew. During her free time, she did the detail trim on the crown molding and baseboards or worked on stripping the woodwork in the butler's pantry. Bryce called just as she was wrapping up the afternoon scraping layers of oil-based paint.

She almost ignored the call when she saw his name on the screen, but she did need to talk to him. They'd been short two painters for several days and the crew's momentum was starting to slow.

Bryce said he was stopping by to talk to Marty and would work on the crew roster. He sounded distracted and disconnected quickly. Grace let Marty know and went up to the apartment to shower and change. She was taking herself out to the Tavern for dinner. The soup and salads she'd been living on had taken care of the ten pounds she'd wanted to lose, but she was hungry for a hot meal that wasn't from a can. She could take her time cleaning up and maybe Bryce would come and go by the time she was ready to leave. She wanted to keep their tenuous hold on civility.

At first, she thought her plan had worked. An hour later when she started down the staircase, the house was quiet, but it didn't feel empty. She paused on the second floor, leaned over the railing and listened.

As if on cue, Norah Jones started to sing.

CHAPTER FORTY

"I brought you a present and it needs atmosphere to be appreciated." Bryce stood in the dining room, his arms wide open.

Grace didn't know if he was offering himself up or trying to showcase the fabric he'd tacked up over the room's tall windows.

Norah finished *Come Away With Me* and moved into *Don't Know Why*. Grace thought the music selection was spot-on, but probably not for the reasons Bryce had intended.

"Well, what do you think? Another client of mine is a decorator. I was at his shop and I saw some drapes made out of this. I thought it looked like you and..." he broke off in mid-sentence, his eyes searching her face. "Okay. Poor decision. I'm sorry. I'll take them down."

"No, wait," Grace said as he went to the window. "The fabric's beautiful. It suits the room." She ran her hands over the pale green watered silk, stopping to trace the outline of a tiny embroidered dragonfly. Hundreds of the golden creatures covered the delicate silk and shimmered in the light from the room's single naked bulb. "It will be something when we get the chandelier hung, won't it?"

He'd moved behind her, but didn't touch her. "I brought a picnic dinner, too. We could start with a glass of wine and talk a while. Down here," he added hastily. "Nothing serious, just talk. Friends, okay? And then, if you're hungry, I have cheese and crackers, and a crab quiche."

She was starved.

He had a plaid blanket which they spread out on the empty dining room floor. The Merlot had a bite to it, but the Talbot Reserve cheddar cheese was exquisite and the smell of the warm quiche was tantalizing. Bryce kept the conversation frivolous, teasing her about saving the crooked doorway as Emma's 'signature' and proposing wild color combinations to replace the neutral palette she was using.

"Let me top your wine off," he leaned closer as he held the bottle out toward her.

The memory of the staircase flashed through her mind; she knew her face was red. "I have plenty," she said, moving her glass away. The wine was bitter, and the half glass she'd had felt sour in her stomach.

Bryce shrugged and sat back. "How would you like to go to Rehoboth tomorrow? We could do the boardwalk, walk on the beach, have a nice meal. How does that sound?"

Grace sat up a bit straighter, her stomach clenching in earnest. Why couldn't he have left it alone? "It sounds like a date and we've had that conversation. I don't want to start anything."

"I only want to spend some time with you. I think you'd enjoy it."

He was still smiling, but Grace sensed something else, a wariness. "This is nice," she said and raised her wine glass in a salute and took a small sip. "But this is all there is, okay?"

"Okay," he agreed. "But, you know, you could keep the house as a weekend home."

She looked at the silk, then at him, wondering if he was teasing again. She decided he was. "Oh, sure. For all the wild parties I have."

"Well, why not?" He leaned back on his elbows, watching her. "You could have a big rolling house party in this place. Plenty of bedrooms. Privacy. Your neighbors are mostly old and far enough away they can't hear anything."

Grace felt a twinge of unease. Her head was beginning to throb and her stomach was getting worse. She said, "People are in and out of here all day. Niki will be here soon, as a matter of fact."

"Is that so? I talked to her yesterday and she didn't mention it. She just said how hard it was to be in the middle between you and her parents."

Damn. Grace tried to shut out the increasingly urgent messages from her body and think clearly. "That's why she's coming over. Besides, I didn't know you two saw so much of each other." Now, why had she said that? He was grinning. Too late, she realized he thought she was jealous.

"She isn't coming, Grace. No one is."

He suddenly sat forward and reached for her. She tried to scoot away, but her feet and legs were heavy and uncooperative. Bryce's fingers closed around her wrist and he yanked her toward him.

The pounding in her skull increased as Grace's feet finally got traction. She scrambled backward, kicking food and sending the bottle of wine sailing across the floor at Bryce.

"Hey!" He let her go and jumped to his feet, wiping wine from his jeans. "I only wanted to kiss you."

Grace rose unsteadily, then bent at the waist as the room tilted.

"Let me help you," Bryce took a tentative step toward her.

She wanted to tell him no, but she was trying not to pass out. "Get away from me!" she pleaded in a whisper. As he reached her, she felt bile rising in her throat and the floor fell away.

———

Her mother stroked her hair. She was wrapped in her old quilt. Where had it been? It didn't matter, she had it now and it kept her warm. A hand touched her cheek.

"Mama?"

The slap split her lip and brought her face to face with Winston. "Not your mommy, cousin. Your worst nightmare."

"Christ, Winnie! Could you be any cornier? What the hell are you doing?"

Bryce's face swam into focus.

"Not another mark on her, understand?" he shouted over his shoulder. "The ones she has will be hard enough to explain."

Winston's voice came through the fog. "A fall down those stairs could have broken her neck. I say a couple more taps won't hurt."

Grace steeled herself, but instead of a blow, she heard a thud of muscle on flesh and a howl of pain that didn't come from her.

"We wouldn't be in this fix if not for you," Bryce shouted. "You leave her alone. Anyone's gonna do her, it'll be me. Understand?"

Grace's vision was clearing. She was in one of the small basement rooms, bound up in something soft. The picnic blanket. She tried to wiggle her hands, but they were clumsy. The scuffling and howling from Winston petered out. She closed her eyes and hoped she looked unconscious. One of the men was moving toward her again.

"I know you can hear me." Fingers brushed her forehead. She flinched but didn't open her eyes. "I'm sorry about all of this. I did try to make it more pleasant for you, but you're a hard woman. At least I kept your cousin from killing you." Suddenly, his mouth was near her ear and she smelled licorice as Bryce's warm breath fell across her face. "You should have let me make you happy, Gracie."

———

"DOWN HERE! HURRY!"

Grace woke to the sounds of thundering feet and shouts. She covered her face with her hands as people moved to her side.

"Don't move now," a man said as he knelt beside her.

She was thrilled that she *could* move. As she'd gone in and out of consciousness, she hadn't been able to move her arms or legs. She'd cried, thinking she was paralyzed.

A cervical collar was slipped around her neck and strong hands maneuvered her onto a backboard.

"Ms. Reagan? Can you talk to me?"

She was being lifted. She wanted to go back to sleep, where she was safe. Something was terribly wrong.

Bryce and Winston.

CHAPTER FORTY-ONE

Cyrus Mosley and Lee McNamara had a standoff at the foot of Grace's hospital bed. If her head hadn't hurt so much, she would have laughed. The police chief won, but just barely.

"I'll be in the hall, Grace," Mosley said. "Unless you'd reconsider my offer?"

"I don't need a lawyer, Cyrus," Grace sighed. "But thank you. I need to talk to Chief McNamara alone."

Mosley narrowed his eyes but said nothing more as he left the room.

"He seems to be worried about you and he has a right to be," McNamara said as he pulled up a chair and settled where Grace could maintain eye contact without moving her head. "Does it hurt a lot?"

"Like the devil," she said and squeezed her eyes shut to stop the tears that welled up. In addition to the lacerations on her face, her left shoulder had been dislocated, her wrist was sprained and she had a cracked rib. She'd made it to the bathroom with the help of a nurse, only to discover that the bathroom had a mirror. The sight of her battered body had made her throw up.

"I'm so sorry."

McNamara's soft voice broke the last of her reserve. He found a box of tissues on the counter and pressed a wad into her hand.

"I thought he was going to rape me," she said when she could finally speak. "The doctor said he didn't. But he did give me something that made me pass out and when I came to, I couldn't move and they'd wrapped me up and I couldn't move and ..."

"Wait now, slow down." This time McNamara got her a small bottle of water. When she'd had a few sips, he said, "Tell me who 'he' is."

"Bryce Cutter."

The surprise on McNamara's face made her cry harder. "I know," she sobbed. "I was so shocked. I mean, looking back, I think I knew as soon as I got sick that he'd put something in the wine."

"You said 'they' had wrapped you up. Who else was there?"

Anger made her voice stronger. "Winston did this," she pointed to her mouth. "I don't know what else he did, but Bryce told him my injuries would be hard to explain and to leave me alone. He even hit Winston. I passed out again before I learned what they were doing."

McNamara wrote for a moment before saying, "Well, Grace, this is odd. Bryce and your cousin are the ones who found you and called 911. Bryce is in the waiting room and has been since you were brought in. He's driving the staff crazy, but I told them no one was to see you until I got here. I didn't reckon on Cyrus as a pit bull guard, but I don't think anyone else has been in here."

Grace tried to gather her thoughts. She had to make McNamara believe her. Finally, she said, "You remember I'm an attorney, right?"

McNamara nodded.

"I'm admitted to practice in Maryland, Virginia, and the District of Columbia. You know that means I am an Officer of the Court. I have a responsibility to report a crime. Unless I screw up big time, a judge is going to take my word."

It seemed important to remind McNamara - and herself - of her credentials. She was broken and battered and confined to a hospital bed without so much as her own underwear. She had to make him believe her.

She said, "Bryce Cutter showed up at my house and surprised me. He'd brought ... oh, God!" The drapes. *Your neighbors are mostly old and far enough away they can't hear anything.* He'd made sure they wouldn't see anything either.

"Grace?" McNamara put a large, warm hand over her bruised one.

She told him about the fabric and the picnic dinner. The bitter wine. "Bryce may have had a sip, but I don't remember him drinking. At first, he was fine. Then I started getting sick. He grabbed me. I fought and got away, but when I stood up, I was so dizzy. It was awful. I vomited all over myself. The nurse told me between the mess and the emergency room treatment, everything I had on was ruined." For some reason, losing her clothes upset her as much as her injuries. She clutched at the neck of the hospital gown.

"I woke up in the basement, wrapped up in the blanket he'd brought for the picnic. It was like I was swaddled. And I couldn't get out because my hands and feet were so heavy and my left arm wouldn't work. It hurt so much, I kept passing out. I was scared I would vomit again and choke."

"Take a minute," McNamara said.

But Grace wanted to get it all out. "At one point, I was dreaming and Winston slapped me awake. Split my lip. I think he wanted to kill me. Bryce wouldn't let him, but then said it was all my fault. Said he'd tried to be nice. When I woke up again, the paramedics were there, but I was on the concrete at the foot of the basement steps and the blanket was gone."

McNamara wrote as she talked. When she finished he said, "Why would Cutter and your cousin do this?"

He didn't believe her. He had to believe her. She said, "I don't know. Not for sure. But Bryce insisted I hire Winston. And that I take him back after I fired him the first time. Bryce was always taking up for him. After the fire I found Winston arguing with Bryce in the kitchen. Just as I walked in, I heard Bryce tell Winston if he ever pulled a stunt like that again, Bryce would kill him. No!" It was important to get it right. "Bryce said, 'if you ever pull a stunt like that again, I'll make it your last.' I thought he meant the fire and the graffiti on the kitchen walls. Now I think there's a lot more to it than Winston vandalizing the house."

"Like what?" McNamara asked. He was writing down everything she said and she wanted to hug him for that. For listening.

"I don't know," she said. "But Bryce is tied to Winston somehow."

"Grace, you yourself said Bryce stopped Winston from killing you. And he called 911."

"But Bryce poisoned me!" she hated that her voice went into a panicked pitch. "He was going to rape me. If I hadn't thrown up on myself - wait, I'll bet I got him, too! Make him show you his clothes!"

"Are you alright?" The door flew open and Mosley was at Grace's bedside. "That's enough, Chief."

"No, Cyrus, please. I have to make him understand."

"Grace, please calm down." McNamara patted her hand. "I do believe you mean every word you say. And I want you to rest easy. You're safe here and I promise you everything will be fine. I'll be back tomorrow." He stood. "Counselor, could I see you in the hall-way, please?"

Grace watched them go, the policeman who wasn't sure she was sane and the old man who'd appointed himself her bodyguard. Reality was too hard to deal with. She closed her eyes and faded away.

On the other side of the door, McNamara and Mosley struck a deal.

"I CAN'T BELIEVE YOU!"

Grace winced. Even after a night of IVs and painkillers, she was in no shape to defend herself, so looking pitiful was what she went with. It didn't work on Niki.

"Winnie and Bryce tried to save your life, even after you fired

Winnie and lied about him. You had too much wine and fell down the stairs. Why can't you admit it?"

The nurses who pestered her every time she went to sleep and the officer who peered in each time the door opened all seemed to be okay with screaming visitors in her room. Grace searched in vain for the call button. She finally gave up and answered Niki.

"I won't admit it because that isn't what happened. Didn't you notice the police officer in the hall? Bryce drugged me and assaulted me. Your brother only assaulted me, if that makes you feel any better." Apparently, she had two weapons - looking pitiful and her mouth. She felt a little better.

Niki moved closer to the side of her bed, her face etched with worry. "Grace, I'm sorry you're hurt, however it happened. I want you to come home with me and I'll take care of you. You don't need the police. Tell them it's all a mistake and let's go."

Grace thought she'd sooner stay in the basement at Delaney House. At least there she knew all the dangers were. Most of them, anyway.

"Thanks," she said, "but I'll keep the police protection. As soon as I can walk without falling down, they'll discharge me and I'll go back to DC for a few days." She was going to the Egret Inn and live off room service for a week, but she didn't see any need to tell Niki.

"Where in DC? You've sublet your condo. And you shouldn't be alone."

"Because I'm so safe here?" Grace had had enough. "I should come stay with you where your brother who used me for a punching bag and your parents who accused me of stealing Emma's jewelry can have another go at me?"

"That's not true." But Niki's downcast eyes and tightly clasped hands undermined her words.

"I am so sorry to hurt you. Again." Grace struggled for words. "I want... I want to be your cousin, your family. I appreciate that you accepted me and took me in. I'm not ending our relationship. If that happens, it's your choice. But I'm telling you, Bryce and Winston are dangerous. They're working together and they're dangerous. They nearly killed me, Niki."

Niki's head came up. "No! Not Bryce." She turned away but paused in the doorway. Her eyes glittering with tears, she said, "Take care of yourself."

After she was gone, Grace thought about all the possible reasons why Niki would defend Bryce but not her own brother.

July 1, 1960

Dearest Mother and Papa,

We are all fine, so don't worry. I know I sounded miserable on the phone yesterday and I am so sorry about that. You are right, Papa. I have to stop caterwauling, as you so aptly put it. The baby is precious. Our sweet Fiona here at last. Even if Ford insists we call her Julia, we know who she is, don't we?

I swear to you I was doing well up until Clancy died and now I can't seem to stop crying. Poor old soul. He stayed until my little girl was home safe and sound before his big heart gave out. I could have borne it better if Ford hadn't made such a fuss about having to bury him in the woods, but as you pointed out, Papa, he was the one who had to do all the work. He could have hired a laborer, of course, but he said the whole affair was tacky and the fewer people who knew about it the better.

Well, it might be 'country' as Ford put it, to bury your animals on your property, but I wasn't sending my Clancy to the dump which is what Ford wanted to do. Can you believe it? Sometimes I think my husband is from another species. And, no, Mother, it's not the 'baby blues' talking. That's my life with Ford. He is a difficult man to live with sometimes. Most times, to be truthful.

I have a non-baby reason for being blue: Audrey has cut all ties with me. I know you don't think that's a bad thing, Mother, and really, we've grown so far apart, I'm not as surprised as I would have been even a few months ago. But still, I miss her company and she kept me up on the social circuit while I'm confined to the nursery circuit. I don't know what happened. The last few times we talked before Julia was born, she was distant but pleasant. She even played with the boys a bit. Then she started cutting me short when I'd catch her on the phone or out in town. Now she won't return my calls. So, I suppose that's that. I thought we'd be best friends forever, but it seems you were right, Mother. We are just too different.

Julia will be awake soon, so I will hurry and close with some happy news. The boys are adjusting well to their sister. The baby nurse seems to love the boys, but after the first week announced she couldn't handle all three children. So, I have moved Julia into our room (which is what I wanted, anyway) and Ford has huffed off to sleep in one of the guest rooms where we won't bother him. The nurse is now a nanny, and she keeps the boys occupied when they aren't in school. They love having someone at their beck and call, and I love being able to sleep and play with my baby. I'm fine if I don't think about Clancy. It is all getting better, I promise.

The girls from the Garden Club are coming over tomorrow to bring a picnic lunch and meet Julia. Should be lots of fun. Normal, see? Don't worry.

Love,

Your silly daughter, Emma

CHAPTER FORTY-TWO

Her head finally cleared, and she felt stronger after another day of hospital care and the security of an officer posted at her door. Even though she was tormented by nurses, she could walk straight without help and was occasionally able to sleep without nightmares. She knew she was ready to be discharged when the hospital social worker showed up. *Are you in an abusive relationship? Do you need a safe place to stay? Do you want an advocate?* Grace wanted to say 'yes' to everything, but instead gave the kind woman answers which would send her on her way, all her forms completed with the proper boxes checked.

As the social worker was leaving, a hospital aide arrived with a delivery from a dress shop in Easton. Cyrus Mosley might have arrested taste in his own fashion, but he'd purchased a simple and stylish outfit of velvet leggings and a matching tunic for her. There was a bad moment when Grace saw panties and a bra in the bottom of the box, but then she found a business card stapled to the tissue paper. Someone named Lily Travers had done the shopping and sent her best wishes. Whoever Lily was, she was amazing. Everything fit.

At some point since her arrival, Avril had delivered her leather tote. It had appeared during one of her many naps, along with a note scrawled in a spidery, arthritic hand. *Call me if you need me.* Grace prayed that wouldn't be necessary. Just having her bag made her feel better.

Her small makeup clutch yielded moisturizer, mascara and lipstick. A comb and two clips tamed the wild nest of her hair and caught it in a tidy twist. Nothing could help her swollen and bruised mouth, but she no longer looked like a refugee. Her benefactor arrived as she was signing the last form for her discharge.

"Well, someone's better," Mosley said as he laid a huge bouquet of roses on the table by her bed and set a large shopping bag on the floor.

"I should," Grace said. "I have a lovely new outfit. I can't thank you enough. I'll repay you, of course."

He waved away her words. "Avril called and told me she'd looked through your closet at Delaney House, but nothing was loose enough for your injuries. She did find some shoes and your coat, though." He gestured to the bag. "Your laptop's in there, too. Avril said you'd want it."

"Please, thank her for me." Grace made a mental note to change the locks. Her house had more keys out in the universe than she'd realized, and no security system worked if you couldn't set it.

"What's wrong?" Mosley asked, drawing her attention back to his worried face.

"Nothing. Thank you for going to all that trouble." She had a sudden image of Cyrus and Avril conspiring to pick her wardrobe and gave him a lop-sided smile with the uninjured side of her mouth.

"Excellent!" Mosley said. "You stay in a good frame of mind. Positivity is important to healing. And I heard you were going back to DC to recover. That's a good plan. Gives us time to figure out what's happening here. No sense exposing yourself to any further risk unnecessarily."

Grace found herself getting teary and decided the pain medication was still in her system. She let him fuss over her and tried to distract herself by wondering how long he'd had the orange windowpane checked golf shirt he wore with his ubiquitous khakis and penny loafers. Did he have a storage room with an unlimited supply of leisurewear from the eighties?

It took a minute or two before her normal thought process kicked in. "So when did you talk to Niki?" she asked. The beauty of only lying to one person was she knew who'd spread the news of her purported departure.

Mosley didn't blink. She thought they might be getting used to each other. "I went by your house to check on things. Niki saw me in the driveway and stopped to ask if I was in charge of the house since you were leaving."

A wave of disappointment rolled over Grace. She was still hoping for a relationship with Niki.

"And what did you tell her?"

"I told her yes, I was. I saw no need to let the world know there wouldn't be anyone to oversee a vacant house. I flattered myself in assuming you wouldn't mind."

To her surprise, she found it didn't. "Thank you," she said. "I'll be back in a week or so. Could you handle getting the keys from Bryce? I'll talk to Henry and see if he's willing to keep the job going with Bryce banned from the premises, but I suspect I'll need a new contractor."

"I can handle that. But there is another option."

"Okay," she drew the word out into a question.

"You can sell right now. I have a buyer and the price is excellent."

She might have known. The disappointment wasn't as strong as what she'd felt for Niki, but Mosley had been growing on her and once again she'd been fooled. He had a buyer, which meant a commission. Every man for himself.

"How excellent is excellent?" she asked.

He named a price more than twice the appraised value of the property and the money she'd put into it so far. Despite her skepticism, she perked up. She could recuperate in Ireland. Or Italy. Or both.

"Who would want it that badly?" she asked.

He didn't hesitate. "I do."

Her travel bubble burst. "Good God, Cyrus! First, you shell out a fortune to repair the damage from Winston's leak and now you're trying to rush me out of town and buy the house. Why?" She'd misjudged him, but he was hiding something.

"I'm very motivated," Mosley asked. "I don't have a family, but I've watched over your mother and Stark and you children from the day each of you was born."

"You'd pay me twice what the house is worth because you want to help me." She said it flatly, her disbelief clear.

He huffed as if insulted. "I would much prefer to pay you exactly what it's worth. Will you take it?"

"No."

"That's what I thought. But you'll consider my latest offer? It would make Emma so happy."

Grace considered this statement and the old man who had pulled a chair to the side of her bed. After a minute, she cranked the top half of the bed up until she was eye to eye with Mosley. She said, "Are you saying Emma would want you to give me all that money? Just me. Not Winston or Niki. Why?"

"They aren't in the house," he said, as if the answer was obvious. "You won't go until you sell it."

She wanted to go. She *was* going. Still, his words stung.

But he wasn't finished. "Besides, they got their share," he said.

"What? Do you mean Winston and Niki?"

Mosley nodded. "She sent them both to college, all expenses paid. Winston played for three years before being arrested in a fraternity melee and expelled. Niki took six years and tried three different campuses before she got a degree in sociology and a husband who was older than her father."

"But how? How could Emma pay for all of it? She didn't have the money, did she?" Grace asked, uncomfortably aware of where a significant part of Emma's assets had gone.

"She'd put the funds aside years ago when she set up your trust."

Grace felt her heart ease a bit as one of the mysteries of her grandmother's long-distance support was cleared up. Emma had treated all her grandchildren the same. But the story didn't ring true. "I'd believe it of Winston," she said. "But I don't think Niki would take money from her grandmother when she knew how little Emma had."

"What has Niki told you about her grandmother?" Mosley asked. "I'll bet she said Emma was eccentric, wore old clothes and refused to spend money on anything, right?"

Grace nodded.

"Well, she spent plenty, but not on herself. She funneled the money through Stark," Mosley shook his head. "The children believe their father paid for their education. We, I, wouldn't want Niki to ever learn otherwise. Emma also paid for Winston's rehab stints and made his bail when he was arrested. Every time he was arrested."

Grace remembered Niki's description of her marriage and its end. "Did she also arrange for a generous divorce settlement for Niki?" she asked.

Mosley smiled, but it was sad. "And money to turn the house into an inn."

"Which Niki believed came from Stark."

"Emma thought if she made sure you all had happy lives, away from Delaney House, you'd be protected. No one is safe like that, but Emma tried."

Grace's head hurt and her body ached, but Mosley's words had jogged something loose. "You're still trying, aren't you?" she asked.

"I promised," he said. "I promised my client her last wishes would be honored."

"Her money's gone, Cyrus. You're using your own. That's not right."

"You give me far too much credit, my dear." He rose and walked to the door. "I'll hand Delaney House over to the Eastern Shore Historic Preservation Commission. Avril can take charge of finishing the renovation, and I'll take the donation as a tax deduction for the rest of my life. Win, win."

It was so, so tempting.

CHAPTER FORTY-THREE

The hospital was happy enough to let her go and the staff at the Egret Inn was gracious, but the law of small town life subverted her plan before she could get to her room. Avril Oxley emerged from the hotel dining room just as Grace finished checking in. There was no denying she was staying at the hotel, she had the room key card in her hand.

Her head was pounding and her back hurt. Sleep was an immediate need. She let herself be corralled into the adjacent bar, partially because the chairs by the fireplace looked so comfy, but mostly because Avril was on her like a hyper terrier after a bone. Also, the bar served food and she was starving.

"Why are you here? What happened?" Avril demanded. "That police officer at the hospital wouldn't let me in to see you. Nazi! Were you under arrest?"

Grace said, "I hope you didn't tell anyone else that."

"Of course not," Avril snapped. Grace would have liked to hear more sincerity in her voice. "But why did you have a police officer at your door?"

Grace adjusted her sling, giving an overly dramatic wince in hopes of some sympathy. Avril just leaned in closer.

"Winston attacked me. He caused the fire and other vandalism and he did this." Forgetting her injury, Grace used the wrong hand to motion to her face. This time the wince was genuine.

"I knew it! That boy is a bad egg. But why wasn't he arrested? I saw him out and about yesterday, free as a bird."

"A turkey vulture maybe," Grace muttered.

"What?"

"It's a serious charge and the police are investigating. He and Bryce Cutter are in some kind of scheme together. Bryce was there when Winston did this. Bryce also drugged me. I don't know how I fell down the steps and dislocated my shoulder, but I was unconscious when it happened."

Avril sat back and stared at Grace in frank disapproval. "I heard you were saying that. Also heard you were drinking - not that anyone would blame you, but still. Nobody believes Bryce Cutter is in cahoots with the likes of Winnie Delaney."

Several people turned to stare at them, but Grace was too tired and sore to care. Everything hurt, including her heart. She said, "They were clever. They pretended to find me in the basement and they spread the lies about the wine. No one believes me, so you're in good company. I want to thank you for all you did for me. You were kind to let me stay with you, and to help Cyrus with my clothes. Right now, I need a place to recuperate and I'm doing it here. I've told everyone, including Cyrus, I'm going out of town and I would appreciate it if you helped me keep that secret. It's important."

"Why?" Avril was still pugnacious, but she was listening.

"Chief McNamara wants me out of town so he can remove my police protection." It was partly true. McNamara had sounded happy when she'd told him she was leaving town.

Avril's shoulders slumped and she seemed to lose some of her steam.

"Cyrus also wants me out of town for my safety. I don't want the Delaneys or Bryce to know where I am for obvious reasons."

Avril's chin came up and she started to protest. "Bryce wouldn't —"

"Listen to me!" Grace demanded, then lowered her voice to a hiss. "I can't use my left arm and I have a concussion, fourteen stitches and a cracked rib. I need to take care of myself without constantly looking over my shoulder. So can you keep my secret or not?"

Avril's agreement was terse and anything but comforting, but Grace took it. Once in her room, she left instructions at the desk to not give out her name and to hold any calls. Then, using her one good hand and a lot of swearing, she managed to wedge a chair under the knob of the locked and chained door before she crawled in between the crisp linen sheets and into oblivion.

EITHER AVRIL KEPT HER SECRET, OR NO ONE CARED ENOUGH TO LOOK for her because Grace spent the next three days in her room without interruption from anyone other than the hotel staff and room service. Avril dropped off a small suitcase of her clothes but sent it up with the porter.

Grace called McNamara once, to let him know where she was and to learn no action was being taken on her complaints against Bryce and Winston. They had alibied each other and Bryce had the additional support from Henry, who claimed to have been with his cousin during the time Grace lay unconscious on the basement floor. While technically possible, the time frame was tight for Bryce to meet with Henry in between drugging and assaulting Grace.

"It happened," she said wearily.

"Arguments, bad ones, certainly can seem like assault." McNamara's tone was irritatingly calm. "And you said you don't remember him hitting you or pushing you down the stairs."

"He drugged me!"

"Yes, well, about that."

She knew what was coming and wanted to cry.

"Your tests at the hospital didn't reveal anything conclusive other than alcohol in your system."

"How much alcohol?"

"You could drive legally, but if you're sensitive to alcohol or taking medication, it could be enough to make you unsteady."

"Chief, please listen. I remember everything before I passed out. Everything. Could a drunk say that?"

There was silence from McNamara's end. Then, "Possibly. But what are you suggesting?"

"You're familiar with Rohypnol?"

"Of course. Are you saying Bryce Cutter gave you a date rape drug?"

"I am. I've had plenty of time for research, and I definitely believe Bryce laced the wine with something. I don't know when they tested my blood at the hospital, but Rohypnol leaves the system quickly, if that's what he used."

More silence. Then he said, "Why don't you stay put at the Egret until you hear from me. No calls, no visitors. Not even Mosley, unless you insist on legal counsel from him."

"I don't need legal counsel," she said through clenched teeth. "No calls, no visitors. But Chief?"

"Yeah?"

"I'm trusting you." She meant it as a warning, but it felt like a plea.

HER PHONE GLOWED WITH THE GREEN DOTS OF UNOPENED VOICE mail. She called Mosley so she could remove half of the stacked up messages without having to listen to them.

"Are you alright?" he demanded by way of a greeting.

"Yes, better every day, thanks." Her shoulder and arm still ached and her head still pounded when she stood too fast, but she was healing.

"I've been trying to reach you and I was worried. You were supposed to stay in touch."

"And here I am." She tried to sound sincere, but Mosley's sigh said she wasn't successful.

"My receptionist has been retrieving your mail from your post office box as you requested. There's a letter from Cutter Enterprises. Should I open it?"

Grace thought he probably was looking at it, but told him to go ahead. After a pause, he said, "You must have expected this. Bryce Cutter has withdrawn his crews and equipment and canceled your contract."

"I don't suppose there's a check for the remainder of the last advance I gave him?"

"Hardly. A bill for a balance due on the account, $347.00 and an accounting of the expenses."

Grace tried to imagine the state the house was in. "I'll be interested to compare it to my records. I'd estimate he owes me at least ten thousand, depending on the value of the materials left at the house."

"I can go over and have a look," Mosley offered. "No need for you to come back to handle this. Have you thought any more about my offer?"

She had. A lot. "I'll be back in a day or so, but I'd like to keep that between us. I'll have an answer for you then."

"I can get the paperwork ready quickly. You could be on your way in the blink of an eye."

She groaned and said, "You're quite a salesman. I hate not to see the project through, though."

"Understandable, but neither wise nor necessary. I'll finish restoration with a new contractor and then turn it over to the Historical Society with an endowment to maintain it."

Something was off in his voice.

"I thought you were going to let Avril handle all that."

"Yes, well. It's not the best time to approach her. She's a bit upset with me."

"Me, too," Grace said. "But why is she upset with you?"

"She's planning a funeral for her sister and we don't see eye to eye on the details."

Audrey's funeral. Grace had forgotten all about it. "I'm sorry," she said.

"It all happened a long time ago and should stay there." His words were hard and didn't invite her comment.

She agreed to meet Mosley on Monday at ten. She had a day and a half to recover her fighting strength and decide if she should finish Delaney House. After Mosley, she handled the few calls from DC friends and work colleagues and ignored two calls from Stark. Avril's rambling message said she believed Grace was confused about Bryce's role in her accident, but to call her if she wanted to move back in. There was warmth in the old woman's shaky voice and a note of genuine regret.

The message from Henry Cutter she saved until last. It was brief - he wanted to talk.

"Thanks for returning my call," he said when she reached him. "I mean, I wasn't sure you would and I really wanted to talk to you again." The sound of his voice made her want to cry. She had missed him.

"How are you?" she managed.

"I, uhm. Well, I know you got a letter from Bryce and I know things aren't settled between you yet, but I wanted to tell you I reviewed all of the expenses and the labor costs and you don't owe us any money. In fact, we'll be issuing a refund to you. I wanted you to hear that from me."

She was a lawyer. She knew to keep her mouth shut and put her carefully considered responses in writing. She said, "They hurt me, Henry."

"Grace, please..."

"It was calculated and vicious. Winston wanted to do more, but Bryce stopped him." He didn't respond, but she could hear him breathing. "He said any more damage would be hard to explain with a fall." She strained to hear something, any reaction from Henry, but he was silent. "I had police protection," she rushed on, anger rising. "Just because there wasn't enough evidence to charge Bryce and Winston doesn't mean the police didn't believe me. Talk to Chief McNamara."

"I wanted to let you know I'll take care of the money, but I can't..."

"My blood alcohol level was negligible, Henry! McNamara has the report. Please, Henry, talk to him." She was begging now, unable to stop the words. "Bryce drugged me. Put something in the wine. I can't prove it, but I know he did. I passed out. I... I think they threw me down the stairs."

The silence had changed. Henry was gone.

CHAPTER FORTY-FOUR

S he could only hide for so long. As disturbing as it was, the call from Henry was a catharsis. As her body healed and she grew stronger, the release of the last tie of friendship gave her wings. Henry - sweet, kind Henry - had made her mad, and anger made her move.

The hotel room lost its sickroom air and became an office. *Get moving! Do something!* The words came at her on Sunday when she opened her laptop. Using what she'd learned during the initial restoration of Delaney House, she worked out a basic, but thorough, plan to complete the renovation. She even calculated an over-run budget and schedule. She'd never again assume anything would work as planned where the house was concerned.

On Monday she called Mosley and declined his latest offer to purchase the house. She braced herself for an argument, but he only sounded disappointed. She agreed to let him know if she changed her mind and on impulse invited him to dinner.

"I'm staying at the Egret," she said, carefully avoiding an outright lie about her non-existent trip to DC "We can have dinner here and I'll tell you my plans."

"Alright." Mosley sounded as if he expected a catch to the rare overture. "In the meantime, promise me you won't be in Delaney House alone."

In spite of Mosley's unsettling warning, a week after the attack, she let herself into her house and locked the door behind her.

CUTTER ENTERPRISES HAD LEFT A NEAT WORK SITE. NO SPRAY painted messages, no 'accidents'. All of their equipment was gone and the house had been swept clean. Just a half finished job waiting for the next round of workers. The third-floor apartment seemed to be undisturbed, except that someone, she prayed it was only Avril, had been through her clothes.

She called the security company and agreed to pay an emergency premium for immediate service. While she waited, she slowly packed up her clothes and loaded the BMW. By the time the locksmith arrived, she was weak with exhaustion and her shoulder and ribs ached.

Keep moving.

Two hours later, new keys in her pocket, she changed the security code, set it and locked up. She couldn't stay at the Egret Inn forever, but her budget could handle another week. Surely she could grow a backbone and sleep in her own bed by then.

IF SHE'D HAD ANY DOUBT OF THE POWER OF A SMALL TOWN RUMOR mill, it was settled that afternoon. As she made call after call to local construction companies, she got variations of the same response. Those who were polite said they were too busy to take over the renovation. The others just said no. She and Delaney House were pariahs.

"I'm not surprised," Mosley said when she relayed the news over dinner. "It isn't only the accusations you've made against Bryce. "I've had three calls today from people in the business community wanting to know if it's true the ownership of Delaney House is in question. Someone, I'm guessing Stark, spread the word there would be a suit over the sale."

"On what grounds?" Grace demanded.

"That Emma was *non compos mentis* when I executed the sale to you, and I knowingly accepted a sale price below market value without considering better offers."

"Were there better offers?"

"No, but it's hard to prove a negative. If Stark's behind this, he's on a fishing expedition to see if my malpractice insurance will settle something on him."

"Does he have any proof Emma wasn't capable of representing her own best interests?"

Mosley laughed, but he didn't look happy. "He may think he does, but I can prove she was cognizant and legally capable. Not my first rodeo, isn't that the expression? I had her physician and the social worker assigned to the assisted care facility talk to her outside of my presence and I have their affidavits. I also did exhaustive comparisons of property sales. Your price was low but given the work the house needed, not unreasonable. And there isn't exactly a booming market for houses that size. Emma knew all of the details and was able to explain everything to her doctor and the social worker."

They ate in silence for a moment, and Grace thought about Henry's call. Did he also believe Stark? "So, between Bryce, Winston and Stark, word's gotten around that I'm a deadbeat client and I may not own the house I'm working on."

Mosley smiled. "You also accused your contractor of assault. Bound to make other firms skittish. Are you sure you don't want to sell?"

Grace glared at him but decided it was just his awkward sense of humor. He'd eaten prime rib and was tucking into an apple dumpling and vanilla ice cream. For Mosley, it appeared to be a big night out.

Around a mouthful of dessert he said, "Perhaps if you enlist Avril to help you, you might make headway with one of the specialty contractors. The ones that are Bryce's direct competitors. Any of them should want to see their name on a historic building like Delaney House."

Grace toyed with the last of her Cobb salad and resisted the urge to lean over and wipe the dollop of cream from his chin. Mosley had definitely grown on her. Probably because he was the only person who was speaking to her.

"Afraid that won't work," she said. "Avril thinks I'm lying about Bryce and she isn't happy with me. I don't think anyone will ever believe me unless he attacks me again in front of witnesses."

"Are you afraid, my dear?" Mosley stopped eating and studied her. "I can have the protection detail reinstated if you'd like."

She blinked at the change in conversation. "Protection detail? You make it sound like I'm the president. The police watched my hospital room for a couple of days, but they're not likely to start up again."

Mosley gave the ice cream his full attention.

"Cyrus?"

He waved for the waiter and pointed to his coffee cup.

"Cyrus!" She waited while the waiter poured more coffee but put her hand over the sugar bowl when Mosley reached for it. "Whatever it is, tell me."

He slurped his unsweetened coffee before answering her. "You're a Delaney. Or an Anders. I don't know which bloodline influenced your mother more. Ford and Emma were the most obstinate people I ever knew and their offspring are just like them."

"Tell me."

"Lee McNamara likes you. And since he's a police officer, he distrusts Winston. But there was no proof to substantiate your claims. Henry Cutter's statement all but completely alibied his cousin. Bryce and Winston backed each other up and now Winston's gone off the wagon and Stark and Connie say it's due to your allegations. He's back in the substance abuse center, and it's an expensive place."

"Don't change the subject. What does any of it have to do with the police officer at the hospital?"

"You need to understand. It isn't whether or not Chief McNamara believed you. He simply couldn't give you protection based on what you could tell him. The emergency room doctor couldn't say if your injuries were from a fall or a beating."

"I know what she said," Grace blushed. How could she forget the doctor's words? *Do you drink regularly? Are you allergic to alcohol? Have a sensitivity to sulfite? Do you pass out often? There are drugs that leave the system quickly, Ms. Reagan. Are you sure you don't remember taking something...?* "But there was a police officer in the hallway the whole time I was there."

Mosley glanced around, then leaned toward her. "I convinced the hospital to keep you an extra day and I arranged for their security to post one of their officers at your door. Private detail."

Grace stared at him. "I see. Please send me the bill and I'll reimburse you," she said as she carefully folded her napkin and placed it on the table.

It was Mosley's turn to stop her. "Please let me take care of you, Grace. This situation, I mean. It would be my honor to do that for Julia's child."

His honor to take care of her. To keep her safe. To continue where Emma Delaney had left off.

She wanted to ask why, but she said, "I'll be fine, Cyrus. I'll be careful. I'll stay in touch and I'll come to you when I need help." She reached out and patted his spotted, leathery hand. "Thank you," she whispered.

CHAPTER FORTY-FIVE

I njuries which aren't fatal eventually heal, in one fashion or another.

Grace's aches and bruises faded, aided by regular sessions in the hotel's sauna and long walks under gray January skies. She continued to call contractors, but the word had spread. Those who knew Delaney House were suspicious, and those who didn't put her on a waiting list for an opening. A half-completed project at a standstill was not an attractive proposition. Time and again, Grace considered calling the contractors she had used in DC, but they were all small firms who operated in a small footprint. And the Mallard Bay rumors might spread back home to her professional circles. No, it was better to contain her humiliation to the eastern side of the Chesapeake Bay.

Each day she went to Delaney House and worked. Sooner or later, the talk would die down, or a contractor would need work and the renovation could start up again. Until then, she would get as much painting done as possible. At first, it was awkward, working one-handed, but as her left arm healed, she picked up speed. After three days of solitary work, and listening to every sound she made echo through the old house, she was delighted to find Benny Pannel on her doorstep.

"Hey, Miz Grace. Hope it's okay that I didn't call first. I was in the area on another job and thought I'd take my chances on finding you. Henry said I should pick up the rest of the traps."

She'd completely forgotten about the mice. She watched while Benny brought out empty traps. After a quick inspection, he declared the house to be critter-free. "I guess the little guys we found got into something they shouldn't have and crawled inside to die. Doesn't look like there are any more."

As they walked to his truck, Benny said, "I saw the big room in the basement is still sealed off. I thought Bryce was gonna handle that." His faced reddened a bit at Bryce's name. "Anyway, I stayed out of there but sprayed around everywhere else - my own blend, non-toxic. It won't hurt anything but the creepy-crawlers."

Grace shuddered. "You said you knew someone who might be able to clean up the front room?" she asked.

Benny broke into a wide smile. "Maybe. I could make some calls if you want."

On a whim, she asked if he knew any contractors looking for work.

"Yeah. Heard about your troubles."

"Then you know I don't have anyone to finish the house."

Benny didn't avoid her gaze. She decided when he wasn't being the Verminator, he looked older.

"Can't you get someone from over the bridge? Heard you had a company, and you being a lawyer and all, I figured you'd be set for help."

"I'll have to make some calls if I can't find someone local soon. But the added expense of using a western shore firm will knock out a lot of the finishing touches I wanted to add. I'll have to sell it as a shell, not a turnkey property."

"You're selling it?"

"I was always going to sell it, Benny."

"I wasn't sure. You hear things, you know?"

Grace said she surely did.

She couldn't tell what was going on behind Benny's guileless expression, but wheels were definitely turning. "Hard to sell a house with a contractor's lien," he finally said.

And easier for a contractor to get paid through settlement on a sale, Grace realized. Why hadn't she thought of that? She felt a glimmer of hope.

Benny said, "I need to ask something if you'll forgive me for being blunt."

Grace suppressed a smile. He was actually waiting for her answer. "Oh, Benny. I know what people are saying. I can prove I own the house free and clear."

He nodded slowly.

"So," she prodded, "do you think you might know a contractor who'd be interested?"

"Contractor? No. But I know some people."

The glimmer faded. Grace shook her head. "I can't compromise on the quality of work. I need licensed tradespeople."

"But you don't need a license to be a general contractor in Maryland. You could act as your own contractor and hire your own licensed subs. Not like you haven't done it before. From what I understand, I mean."

Benny was wrong. Her mother had been the general contractor. "I guess I could," she said, and immediately thought of a dozen reasons why this was a bad idea.

"Let me make some calls." Benny climbed into his van and leaned out the window. "If I can put some folks together, I'll call you in a day or so. If not, maybe everything will die down before long and you can get a local crew."

It was a wobbly plan, but a plan nonetheless. Things were moving again.

IT WAS NEARLY A WEEK BEFORE BENNY CALLED. A WEEK IN WHICH

Grace finished scraping the woodwork in the butler's pantry and begin the tedious job of painting it. An ad in the help-wanted section of the newspaper solved her immediate problem. By agreeing to pay cash at the end of each day, she secured three workers to finish the landscaping and the reconstruction of the brick walk. If she couldn't complete the interior renovation, the exterior would have to be a show stopper.

She was putting the first coat of paint on a built-in linen cupboard when her cell buzzed. She caught the call and heard Benny's voice over a background of crowd noise. "Do you still want to be a general contractor?" he shouted into her ear.

Did she? She could hear the voices of the workers in the yard. The progress they'd made so far gave her hope. She walked out to the entry hall, looked up to the domed ceiling and slowly turned in a circle taking in the turret window, the circle of ruby glass over the front door and finally, the cantilevered staircase. It was the crooked doorway near the second floor landing that made her decision. If she did nothing else, she'd remove that abomination.

"I'm listening." She sat on the bottom step and admired the staircase while the Verminator talked.

Benny, it seemed, had always had a plan. Lining it up had just taken a while. "You're gonna need some imagination. And faith. You're gonna have to trust me, Miss Grace."

Grace rolled her eyes. He'd 'ma'am'd' her, 'Miz Delaney'd' her and eventually wrapped his head around 'Reagan'. Now that he had a plan, she was 'Miss Grace'. She smiled in spite of herself.

And then she saw it.

"Benny! I have to call you back. I want to hear all your ideas, but I have to do something." She disconnected as he was offering to come to the house.

It was in plain sight at the base of the crooked doorway. A slight recess under the lip of the threshold; a shadow to the casual observer. Grace scrambled up the stairs, dropping to her hands and knees as she drew even with the doorway. Reaching under the threshold, she felt along the narrow edge, gasping as her fingers found the gap between the wood and the wall plaster below it. The next surface she touched was different, rougher. Sticking her fingers into a dark hole was nerve wracking, but she couldn't wait to find a flashlight. She wiggled a forefinger into the gap and felt something shift. A moment later she had a small, flat box in her hands.

"Good one, Mom," she whispered. Or was it Emma's?

THE FRONT END OF THE CARDBOARD BOX WAS PAINTED THE SAME color as the wall and was only visible to someone sitting on the steps below. Even then, it looked like a crack in the plaster from the haphazard construction of the doorway. But as soon as she'd seen the 'crack', Grace had known it was a hiding place. She carefully pried the stiff lid off the little box and looked at the treasures it held.

A thin gold ring caught the weak afternoon sun streaming through the turret window. She picked it up and let its blue stone wink and sparkle in the sunlight. Sapphire. Her mother's birthstone. Grace slipped it on her pinky finger and caressed it before turning back to the box.

The photographs were clear enough, in the slightly murky, overly orange tones of old Polaroids. Her mother couldn't have been more than seventeen or eighteen. She vamped for the camera in an off-the-shoulder ball gown, her golden hair fluffed out in a cloud of curls. Prom night? A man stood in the background, caught mid-laugh, hands clapped together. Julia was entertaining, as usual.

It was the second picture, placed face down in the box, that stopped Grace's heart. Seconds and then minutes ticked by as she sat and stared at her mother wrapped in the arms of a man who was kissing her forehead. The man from the first photo. Two words were written in faded blue ink on the white paper band at the bottom of the Polaroid. *Love always.*

Her mother and Cyrus Mosley.

CHAPTER FORTY-SIX

I t all fit so nicely. Or would have, if it had made any sense.

Her mother in a middle-aged Cyrus' arms, the tenderness between them captured on film and hidden away with a ring. *Love always.*

By the time a knock on the front door brought her back to the present, Grace had run through dozens of explanations for the photographs. She didn't like any of them, and a couple made her nauseous. She tucked the box and the photos into her tote before answering the door to find Aidan Banks.

"Niki isn't here," she snapped and immediately felt ashamed. He hadn't done anything to deserve her tone of voice. Yet.

His jaw worked, but he didn't respond immediately. Instead, he handed her an envelope. "Chief McNamara told me to drop this off. I thought Mr. Mosley would be here. The Chief said he was your agent."

Any other time Grace might have wondered at his deferential tone, but as it was, she only wanted him to leave her alone with her discovery. "Mosley, my agent? Of course." She'd give everything she owned if that's all he was.

"It's your occupancy permit," he gestured to the envelope. "You're cleared to live here again. If you aren't already."

"I'm willing to bet you know I'm staying at the Egret."

"Yeah, well, now you can live here." It wasn't only that his tone was different, the belligerence was gone. As he spoke, his eyes kept drifting to her mouth. To her scabbed-over lip, which was all that remained of her injuries. The visible ones, anyway.

"Thank you for bringing it by," she managed. "I guess you heard what happened?"

"Yes." He flushed and lowered his gaze.

"I didn't - I don't know what they're up to. Bryce Cutter and Winston." It seemed important to tell him that.

Banks nodded once and turned to leave.

As she was closing the door behind him, she heard him say, "I did."

"Wait! What?" She yanked the door open and ran after Banks, catching his arm as he reached front walk. "What do you mean? You knew what?"

"What everybody knows." He pulled out of her grasp but didn't move away from her.

"What! What does everyone know? You've been hostile since day one, and I want to know why."

She'd gone too far. His face hardened. "Ask your cousin."

He got into the truck, slammed the door and was rolling down the driveway before she thought to ask which cousin he meant.

She found Stark at Niki's house.

She hadn't meant to force a showdown so soon, but the sight of her uncle's sleek Mercedes parked in front of the Victory Manor Inn made the decision for her. She drove around back to the guest parking and pulled in next to a gold Lexus. Mosley.

Could she barge in there and demand answers? Did she really want the truth she might hear? In Julia's snapshots, she might have found her father. Or she might have a lot of misconceptions. The pictures could be innocent. Cyrus had certainly tried to step into the role of father and protector for the Delaney offspring. A teenager would hug her dad like that, wouldn't she? Grace realized she had no idea.

Wailing sirens blasted her out of her inertia. Instead of fading away, the noise reached a crescendo before cutting off. She tucked her tote with its dangerous contents under the passenger seat and ran, rounding the front of the inn as paramedics entered the front door.

THE HOUSE WAS IN CHAOS. CONNIE WAS CRYING WHILE STARK shouted over her, demanding that someone give him answers. The paramedics blocked Grace's view of their patient's face, but she would have known the lime green golf pants anywhere. Mosley was the only quiet person in the room.

She found Niki in the kitchen making coffee.

"They'll all need some when they bring him around," Niki insisted when Grace tried to get her to sit down. "Cyrus likes his coffee and Dad will always take a cup." Grace watched her cousin heap scoop after scoop into the brewer basket, stopping only when the can was empty. Niki shoved the basket into place then walked out of the room, leaving the coffee maker to chug fruitlessly with an empty water carafe.

Grace turned the machine off and followed her cousin into the living room. Connie had finally quieted and even Stark was silent while Mosley was rolled out to the ambulance.

"Why're you here?" Connie asked Grace when the door closed after the last of the emergency personnel.

"It's not important now," Grace said. "What happened?"

"What do you think?" Stark answered. He rubbed his face with his hands and abruptly sat down on the arm of the sofa. Connie moved toward him as if to offer comfort, but he made a swatting motion in her direction.

"What happened to Cyrus?" Grace demanded.

"He stopped by uninvited like you just did." Stark again made air-swatting motions when his wife and daughter protested his rudeness.

"We don't know, Grace," Connie finally answered. She sank onto overstuffed brocade couch near Stark. Niki came to sit next to her and held her hands. Stark got up as if they'd crowded him, walked to the windows overlooking the side garden and turned his back to everyone.

Niki said, "Mom and Dad and I were, uh, visiting in here when Cyrus stopped by. And Dad's right, it was odd. Cyrus's never done that before, but he said he had to talk to us."

Connie added, "Cyrus asked Niki for some water but before she could get it, he said he didn't feel well and then he collapsed." She looked down at her hands, which were still intertwined with her daughter's. "I stayed beside him. He never opened his eyes or spoke again."

Out of the corner of her eye, Grace saw Stark bow his head for a second before turning to face them. "It's a shock," he said. "He's always been here, good times when you wish he wasn't hanging around, and bad times when he handled everything, took over."

Grace thought he was stating facts, not conveying gratitude.

"Maybe we should go to the hospital?" Niki asked.

"What for, girl?" Stark said, some of his belligerence resurfacing. "We aren't family, and he wasn't dead when they took him out. We'd only be in the way and they aren't going to tell us anything."

"But, I still —"

"I'd rather find out what Grace came to see us about," Stark said, rolling over his daughter's protest.

"It can wait," Grace said, rising from her chair. "I'll go to the hospital."

"I thought you would," Stark said. Connie and Niki looked at each other and back at Stark, who gave them a sly smile. "She's the only one of us who has any reason to go, right, Grace?"

Grace couldn't tell if he was serious or ridiculing her. He was watching her intently.

"You're the perfect blend, you know?" Stark went on. "Tall and

eyes blue enough to be a real Delaney, but your hair and your face...
By God, you look just like her. You're an Anders on the inside, I'm
thinking. But of course, there's that little something extra you alone
are blessed with."

The challenge hung in the air between them, but only for the
second it took Grace to cross the room and stand toe to toe with her
uncle.

"Is Cyrus Mosley my father?" she demanded.

She heard Connie and Niki gasp, but Stark didn't hesitate with
his answer. "Yes."

———————

SHE WASTED TOO MUCH TIME ON STARK. "I JUST KNOW, OKAY?" WAS
the only response he gave to the barrage of questions Grace hurled
at him.

With Niki right behind her, she raced to the hospital in Easton
only to find Mosley had been swept into a labyrinth of medical care.
After an hour of being shuffled from waiting rooms to offices, Niki
finally shouted the magic words, "She's his daughter!"

The beleaguered emergency room clerk gave Grace a 'why didn't
you say so' look and picked up the phone. Minutes later, a harried
young doctor joined them.

"Your father had a stroke, a rather major one, I'm afraid. We did
what we could —"

"He's *dead?*" Niki cried.

"No, no. We did what we could *here*, I was going to say. But we
aren't certified to handle that kind of surgery and post op. He's on his
way to the University of Maryland Stroke Center in Baltimore. Do
you know where it is?"

They found it, and two hours later, Niki repeated what Grace still
prayed was a lie. They were led to another waiting room with
another sympathetic doctor. There, they waited through the surgery
to remove a clot and the heart attack that followed. Dawn was
breaking as they left the hospital. Cyrus was alive, but just barely.

The odds were slim that he would survive, even less that he would wake up. Grace would have stayed, hoping for a chance to ask her question, but the doors to the post-surgical unit didn't open for visitors. Not even for daughters.

Mosley didn't wake up.

When Grace called the hospital later that afternoon, she was met with a wall of evasion. She was getting into her car for the drive to Baltimore when her cell rang, displaying office number for Mosley, Kastner and Associates. Her conversation with Mosley's partner was short and to the point. She sat in the car for a long time deciding what to do next.

November 1, 1973

Dear Mother,

I know I'm not making sense on the phone and I'm sorry for scaring you. You have your own problems I know, but this time I have to have your help. If there was any way not to burden you with the children, I would keep them here. But Stark is so withdrawn he scares me with his silence and Julia is underfoot constantly trying to 'help' me. I can't make the arrangements and care for them, too.

As bad as Ford's death was, it was his choice. He wanted to leave us, God alone knows why, and I won't grieve for him, only for what might have been if he'd stayed.

But this loss, my Tony. My baby.

Stark says he's nearly grown, but a boy of sixteen should not have to bury his brother and comfort his mother. It has been two weeks since the funeral and I have to do something. Anything to break out of this paralysis.

Stark and Julia packed up Tony's room. Can you believe it? I walked in there yesterday and it was as neat as a pin. All the boxes stacked in the corner were labeled in Julia's neat little letters. I wanted to die right there. But, of course, I won't. And I won't let my babies take care of me, either.

We have to get out of here. I'm telling Julia and Stark they are going to you for a long holiday break, but I will close everything up here, get the house on the market and then join you all in Asheville. Maybe then I'll be able to breathe. Leaving here will be hard for them, but not for me. With the children all gone - to you and to God - there won't be anything here I care about. The hardest thing will be packing up Ford's clothes and the papers in his desk. I haven't touched them since he died. I need to be able to go through that grief alone, not while there are children in the house.

Breaking the news of the move to Cyrus will be painful, too. He's tried to handle everything I needed, but he couldn't mend the hole in my heart. Now I'll finish breaking his when I tell him the children and I are leaving.

I'll get the house sold as quickly as possible, and then I'll join you in Asheville. After all this time, I am really coming home.

Love,

Emma

CHAPTER FORTY-SEVEN

Mosley's partner, Paul Kastner, was very clear. He held Mosley's legal and medical power of attorney and was the executor of his estate. He didn't sugarcoat his message when he told Grace she wasn't Mosley's daughter and any further representations to the contrary would land her in serious trouble. Grace knew it was legal hot air, but was so relieved to hear the magic words 'not his daughter', she quickly agreed with Kastner's demands. She hadn't heard a word from him since.

With Cyrus off limits and Stark refusing to cooperate, she was left with a lot of agitation and only work as an outlet. On Saturday, she threw herself into painting and by the time Benny Pannel showed up, she had finished the butler's pantry and was halfway down the hall.

She was taking a break on the front steps when the Verminator van pulled into the driveway behind her car. Grace didn't know whether to be relieved at the sight of help, or afraid of the plan Benny had come to tell her about. Still, she needed carpenters, painters and electricians, and no one else wanted to work for her. She forced some enthusiasm for the Verminator.

"I come from a large family," he began. "My mom and dad have a lot of brothers and sisters, so they wanted a big family, too, and there are seven of us." Benny rambled on about his far-flung relatives and how they all wished they were closer to each other. Grace tried to be polite, but when he started in on a cousin's problems finding reliable daycare, she finally ran out of patience.

"Benny, my imagination is trying, but you aren't making it easy. What does this have to do with me needing subcontractors?"

"Stay with me, Miss Grace. My sister, Joan, is a lawyer like you. And my brother Phil is a pediatrician. With all us kids, Mom said someone had to be."

"Benny —"

"I'm gettin' there. See, the rest of us are tradesmen or entrepreneurs." The Verminator took a deep breath and spilled his plan. "I've got an uncle in Cecil County who does window installation and repairs, another one in Harrington who works for a heating and air conditioning contractor. I've got cousins who are painters, and carpenters. My brother, Joe, is an electrician. He's trying to get his own shop off the ground down in Berlin. And then there're a few folks, mostly related by marriage, you understand, who'd be happy to work if anyone would hire them. We'd keep a close eye on that bunch, so don't worry."

"Benny —"

"Now, think about it, Miss Grace. Work's good right now. Which is another reason you aren't getting any callbacks. Guys are finishing up indoor projects and have outdoor work waitin' for the good weather days. Oh, now, you'll eventually get somebody. Like I said, this thing with the Cutters will die down. It already has, a little bit anyway. But what I'm sayin' is, I can provide most everything you need to finish up here. My folks're lined up and ready to go, I just have to give them the nod. A couple of them'll have to take vacation days to do this project, and others are giving up plans they had for other jobs. But everyone we need can work in the next three weeks. Maybe some odd schedules, but they'll get 'er done. We should be able to get you wrapped up pretty well inside the house in that time. It's kind of a test for us. If this works out, some of us are thinking about forming our own company." He stopped. The sales pitch was over.

Grace told herself she had other options. She didn't. Short of selling the house unfinished, the Pannel family was the only game in town.

THE EXTENDED PANNEL FAMILY MEMBERS WERE AN ECLECTIC LOT who fit Benny's description down to the last detail. What Benny had failed to mention was that all the Pannels talked as much as he did.

Delaney House reverberated with voices and the noise of carpenters, painters and assorted handymen. Their family and friends appeared throughout the day to bring food, run errands and provide critiques of the latest projects. A carnival atmosphere reigned and Grace was charmed by all of it, even though a less professional work site would be hard to imagine. She worked alongside the laughing, yelling, constantly moving Pannels and watched their lives bubble and churn, dispelling the last of the gloom in the old mansion.

At night, she lay in her room in the third-floor apartment and tried to channel the day's enthusiasm and optimism into the rest of her life. If a change in attitude and energy could make such a difference to a brick and mortar structure, surely it could solve her dilemmas with her family. Every night she tried, and every night she floundered. Even defining 'family' was problematic. With the wavering exception of Niki, the remaining Delaneys had no use for her. Everyone she'd ever loved, or who had ever loved her, was gone.

But then there were moments like the morning she stood in the entrance hall and watched the plasterers skim away the last evidence of the crooked doorway. Spontaneous applause broke out when one of the Pannels shouted congratulations to Grace, and the crew on the staircase turned and took a bow. As she clapped and laughed, Grace realized she had made it too complicated. She didn't have to answer every question, solve every problem. Life was messy and she would never smooth out all the wrinkles.

But she could restore Delaney House.

CHAPTER FORTY-EIGHT

Audrey was buried in the Oxley family cemetery on a sunny Wednesday morning in the last week of February. Avril said she waited for a stretch of good weather so the nosy townspeople and the police wouldn't sink to their ankles in soft ground that held ten generations of her family.

Following her directions, Grace drove out into the heavily forested countryside, taking turn after turn until she was thoroughly lost. She nervously eyed deep ditches that ran along the edges of the increasingly narrow roads.

"Almost there," Avril said. "Left up here at that willow and slow way down if you want to keep the bottom of this pretty car intact."

Grace was only doing fifteen miles per hour as it was, but she slowed immediately. Five minutes later, they pulled up beside a beautifully landscaped acre of land at the end of the pitted gravel road. Grace estimated they were at least a half a mile from the nearest house if you didn't count the vegetation-covered foundation Avril pointed out near the edge of the woods.

"The family place burned down in the fifties. That's all that remains of the house. Oxleys have owned this property since the 1700s, but my father's father moved into town and left this to his oldest son. The home place eventually made its way to me. I'm the only one left."

An oyster shell pathway led from a little footbridge arching the roadside ditch to the gate in a wrought-iron fence that enclosed several dozen graves. Every blade of grass in the cemetery was neatly trimmed, and rose bushes ringed the perimeter. "Do you maintain this?" Grace asked in amazement.

"A friend helps me," Avril said with a shrug. We keep at it year-round so there's never too much to handle."

A car pulled up behind them, followed by a steady stream of vehicles. Even with short notice and a remote location, Audrey Oxley's funeral would be well attended.

"Ghouls," Avril hissed to Grace, who had the dubious honor of escorting the lone surviving member of the Oxley family to her seat at the graveside. Avril gave Grace's arm a yank and didn't let go as she sat down. Having no choice, Grace joined her, taking the only other chair under the small tent.

"Did it occur to you," she whispered to Avril, "these people might be here to show their respect for you?"

"Don't be ridiculous," Avril said. She scanned the crowd again, her gaze resting on each person who made their way across the clearing to the graveyard. "They came for the show. See the group over there?" She pointed directly at four well-dressed women who'd had the foresight to wear boots suitable for tramping through the late winter countryside. "Look really broken up, don't they?"

The women talked excitedly among themselves, pointing at first to one tombstone then another.

"Local grave hunters," Avril said. "Their mission is to catalog every cemetery in the county. I gave them photographs of the legible stones and rubbings of others that still had some engraving as well as a complete listing of everyone buried here. But was that good enough? No. They wanted to *see*. Well, I didn't want them traipsing around my family. I *don't* want them here today." She looked around again. "Not a soul here knew Audrey. Ghouls, every one."

Grace patted the bony white-gloved hand that clutched her arm.

She could truthfully say the cemetery hunters had nothing on Avril when it came to pushing into other people's family drama, but she didn't. She'd grown attached to the old woman, and on the rare days when Avril let her frailty show, it was unsettling.

Lee McNamara made his way through the groups of people and came to Avril's side. Grace barely had time to notice how different he looked in his dark navy suit and bright yellow tie before he leaned down to kiss Avril's cheek.

"I'm sorry, Miss Avril. I should have expected the crowd and left earlier." He nodded to Grace before turning to Avril. "Are you ready?" he asked.

"I've been ready for a long time, Lee."

Grace didn't know why she should be surprised at the tender moment, or that the Chief of Police delivered the eulogy and lead the mourners in the Lord's Prayer. Every time she thought she had Mallard Bay and its inhabitants figured out, she tripped over another facet of village life that changed her view. Lee McNamara and Avril Oxley were the only real mourners at the service, she realized. One grieved the loss of a sister, the other the loss of justice. No matter how his investigation turned out, the Chief wasn't likely to find anyone to punish for a murder that had happened half a century before.

"I WANTED TO WAIT FOR CYRUS," AVRIL SAID. THEY SAT IN THE BMW waiting for the last car to make its three-point turn and head back down the pitted road toward a real asphalt surface and civilization. Avril refused to leave until all the interlopers were off Oxley land.

Grace pulled two bottles of water from her tote, opened one and handed it to Avril, who frowned at her. "I could have done that myself," she said, but took the water and sipped it.

"You're welcome," Grace responded. "I always opened Mom's, it was reflex, I guess."

A smile, her first of the day, lit Avril's face, then was quickly gone. "Is it too much?" she asked. "I realize I'm trampling on a painful anniversary for you."

Grace didn't know how to explain that helping Avril with all of her last minute funeral arrangement emergencies had been a welcome distraction through the anniversary of her mother's passing, so she changed the subject. "It was a lovely service and the Chief did a wonderful job."

"Everyone thinks this is so sudden," Avril said. "But as I told Lee, I've had bits and pieces in my mind for years. I never thought I'd see Audrey again, except like this." She nodded toward the cemetery. "Of course, I thought she'd have a family somewhere, and I'd travel to her funeral, not plan it, but I always have contingencies for everything. I like a good backup plan, cuts down on worry, you know? This was my backup plan for Audrey. It went well enough, I think, except for Cyrus. I'm sorry, Grace, but it didn't feel right to make her wait any longer."

Avril had connections to the hospital in Easton. The story of Niki's dramatic announcement in the lobby of the emergency room had reached her in short order. Avril said she understood the situation but still treated Grace as if she had proprietary rights in protecting Mosley. He'd been moved to a nursing home where he remained unconscious, but clinging to life.

"Who's that?" Avril asked. The irritable tone was back in her voice.

Grace followed her gaze. A slender woman in a conservative business suit stood off to the side of the car, watching them. "I'll see," she said, lowering her window and learning out. "Can I help you?"

Without her stilettos and full face of makeup, Mosley's secretary was hard to place, but as soon as she spoke, Grace knew it was the Gum Snapper.

"Miss Reagan, I'm sorry to bother you. Do you remember me?"

"From Cyrus' office, right? I'm afraid I don't remember your name, though."

"Lily Travers. I know this is a bad time, but I wonder if you could talk to me for a few minutes?"

"It's not a good —"

Avril poked Grace in the ribs and called out, "Of course she can, dear." Lowering her voice, she said, "Go see what she wants. This could be news about Cyrus."

After another sharp jab from Avril's supposedly arthritic finger, Grace got out of the car and followed Lily Travers to the footbridge.

"I'm sorry," Lily said. "This is so inappropriate, but I don't think it's good for either of us to be seen talking. Mr. Mosley was close to Miss Avril, so I had an excuse to come today."

Grace didn't need to ask why Lily was behaving so secretly. She had tried to visit Mosley in the nursing home and had been met with a polite but firm refusal. The management had a written order from Paul Kastner to keep her away from his business partner.

Lily said, "I know how fond Mr. Mosley is of you, and I know he would want you with him. It's wrong what Mr. Kastner is doing, but it's not my place to contradict him, so this is hard." Without her makeup, Lily appeared both older and more vulnerable. Grace realized she was very pretty, even with dark circles under her worried eyes. She glanced over her shoulder to see Avril walking away from them toward the foundation of the old house.

"I was Mr. Mosley's personal secretary."

Grace turned to Lily, who was hesitating, appearing to reconsider her next words.

"I'm sure it was a shock," Grace offered. She cast about for something else to say. "Will you be reassigned to another attorney?"

"I doubt it. I think the firm is winding down. The only reason I still have a job is because Mr. Mosley insisted I stay. I heard them arguing, Mr. Mosley and Mr. Kastner, I mean. Mr. Kastner wanted to keep a more senior secretary, but Mr. Mosley said he didn't like her. Said I was more personable." She smiled. "He likes short skirts and high heels, and that's how I got the job to begin with. He likes a certain look in a girl."

Grace tried not to picture her mother in the Gum Snapper's clothes.

"I make sure I'm the best secretary they have. Mr. Mosley was, *is,* the senior partner, so Mr. Kastner gave in. But now, well, I've started looking for another job. Even if he lives —" her hand flew to her mouth. "Oh, God! That sounds awful. I only meant even if Mr. Kastner doesn't fire me right away, he doesn't want me there, and I deserve better than that."

"I understand," Grace said. "All too well."

"I know you do." Lily's hand dipped into the pocket of her jacket. She was silent for a moment, then said, "There is a strip mall on Kent Island. On the right, just before you go over the Bay bridge. You know the area?"

Grace nodded.

Lily took her hand out of her pocket, her fingers closed around something. "Go to Daily's Office Supply. They rent mailboxes. You want Box 419. I put it in both our names. I have a key here for you, but you'll need a driver's license for identification. Take everything in the box."

CHAPTER FORTY-NINE

"I'm not comfortable with this. Why can't you just tell me what it is?" As much as she wanted to fly straight to whatever it was Lily Travers had left in the post office box, none of this made sense. Grace desperately wanted something, just one thing, to make sense.

"I know this is weird." Lily looked miserable. "But I think we have to be careful. A few days after Mr. Mosley's heart attack, I was looking through his desk for a file Mr. Kastner wanted and I found a package with your mother's name on it. I didn't want to leave it there, and I didn't feel right keeping it. It's been hard to decide what to do. So I put it where it would be safe."

"What's in it?"

"I don't know. It's sealed." Her tone said Grace should know better than to think she'd looked. "Your uncle came into the office the last day Mr. Mosley worked. I could hear them arguing even though the door was shut. He isn't a client, so I'm not breaking confidentiality. Your uncle kept saying he wanted it."

Grace shook her head. "Wanted what?"

"I don't know. Maybe the package I found, but I'm not sure. Mr. Delaney has been to the office several times in the past year. Usually with his wife, but this time, he was alone. I've heard him accuse Mr.

Mosley of altering your grandmother's will. That didn't happen. I was a witness to both of her wills. The one she made about three years ago and the one she did last year. I filed the final version with the Register of Wills after she died, and I saw it was the same will I witnessed last year."

"Do you know what changed?"

"No. That was between Mrs. Delaney and Mr. Mosley." She hesitated and then said, "If I could, I'd give the package to your mother, but Mr. Mosley told me you inherited everything she had, so I think you should get this, too."

"Why aren't you giving it to Mr. Kastner?" Grace asked.

"I saw the package once before. Mr. Mosley took it with him when he went to Washington last spring. He brought it back again and told me to put it in his personal safe. I was surprised to find it in his desk. He must have planned to do something with it but didn't get around to it. Since he didn't give it to your uncle, I think he'd want you to have it."

Grace could see there was more, but Lily was struggling. And she still had the key.

As if she heard Grace's thoughts, Lily reached over and clasped Grace's right hand. "Mr. and Mrs. Delaney have been very angry with Mr. Mosley, and he had his stroke while he was with them. If I leave the package in his desk, they might be able to get it." With a gentle squeeze, Lily released her hand, leaving the key behind. "Your grandmother was special to Mr. Mosley. I saw them together a lot over the years. I believe he loved her."

Grace's hand burned where the little piece of metal pressed into her palm.

Grace dropped Avril at home, promised to stop by later in the evening and tried not to gun the engine as she peeled away from the curb, headed for Kent Island.

Surprisingly, Avril bought Grace's story that Lily wanted to talk about Cyrus but had no real news. The old woman seemed lost in her own thoughts when she returned from walking around the ruins of her family's ancient homestead. She agreed a nap was in order and didn't ask Grace in when they reached her house. Less than an hour after Lily gave her the key, Grace was back in the BMW with a small package wrapped in brown paper and a large white envelope. Both were addressed to her mother.

The spidery handwriting on the package was an arthritic version of the one that penned the letters she'd found in the secret room. Emma. The envelope was Mosley and Kastner stationary. Cyrus. She set the package on the seat beside her, opened the envelope and withdrew two thick documents. Wills. Emma's and Mosley's. She turned to the last page of each document. Both were executed and both had been notarized by Lily Travers.

Grace hesitated. The parking lot of a strip mall didn't feel like the right place to go through the documents, which might hold the answers to all of her questions. Still, she let herself skim over Cyrus' will before refolding it. She found what she was looking for at the end of three pages of detailed bequests.

All my remaining property, possessions and assets of any kind I leave to Emma Fiona Anders Delaney. Should she predecease me, Julia Fiona Reagan and Grace Fiona Reagan, in equal shares, shall inherit in her stead.

She leaned forward and rested her head on the steering wheel. Mosley had said plenty in his last will and testament, but he hadn't said she was his daughter.

A shadow fell across the dashboard. She looked up to find Bryce Cutter peering into the passenger side window. As she instinctively reached for the lock, he opened the door and leaned in.

"Now, Grace, don't be that way. I only want to talk."

She opened her door and jumped out. As Bryce rounded the front of the car she yelled, "Stop or I'll scream."

He hesitated. She backed up, putting another five feet between them and yelled, "Get away from me!"

He gave her one of his lazy smiles. She couldn't believe she'd ever found them appealing, even his dimples seemed menacing now. He said, "I feel bad about how things ended and I want to finish the house for you."

"How things *ended?*" She hated that her voice cracked. "You tried to rape me!"

His smile grew. "Is that what you call it? We were having fun and then you got too drunk." He raised his voice, "But no need for everyone to know. I can be a gentleman. Let me finish the job, Grace. Material costs only. That sounds good, doesn't it? Get rid of Benny's group of yahoos and I'll bring a professional crew in to wrap everything up right."

Despite her fear and racing heart, curiosity won out. "Why? You've spread so many lies about me, why would you want to do that?"

"I told you, I feel bad. You need me. I'll be in and out in a week and you can get the house on the market. That's what you want, isn't it? To be away? Out of here with a lot of money from the sale? I can make it happen fast."

Grace glanced around again. No one was close enough to hear them.

"Say yes, Gracie," Bryce wheedled. He took a tentative step toward her. "This is a good deal. I'll come by this afternoon and bring some materials. You don't even have to be there, just leave the back door and basement unlocked."

"That would be convenient, wouldn't it?" Now she knew what he wanted. She'd changed the locks and he couldn't get in the house.

He yanked the bill of his ball cap lower on his forehead and studied her before finally saying, "I'm trying to make up for bringing your crazy-assed cousin back into the picture when you didn't want him. You were right. Is that what you want to hear? You were right about Winnie and I was wrong to try to keep him on the job."

"And everything was his fault?"

"That's what I'm trying to tell you. I don't know what you thought you heard while you were passed out, but Winnie and I were fighting about work, okay? Nothing to do with you."

"You told everyone you and Winston called 911."

"*I* did! I saved your life! The ambulance took a long time. It felt like forever."

What little control she had disintegrated. "I heard you tell Winston if anyone was going to *do* me it would be you! You even hit him! And now he's in rehab and you don't have access to the house and you need to get in there." She knew she was right; she could see it on his face. What *had* he left behind?

"You're crazy!" Here was the angry man who'd taunted her while she lay immobilized in the basement. *I would have made you happy.* "Get in the car. Now." He jammed his hand into his jacket pocket and pointed his covered fist - and whatever it held - at her. "I said now!"

She turned and ran.

CHAPTER FIFTY

Dodging and weaving around and behind vehicles, Grace put as much metal as possible between them. She ran inside a grocery store before finally slowing and risking a look over her shoulder. After ten minutes of scanning the parking lot, she was calmer. There was no sign of Bryce Cutter.

Only the realization she'd left Cyrus' package and her tote in the front seat of her unlocked car sent her back outside, but she took the store's security clerk with her. The nervous young man, whose name tag said he did double duty as a shift manager, wanted to call the police but finally agreed to escort her.

"You know, ma'am, domestic problems can be serious. You should get some help," he said as he followed Grace, providing about as much intimidating bulk as a Golden Retriever.

"I'll do that," she promised, wondering just what kind of help might be available to protect her against a man she couldn't prove was dangerous. She kept coming back to the expression on Bryce's face when she'd asked what he'd left in the house. She felt sure she'd hit on the crux of the entire Bryce/Winston mystery. But try as she might, she couldn't guess what it was he wanted.

Her hands still shook and Bryce's face appeared everywhere she looked. His patronizing grin filled her side view mirror. 'Come on, Gracie' echoed in her ears. Bryce's ability to turn her insides to water scared her more than his physical threat.

She drove past the exit for Mallard Bay and on to Easton. At Tred Avon Bank and Trust, it took a half hour to arrange for immediate access to a safe deposit box. At last she was alone in the small, windowless room allocated for customers who wanted to pack and unpack their valuables in private. She took Emma's package from her tote, peeled the strip of tape away from the top, and then found herself hesitating.

Get on with it!

More letters. Ten envelopes, some thicker than others, but none holding more than a few pages of paper. A few were worn and had obviously been read and reread many times. Others, while opened, were in better shape. Unlike the ones she'd found at Delaney House, all but one were addressed to Emma. A single unopened letter was addressed to Julia in Emma's shaky handwriting. Grace tried not to tear the paper inside in her eagerness to get it open.

February 1, 2015

My beautiful child - My Julia,

I hope you were kind to poor Cyrus. Even after all these years, I wouldn't have sent him to you if I'd had anyone else.

Are you still angry? Of course you are, but I hope you've also grown wiser and stronger. It's time for you and Grace to come home. We need to make peace, darling. I've sold Delaney House. As long as Cyrus and I breathe, we will never be free of it, but it no longer seems so important to maintain its secrets. We've paid the price for our vanity, Cy and I. I hope you'll agree and come home, if only to say goodbye.

These letters I'm sending will explain some of the choices I've made over the years and, I hope, will help you understand I never meant to hurt you. Cyrus will fill in the blanks. Please let him get a word in edgewise, and listen to what he tells you. Forget what you think you know and listen. Please.

You have always thought I put myself and my desires before yours and you were right. I took a vow long before you were born and, for better or worse, I've honored it. Now that it's too late, I see there were other paths I could have chosen, but who is to say they would have turned out any better?

I will not blame your father, or his father, or whichever Delaney produced the twist of personality that ruined my poor Ford. We each had a part to play in this tragedy and we all carry some of the blame. Why do you think I let you go? Because I didn't love you enough to come after you? Because I was happy to have you and Grace out of my life? Did you really believe any of the horrible things you said? You couldn't possibly.

I let you go because Washington is close enough that I could check on you and our Grace from time to time. I could help if you needed me and you would be out of the line of fire when the truth finally came out. I stood guard all of these years, sacrificed a life with you and Grace and watched Stark turn into a bitter caricature of the sweet boy he once was. I've allowed our family name to become tarnished because, while I could protect your father's honor, I couldn't quite manage to hold on to my own.

You'll have to be strong when you come back. Stark won't make it easy. Once he could have handled a reconciliation honorably, but not now. Connie has always fueled his anger. That's how she keeps him all to herself. She's been very successful, but not, I think, very happy.

I tried to protect Stark, too. I realize now I should have just trusted him. He was too much like me. I loved him too much, demanded too much of him and, deep down, expected him to fail. After all, I did.

Love without trust is a prison. Remember that, Julia. Stark has been in a prison of my making. I asked too much of him and too little of your father. I didn't demand anything at all of Tony or Winston. Look what happened to the golden Delaney boys.

Whether you admit it or not, I helped you escape. Now I'm begging you to come and let me say goodbye.

Here is the apology you have been waiting for: I never thought the truth would stay hidden. I was sure every day would be the day I would have to account for what happened, and when I did, we would all be stained. Forever. I thought I could keep it from touching you and Grace. I was willing to let you hate me to keep you away from home until the storm passed. Only there was no storm, just a vicious erosion of our lives. The truth is still buried and now I've waited too long. My time has come and gone.

It's up to you. Try to forgive me.

All my love and my trust.

Mother

IF THE CLERK THOUGHT IT ODD THAT GRACE ENTERED THE VAULT dry-eyed and emerged in tears, she didn't show it. Grace decided a lot of people must store their personal bombs in safe-deposit boxes. By the time she'd paid for copies of the letters and the wills, and had seen the originals locked safely away, she was calmer and had a rudimentary plan.

Back in Delaney House, she was grateful Benny's crew was gone for the day. She couldn't have talked to anyone if she'd had to. Ignoring her desk on the third floor, she took her usual spot on the staircase. She spread the copies of the new letters out over the steps, carefully placing them in the order in which Emma had bundled them. The last letter wasn't in an envelope but was folded into thirds as if ready to be mailed. Grace thought of the empty envelope she'd found in Emma' secret room. *If you have this, I am gone.* Turning the letter over, she saw a note on the top of the first page: *Found and opened November 8, 1973 - E.A.D.*

She itched to read the last letter first, but honored Emma's wishes and started at the beginning - 1952 and 1953 - letters from Emma's father. Each brief note referenced a check he'd enclosed. Robert Anders told his daughter to treat herself to something pretty and to stop complaining. *'Your mother has her hands full and you know how busy I am. You wanted Ford, and now you are a married woman. It's time you acted like it. Treat your husband well and you'll be fine.'* And later, *'Pull yourself up, girl. You're upsetting your mother and I won't have it.'*

Grace hoped there were other letters from father to daughter that were kinder, but these were the ones Emma had wanted Julia to see. Between 1952 and 1955, there were letters to Emma from her grandmother. Nanny Anders' tone was loving, her words kind, but the message was the same as her son-in-law's: Emma was married and her duty was to her husband.

In April 1974, Ingrid Anders wrote of returning all of her daughter's letters.

You've made your decision with no regard for my opinion, as usual. You may as well have these letters. Your father and Nanny are gone now, and I need no reminders of the mistakes we've made or the price you and the children are paying. They are all gone. Mother, Robert, your Ford and our Tony.

Emma, I can't bear it.

I pray daily you'll forgive me for not listening to you sooner and letting my pride keep me from coming to get you while I could still manage the trip. Read the letters you wrote to us, to your Nanny. Come; bring Stark and Julia home to me. You say you have to stay in that God-forsaken hamlet for the children's sake. What could have possibly changed in the months since Tony's accident? Nothing in that house could be worth staying for.

No, not in the house, Grace thought when she finally picked up the last letter with Emma's cryptic note. An hour later, she pulled herself up off the stairs and dug her cell out of the tote.

Her call to Lee McNamara's office went to voicemail. She left her name and number and tried his cell, but had no better luck. She pictured him listening to his messages and hearing her say 'I know who killed Audrey Oxley'. The truth had waited nearly sixty years. Grace decided Audrey deserved more than having her fate revealed in a voice mail. "Please call me as soon as you get this message," she said instead.

Upstairs in the apartment, she changed out of the suit she'd worn to the funeral and into jeans and a sweatshirt. Now that she knew the secret that had been hidden for so long in the woods, it was time to uncover the scheme Bryce and Winston had planned for the house.

CHAPTER FIFTY-ONE

W inston had warned her to stay away from the basement.
Bryce had said there were dangerous chemicals and snakes.
The idea of going into the toxic-smelling sealed room at the street
side of the house scared her. Even Benny's far-flung family had failed
to yield a hazardous materials specialist and Grace had refused to let
his eager, but untrained workers in the room. A Baltimore company
was scheduled for next week, but after her parking lot encounter with
Bryce, she knew she didn't have the luxury of waiting.

She tried McNamara one more time and left a message telling
him about the attack at the shopping center and her plan to search the
sealed room. With nothing more to delay her, she sandwiched three
filter masks from her painting kit and fitted them over her mouth and
nose, praying whatever she inhaled in the basement would be no
more dangerous than plaster dust or paint remover.

She carried a heavy flashlight and turned on all the overhead
lights as she went down the kitchen stairs. It would be full dark soon
and the light in the basement windows would draw attention from the
outside, but all the doors were locked, the alarm was on and her cell
phone was set to call 911 with one touch. If Bryce was watching the

house, he'd know she was in the basement, but she was as ready as she could be to deal with him.

She shivered as she passed the spot where she'd lain wrapped in a blanket as Winston had brutalized her and she'd learned who - what - Bryce really was. They'd led the paramedics down here, so whatever they were hiding wouldn't be in the main area under the kitchen. She briefly checked the rooms which now held the new heating and air conditioning systems and electrical panels. Again reasoning that the areas where plumbers and electricians had installed modern equipment wouldn't be suitable for Bryce and Winston's plans, she moved on to the sealed room. Although she was under the front rooms of the first floor, she was as far from the basement entrance as she could go.

The tape was harder to remove than the first time. Her fingers had been fueled by anger then. Tonight they were clumsy, frozen with fear. When she pulled off the last strip and opened the door, her pulse quickened. The last time she'd been here, the room had been clean and nearly empty, a few boxes and a work table. Someone had been in here since then.

Grace found the pull-cord for the room's single light bulb. After a moment's hesitation, she gave it a yank and was rewarded with a weak yellow glow. The table was no longer clean. Stacks of small sheets of aluminum foil, plastic bags of varying sizes, and a fine layer of whitish-gray dust covered everything.

She felt the air change an instant before she knew he was there.

"You just had to know, didn't you?" Bryce sounded tired, but the gun he held was steady.

Grace still held the flashlight. It was the only thing between them.

"Don't even think about throwing that at me, Gracie. Set it down gently."

"The alarm!" she said, trying to distract him while praying for intervention, or at least inspiration. Her phone was in her pocket. Could she reach it before he shot her?

"It's wireless, sweetheart. Signals can be jammed." He pointed to the flashlight with his free hand. "Drop it. Now!"

The anger in his voice made her jump, and she threw everything she had into a helpless girl reflex. "I'm sorry!" she cried as she dropped the flashlight and crouched down, scrambling further away from him. She had her right hand on the phone in her pocket. Feeling the depression of the 'On' button, she pressed it and wailed, "Bryce! What are you doing with a gun?"

"Oh, for God's sake, shut up!" In two strides, he had her arm and yanked it viciously. The cell phone flew from her grasp and clattered to the stone floor. He released her, his curses bouncing off the brick walls as he crushed the device under his work boot. His tantrum gave her the precious seconds she needed.

She was down the dark hallway and into the light of the main storage room when he caught her and jerked her around to face him.

"The police are on their way," she tried.

"I doubt it." He seemed to consider his options for a moment, and then his features softened. "Now Gracie, don't be afraid of me. I didn't lie to you. All this, what you saw, what you think you heard the day you fell, it's all Winnie's doing. When I realized he was using the house for his heroin sales, I put a stop to it. He is, well he was, a good kid. I gave him another chance and look what it got me. Between cleaning up his mess and dealing with the rumors you started, my business is tanking."

She knew she should play him, go along until she could escape. "Then why are you here?" Her teeth were chattering and she could barely understand her own words.

Bryce chuckled and loosened his grip on her arm a little. "I stopped by to check on things, like I told you I would, remember? The alarm is insulting, and I wanted to show you how easily anyone could get in. And what do I find? Winnie's at it again. You need to move on, Grace. Let me handle Winnie and get our lives back to normal. Can you go along with that?"

"Maybe. If you put the gun away."

"Am I scaring you, Gracie? I just want you to hear me out and then you can go. Sound fair?"

She wanted to scream that he sounded crazy, but she nodded.

"I over-reacted, okay? The gun and breaking your phone. But you've caused such a mess and you've got it all wrong. I've never hurt you, never wanted to hurt you. It's Winnie with the drugs; I wanted to help him get straight. If Mosley was here, he could tell you. He asked me to keep an eye on the kid; keep him out of trouble. I did try. I kept him around and gave him work when no one else would." He paused, watching her. "And I left you alone, you have to admit that, right?"

She nodded slowly. He *had* left her alone, and it didn't make any sense.

Bryce smiled and said, "That's right. You're getting it. I thought Winnie had cleaned up. He told me he had, you know? What he didn't tell me was he had one last shipment. He sampled the merchandise and then went home to mommy who slapped him back in rehab before he could blink. One of his customers called me today. Winnie told them I could get into his stash."

"You still have the gun pointed at me," she said.

With a theatrical sigh, he tucked the pistol into the waistband at the back of his jeans. "There," he held both hands up. "I'm sorry. Really sorry. But I can make it up to you. Winnie told me he'd left a few other things here that I needed to clean up for him." He shook his head in a 'can you believe that crazy kid' gesture. "He said he had some jewelry that belonged to your grandmother. Said he'd put it in a box and buried it in the grave out there in the woods. The dirt was already loose - a bonus for that lazy jackass - and he thought it would be a great hiding place until he could sell it."

"Why would he tell you that?"

"Because he owes me money, and he thought I wouldn't tell the police about his heroin operation if he paid me off. The jewelry is all he has. I can prove it to you. Let's go dig it up. It's yours, anyway, right?"

She saw no value in telling him the jewelry belonged to Niki. "Oh-okay," she stammered, playing into the nerves that locked her jaws. Her mind raced ahead to possible avenues of escape.

"Good girl. I'll grab that shovel by the basement door and we'll make you a rich woman. A richer woman." He made shooing motions with his hands. "Let's go. We can call Chief McNamara as soon as we've gotten the jewelry."

Now she knew he was lying. He would never lead the police to the heroin; she could see it in his face, his body language. The hands on his hips, so close to the gun. She prayed he couldn't read her as easily.

"So let's go." Again, he waved her toward the steps.

She would have to turn her back to him and walk ahead of him out of the basement. But then she could run for the street and help. She tried to look as if she believed him. Like she wanted to go into the woods with a man with a gun.

"That works for me," she managed and turned for the stairs. She could feel him behind her, but he didn't touch her.

It was darker outside than she'd expected. The basement lights only created shadows beyond the window wells. She stopped a few feet into the yard to let her eyes adjust. A mistake.

Bryce grabbed her hand. "Come on!"

The tree line was closer than she remembered.

"Come on, Gracie. Let's go get the jewelry." His breath was warm against her face. No sweet candy smell tonight. He smelled of musk and adrenalin. He smelled like fear.

She tried to pull away from him but his grip tightened. He pulled her forward.

"Let go! Stop!" she yelled as loudly as she could.

He dropped the shovel. The gun was back before she could make another sound.

"Pick up the shovel, Gracie. Don't make me hurt you. Nobody heard you and no one knows I'm here."

Grace saw something move in the shadows behind Bryce. A

shape, lighter than the surrounding bushes and coming soundlessly toward them. She had to keep his attention.

"So now you need a gun again?" she said, hoping her voice was low enough not to alarm him but clear enough to warn whoever was coming to her aid.

"You aren't stupid, are you?" he said. There was a note of admiration in his voice. "Did you buy any of it?"

It was hard not to stare over his shoulder. She fought to keep her focus on him. "I don't believe anything you said." She risked raising her voice. "You're lying about Winston selling heroin. I think it was all your doing and so will everyone else." She'd recognized the person who hid in the shadows behind Bryce.

He laughed. "Everyone will believe he acted alone when you aren't here to contradict me."

The shadow moved. Grace dropped to the ground as a shot rang out.

"Liar!" Two more shots spit from the end of Connie's gun.

Bryce screamed and writhed on the ground.

"Connie, no! No more." Grace tried to push herself up, but sharp pains crippled her right foot.

Move!

She crawled across the grass until her fingers closed over the shovel handle. She used it as a crutch and finally got upright only to see Connie swing toward her, arms still outstretched, but shaking badly. Clods of dirt peppered Grace as a bullet hit the ground a few feet from her.

Connie's gun wobbled like a live thing as she yelled, "He hurt Winnie!" The barrel swung down to Bryce, who was in a fetal position. More dirt exploded near his head.

Grace tried desperately to count the number of times Connie had fired. Did she have any more bullets?

"God, Grace!" Bryce screamed. "Do something! She's crazy -" another bullet and another scream. If he had stayed still, it might have ended differently, but he tried to crawl toward Grace.

302 | CHERIL THOMAS

"You're not going anywhere!" Connie screamed and four loud, impotent clicks sounded in quick succession.

With a roar, Bryce rolled over and Grace saw he had his gun again. "Run!" she screamed at Connie and swung the shovel with every ounce of frustrated, terrified strength she had.

For a moment there was a perfect silence, then the wail of a siren split the cold night air.

CHAPTER FIFTY-TWO

"One murder, two attempted murders, a heroin distribution ring, and God-knows how many assaults. That's before we get into attempted assault, breaking and entering, and theft. You Delaneys like a little variety in your crimes, don't you?"

"Don't forget arson," Grace said. She thought she'd like to talk to Lee McNamara somewhere other than a hospital, about something other than her poor judgment. He didn't seem angry, but she couldn't tell what he was thinking. Surely he wouldn't arrest her while the plaster was still wet on her cast.

"It wasn't my fault," she tried.

"I'm not charging you, yet," he countered in a reasonable tone. "Who knows what I might find before this is all over?"

She tried hard to think what she could be guilty of, but her ankle was on fire. She'd refused painkillers. It didn't seem smart to ease the agony of her broken ankle at the expense of saying the wrong thing to the police. And she had to remember Chief McNamara wasn't her friend, even if he had kind brown eyes and seemed to be genuinely concerned about her.

"Where's Connie?" she asked.

"In a holding cell, but she's fine. She's with Niki and they're waiting on her attorney."

"A holding cell! She saved my life."

"She shot you. You should take some of those painkillers and rest a while."

"She shot at Bryce. I was hit by a ricochet — a freak accident. You can't charge her! I want to see her. I'll represent her." Grace tried to stand but quickly decided that was a bad idea. "Maybe a wheelchair would be good," she said through clenched teeth.

McNamara touched her hand briefly. "Sit still. Connie's in a holding cell because she said she was going to kill Stark."

"What?" Grace gave up and tore the top off of the small envelope of Percocet the doctor had given her. She couldn't handle this mess sober or pain-free, so there was no point in continued sacrifice.

McNamara stepped out of the emergency room cubicle and returned with a bottle of water.

"I'm only holding her until the lawyer Niki got her arrives. She'll calm down, and if Stark has any sense at all, he'll stay away from her a while. Connie learned that he's has been paying off Winston's dealer. Or, rather, he thought he was. He didn't know Winston *was* the dealer and needed the money to buy his next shipment. Stark has gone through most of his and Connie's assets thinking he was helping Winston, when what he was actually doing was financing a drug ring. When Connie found out what Stark had done, it wasn't pretty."

Grace closed her eyes. The Percocet wasn't working fast enough. "We are a pathetic lot, aren't we?" She tried to find a more comfortable position for her ankle, but there wasn't one. So much for avoidance. She asked the question she'd wanted to voice since he'd arrived.

"What happens if Bryce dies?"

"Your story and Connie's match, and the evidence bears you out. I'd say it was self-defense, whether or not he dies."

"Is there any proof that he was in the heroin operation with Winston? I mean, other than what I heard?"

"No. And as you know, what you heard isn't conclusive."

"It's the only way it all makes sense! That's why Bryce insisted on keeping Winston around, sent him on all those errands."

"Maybe. I'll give you a probably. We'll have to see if a grand jury agrees. I'm hoping Winnie'll testify against him, for what that'll be worth." He rose and patted her shoulder. "Try not to worry."

When McNamara left, Grace said a prayer for Bryce to be well and whole. She wanted him to be able to pay for his crimes.

Bryce didn't die and was able to make bail. Connie's lawyer got her out of jail, and Stark talked her out of killing him. Winston was transferred from the comfortable and discreet rehab center in Annapolis to the Talbot County Department of Corrections. The Delaney family's resources finally ran out for the last Winston. The jewelry he'd buried in the grave was only valuable in Niki's eyes.

While Winnie and Bryce waited for their respective trials, the Mallard Bay grapevine destroyed what was left of their reputations and elevated Grace to near sainthood. Between the enthusiastic Pannel family and everyone in town who'd 'always known' she was an upstanding attorney victimized by the perpetually bad Winston and his surprising partner, Grace was overrun with friendly neighbors and helpful tradespeople.

Under Avril's watchful eye and Grace's direction, the Pannels finished the renovations.. When the last crew packed up to leave, Benny gave Grace a large wooden box. A wide brass plate on the lid bore an etching of Delaney House.

"So you can take it with you wherever you go," Benny said. "Look inside."

A small brick from the original 1708 kitchen house foundation accounted for the box's weight. Grace rubbed her fingers over its rough edges in awe, but a neatly trimmed piece of wood that bore the inscription 'Staircase Doorway, Circa 1975' made her laugh out loud. Laughter turned into misty tears as she looked at a handcrafted album made from a miraculously undamaged piece of the paisley wallpaper. The best of her house photos covered its pages, cataloging the work that had gone into the renovation. Grace gave Benny a heartfelt hug, but later she added the box to the items she was putting into storage.

The house was listed for sale. She only had one task left and then she was going home — wherever home turned out to be.

CHAPTER FIFTY-THREE

The Gum Snapper ushered Grace into Mosley's office with a cheerful flourish that seemed out of place in the empty, somber room. Someone had been keeping things tidy, but Grace felt the lawyer's absence all the same.

"Everyone else has gone for the day," Lily Travers said. "That's why I asked you to come by so late. We won't be disturbed."

Grace nodded, took a seat and waited. She had no idea what Lily wanted and had almost refused to come. She had to be in court tomorrow and needed a good night's rest. When tomorrow's chore was done, she would be free of Mallard Bay and the Delaneys. A quick trip to DC to tie up a few loose ends, and she'd be somewhere warm by the end of the week. 'Warm' was all she'd committed to. She didn't know where she was going, but she had time to figure it out.

"I'm happy to say I'm acting in an official capacity for this meeting," Lily said. The Gum Snapper was gone and in her place was a polished, professional woman who handed Grace a folder. "Mr. Mosley asked me to give you this." She laughed at Grace's expression. "He woke up two days ago. Out cold for more than a month and then sitting up and demanding a Scotch on the rocks. Do you believe it? They're trying to keep him quiet, but he's issuing orders right and left and guess who he wanted to see first? Me! Ha! I can tell you that frosted some people around here."

Now Grace was laughing as she hugged Lily. "How wonderful! He's really alright?"

"Well, that's debatable," Lily handed Grace a box of tissues, grabbing one for herself. "As far as being mentally competent, he sure seems like it. He's demanded a psychological work up from an independent firm not associated with the nursing home Mr. Kastner put him in. Mr. Mosley said he wants no question left in anyone's mind that he's able to handle his own affairs. He even knew the doctor he wanted. I set that up for him today. He told me not to tell anyone but you. He wants you to know -" the exuberance left her voice and her eyes teared up again. "He wants you to know he'll be back to take care of you, even if you think you don't need it."

They took a minute to regroup. Lily insisted on getting drinks and Grace walked around Mosley's office looking at the photos and paintings and small pieces of art she'd never taken the time to notice before. She didn't know anything about him, she realized as she studied a framed photo of a young Cyrus and... she squinted and looked closer. Was that Dwight Eisenhower? She could swear she'd seen Mosley in the same golf pants just last month.

"I know it's against the office rules, but Cyrus gave me explicit instructions."

Grace turned from the photo to see Lily standing behind her holding two cut-glass whiskey tumblers. "Johnny Walker Blue," she said and held a glass out to Grace. "His private stash. I told him I gave you the package and the envelope. And I told him what people had been saying. About you being his daughter."

Grace held her breath, then let it out. They touched their glasses, smiling at the crystal's clear ring and sipped their Scotch. "Well?" she finally asked. "Is he my father?"

"He said you should have this, too." Lily picked up a manila envelope from the middle of Mosley's desk and gave it to Grace. "I'll leave you alone. Take as long as you need."

The folder held two photos and a battered greeting card. Grace swallowed the rest of the Scotch and sat down before her legs gave way. The Polaroids looked like the ones that had been hidden under the crooked bathroom door. In the first picture, Julia was still going to the prom, still laughing and vamping for the camera, but the boy who held her arm was a stranger. The mirror behind them caught the reflection of another couple. A thin woman with curly brown hair was smiling at the man who held the camera. Cyrus and Emma.

In the other photograph, Emma and Julia cuddled around a toddler with a cap of curls and a wide, gapped-tooth grin. On the white strip at the edge of the picture, a firm hand had written "My Girls 1981".

Grace picked up the worn card, her hands shaking as she read 'Happy Father's Day' and smiled at a faded scene of a golfer lining up a putt. The ink on the note inside was surprisingly clear. She had no trouble at all reading the inscription.

To the man who has always been a father to me, even though I didn't and still don't deserve him. You have taken better care of me than my own parents and I will always love you for it. Thank you for not asking 'who' or 'why' or 'what next'. Thank you for trusting me to do the right thing. I will try to make you proud.

Love always,

Julia

THE HISTORIC TALBOT COUNTY COURTHOUSE WITH ITS STORIED PAST seemed a fitting site to pay her family's debt and set the record straight. As Grace waited to testify, she hoped her grandparents' letters would be enough to answer the grand jury's questions. Fifty-seven years after her death, Audrey Oxley was about to have her day in court.

"Ready?" Lee McNamara asked as the courtroom doors swung open and a young, red-faced bailiff called her name.

"Yes, I am," Grace said.

And she was.

June 28, 1961

My Emma,

I have loved you more than my life, something you will doubt after reading this letter. Please try not to think of how I left you, but only how I first loved you. We've changed so much in the decade since that wild day in North Carolina when you gave yourself to me. You have become a mother - a parent. I have become the man my father always said I would be. For that and so much more, I apologize.

I can hear you admonishing me, but I am not being maudlin. I am being truthful. For once, I am going to tell you the truth. Not all of it, but the parts you need to know. The parts that will matter to you. You are always asking me to talk to you. This letter is the best I can do.

So, first, I loved you. Why past tense? I know I loved you fiercely in the beginning, but I must have lost it somewhere along the way. How else could I have done all these things to you? I am numb now, no love and surprisingly, no fear either. I've found one doesn't exist without the other. Perhaps that's the trade-off.

Second, I'm the reason you lost Audrey. I think you knew, somehow, that it was my fault. I swear to you, no one else knows. Well, except for Cyrus. He has been a true friend all along. You'll tell him I said so, won't you? He's always been sweet on you, but we've been friends our whole lives, so of course, he'll never say so. Let him help you out of this hell I've put you in.

Third. Also Audrey. If you didn't hate me before, you will now and I hope it gets you through the days to come. I want to tell you that she didn't mean anything to me, but I am telling the truth here and the truth is she meant enough that I risked everything for her. She was what you weren't. She was like me: selfish and calculating and deceitful, and I couldn't keep away from her. I thought she knew how things stood with us, but she convinced herself if we told you,

you'd take the children and leave me. When I told her that wouldn't happen, she latched onto poor Cy. But, even then, she didn't leave me alone and, God help me, I didn't try to stop her until the night Julia was born.

I gave our baby my mother's name because those huge eyes of hers seemed so familiar, but she's just another love I can't measure up to. The boys will be fine - they are boys and will be men. But Julia gives me pause. I'm still leaving, but there is a little something left where my heart should be and I believe it belongs to her.

But Audrey's story isn't finished. It was an accident. We were fighting - about you, as it happens. I hit her. She said things, and I lost control. I always lost control when I was with her. I carried her to the back woods and buried her right on top of Clancy. Everyone knew there was a grave there, so in the end the old boy took care of me, too. I wish I'd been kinder to him. I wish I'd had the nerve to tell you. I am so sorry. Or I would be if I could feel anything.

Now you know why I am leaving. I'm not glossing over the act of suicide. I really look at it this way. I am finally leaving you so you can live. I should have done it ten years ago. I'm putting this letter in my desk because I know you won't let anyone else go through it after I'm gone.

I've taught you that, right? Keep family private.

Try to have a happy life with the children. Give Delaney House to Tony when the right time comes. You'll know when to tell him everything and he'll take over. He can keep the house - and our secret - safe. You all deserve better than I've given you. You deserve happiness and I pray you find it.

Ford

Before You Go...

Thank you for reading *Squatter's Rights*! I hope you enjoyed your mini-vacation on the Eastern Shore, and that you'll come back to Mallard Bay soon. The Eastern Shore Mysteries continue in *A Commission on Murder* and *Bad Intent*.

Your time is valuable, and I am humbled that you chose to spend it with me. If you have another few minutes to spare and would like to leave a review on Amazon, Goodreads, or anywhere else, I'd be very grateful.

I hope you'll stay in touch with me for the latest updates on the Eastern Shore Mysteries. My website has all the book news, plus a little taste of Maryland's beautiful Eastern Shore. I'm also on Facebook and Twitter. Drop me an email — I'd love to hear from you!

Website: www.CherilThomas.com
Email: Cheril@CherilThomas.com
Amazon Author Page: www.amazon.com/author/cherilthomas

UP NEXT IN MALLARD BAY...

A COMMISSION ON MURDER

One waterfront property for auction and three buyers - then someone narrows the odds.

Until the morning Garrett Bishop is murdered, Grace Reagan only has to worry about the house she can't sell and a business sliding into bankruptcy. She has four months left on her agreement to manage Cyrus Mosley's law firm, a plan that sounded easy enough in September when the weather was warm and she was optimistic. But Grace barely has time to regret the decision she's made before the man who can guarantee her success is killed.

Was the flamboyant, loud-mouthed Bishop shot by a hunter with bad aim or by one of the many people who want him gone from Kingston County and don't care how he leaves? Grace knows that in some parts of the Eastern Shore strangers are guilty until proven otherwise. A near stranger herself, she must prove not one, but two of her clients are innocent of murder.

A Commission on Murder **is available today in eBook, paperback and large print editions. For a sample - read on!**

A COMMISSION ON MURDER

Friday Morning
November 10

The rifle was heavy.

Slippery, wet leaves and tree roots made slow going and weak sunshine did nothing to dispel the cold. It was a perfect day for correcting mistakes, clearing accounts. A perfect day for hunting. Too bad the hunter hadn't planned better, but some things couldn't be helped. When life hands you the perfect opportunity, you take your shot. So to speak.

Overhead, south-bound Canadian geese called to each other in a crashing chorus, but the hunter wasn't tempted. Five minutes later, the desired target came into view, still far away but well within range.

Turn around. Let me see your face.

So. Not the perfect opportunity, after all. The bastard wouldn't turn around.

The hunter took the shot anyway.

Perfect.

CHAPTER ONE

"HE CAN'T BE DEAD," GRACE REAGAN SAID.

"Looks dead to me." The police officer standing beside her sounded pleased. Corporal Aidan Banks hated being bored and a murder guaranteed excitement. Much better than writing parking tickets and wrangling drunk tourists.

"Maybe I didn't do CPR long enough. I should try again."

"He's gone." Banks kept a wary eye on the tall woman who stood next to him, shivering in the brisk autumn breeze. He'd put his uniform jacket over her shoulders when he'd found her pumping the dead man's chest in a frenzy. "You did what you could," he added, but only because he didn't want her to freak out until someone who outranked him arrived to take over.

"He was fine when I talked to him a couple of hours ago," Grace insisted.

"Not fine now."

There was no denying it. The man lying on the scraggly grass behind a decrepit house in the middle of nowhere was dead.

"Look, Aidan, I know I need to stay here, but could you check his pockets? He should have a contract with him and I need it."

Banks didn't bother telling her 'no.'

She knew better, but she had to try. "Sorry. I know you can't. I'm just going back in the house and wash my hands."

"No."

They heard sirens, still far off but getting closer.

"I've got blood everywhere. I'm a mess. Look at me!"

Ordinarily, Grace with her curly dark hair and wide blue eyes wasn't hard to look at, but today wasn't ordinary. Unable to produce a response that wouldn't cause trouble, Banks remained stoically silent. He'd sacrificed his almost new jacket to a blood-covered woman and that was as far as he'd go. Tact was beyond him.

"Fine," she said when he didn't answer her. "I'll wait in my car."

"Stay where you are, just like the Chief said. He'll be here soon with the State Police."

Grace gave up and tried not to fidget as she waited for Banks' boss to arrive and tell her what she already knew – her ticket out of Mallard Bay, Maryland was officially canceled. She wanted to feel horrified, or at the very least *bad* for the dead man, but Garrett Bishop had been difficult from the first moment she'd met him. In the last week he had more than lived up to his notorious reputation and now he'd gone and gotten himself killed, probably without signing the bid he'd offered her. If only she could get her hands on the papers he'd taunted her with this morning, she'd know if she still had a deal.

She took a step back and then another. And then heard tires crunching over oyster shells as vehicles pulled into the driveway at the front of the property. Banks was right. She wasn't going anywhere.

Want more?

Check your local bookstore or library for
A COMMISSION ON MURDER
or
use this link for Amazon:

http://getbook.at/acommissiononmurder

THANK YOU FOR READING!

AUTHOR'S NOTE

Years ago, my husband and I spent a happy summer looking at old houses around Talbot County, Maryland with the intent to open a bed and breakfast. Fortunately, we came to our senses and remembered we didn't like cleaning our own rooms, let alone someone else's, but for a while we looked at huge old houses in various stages of decay and imagined them transformed. I fell in love with one that became Delaney House. I tried to capture the most amazing features of that house in these pages. The wallpapered ceiling, doorway off the cantilevered staircase and basement with servant's quarters exist, or did twenty years ago. We didn't buy the huge, brick money pit, but I've never been able to let 'my' house go, so what to do? Concoct a few new details, put a grave in the backyard and make it the setting for a mystery, of course.

The errors within these pages are my own; the rest is the happy result of my imagination boosted by large amounts of caffeine and the assistance of many kind and talented people. My wonderful story editor, the legendary Helen Chappell, was amazing. She was unfailingly kind every time she sent me back to the laptop to cut, cut, cut. Her edits and suggestions made me a better writer. Miss Helen, I hope I made you proud. Olivia Martin (www.OliviaJuneMartin.com) provided line editing services for *Squatter's Rights*. This sharp-eyed, fact-checking, uber-talented writer/editor is amazing for many reasons, not the least of which is she knows exactly which museums had collections of Monet's work in 1952. Charlene Marcum provided proofreading for the final manuscript. I can't thank her enough for her excellent work and enthusiastic support.

My sister, Clara Ellingson, shared her considerable talent helping me shape this book. Beta readers Kate Thomas, Olivia Martin, Clara Ellingson, Cindy Haddaway and Tara Kleinert – you are the best! I thank you and the characters thank you for your readings, rereadings and copious notes on our behalf.

Finally, it always comes back to family. Mine is flat out wonderful. Patrick, Kate, James and Jack - each of you is a blessing. My sweet husband and very attentive four-legged child, Gracie Mae, make it easy for me to write, to live, to love. Thank you all.

This book is dedicated to the best mother anyone could be blessed with. I miss you, Mama.

May 2017
Easton, Maryland

ABOUT THE AUTHOR

Cheril Thomas is the author of the Eastern Shore Mysteries series. *Squatter's Rights* and *A Commission on Murder* will be followed by *Bad Intent*. She is also the co-author of a mystery novel, *Whispers,* and is a published short fiction author. She lives on the Eastern Shore of Maryland with her husband and a shaggy black dog named Gracie Mae.

SQUATTER'S RIGHTS
© 2016, 2017, 2019, 2020 Cheril Thomas
ALL RIGHTS
RESERVED.

Thomas, Cheril, Squatter's Rights, (An Eastern Shore Mystery). 2020.

TRED AVON PRESS
Easton, Maryland, USA
www.TredAvonPress.com

Book cover by Mibl Art Studio

ISBN: 978-1733412100